HOW TO FIND A ROMANCE IN A BOOKSHOP

Also by Poppy Alexander

The Battle of the Bookshops
Storybook Ending
The 12 Days of Christmas
The Littlest Library
25 Days 'Til Christmas

HOW TO FIND A ROMANCE IN A BOOKSHOP

A Novel

POPPY ALEXANDER

AVON
An Imprint of HarperCollins*Publishers*

HarperCollins books may be purchased for educational, business, or sales promotional use. For information, please email the Special Markets Department at SPsales@harpercollins.com.

hc.com

FIRST EDITION

Interior text design by Diahann Sturge-Campbell

Stack of books illustration © DesignIMT/Stock.Adobe.com

Library of Congress Cataloging-in-Publication Data has been applied for.

ISBN 978-0-06-346342-4

26 27 28 29 30 LBC 5 4 3 2 1

HR 06 08 2026 1256

To Jonathan, for being there always

Chapter One

"I meant 'bibliophile,'" protested Petra desperately. "I meant to say he was the publishing world's greatest 'bibliophile.'"

"Ah," said Petra's boss, Alistair, looking sympathetically at her over the top of his glasses. "Predictive text can be a nightmare. You deleted it?"

"Of *course*, I deleted it," said Petra. As soon as her phone's "do not disturb" clicked off, the tsunami of notifications had woken her. Bleary-eyed, she was initially excited that her final, late-night task of the day—generating some social-media content—had gained traction at last. The huge number of cry-laughing and shocked reactions was puzzling, though. And then there had been the comments . . . And then the sickening re-reading of her post . . . So—yes—she had deleted it. And her account. Not, however, before her mistake had been screenshotted and shared thousands of times.

Petra swallowed, eyeing Alistair's wastebasket queasily as she wondered, in horror, if she was going to be sick. But, on reflection, why even worry? Calling your best client a "bibulous pedophile" beat vomiting into your boss's wastebasket hands down on the "most unthinkable things that might happen" scale. At least when the most unthinkable thing happened, you could stop worrying about the most unthinkable thing happening. There was that.

"I mean, I don't think I actually know what 'bibulous' means," Alistair went on. "It might even be a compliment."

"It means 'drunk,'" Petra informed him.

"I did *not* know that," mused Alistair.

Yup. She had not only gratuitously called her most lucrative client a child molester, she had in fact called him a *drunken* child molester.

"Have you spoken to him?"

Petra nodded miserably. The telephone call had been distinctly one-sided. And shouty. The gist of the conversation, she explained to Alistair, was that she was extremely fired.

"Clients come and go," sympathized Alistair. "And being a little bit infamous? That can be a *good* thing in our line of work."

"Yeah . . . ?" said Petra, trying—and failing—to reflect his positivity. "At least I still have Isabella May," she said. Isabella was her second-highest-earning client, although she was also a spoiled, demanding woman who took up a huge amount of Petra's time and pretty much all of her patience. Actually, patience had been in short supply lately, she admitted to herself.

"Ah," said Alistair again. "You haven't read your emails then?" He screwed up his face into an exaggerated mask of sympathy.

"What? How so?" Petra exclaimed.

"I suspect Henry Atherstone might have gotten to her," Alistair suggested. "He's been hovering."

"That's illegal," protested Petra. Unfortunately, as she knew full well, poaching each other's clients wasn't *literally* a criminal act, but it was seriously frowned upon. As was insulting your own authors online, unfortunately.

"What do I do now?" she asked, her question being directed not so much at Alistair but more at the universe—a universe that had just dumped on her from a great height like a passing seagull would.

"Lie low," he said. "This too shall pass. And even before this happened, I've been thinking you need a change of scene. A fresh challenge."

At this, Petra's eyes filled with tears. She sniffed and gazed out of the window, hoping he hadn't noticed. So now he wanted to get rid of her. Fair enough.

"I'm resigning, obviously," she began.

"Whoa, easy, tiger," he chuckled. "I'm not asking for your badge and gun. I've had an idea . . . Did you ever come across a lovely young woman called Jules Capelthorne on your travels? Assistant editor at Farquarson and Trimble?"

Petra shook her head mutely. Publishing was full of lovely young women. They came and then—often—they went. It was a tough industry.

"Jules was one of the ones who got away," Alistair went on. "Moved to Devon, started running a bookshop by the sea, just got married to the local Romeo . . ."

"Living the dream," snarked Petra. And then she was ashamed. *God*, she was turning into a miserable person; she couldn't even feel positive about the good fortune of a woman she had never met.

"So," Alistair went on, undaunted, "apparently Jules and her new husband are off on a huge honeymoon trip, taking in all the great bookshops of the world, and they need someone to mind the shop for six months. I saw it on Facebook. You get your own little flat above the shop, a reasonable salary, and all the books you can eat. Devon's a funny old place," he mused. "Full of eccentrics . . . I think it would be perfect for you."

Ouch, thought Petra. Rude.

"I'll put in a call?" Alistair's hand hovered over his phone, as he sought her permission.

Petra gave him a tiny nod of acquiescence. Fine. It wasn't like she had any choice. Six months surrounded by books, which were now—she had decided—her personal nemesis. Great. And at the seaside too. With her luck, those incontinent seagulls were going to be forming an orderly queue.

Alistair had seemed mighty keen on getting her out of the office, Petra reflected miserably as she sat on the train. She didn't blame him. She was a Jonah now—a sailor's bad-luck omen—likely to cast their literary agency's boat onto publishing's rocks of failure if she was left to contaminate their little enterprise a minute longer.

There was a sword of Damocles hanging over all those who were on the commissioning end of publishing. A "there but for the grace of God . . ." feeling, knowing how capricious the industry could be. Anything approximating guaranteed success was well beyond the gift of all literary agents—if they were brave enough to admit it.

Of course, they rarely were. And Petra was as guilty as the rest of them.

Which literary agent didn't revel in the moment when they communicated to a breathless wannabe that they were prepared to represent that writer's work? Seeing their little faces light up—faces that were pale after too many years bunkered inside with their laptops, hammering away on work that might never see an audience—work that *still* might never see an audience.

Naturally, those involved would do everything they could to increase its chances. The new acquisition would be edited and polished to the best ability of all, and then the manuscript would ping into the inboxes of half a dozen overworked editors with too much power at their fingertips. And then—when that bunch ghosted her—another half dozen editors would be selected, and so it would continue . . . Finally, when even the obscure little presses had declined—including the ones that never got their print books into the shops and the ones that never paid the pitiful royalties on time, or at all . . .

Only then would Petra put the author's dying hopes out of their misery. Then they would both pretend to believe her excuses: that the market was unbelievably tough at the moment; that no one was buying anything; that there had been near misses, rave rejections—that it might even get picked up in the future, when the zeitgeist caught up with this particular writer's vision.

After a suitable period of mourning, the writer would pluckily begin something new, something that would perhaps more closely echo the current trends, both telling each other that next time the outcome would be entirely different.

Was Petra such a terrible judge of talent? Just lately it would seem she was. And with the contracts she *had* managed to procure, the advances had been abysmal or just full-on nonexistent. Alistair had been generous for far too long, continuing to pay her a subsistence wage until she started generating some proper income for the little agency. If it wasn't for her bigger clients—well, her ex-clients—she would not have been justifying her existence there at all. No, he was well rid of her and had been more than kind in offering his counsel to her remaining clients during her sabbatical. She couldn't help thinking they would all be cracking open the champagne with their cornflakes on reading their emails that morning, learning they were going to be being represented by a real agent at last.

Where on earth *was* Portneath, anyhow? All she knew was, if she got to Penzance, which was practically at the farthest tip of Cornwall—next stop America—she had gone too far. Ooh, Penzance though, she mused, her mood brightening momentarily. When she thought about Cornwall—and especially Penzance—she thought "pirates," and pirates were seriously cool . . . even a little bit sexy? She had always had a thing for them. *Treasure Island*! *Peter Pan*! Both were among her all-time favorite childhood books, and when she got around to reading du Maurier's *Frenchman's Creek*, her weird little pirate kink had been cemented forever. An actual sexy *French* pirate? *Ooh la la.* Literary heroes didn't get any better than that. She wondered if there were Devon pirates too. Surely there would be, with it being Cornwall-adjacent. She might do a bit of research. But first, where the heck *was* Portneath, anyhow?

She held up her phone, looking anxiously for some bars. Seriously, no signal? She wasn't in London anymore, that was for sure. Petra impatiently logged her phone onto the train's pitifully weak

Wi-Fi and googled. Here it was at last, a Tourist Information Office listing.

> Portneath is a pretty little seaside town, nestling on the coast at the foot of the rolling hills of Devon's South Hams. It offers charming beaches and plentiful vacation rental accommodations—both in town and in nearby villages such as the delightful Middlemass. The town is a magnet for lovers of good, locally produced food. It has a Saturday market and a range of excellent independent stores, including a well-regarded bookshop.

Ha! thought Petra. A "well-regarded bookshop" now, maybe. Just wait until she had had her hands on it for six months. What a pity. And Jules had seemed so nice on the phone too, breathlessly thanking her for stepping in at the last moment, apologizing that she and Roman would not be there to greet her, but explaining that they would leave the keys for the shop with a friend who ran the restaurant across the street.

There were heavy clouds, purple with yellow underbellies, pressing low onto the horizon now. Would it rain? Would it snow, even? Being January, that was entirely plausible . . . The tourist information definitely seemed to be positioning Portneath as a *summer* holiday destination. It was probably one of those seaside towns that was derelict and bleak through the winter. Most of the "excellent independent stores" and fancy restaurants probably didn't even bother opening until Easter. Great. No wonder Jules and Roman had decided to vacate until the beginning of August. If she were them, she would probably do the same.

Her mind swirling with these bleak thoughts, Petra rested her head against the glass and gazed unseeing at the countryside, the craggy, desolate landscape of Dartmoor perfectly echoing her plummeting mood. This must be Bodmin Moor, she thought bleakly. Would she be able to see Jamaica Inn from the train? Somehow that didn't fit with the mental image of its dour isolation, captured so beautifully in du Maurier's novel. Which brought her back to thinking about pirates again. Or smugglers, anyhow. Weren't they basically the same thing? Petra was hazy about job titles. But—pushing pirates out of her mind—as the train wended slowly on its way, taking her to her fate, she punished herself with a well-worn litany of every self-inflicted catastrophe over the whole of her twenty-eight years to date. It was quite the list. The unifying aspect was—as usual—her inability to engage her brain before opening her mouth. Would she ever learn not to detonate her own life through a misspeak, or—as in this case—a mistype? Doubtful.

As she continued to castigate herself, Petra's eyelids grew heavy, and the view grew blurry.

She had better not fall asleep and end up in Penzance.

"Wait! Don't! Stop! I mean, don't go!" Petra shouted desperately, as she scrambled for the door, having woken to see part of a platform place name outside the windows—a place name that definitely started with a *P*.

She threw her backpack onto the platform and launched herself after it, just as the whistle blew and the train started to pull away. Landing heavily, she lay prone and winded, trying to decide whether she had injured herself. After gathering her wits, she started to get up but froze as a voice bellowed:

"Stay down! Don't move."

Petra squeaked in alarm. What fresh hell was this?! Had she just thrown herself headlong into a police raid? A gunfight? At a little country railway station? What were the chances? Terrified, she hunched and put her arms over her head. Feeling a heavy hand on her shoulder, she jumped violently.

"Whoa, easy . . ." came that deep voice again with its very un-Devonshire Scottish burr. "That was a hell of a—actually, I don't even *know* what that was—just take it really slow," the voice counseled. "You could be injured."

It was rather a lovely voice, she decided, authoritative and soothing. The kind of voice that made you feel safe.

"Where am I?" she asked, still not daring to move.

"What? Did you hit your head?" the man replied anxiously. "You're in Portneath. Okay—let's not panic—what's the last thing you remember?"

"Portneath? Oh, thank God for that. I fell asleep, thought I'd ended up in Penzance," Petra chattered, feeling much better. Finally, something had started to go right. "Ow! Oof, ouch!" she exclaimed as she tentatively stirred, not at all enjoying having to put all her weight on her bashed-up knees, but then she urgently wanted to remove her right boob from whatever in her backpack had been sticking into it. Plus, it wasn't practical to just stay there for what remained of the day.

"Here, let me . . ." A hand under her elbow propelled her to standing as if by magic. Strong too, eh? Very promising.

Petra turned to thank her savior but, as she caught sight of him, her jaw dropped and her eyes bulged in amazement. Well! This may not be Penzance, but who would have thought . . . "Omigod, you're a pirate!" she blurted, thrilled.

The man—several inches taller than her, with an abundance of chestnut brown, wavy hair—may or may not have been handsome. It was hard to tell what was going on under the proliferation of facial hair, although the heavy brows framed a compelling pair of eyes. Entranced by them, Petra noticed they were—appropriately enough—the color of the sea on a stormy day. A long, greenish-but-might-once-have-been-black great coat, somewhat moth-eaten, and dun-colored wide-legged trousers tucked into thick socks and chunky black boots together lent a swashbuckling air. A thick black-leather belt with a brass buckle did not—sadly—sport a cutlass, but other than that, the picture was absolutely joyful.

"Um—no—not a pirate," the man replied at last, apparently taken aback.

"Are you sure?" Petra pressed him.

"Yes, thanks."

"But definitely dressed as one, though," Petra doubled down. "Filming a movie?" she scanned the area for the usual filmmaking paraphernalia. "Actor?" she went on. "Maybe just an extra? Nothing wrong with that . . ." Wow, he had a fabulously piratical glower, she observed delightedly. He was totally wasted as an extra, for sure.

Although they did seem to be alone on the platform, which was weird. Usually filming meant crowds of people and tons of equipment.

"Nope," he said. "Not a pirate. Not even pretending to be a pirate."

"Children's party?" she hazarded, slow to process what he was saying. Although, to be fair, he looked a bit too scary to be a kids' entertainer.

"This," he said heavily, gesturing at himself, "is *not* a costume. These are my *clothes*," he emphasized.

"Then, why . . . ?" Petra was genuinely confused. Sure, he was missing the tricorn hat, she conceded. And the parrot. And the wooden leg . . . Doubt began to creep in. Could it possibly be that she had done it again? She stifled a groan. Nice start, Petra.

"And please stop jumping out of moving trains," he added stiffly. "Because, as far as I can tell, *you're* not in the movies, either. And get those skinned knees cleaned up, okay?" At that, with one last glare, he turned, striding down the platform, long coat flapping, his rear view radiating offense.

Petra groaned, hanging her head. There she went again, with her unerring ability to insult everyone. She should come with a government health warning. Although he need not have *been quite* so annoyed. It wasn't like she had called him a pedophile or anything. He got off lightly. As far as she was concerned, being called a pirate was a compliment. And anyway, people shouldn't go around with bushy beards and swirly coats. It wasn't that much of a leap. Other people were *bound* to get confused. Maybe even people who *hadn't* just been dreaming about them. Maybe.

Sighing, she hoicked her backpack up onto her back.

By the time she was ready to look for the station exit, he had vanished.

Chapter Two

The taxi rank was unhelpfully empty, but Google maps told her it was only an eight-minute walk. Casting a doubtful look at the lowering sky, Petra adjusted her backpack more comfortably on her shoulders and set off, trying to ignore her protesting knees.

It may only be January, but Portneath really was picture post-card stuff, she thought as she crossed the bridge over the wide river mouth. The little town sprawled decorously on either side of the estuary, with the town quay on one side, and wide sandy beaches on the other. The light was fading rapidly now. On the horizon, the sky was stained red and gold, with stars already piercing the inky blue velvet above. Lights had twinkled into life in the windows of the fishermen's cottages lining the road along the shore, and an avenue of streetlights delineated the main street that stretched up the hill from the quay to a little castle on the summit.

From Jules's instructions and Google maps, Petra knew Capel-thorne's was near the bottom of this hill, and she found it easily. It was a cute little shopfront, with its rose-colored limewash and a multipaned bow window. It was clearly freshly painted, sporting a coat of green gloss paint with the name picked out in bright gold lettering above. It looked like a remnant from a Dickens novel—utterly charming—but the shop window was dark, and the sign, hanging askew in the doorway, was turned to "closed."

With her back to the shop, Petra surveyed the scene. There! The restaurant Jules had told her about was just yards away. Freya's. It was early evening still—not quite six o'clock—and there were no customers at tables, but Petra could see the staff, in neat slate gray aprons, flitting around the little wooden tables in the warmly lit interior, straightening the knives and forks, and laying down starched white napkins in preparation for evening service. One member of the staff was standing behind the bar area, polishing glasses and surveying the scene. Here, Petra had been told, they were keeping the key to the shop and to the flat above. After her peculiar interaction with the man at the train station, she was dubious about further conversations with the Portneath natives, but—hey ho . . . She walked over and pushed confidently at the restaurant door.

It was locked, causing her to rebound with some force, but a member of the staff hurried over to unlock it, opening their mouth to explain the obvious, but Petra interrupted—she was cold, tired, and the grazes on her knees were burning. "I think you have the keys? To Capelthorne's? I'm—" but before she had a chance to explain, a little blond figure in chef's whites who had just appeared out of the room behind called across:

"Hellooo! Are you Petra?"

Petra nodded wordlessly as the woman trotted across the room and enveloped her in a warm hug.

"Gosh, poor you, you must be exhausted," she chattered. "I'm Freya. I've promised Jules and Roman that we'll take really good care of you. Oh no!" she added, having stepped back to take in Jules's entire appearance. "Your poor knees, what happened? We need to clean you up. Lucy, will you fetch the first-aid kit for me? Come and sit . . . Glass of wine? We've got this amazing local Chardonnay; you've got to try it."

"Do you ever breathe?" interrupted Petra. Oops, that was unintentionally rude. Again.

"Sorry!" Freya replied, unabashed. "Finn tells me all the time that I talk too much—when I let him get a word in." She giggled. "Jules was so thrilled you were coming. We all are."

"Who is we?"

"Oh, you know. The crowd. Obviously, Jules and Roman aren't around, but everyone else . . . you'll get to know us."

By this time, Lucy had quietly slid a green plastic first-aid box onto the table, and Freya was rummaging through it efficiently, lining up scissors, sterilizing wipes, and strips of bandage material.

"Ouchy, sorry," she crooned in empathy as she gently dabbed Petra's scraped knees, cleaning off the blood and grit. Underneath, the flesh was pink and oozing, but there were no deep cuts. She would live.

Cutting bandage strips and tenderly placing them over the grazes, Freya chattered away guilelessly.

"Capelthorne's is *the* best bookshop in the world," she was saying. "Jules and Roman have really turned it around. Well, it was Jules mostly, not that Flo wasn't doing a good job, but she's ancient, bless her, and she's adoring her retirement. That said, she won't resist coming in to have a good look at you, and she'll be itching to help if you let her."

Soothed by Freya's chatter and succumbing to the blissful

warmth, Petra was breathing in the most intoxicating scent of fresh garlic and butter. In response to the possibility of food, despite having felt too sick to eat since the awful disaster struck, her stomach gave an enormous, resonant, and extended growl.

"Gosh, sorry," muttered Petra, putting her hand over her abdomen.

Freya giggled again. "Music to my ears," she said. "I love hungry people. Now, for an early supper, I recommend the lobster linguine. Absolute simple perfection," she declared. "And the lobster is fresh off the boats this morning," she went on. "Roman's paying, by the way. He said to make sure you had a good meal on him when you arrived."

That was lucky, thought Petra. She reckoned Freya's wasn't the cheapest and she was going to have to be really careful with money.

By the time Petra had finished off a huge plate of pasta and a large glass of wine, a contented glow had suffused her. She regretfully turned down sticky toffee pudding for another time but accepted the suggested cup of chamomile tea to round off her meal.

Now, with her cup drained, and the key to the shop sitting by her saucer, there could be no further excuses to linger.

The little restaurant had filled up gradually as Petra ate and was now humming with life, the clinking cutlery and low rumbles of conversation all but drowning out the gentle, rhythmic roar of the sea. All around her were rosy-cheeked groups of friends and couples of all ages, some with children or grandchildren, and all looking as if their lives were quietly delightful. Which they probably were.

Petra began to wonder why she had clung to her life in London. After all, rents were exorbitant, property prices made buying somewhere to live totally unattainable, and only people with disposable income far exceeding hers could really take advantage of the delights that the city had to offer. But then she remembered, even with the whole post-Covid working-from-home thing, it surely must be unrealistic for a literary agent to base themselves so far from where the action was. Those human relationships, those business contacts, were key to success. And success had been pretty elusive for her, even when she was on the spot. So that was that.

Anyhow, thoughts of her old life, and how it had imploded, were enough to make her cheeks flush scarlet again. She was now allergic to books, and the entire publishing industry, she decided, draining her cup and placing it carefully back on the saucer in a decisive gesture. A complete change of career was probably in order. And she had six months to think of what that might be.

Yawning, and shivering just at the thought of venturing outside again, she gathered up the keys, hauled her backpack onto her shoulder, and slipped out without interrupting people to say goodbye. She would have liked to thank Freya, but she could see her through the hatch into the kitchen—a whirling dervish as she produced plate after plate of delicious food.

Petra could see herself eating at Freya's rather too often.

The lock was tricky. So tricky Petra thought perhaps she had been given the wrong key, but just as she was seriously beginning to wonder where she was going to sleep that night, the door succumbed, flying open so unexpectedly she nearly ended up sprawling headfirst onto the floor for the second time that day.

Her more pleasant childhood dreams had included one where

Petra was locked in a bookshop overnight. And this little shop, with its squeaky wide-oak floorboards, crammed shelves that reached the ceiling, and twisted oak beams, dark with age, was pretty much that dream. If the horrors of the last twenty-four hours had not happened, Petra would have been flinging on all the lights and delighting in her new domain, but now she yawned again and wondered if Jules and Roman had left her bed made up.

She trailed wearily up the steep wooden staircase, finding herself on a second floor of books—this time used ones, judging by the faintly musty smell.

The second flight of stairs—marked with a polite sign saying "private"—delivered her straight into a narrow hallway with doors on both sides. A quick exploration revealed a neat little kitchen, a tiny bathroom with an old-fashioned, claw-footed tub—no shower—and a cozy sitting room with a pretty fireplace, plump blue sofa, and a dormer window with a view all the way up the main street. It had a cushioned window seat built into it too—the perfect corner to curl up with a book.

Ah yes, reading . . . At that moment, Petra didn't think she would care if she never read another book in her life.

All she wanted to find was a bed to sleep in. Right away. Trying the last doorway, she found herself in a windowless hallway, with two further doors leading off it. The smallest room—tiny, actually—housed little more than a low wooden single bed with a faded patchwork quilt and a hole in the shape of a heart carved into the painted wooden headboard. It was obviously a child's bed, and Petra was not at all sure that her feet wouldn't be sticking out of the end. Thankfully, the final room was an absolute delight: In pride of place was a high, wrought-iron bedstead piled with plump feather pillows and made up with blankets, a silky eiderdown quilt, and impeccably ironed white sheets. Whoever ironed their sheets these days? Whoever *had* sheets and blankets these days? Not that she was complaining. The bed was positioned in the middle of the wall opposite the window and was high enough to allow the occupant to gaze out of the open curtains and survey most of Portneath, or at least the same jumble of pastel-painted cottages she had seen on her walk into town. In daylight, there would surely be a clear view of the beach and the cliffs beyond.

It was quite dark now, though, with just the glow of the lights in the cottages and a silver moon lighting a wide, shimmering path across the sea. Who needed books? Petra felt she would be happy if she spent the rest of her life cocooned in that glorious bed with its stunning view. Other than the bed, the furniture in the room comprised a dark brown wardrobe, so tall it barely fit under the sloping ceiling, a chair and dressing table under the window, and a highly polished rosewood chest of drawers that doubled as a bedside table. Clearly Jules—or someone—had prepared for her arrival. Not only were there two fluffy white towels on the bed, but the bedside light was glowing warmly through its pink silk shade and there was a little posy of flowers in a rose china jug beside it. There was even a glass and a carafe filled with water sitting ready. Petra discovered the drawers were empty, as was the wardrobe, other than a handful of wooden hangers that rattled like bones as she opened the door.

Unpacking could wait. Petra quickly undressed and—chilled, in nothing but her underwear—dived into the bed. She moaned with gratitude on discovering that there was an electric blanket *and* that her mystery benefactor had switched it on for her.

Cocooned in the most comfortable bed she had ever encountered—and used to battling insomnia in her London flat, where traffic noise and sirens roused her repeatedly throughout the night—Petra was soothed by the gentle sound of the sea, sucking and roaring like a giant snoring in the background.

Sleep claimed her in minutes.

PETRA JOLTED AWAKE, adrenaline pumping. For several moments, she had no idea where she was, then her memory of recent events returned, and her stomach lurched with anxiety. She groaned aloud. Maybe she would just stay in bed with the covers pulled over her head today? She was sure she must be ill. Her head was definitely aching a bit.

Some considerable time later, bored and too hot, Petra poked her head out again, reluctantly admitting to herself that a) she was basically fine—if her head was sore it was because of the wine she had with supper, and b) she owed it to Jules and Roman—her saviors—to actually do the thing she had come all the way to Devon to do. What day was it? Thursday. Definitely a day when the shop would be—should be—open.

Sighing, Petra climbed out of bed. Taking just a few moments to unpack, she dressed in yesterday's clothes and went to explore the kitchen. Astonishingly, even after her hearty supper, she was hungry again. Either that or her churning stomach was a precursor to an ulcer brought on by all the stress. Petra mentally prepared herself that breakfast was unlikely to be on the agenda until she found somewhere to shop for provisions, but she discovered her hospitable hosts had—once again—been extremely kind.

Sitting on a scratched wooden board that rested on the countertop was a delicious-looking crusty sourdough loaf alongside a dish housing a slab of primrose yellow butter, speckled with salt crystals. After flicking on the kettle, Petra opened the fridge to discover an old-fashioned glass pint bottle of gold-top milk for her tea, along with a carton of half a dozen eggs, and a greaseproof parcel of streaky bacon. Wow! Bacon and eggs for breakfast? Both items were apparently from a place called Hollytree Farm in Middlemass. Middlemass? Wasn't that the nearby village the Tourist Information Office had mentioned? She was sure it was.

Petra rarely ate breakfast, but fresh local eggs and bacon? This was appealing. Glancing at her watch, she realized reluctantly she had slept too late to indulge in the full "hearty English breakfast" experience, but she did pop some bacon under the grill and slice some bread while she waited for the kettle to boil.

Just minutes later, after a quick face wash and toothbrushing, she carried her bacon sandwich and tea downstairs to eat while she figured out how to open up the shop.

Seeing the shop in the cold daylight, Petra's anxiety returned. She wasn't completely green, she reminded herself: Her first sortie into the book trade as a teenager had been a Saturday job working in the local branch of Waterstones bookshop. And then, after university, there had been several years in junior editorial roles. But it felt now that those experiences, plus being a—not very able—literary agent had in no way prepared her for this. Even an old-fashioned bookshop like Capelthorne's would have more up-to-date systems than Waterstones had had, back in the day. She probably wouldn't even be able to work the card scanner, let alone having the first clue about ordering and deliveries.

What on earth had made her think she could do this?

The one thing she *was* good at was letting people down. She was bound to achieve that, at least.

It took a couple of minutes to find out where to switch all the lights on, and another couple to figure out how to power up the cash register, which didn't—to be fair—look too different from the ones she remembered from ten years earlier. Whatever this bookshop was, it wasn't on the cutting edge of book retail IT systems, that was for sure.

"Door unlocked? Check. Sign turned to 'open'? Check," Petra said aloud, to give herself confidence. Then she sat expectantly on the stool behind the checkout desk.

Let them come, she thought.

Nobody did.

Chapter Three

She *had* turned the "open" sign around, hadn't she? Petra glanced over to it repeatedly, like a nervous tic, fully expecting a Devonshire gremlin to have flipped it around to "closed" as soon as her back was turned. Devon was supposed to be a mystical place, with magical goings-on, wasn't it? Druids and stuff . . . ? Portneath's main street, in broad daylight, didn't look particularly fey, but you never knew . . .

It wouldn't do to desert her post, she told herself repeatedly, staring at the door in an attempt to will people through it. But eventually boredom won, and she began a tour of the shop.

Petra was impressed. This was a "highly regarded" bookshop for good reason. The shop window had a clean, bright, and impactful display of "new year, new you" books ranging from get-fit guru six-pack shortcuts to step-by-step guides on how to realize the next big business idea. The less said about Petra's abandoned New Year's resolutions the better. If only one of them had been "blow your career to smithereens," she would have beaten her own deadline. It wasn't even February yet. Still, no point dwelling . . .

There was a large and mouthwatering cooking section, she discovered. Petra was a sucker for a beautifully photographed cookbook, although she rarely cooked; it never seemed worth the bother, just for herself. The other reference book sections were similarly compelling—but fiction always had been Petra's first love. She skimmed the alphabetically ordered novels lining the walls to see all the usual suspects, with some more unusual choices too, suggesting confident and intelligent buying. The shelves were flanked with tabletop displays categorized by genre: cozy crime, romance, science fiction, romantasy. She couldn't resist looking for her clients' work and saw nothing to encourage her on the tables. There was her failure again; she swallowed miserably, remembering. She had hardly ever managed to get any of her clients the kind of marketing spend that would put their stories on those coveted table spaces.

Turning back to the shelves, she *was* encouraged to find a couple of books she had played a part in producing, tucked in, spines facing out. From long habit, she guiltily looked over her shoulder as she turned them face out. Screw it, she told herself. *She* was in charge now, and she could display the books however she darn well liked!

Momentarily giddy with the power, her hubris was interrupted by the bell signifying an arriving customer. At last! Skittering back to her seat, she pasted on her brightest, most welcoming smile and turned toward the door to see . . . nothing. Actually, not nothing, but it seemed the only living being entering the shop was a dog. Goodness knows how it had reached the door handle, because it was a small white-and-brown Jack Russell, standing barely twelve inches off the floor. It trotted toward her, confident and bright-eyed, gracefully accepting a pat on the head, before wheeling away to do a circuit of the shop. Petra watched it narrowly, alert to any attempts to lift a leg on the merchandise. Or worse.

She resisted the urge to ask if it was looking for anything in particular or just browsing, and was still sitting, nonplussed, when the doorbell sounded again. This time, a tall, elegant older lady entered in a rush.

"Digger?" she called, as she closed the door. "I really do hope you're in h—ah, *there* you are, you little monkey," she went on, obvious relief in her voice as he scampered toward her before throwing himself down on the floor and licking her ankle lovingly.

"When I require you to dribble on my foot, I will be sure to let you know," the lady informed him as she gently moved her foot away. "I'm so sorry," she said to Petra. "I opened the door to come in, then saw someone I had to buttonhole about the village jumble sale. I was chatting away when I suddenly noticed he wasn't with me, and I wasn't sure *where* he had gone. He gave me quite a fright."

"Me too," Petra admitted. "At least—I was a bit confused . . . although dogs *are* very welcome," she added, so as not to seem unfriendly.

"Oh, I know that," the lady said. "We even let children in, sometimes. I'm Flo," she went on, extending an elegant hand, bony and frail with advanced age.

"Aha!" said Petra, remembering Freya's information dump the previous evening. "Bookshop Flo?"

"Indeed," Flo inclined her head. "You are very well briefed. I'm flattered Jules took the time to mention me . . . she was in such a fluster before they left."

Jules in fact had not, although Petra decided to let her take the credit anyway; she was sure Freya wouldn't mind. "So you worked here when you were—well—younger?" she probed and then clamped her hand over her mouth in a too-often-used gesture. Lesson one: Don't mention a person's age. Especially in expressions of awe. But then, to be fair, surely this lady was ancient? In her eighties, perhaps, but Freya had given her the impression that Flo's retirement was only recent. She must have misunderstood.

"It would be nice to be regarded with awe for reasons *other* than my antiquity," Flo chuckled. "Fair enough, I must seem ancient to you, but I retired, just a couple of months ago, as it happens. I've been sitting on my hands," she confessed. "Important not to interfere, to let the young ones get on with things, fresh ideas and all that."

"Well, *this* young one would be better off *not* being left to get on with things," admitted Petra.

Flo seemed to be trying—and failing—to hide her delight. "Of course, I would be *more* than happy to assist," she said, with a courtly nod of the head. "Jules kindly let me get the flat ready for you, at least."

"Did you leave those heavenly snowdrops and"—Petra faltered—"whatever those other flowers were, by the bed?"

"Hellebores. All from my garden at Nightingale Cottage. There isn't much blooming in January, but the previous occupant was a gardening genius. I can't take credit. I haven't been there long."

"They're beautiful though, thank you," said Petra. "And the delicious food too? Such a lovely welcome."

"We are all very grateful to you, my dear," Flo demurred. "And—as I say—I'm more than happy to give you a few hours a week—if you're sure that would be helpful?—but not too much longer than that, because I have Digger to care for now." She gave Digger a fond look. It was wasted on him, because he had, in just the few minutes they had been talking, draped himself devotedly across Flo's feet and fallen sound asleep.

"But you could bring him!" said Petra, her heart melting at the sight of the dozing little dog. She had always longed for a dog of her own.

"Of course, I could bring him, how silly of me," Flo berated herself. "Well, that's decided then. He can be the official shop dog, as long as he behaves himself."

The two women agreed that Flo would come in to help just on Saturdays, at least at first, because that was the busiest day. From Easter onward she might need to help out a little more—Flo suggested—as the summer season would generally get very busy. Petra didn't like to admit that with her recent record, she was likely to have single-handedly tanked the business by then.

But if Petra's presence was a bad omen, it seemed Flo's visit might have been a good one. After she left, promising to be back on Saturday at nine o'clock sharp, Petra found herself quite respectably busy.

By day two, Petra had begun to pride herself on predicting what people might buy as they walked through the door.

Wiry-looking older couples with walking boots and matching rain jackets were after ordnance survey maps and more information about the castle at the top of the hill. There were grandmothers keen to buy picture books for grandchildren, stout purple-nosed older men looking for history books and biographies, and frazzled young women drawn to the rom-coms about sweary mothers of young children who rely a little too heavily on wine—the mothers, not the young children.

"My goodness, Roald Dahl wrote so many more books when I wasn't looking!" exclaimed a plump, sweet-faced grandmother who was stocking up for a much-anticipated grandchild visit. "And the Just William books too! Heaven, I used to be in stitches, reading these as a child."

"Gosh, really?" blurted Petra. "Surely they must have been old, even then?"

"*Even* then," agreed the lady, with a wry smile.

Petra consciously repressed the instinct to smack herself on the forehead. She had been doing that so much today she was giving herself a headache. Maybe she could style it out. "I mean, the Just William books are *really, really* old," she added, before she realized she wasn't sure where she was going with it.

Luckily, the lady just laughed. "Help me find some authors I *don't* know about too," she invited Petra. "How about these David Walliams ones? I've heard of him . . . but I'm not sure how I feel about his comedy, if I'm honest."

Finishing up with the grandmother and then helping a lady who was going on a winter cruise and who bought a whole stack of books about the places she was visiting, Petra was surprised to see it was ten minutes past closing time. The day had not dragged at all. In fact, she had enjoyed it more than she thought she would, and the time had flown. Of course, books were still a painful reminder of everything that was bad in her life, but dealing with the public had been quite fun, if you discounted all her usual inadvertent insults. It made her realize how few people she encountered in an average literary agency day. The majority of her time had been spent alone, reading unsolicited submissions that were mostly rather bad and trying to find nice things to say to the people who had written them.

She had become isolated. She saw that now.

Petra locked the door and turned the sign to "closed." It had been a good day's trade. Not many people seemed to be quite so interested in the old books upstairs, though. She did think she had seen a glimpse of someone in a long dark coat and a beanie hat slip up the stairs earlier that afternoon, but it had been much earlier. They must have slipped back out without buying anything, while she was distracted.

She was looking forward to going up to the flat to make a cup of tea and try out the inviting blue sofa. She had had no time for lunch and was starving too. Maybe lovely Flo had tucked a packet of cookies, or some chocolate, into one of those kitchen cupboards. Perhaps she would even install herself on that lovely window seat to watch the world go by. She fleetingly thought about curling up there to read a book, until she remembered that she didn't read anymore. Reading had become work. And work had been stressful enough for her to avoid doing anything connected with it for relaxation.

Walking through from the office at the back to the stairs, it occurred to Petra that she hadn't checked for customers up here before she locked the door.

She glanced through the bannisters as she climbed the first flight, and her heart jolted to see a pair of heavy walking boots beneath the table that customers could sit at to read. Definitely a man's foot as well, she realized with a gulp—they were too big to be a woman's. The bottom part of a strangely familiar, thick, dark green wool coat above the feet looked as if it might belong to the figure with the beanie hat she had glimpsed. But that had been literally hours ago. Surely, he would have left already? And then a thought struck her. Of course, it was so bitterly cold outside, this person had come in to get warm and had snuck upstairs where he wouldn't be disturbed. Maybe he had nowhere else to go? Bless him. He hadn't even moved in response to her approach. She was going to have to ask him to leave.

"*Ahem.*" Petra cleared her throat politely as she climbed the last step. Yes, it was definitely the beanie-hat man. She could see just the top of his head, because his face was right down over the top of a book, opened in front of him on the table. He seemed to be taking a nap. And then a terrible thought occurred to her. What if this man was elderly and in ill health, with no one to care for him? What if he had dragged himself into the shop, feeling unwell and instinctively seeking sanctuary, and then his spirit had—this precise afternoon—slipped away from this cruel world to reside permanently in a better place?

Just at that moment, his head shot up and Petra screamed.

"Christ!" he yelled back. "What on earth is the matter with you, woman?"

"I thought you were dead," she gibbered. "Hang on, I know you!"

"No, you don't," he snapped.

"Yes! From the station—you're the pirate guy."

"Ah." He faltered for just a millisecond, his eyebrows shooting up, and then, "You mean the plundering, murderous, tyrant of the seas—or, alternatively, the dressed-up children's party turn, balloon cutlasses and walking the plank game my specialty?" he reminded her wryly.

"Yes. No! I mean, I really thought you were . . . sorry, that was ridiculous of me," she said, chastened. Although, if he only knew, accusing someone's everyday wardrobe of being a costume was quite mild in the Petra playbook of insults. "I honestly didn't mean to offend," she apologized. "You were being very kind, and I jumped to conclusions, because, well," she gestured at his clothes, and then struck herself on the forehead. "Oops, sorry again . . ."

He laughed but immediately stopped, as if he had just remembered that laughing was not something he did.

"You just scared the bejaysus out of me, by the way," she added, with a hint of reproach.

"Likewise," he countered. "How are your knees?"

"Oh, fine," Petra made a dismissive gesture. "Thank you. What are you reading?" she nodded her head at the book on the table and peered at the spine as he lifted it for her to see. "*Paradise Lost*!" Petra clasped her hands to her heart and sighed.

"You know it?"

"Of course! 'The mind is its own place, and in itself can make a heaven of hell, a hell of heaven.' Ain't that the truth," she added wholeheartedly.

His eyes widened. "Extraordinary . . . look." He showed her the page he had been reading, pointing to the words she had just quoted.

Petra nodded emphatically. "I think it's the truest thing I've ever heard, don't you?" she went on. "And the precision of his language! Like where he talks about 'darkness visible'? He's writing more than three hundred years ago, and we know exactly what he means—this idea that it's so pitch-black the dark has a physical presence of its own?"

"E*xac*tly! And that brutal spareness, it just kills me. I always try to get near that myself, to use the most direct, unadorned language I can. So much more powerful . . . I ask myself, what would Milton do?"

"You're a writer!" Petra exclaimed, delighted.

"No," he snapped. "Absolutely not."

"Oh, okay, I thought you just said—"

"No," he interrupted. "I meant, when I was at school. English essays. We had quite a good English teacher. It was like something out of *Dead Poets Society*, but then I grew up, so . . ."

His manner invited no further questions on the matter, and this time even Petra could take the hint. Plus, she had put her foot in her mouth once too often with the poor man, the last thing she wanted was to subject him to any further insults.

"I should be going," he said, glancing at the clock on the wall. "You'll be wanting to lock up."

"Ah yes," she said, realizing, "I already have. I'll come and let you out." It occurred to her that she was alone with him, and the shop door was now locked, but—despite her initial mistaken impressions—she felt entirely safe in his company.

"So, whenever you want to just come back to hang out and—I dunno—find your land legs, you're more than welcome," she told him as she held open the door.

"Not a pirate, remember?"

"Ah yes," said Petra again, clapping her hands to her cheeks in confusion. "In that case, do just come back and spend a squillion pounds on books," she joked. "I'm on commission"—she wasn't—"so that would be very nice."

"You're right, I should buy something," he said. "How much do you want for the Milton?"

"Eleventy-billion pounds, please," said Petra solemnly, holding out her hand. The register was all shut down now, and she was pretty sure he didn't mean it.

Instead, he shook her outstretched hand. His own hand was strong, warm, and dry. "Ross," he said. "How do you do?"

Actually, maybe he was incredibly rich, she thought, as she climbed the stairs to the flat a minute later. So, basically, she had just insulted him. Again. Didn't eccentric rich aristocrats sometimes dress weirdly because it amused them? But then, replaying their interactions, she thought it through. Discerning the mood of the "mind's own place" hiding behind those sea-green eyes, this was not—she felt sure—a man who considered himself amused, or in heaven.

In fact, he looked more like a man who was in hell.

Chapter Four

Ross shook his head as he walked up the hill, smiling despite himself. That woman had an even worse foot-in-mouth problem than he did. Hilarious! And it was kind of nice to meet someone who knew their Milton too. He had missed that bit of his old life—hanging out with other people who loved good writing. They were his people.

He had so nearly given himself away to her, though, biting her head off because she said she recognized him. And then letting slip that he was writer . . . She must think him very odd. Or—worse—just rude. Not that it mattered what she thought of him, of course. That aspect of his new life had been quite freeing, the "not caring what people thought." It was that, versus the oppression of people's expectations, constantly trying to second-guess what his readers wanted so he could give it to them, like a particularly people-pleasing dog. It had been exhausting.

Although, as the antithesis of keeping a low profile, he had gone and unnecessarily given her his name. Just knowing his first name wouldn't get her far, though, he reassured himself. Somehow, he had just wanted her to know. He couldn't remember the last time he had heard someone say his name out loud.

Which was weird because he had always found it so intrusive—the discombobulation of realizing that people he had never met clearly thought, somehow, that they knew him? Hearing strangers say his name. Shouting it in the street, even. He had hated that. When you pour out your innermost thoughts into your work, it doesn't feel like you are announcing them to the world. You don't imagine your words will be read by all those strangers, who then think that—in owning your book—they somehow own a piece of your soul.

It was a strange, Faustian pact he had entered into then. He felt so obligated—so grateful—to his readers that even their most ridiculous expectations had seemed eminently reasonable.

Until they didn't.

Yes, cutting himself off from the world had been a relief at first. No, actually, it had been terrifying at first. *Then* it had been a relief. Then . . . ?

Then, it had become lonely.

But there was nothing to be done about that, because the only legitimate way back to the world—to *his* world, and *his* life—had been to write another book.

And that hadn't happened, had it?

Ross sighed. It was all just too big a problem. It had been five years—five years!—and he had not lighted upon a solution to it, not yet. But—he smiled as he strode—even being in a bookshop had been surprisingly nice. For a long time, being surrounded by other writers' words when he had none of his own—nothing worth saying—had been a torment. Today, though, it had begun to feel like something else. A comfort. A fragile trail of white breadcrumbs in a dark forest . . . Leading him home? Leading him somewhere, anyhow . . .

Smiling to herself, Petra checked all the doors and windows again before going upstairs in search of food. She really must find out where the nearest supermarket was tomorrow, but just for tonight she was hoping to scavenge whatever she could find in the kitchen.

Settling for a can of someone else's oxtail soup and making a note on her phone to replace it when she went food shopping, Petra stood stirring the saucepan in one hand and doing Wordle on her phone with the other. She was perplexed. It took longer than usual, which was ironic, she realized, as inspiration struck.

"Novel."

Ha.

Still, at least she got it in three tries. Not bad.

While shoveling in soup and a thick slice of bread and butter, Petra made a list of all the things she needed to ask Flo the next day. The shop had better not be *too* busy. It was a long list.

Once planning ahead was done, the silence in the flat felt oppressive. It was too early to go to bed. There was no Wi-Fi, or at least not a strong enough signal to make it upstairs from the office at the back of the shop. No Wi-Fi! Who didn't have Wi-Fi these days? It was barbaric. Also, there was no terrestrial television of any kind. Petra had been forced to fall back on a disgracefully patchy phone signal that was far too intermittent to stream anything, denying Petra her usual mind-numbing binge-watching of

Friends and *The Good Place*. Tonight, though, her phone informed her she had hardly any data left either, so TV was out. Great.

What the heck did people *do* in Portneath?

She had deleted TikTok on the train coming down, because the algorithm delivered nothing but BookTok—which now caused her actual physical pain—and she didn't know how to train it to show her anything else. This seemed to gloomily confirm that—without books—she was a nobody, with no personality and no interests. Instagram was no better but at least included a million ads that were fascinating in their randomness. Why—in the name of all that was holy—did Insta think she wanted big underpants and comfy bras, to the exclusion of everything else? What had led it to this conclusion? Had her account been hacked by a busty middle-aged woman with an addiction to cake and underwear?

Doomscrolling endlessly anyway, Petra glanced up and—horrified to see she had allowed an hour and a half of her life to trickle away pointlessly—put down her phone and jumped to her feet. Books! She would read. That was what she used to do, for hours, weeks, months . . . her love of books had propelled her through most of the first twenty-eight years of her life. They had been her hobby, her friends, her career, and her solace. She found herself on the shop floor without further conscious thought, but that was where the enthusiasm drained away. Cozy crime, romance, literary feminist retellings of Greek myths . . . all delicious, tempting, absorbing stories, but each possibility left her filled with ever increasing ennui.

Trying again on the second floor, looking this time for the comfort of something she had read a dozen times before, she dismissed du Maurier, George Eliot, Agatha Christie, or even

Conan Doyle, although Holmes and Watson were her go-to absorbing read throughout her childhood. She had happy memories of lying wrapped in the sofa throw on the hearth in front of the fire, totally transported by *The Hound of the Baskervilles* or "The Speckled Band."

Everything she might re-read now felt stale and dry. Eventually, her eye lighted on the Milton book still on the table. An epic poem might fill the void where a novel felt too large a commitment. Maybe that was the problem? A lifetime of tiny doomscrolling dopamine hits had broken her ability to focus long enough to read a ninety-thousand-word story anymore. Unless it was for work, which had—perhaps for that reason—become increasingly joyless.

The sonorous, magnificent language of Milton would draw her in and fill the emptiness in her mind, she decided.

Petra carried the book upstairs and settled herself, in pajamas, in her new, fabulous bed, with a cup of tea and a packet of chocolate biscuits. Crumbs on the sheets? Who cared! She knew how to live!

Lucifer's journey echoed her own all too closely, she realized. Hubris and pride had caused her descent into hell. But hell wasn't all fire and brimstone. As Milton knew all too well, hell was mostly a cold and lonely absence from the world. A casting out. Yup. As delightful as Portneath appeared to be, the mind was its own place. And she was in hell.

LATER, BACK IN Ross's stone cottage, where the top of the main street petered gently into a country lane, he slipped, out of habit, into his normal evening routine. The house—his latest rental in a series of frequent moves—was probably pleasant in the summer. In January, it was damp and dreary when he allowed the wood-burning stove to go out.

It was out.

After getting it burning again, he cooked up some supper and ate it without relish straight out of the pan while he had a crack at Wordle. This was usually the one pathetic sense of achievement he obtained all day.

The word was "novel." Oh, the irony. *And* it took him six tries.

Staring sightlessly into the flames and spending too much time thinking about the woman in the bookshop, he decided to look on Netflix for something distractingly bad to bury himself in. This evening, though, the gloomy Swedish detective shtick was too predictable, even for him. He guessed the murderer during the first half hour, and the woman detective's back story didn't engage him at all. He decided to call it a night, shut down his laptop, and went up the creaking wooden stairs to get ready for bed.

Ross studied himself dispassionately in the bathroom mirror, toothbrush in hand. No wonder that woman in the bookshop thought he was a pirate, although she was definitely a bit eccentric, in a strangely appealing way, he thought, suppressing a smile as he squeezed the toothpaste tube. He turned his attention back to his reflection, sobered at the sight. The state of him! He turned his face this way and then the other, as if seeing it for the first time. The beard was a disaster. Less of a fashion choice, more an absence of the will required to shave, it had grown bushy and unkempt. He also noticed in the harsh bathroom light that there were more than a few gray hairs in it. He was only thirty-four, for God's sake. The hair on his head wasn't great either. There was plenty of it, at least—no sign of thinning—but he couldn't remember the last time he had gone to the barber, and it didn't know what to do with itself. He looked like the wild man of the woods.

And his clothes weren't going to speak up for him either, he thought, unable by now to stifle the critical voice in his head. He had that morning—while giving it the usual zero thought—put on the ragged-hemmed dun-colored trousers that she had first seen him in, a once-white T-shirt, and one of his several crumpled khaki shirts. This one had faded quite badly, he noticed now, and the pocket had started to become unstitched. Also *why* was his T-shirt so dingy? Could it be that washing your colored clothes separately really *was* a thing?

Ross didn't separate his whites. And he didn't do ironing. So sue him . . . But—hmm—the shaving and showering? The occasional haircut? Yeah . . . he should really raise his game. Not because he had a reputation to maintain; not because he was an award-winning writer; not because he was Ross McCloud; but purely because he thought he might like to have further conversations with this bookshop woman, who made him laugh and knew her Milton. And he had a sneaking suspicion she seemed interested to know him too. Just him. Without that crushing "literary genius" nonsense, a label hanging around his neck like he was a prize bull.

First impressions counted, wasn't that what people said? Oh dear. It might already be too late to persuade bookshop woman that he was someone worth knowing. Although she currently believed he was a grown man who thought it was cool to dress up as Bluebeard, surely one of the most misogynist of all the serial killers. Which might be even more off-putting than the truth. And hey, from such a low bar, the only way was up, right?

On Saturday morning, Petra was feeling refreshed, purposeful, and maybe a little bit optimistic. Actually, the optimism might just be relief, because she knew Flo was going to be in. Whatever . . . Petra skipped down the stairs bright and early to get everything perfect before Flo arrived.

"You're here!" she blurted witlessly, finding Flo looking elegant and serene, waving a duster around in the Booker Prize short list compilation.

"I promised I would be," said Flo, raising impeccably arched eyebrows. "Just having a whizz 'round, before we open. I hope that's all right?"

"You don't have to ask me! This is your shop."

"Was," corrected Flo, sounding perfectly cheerful about it. "I know it will benefit enormously from what you have to offer. Jules tells me you're a literary agent."

"Was," said Petra, inadvertently echoing Flo. "Long story," she added, shaking her head repressively. Thank goodness, Flo took the hint and was too well-mannered to push for more.

Checking her watch, Petra went to turn over the sign and noticed how bustling Portneath was, even though it was barely nine in the morning. Today a central spine of dark green awnings had sprung up along the wide cobbled street between the two rows of shops. It was hard for Petra to see what each of them was selling, as they were obscured from view by a mass of shoppers in brightly colored coats, hats, and scarves, muffled against the chill.

There was a man in a dark blue coat, with a small child hanging off each hand, both of them wearing matching woolly hats with pom-poms. He and his pretty blond wife looked as if they were laughing together at something one of the children said. She pinched the child's nose fondly before packing another white-paper-wrapped parcel into the backpack her husband was wearing.

Petra was overtaken by a wave of longing to be that woman, with her partner and her children, doing normal Saturday morning things. She imagined them all going off to a café for coffee and—for the children—hot chocolate with whipped cream and grated chocolate on top. Maybe they would have a late breakfast there too: pancakes with bacon and maple syrup or eggs Benedict. Perhaps then they would take their dog—a fox-red labrador, Petra decided—for a walk on the beach, before returning home for homemade vegetable soup and fresh bread bought from one of the stalls that morning. She pictured what they would do later too: perhaps a family board game, or baking, or an invitation to another child's birthday party, then supper and bedtime, and the couple finally sitting down in front of the fire with a glass of wine, sighing in relief, and settling to watch something on television together, snuggled up in each other's arms.

Petra blinked away her daydream and made to move from the window, just as a graceful older lady in a trailing aquamarine scarf and tumbling blond-gray hair waved cheerily in at her. Petra turned to see Flo waving back before the woman carried on up the steep hill of the main street, a basket on her arm already packed with goodies.

"That was Diana," Flo explained. "A great friend, and tremendous fun. You'll meet her soon, but she looks like she's on a mission this morning. Probably heading up to see Vanessa in the flower shop."

"Talking of shopping, I was going to ask you where there was a supermarket so I can stock up with some groceries," said Petra, "but I hardly need a Sainsbury's with all this on the doorstep."

"Oh yes, Portneath is famous for its food. You'll see everyone in town on market days," agreed Flo. "But for the boring stuff, you'll want to pop over the bridge to the Co-op. And there's Finn's deli next to Freya's too, of course. I shouldn't say this, but he stocks goods from half the market stallholders, so he's very convenient if you don't manage to buy from the producers direct. His prices are slightly higher, naturally enough."

"Of course," agreed Petra vaguely, still half lost in her day-dreams about what a wonderful life she would have if she lived here properly. She felt unable to pull herself away from the window, such was the allure and vitality of the scene.

"Why don't you pop out now, with my basket, and find yourself some nice things to keep you going," suggested Flo. "Now's the time, before the baker sells out."

"But I don't want to leave you on your own," said Petra.

"People only really drift in here once they've bought their fresh food and had a coffee in Finn's shop. We won't get busy until late morning at the earliest. You'll see."

"Really?" said Petra guiltily, but Flo had turned away, returning quickly with an old-fashioned basket like the one Diana had been carrying.

A minute later, wrapped up against the chill and giving Flo a grateful look, Petra launched into the crowds.

There was one stall selling nothing but mushrooms. She had never seen such a variety of shapes and sizes. They were all quite beautiful, but to Petra they seemed prohibitively expensive. The stallholder was a red-faced, beefy man, stirring a huge pan of steaming risotto that was glistening with mushrooms and speckled with herbs. It smelled absolutely delicious—earthy and rich. He was ladling it into paper containers, with little wooden forks to eat it with, and several people were standing around, warming their hands on their pots as they tucked into an unconventional late breakfast.

Petra bought a small portion of oyster mushrooms wrapped in a brown paper bag. She would fry them with butter and garlic and make them into an omelet for her supper that night. With her purchase stowed away in the basket, she moved on to the baker, who was standing, beaming, in front of shelves piled high with crusty loaves of bread. It was the huge trays of pastries in the stall in front of him that had piqued Petra's interest. She sniffed appreciatively while she waited for him to deal with another customer, breathing in the delicious aromas of toasted almond, apple, cinnamon, and caramelized sugar, overlaid on a warming base note of yeast and flour. She was determined to have one of the puffy, lopsided, and utterly delicious-looking cinnamon buns. In the end, she decided on two, so she and Flo could have them with their coffee later and then—on impulse—she added a foot-long skein of Danish pastry twist, threaded through with chocolate pieces and dusted with a snowfall of icing sugar.

Speckled brown eggs from a comfortably plump and aproned lady at the next stall completed her supper plans, and there was milk and yogurt from the stall at the end of the street nearest Freya's. The live crabs and lobsters at another stall made Petra feel terrible about the linguine she had eaten at Freya's. She vowed to eschew seafood henceforth. With all these delicious alternatives—locally grown organic vegetables and a huge selection of cheeses—it would be no hardship. Petra didn't feel she needed to eat anything with a face ever again.

That said, a life without bacon was no life at all . . .

Dreamily browsing a stall selling local honey in jars and chunky squares of honeycomb, Petra suddenly became aware she had left poor Flo on her own for ages. She had been drifting around the photogenic marketplace like the heroine in a rom-com montage, squeezing a perfectly ripe peach here, sharing a joke with a stall-holder there. But this was real life, and she had a bookshop to run. She spun around to hurry back, accidentally knocking into a tall, dark man in a green army jacket with her basket.

"Oops, sorry," she blurted. "Oh wow," she breathed—hopefully not out loud—as he turned, and she looked up, her eyes locking with his. Never mind real life, she decided, if this was her rom-com meet-cute, then Petra was all in. This man was *ridiculously* beautiful, with his broad shoulders and sleek dark hair, brushed back, but with a heavy lock falling across his forehead as if designed to emphasize his sea-green eyes and chiseled, dark-stubbled jaw.

A bubble of nervous laughter escaped her. She made to break eye contact and found that she couldn't.

"Hello," she said inadequately. What was the correct response in these situations? Would it be rude to just go in for a full-on snog? Would a handshake be more appropriate? I mean, he'd seen the movies, right? He too must realize this was a moment full of huge portent. A moment dividing "then" and "now" as decisively as the big bang would have done.

"Do I know you?" she heard herself say, perplexed. She felt like she had *definitely* seen this ludicrously handsome face before, and yet that was nonsense because, if she had, she would hardly have forgotten. Only somehow—in her memory—she was seeing this same face artfully lit, jaw even more pronounced, eyes even more brooding . . . Oh God, she suddenly realized, it must be because he was an actual actor, someone who was probably used to playing the rom-com hero, and now there she was like a clucking super-fan, simpering and claiming familiarity. He must be so bored with all that from practically every woman he encountered. And yet . . . "*Have* we actually met, in real life?" she asked, unable to stop herself. "Or are you a famous actor?" Or is this just me recognizing my life partner . . . soulmate . . . the man I am going to marry? she thought and managed not to say, but only by physically placing her fingers over her lips.

"Er, *no*," he was insisting. "That is 'no, I'm not an actor' and 'yes, we've met,' first time when you were face down on a railway station platform." A thought occurred to him. "Are you *sure* you didn't hit your head?"

"Ha! Pirate man!" she exclaimed. And then, scraping what remained of her brain for further information, "You're Russ," she proclaimed proudly.

"Actually, it's Ross," he reminded her, emphasizing the "o" with a mouth so beautifully kissable, Petra realized she was staring at it with hers hanging open.

"Yeah, Russ," murmured Petra, giving herself a metaphorical pat on the back. "Short for Russell, I assume?" she went on, hoping the witless inanity might pass for conversation.

"No, because it's Ross, not Russ," he told her patiently.

"Short for Rossell?" she asked, puzzled.

"No, just Ross—not short for anything,"

"Oh, come on, it must be short for something," Petra's mouth went on doggedly as her brain continued to refuse to engage. "Rossie, maybe?"

An indefinable expression washed across his face. Anger? Pain?

"Well—no—because 'Rossie' isn't actually a name, is it?" he said, in a tone of superhuman patience. "Also, not even my mother calls me Rossie," he told her firmly. "Thank God."

Apparently, unable to stop herself from talking crap, Petra decided all she could gracefully do was apologize and explain: "It's just that you suddenly look . . ." She gestured to his face, unable to summon further words.

"Yeah," he admitted. "I'd been kind of . . . letting things slide."

"Okay—well—now you look, erm . . . great," Petra observed inadequately, certain he could feel the heat from her now flaming face. But that pirate-fetish motormouth had not yet done with her it seemed. "Ooh, I've just remembered a really funny joke," she heard herself announce. "To 'err' is human, to 'arr' is pirate. Geddit?"

Silence fell. This was weird! Surely the man was not impervious to the best pirate joke in the whole world? Sheesh. Tough crowd.

"Anyhow," Ross continued briskly, "I'm glad we've bumped into each other."

Petra couldn't imagine how this was true, but it was nice of him to say so.

"I was thinking about dropping in to the bookshop," he went on, "to buy the Milton, but you're here . . ." He raised a perfectly formed eyebrow. The effect was devastating.

"Okay! So . . . I am going *right* back there, *right* now," gabbled Petra. "See you in a minute?" she called over her shoulder, not waiting for a reply.

Chapter Five

Panting, Petra burst into the shop, closed the door, and then leaned on it, closing her eyes.

"Are you quite well?" came Flo's voice, laced with concern.

Petra opened her eyes and stared at Flo, unseeing. "I. Have. Just. Met . . ."

"Who?" pressed Flo. "Your maker? The abominable snowman? The Loch Ness Monster?"

"Ha! Scottish, yes! But 'Rossie' not 'Nessie,'" mumbled Petra, staring into space. The voice—the Scottish accent—*had* been the same, she was able to appreciate that now. The physical appearance? Unsettlingly different. And, of course, she couldn't possibly have met the "hot Ross" iteration before, but she still struggled to dismiss the déjà vu vibe—that version of his face with the moody lighting that she felt she was dredging up from her memory banks. It made no sense, though. How would it be possible to meet someone that stunning and not have his image burned onto her eyeballs to the exclusion of everything else from that moment on? It would have been the most memorable event of her life to date.

No, the unsettling familiarity must have simply been her brain telling her that—despite being almost beyond comprehension—this demigod and the costumed Captain Hook guy she had been so amused by were one and the same.

"You look as if you've seen a ghost," Flo persisted, her brows knitted, clearly desperate for some better-quality information from Petra about why she was in such a state.

It was too ridiculous to admit to feelings she barely understood herself, thought Petra. And she hardly knew this woman, who had probably now decided she was completely unstable.

"So," Petra clasped her hands in a parody of enthusiasm, "I think I've sold a book," she explained, trying to adopt a businesslike tone. "That's all. There's a man coming in shortly. I just bumped into him. He was looking at a copy of *Paradise Lost* the other day, and he wants it. Ooh, do the secondhand books have prices on them, by the way?" she added.

"They should have," said Flo, giving Petra a strange look but then visibly deciding to let it go. "But if there's no sticker on the book itself, all the secondhand books should be on the system, and the price will be there as well."

"I'll go and see," said Petra, glad to have something to do. She scampered upstairs to find the book still lying on the table where they had left it and—yes—as good as Flo's word, there was a fresh price label on the back. Yikes. Fifty pounds, though . . . The scruffy version of Ross didn't look as if he would have been good for fifty pence, let alone fifty pounds. However, handsome Ross looked as though fifty-pound books were very much part of his world.

"Does that sound about right?" she asked Flo, showing her the label.

"I wouldn't have a clue," Flo admitted, "but that's Charlie's writing, for sure. Charlie," she explained, "was our antiquarian book expert. He worked here for a few months last year then he got snapped up by Sotheby's, so he's in London now. He knows his stuff."

"Sure, sure," said Petra, anxious for Flo not to think she was second-guessing former staff. What did she know about secondhand books, after all?

"But it's totally up to you," Flo reassured her. "A sale's a sale. If you want to offer a discount."

Could she? Should she? Was it really her place to be giving away stock at rock-bottom prices? Surely there were *so* many other ways she would damage poor Jules and Roman's business. Doubtless she would soon find out what they all were.

The shop doorbell clanged, and the doorway darkened. The silhouette was unmistakable, those broad shoulders and long legs . . . If she hadn't appreciated the sheer physical perfection of the man on first meeting him, it would have been that the enveloping great coat had been relinquished in the spring sunshine for this khaki jacket. And it suited him. Very, very much.

Petra drew in a shuddering breath. "Fifty!" she blurted, holding the book out toward him. "But," she added on reflection, "to you—um—forty-nine pounds . . . and—er—ninety-nine pence," she went on, lamely, losing her nerve.

Ross chuckled, taking it from her, their fingers touching briefly. He seemed not to notice how Petra froze and then snatched back her hand as if it had been burned by the contact. "A penny off?" he said, examining it critically. "What a tempting offer. I'm going to have to grab it before you change your mind," he said, grinning at her, apparently relaxed, although he broke their gaze after just a moment.

How could he behave so normally? she thought, resisting the temptation to place a steadying hand over her racing heart. But then, this was *her* gazing at *his* beauty; he was hardly going to be having a similar reaction to the sight of her. She, with her London-in-winter pallor and total absence of makeup. Today, having brought few clothes with her, she was in the saggy brown sweater she had been wearing the morning of the unspeakable social media gaffe.

Ross's newly revealed beauty almost made her want to raise *her* game.

But the raw material—pale skin, poker-straight black hair in a nondescript bob, and an okay figure, not best served by her normal uniform of jeans and sweater—was never going to elevate her to his levels of personal attractiveness . . . She could maybe iron a shirt or slap on some mascara occasionally, though.

She had her pride.

While Petra was taking the opportunity to examine Ross unobserved, he was engaged in further examining the book, turning it this way and that. "Worth every penny of forty-nine pounds and ninety-nine pence," he declared. "And I need to build up my collection," he added. "I've probably only got about four copies already. Not this edition though."

"I'm like that with *Jane Eyre*," Petra admitted, as he reached for his wallet, peeling off tens from what looked like a decent roll of cash.

"Please come again," she said, as she handed him the penny change, grateful that there was no inadvertent touching this time.

In fact, he took it with comic precision between finger and thumb, squinted at it, as if to check that it wasn't counterfeit, then dropped it into the charity collection pot on the counter.

"Maybe I will," he said, waving his new book in salute as he left. "And by the way," he added, over his shoulder. "That joke? It was pretty funny."

"Well!" declared Flo, after a pause. "He *was* handsome."

"He was all right, I suppose," said Petra, hearing all too clearly how unconvincing she sounded.

"We had better keep Diana away from him. She'd have him for breakfast," Flo went on, examining Petra's demeanor shrewdly and looking as if she would like to say a lot more on the matter.

Thankfully for Petra, the two women were kept busy by a steady stream of customers after that, although Flo kindly stayed, once the shop went quiet in the afternoon, to answer all the questions on Petra's list. Even the silly ones.

The more Ross thought about his interactions with Petra that morning in comparison with the two prior meetings, the more depressed he became.

And when he was depressed, he walked.

The rented cottage was damp and poky, for all its thick-walled, oak-beamed charm, but the aspect that had really attracted him to the little house was through the gate at the end of the garden. The gate opened onto a narrow muddy path that led directly to the summit of the nearest hill. It was steep and rocky, but this walk had become his escape. His daily meditation. It was his opportunity to think and his opportunity to stop thinking. On this particular afternoon, it also led to needle-sharp rain, low clouds, and finger-nipping cold. But Ross didn't mind. He barely noticed. He strode quickly, splashing through the puddles, the fragile, striated ice layer shattering under his boots. The icy water seeped inside, through the lace holes, but he welcomed the distraction of rapidly numbing feet. His face quickly felt numb too, with no beard to lend its warmth; the newly exposed skin felt raw, and then it felt like nothing at all. Ross welcomed numb. Numb was good. Eventually numb turned to pain. But pain was good too. It was all a distraction from the complicated, swirling feelings that had started racing through his brain again, scattering his thoughts and settling, as always, into a thick, blanketing fug of self-loathing.

And shame.

His mates had laughed, of course. Back in the time when he actually *had* mates, this was. Before he had kept saying no to those nights out. Before they got tired of asking him and drifted away. Before then, they had torn out the newspaper articles and brought them along to their pub meet-ups, those hateful, artsy, black-and-white photos of him that the literature review picture desks loved to use. His friends would deface them with speccy glasses, zits, and comical mustaches. "Not just a pretty face," one article headlined. "Not *even* a pretty face," they had bantered, joshing, punching him on the shoulder.

"Nice problem to have, buddy," seemed to be the general consensus when he demurred at how the arts correspondents had gazed in wonder at his beauty and talent, gushing about his setting the scene for a new wave of talented young writers. To a man and a woman, they were rapt, not only burdening him with the weight of his own work but also casually loading onto his shoulders the dreams and aspirations of the entire literary world. He was, they informed him, the lodestone of an entire generation of young British writers.

So, no pressure.

And then, of course, there was the casual objectification: the deliberate placing of a heavily ringed hand on his knee by the mascaraed, leopard-printed literary page editor who invited him to have dinner one day soon, fluttering her lashes suggestively. Then, there was the esteemed arts critic of a national Sunday broadsheet who proposed Ross should come to his home because he, Ross, and his husband would "get on well" together. As a threesome.

Some of these people had clearly not even read his book. And that hurt, because he had been proud of his debut: a slim, dense, literary novel, crafted over the course of several years and a creative writing MA. The book had been endlessly described as a bold, brave concept, "a story of our time, told with precocity and exquisitely poetic wisdom," as one reviewer had put it. He had poured out his heart to the world. And it had listened. And then . . . when the clamor and the flattery and the acclaim of his first novel had fallen silent?

Nothing.

He had—he discovered to his horror and bemusement—nothing further to say.

He had tried, of course. At first, flexing his writing muscles, allowing himself space and solitude, had been a relief after more human contact and fuss than had ever felt comfortable. Patiently—at first—he had waited for fresh writing ideas to take root. But they did not. And then being alone had gradually become painful, even more enervating than all those interminable discussion panels, readings, and interviews had been. Once the darling of the literary world, he found the commentators and the influencers had quickly moved on. Within its diurnal round, the publishing world had inevitably discovered newer award-winners, even younger geniuses, fresher and shinier ideas.

His agent had been supportive—he couldn't fault her. His editor was less so. She, in the warm spotlight of success, quickly moved publishers for an even more elevated job title, and had leveraged her connection with him to suggest his second novel would come with her. But then their bond had soured in a blizzard of unprofessional bitterness and spiteful recriminations.

It had hardly even mattered in the end that he had been silly enough to mix business with pleasure. Because there had simply been no second novel.

For a year, two years, three years, the "just checking in" phone calls and emails from his highly regarded agent had become less and less frequent. The agent's pep talks had morphed from euphoric anticipation to gentle enquiry, through bracing statements of expectations and then—finally—to imploring. It was Ross who had ended it formally. What use was an author to a literary agent when he was producing nothing they could sell? He wasn't even producing something they could help to develop, to edit, to brainstorm . . . There had been nothing. Well, not *totally* nothing, but nothing the agent could go out on submission with. At one point, Ross had tentatively shared a couple of half-formed ideas with her, a panacea he had hoped would buy him some peace for a while. But—gently—the agent had declined to endorse these fragments with any confidence. "Not high concept enough," she said. "Too quiet," "Too derivative," "It's a brutal market."

And Ross had agreed with her, he reminded himself, running his frozen hands through his soaked hair, tipping his head back to the lowering gray sky that nearly touched the summit of the little hill as he reached it, welcoming the needle-sharp rain on his face. Now very decidedly into his mid-thirties, he was no longer even the young, fresh-faced emperor of the literary world—he had nothing to say. Nada.

And what was the use of a washed-up writer to anyone?

Even if he *did* still have the looks.

Chapter Six

It had been a good day's trade, and Petra felt much better about running the shop after Flo's briefing but—alone again in the flat—cooking her supper, the anxious swirl of negativity infected her brain again.

As she peeled the garlic and chopped the mushrooms for her carefully planned omelet supper, Petra's mind played an endless cine-reel of all her most recent and abject failures for her own delectation and entertainment.

The vaporizing of her career was up there, of course. As the inciting incident in the story of her life—a tragedy, obviously—it was an absolute banger. Since then, the narrative seemed to be spooling out as a series of opportunities to mess up any chance of a friendship with Ross. And that really hurt, she admitted to herself as she dropped the butter into the hot pan with a sizzle. Six months was going to be a long time without companionship. Although it wasn't that people hadn't been friendly. They had. Freya was a sweetheart but far too busy with the restaurant to entertain her, and Flo was fabulous, but Petra was wary of taking up time in her precious retirement, which was obviously full and delightful. Flo didn't need Petra hanging around, being a burden.

Ross would have been the most likely contender for chief companion, but each and every one of their interactions so far had been a disaster. If he hadn't been put off by her accusing him of being an alcoholic drug addict, no emerging friendship was going to survive her turning into a fawning, giggling imbecile at the sight of his freshly revealed good looks. And then there had been the luring of him in with a promised book bargain and then giving him the handsome discount of one penny. Petra groaned at the thought. And the whole "I know you from somewhere" thing must have sounded like a ploy.

Although she totally *did* know him from somewhere . . .

"Anyhow," she said aloud, as she poured in the eggs, dragging the edges into the center as they set—if she knew nothing else, she knew how to make an omelet—she was going to be in Portneath for six months, and she needed not to spend the whole time alone, letting her thoughts and memories drive her mad. Tomorrow the shop was closed, and she needed to find something to do. The weather was set to be dry but fiercely cold. She would take the opportunity to explore the area, starting with the countryside just inland. The beach could wait. Flo had been telling her there were multiple footpaths on the hills she could see from the flat's sitting room window: gentle, conical slopes, the closest of which was the hill just behind the castle at the top of the main street. She would put on her walking boots and see how far she got.

Feeling slightly better after having made a plan, Petra wolfed down her omelet, which was—if she said so herself—absolutely delicious. Then she filled the bathtub and wallowed until her fingertips went white and were as wrinkly as prunes. By the time she climbed into bed, she was yawning. She used to read herself to sleep, but that habit had irreversibly slipped it seemed. Thanks to topping up her cell phone data, she had been able to download TikTok again, probably ill-advisedly.

Ten minutes in to scrolling videos of dogs that "talked like humans"—only they didn't really, it turned out—Petra fell fast asleep with her phone still in her hand.

A HIGH, PALE blue sky and a hard frost greeted her on Sunday morning. She shivered as she dressed, layering on a thermal vest, two sweaters, and thick, fleecy leggings under her jeans. Porridge with cream and golden syrup warmed her from within, and by the time she had drained her mug of tea, Petra was raring to go.

A minute later, she was marching up the near-deserted main street, discovering the gate to the network of public footpaths just where Flo had said, on the far side of the graveyard at the top of the hill. The gate led directly to a crossroads of three paths, each marked with a finger post pointing roughly north, east, and west. The northerly path looked as if it would take Petra most directly through the valley to the funny little conical hill that was nearest, so she strode off confidently in that direction.

Soon she was panting, her breath turning to clouds of mist in the frosty air. By the time she stood at the foot of the hill, contemplating the climb, she was ready to peel off some layers. She looked around her, catching her breath. Lower down in the valley, she had passed a little cluster of stone cottages, but here there was no sign of human habitation, just some rabbit tracks and burrows, with a brave robin singing to frighten her away while perched in a bare thorn bush by the path.

Her oxygen levels restored, Petra set off up the path at a brisk pace, looking forward to seeing the view from the peak. The sky was so clear today she was sure she would be able to see for miles.

It was when it was too late to turn back that Petra spotted two things on the peak. The first was a bench, and the second was its occupant, a man—judging by the broad shoulders. He was facing away from her toward the view she was so desperate to see herself. Making polite conversation with a stranger had not been on the agenda. But she mustn't be rude, she told herself. A few remarks about the weather were all she needed to summon up. Being polite to strangers was an important life skill, she reminded herself. Not a biggie.

Only it wasn't a stranger. By the time he had stood and turned to see who was approaching him, she had already recognized the khaki jacket, and her heart sank as she remembered her behavior the previous day.

"Fancy meeting you here," he said, eyebrows raised in what looked like genuine pleasure. "Join me?" He waved gallantly at the narrow wooden bench.

"I wasn't following you," Petra said, and then realized she had made it sound like that was exactly what she was doing.

Thankfully, he didn't hear, or at least pretended not to, instead busying himself wiping the frost off the other end of the bench for her with his scarf.

Sitting down with a decorous distance between them, Petra was glad to be excused from eye contact by sitting side by side. It was eye contact with this man that had made her behave like an idiot the day before. Instead, there was the view she had longed for, and it did not disappoint. "It's beautiful," she breathed.

Below them was a patchwork of farmland, harvest-striped fields, and copses of trees checkered with neat hedgerows. In the clear winter sunshine, the river gleamed silver-blue as it widened toward the harbor below them.

"Do you come here often?" she blurted and then giggled. "Oops, world's worst chat-up line ever," she added, hoping he would put her pink cheeks down to the bracing cold. "Not that I *was* chatting you up, obviously," she went on, resisting the urge to slap herself on the forehead.

"In answer to . . . whatever that was," he replied patiently, "I *do* come here often. My cottage is that one down there." He pointed to a red-clay tiled roof down below.

"Practically your back garden, then," Petra said. "Such a funny little hill. Like a child's drawing almost."

"It's volcanic apparently," observed Ross.

"No way!"

"Way."

"Kind of makes sense, though," said Petra. "Actually, I can imagine it like a big zit on the landscape back when mankind wasn't invented." Dear God! What an allusion, she chided herself silently. What was the matter with her? There they were, enjoying the amazing view on a beautiful winter's day, and she starts talking about pus. What was it her dad used to say? Sometimes it's better to stay silent and have people think you are an idiot, than to open your mouth and remove all doubt.

"Nicely put," Ross observed, nodding politely.

She stole a glance, sensitive to any suggestion of mockery.

Although it wasn't even the stupidest thing she had ever said to him—not by a long way, unfortunately. He had the most ridiculously handsome profile, she observed, even in his slightly dodgy maroon beanie hat. And—still—familiar . . .

"We *have* met," she insisted.

"Yup. Station. Bookshop. Market. Bookshop again," he reeled off, counting on his fingers.

"No, I mean . . ." hazarded Petra. But of course, he must be right. She had lived in London for years, and now here she was, hundreds of miles away, in self-imposed exile. It was ridiculous to think she was going to bump into someone she knew. Wasn't that the entire point of coming here?

"I get it all the time," he said. "I guess I've just got that kind of face. Here. Coffee?" He reached around and produced a thermos flask with a flourish.

"I can't drink your coffee."

"It's not *that* bad," he retorted, deliberately misunderstanding. He was opening it now, releasing a plume of steam as the hot liquid interacted with the freezing air. He handed the cup to Petra, and she sniffed it appreciatively.

"Black, no sugar, I'm afraid," he said.

"What about you?" said Petra. "You haven't got a cup."

"I'll have some when you've finished," he said.

They sat, companionably, as Petra admired the view and sipped rapidly at the coffee, not wanting to keep him waiting.

"How long have you worked at the bookshop?" he asked.

Petra told him.

"You're a blow-in, like me then," he said. "I've been here since the autumn."

"I could tell you're not a local," Petra remarked.

"The accent? Yeah, I'm not from round here," he admitted.

"So, what brings you here?" asked Petra, her curiosity getting the better of her, although she instantly regretted it. Let's not get into a conversation about why *I'm* here, she thought. But it seemed Ross was as reluctant as her to exchange information.

"I just tend to move around a lot," he said repressively. The mood had instantly changed, but it didn't stop Petra from plowing on regardless.

"What about family, though . . . friends?" she enquired.

"I like being alone," Ross snapped, shutting off any further interrogation by standing up and holding his hand out for the thermos mug, which she handed to him, chastened.

"I should get going," he said, screwing the top on the thermos with what looked like unnecessary force. "Don't rush," he added, apparently just in case Petra was thinking about accompanying him down. "Enjoy the view."

Obediently, and keen to make amends—although she wasn't quite sure what she had done, apart from the usual inadvertent insults—she looked fixedly at the horizon as she heard him stomping away. A minute later, when she dared to turn around, it was confirmed that he was gone, and she was alone. Again.

Ross SHOOK HIS head angrily as he stomped back down the hill. Why was all this stuff so complicated now? He was lonely. She was nice. The intention was to be friendly and instead he was gruff and rude. When did allowing other people in his life get so hard? When he started having something to hide, he answered himself, scowling. For the thousandth time he regretted not hiding behind a writing name as his agent had gently suggested. No. His ego had insisted that he bare his soul to the world with his real name, thinking smugly of old school tormentors—teachers and students alike—and of how proud his parents would be . . . It was vanity, of course. And now, in punishment, the identity he would rather escape from dogged him everywhere. He wasn't hiding from *everyone*—just the significant proportion of the population who had seen or heard the interviews, plus the people who might have even read the damned thing. It was too much to expect that someone working in a bookshop wouldn't have heard of him.

"The highest form of vanity is love of fame." Who said that? They were right. It was his own fault.

THE REST OF the day yawned ahead of Petra when she got back to the shop. She was rubbish at being alone and was well aware it signaled a lack of inner resources. As a child she was thrilled to have time on her own; it had given her a precious chance to escape into books for hour after hour. Now, ruined by the tyranny of impossible work expectations along with the distractibility driven by her social media addiction, she could barely read the back of a cereal box without losing focus. Everyone in publishing knew the reality. You enter the profession because of a love of books and then that very thing—the reading—ends up getting pushed into the margins. With whole days spent hustling, editors and agents alike invariably tackled the never-ending "to be read" pile in their own time.

So now, when it came to the simple act of reading, Petra was all burned-out. As for whole books, even picking one up to read it gave her palpitations, unleashing a flood of thoughts about all the people she had let down. What had things come to that she didn't even have the inner resources to make the most of a day off?

Tugging her coat back on, she grabbed her phone and set off to find the little supermarket Flo had told her about. The one just over the other side of the bridge.

The familiarity of the grocery shop interior soothed her. She could be anywhere in the country; it would look just the same. She felt reassuringly anonymous and rootless. Wandering the shelves, randomly chucking things in her basket—milk, toilet roll, a packet of chocolate biscuits—she paused at the newspapers section. Maybe, if she could no longer lose herself in a book, she could at least read the Sunday papers, like normal people did? She hefted the *Sunday Times* into her basket on top of the food, added a copy of the *Observer* to balance out editorial bias, and went off to pay.

Back at the flat, she lit the fire in the sitting room, committed to getting cozy. It was soon blazing merrily, combating the chill outside. Making herself a pot of coffee and then settling on the sofa with the throw wrapped around her, Petra started to read the papers. Usually, if she read them at all, she would read on her phone, but it was strangely soothing to have all the sections of the paper slewed onto the coffee table in front of her. The *Sunday Times* had a great culture section. Knowing about all that stuff in the wider cultural arena other than just books was her job. She needed to bring herself up to speed, and browsing the Sunday papers on a chilly weekend afternoon away from work was what normal people did. She had almost forgotten that.

Now Petra learned from reading that there was a surprising amount of "culture" happening in Devon. She had been snobby in her London-centric assumptions. A couple of important plays were touring in Exeter before their London runs, and there was a huge concert hall with a full program in Plymouth, not too far away. Soon she was wired from all the coffee—Ross's coffee, in particular, had been caffeine-loaded—she needed to eat something. She broke off for a bread and cheese lunch, and then—bringing a large bar of nut chocolate with her back into the sitting room and putting another log on the fire—she braved the literary section with a flutter of anxiety.

She was confronted immediately with a sharp reminder of her own failings. In the column devoted to new releases, there was a debut novel by a writer who had requested representation from her. She had politely declined, and he had gone to another agent who had negotiated him a significant deal, by the look of it. Oops. But she was glad for him. Breaking out with your first book was an amazing achievement. Petra smiled, as she broke off another square of chocolate. She loved sharing those moments with her authors. They were to be savored. Not that a good debut necessarily heralded a stellar career, of course, and sometimes the weight of expectation with a big first publishing deal could be crushing.

Petra turned the page, and her eye was immediately drawn to a "Where are they now?" article. Echoing her thoughts, it outlined how six authors with big contracts had fared after their keenly awaited debuts. It wasn't all bad. One of them was now adapting their own books into screenplays. Another had produced a second novel to a tepid response and had finally, the article reported, returned to teaching English with their tail between their legs. Another broken dream.

And then, the last, brief, example the article writer had chosen to follow up was a novelist called Ross McCloud.

As soon as she read the name, Petra instantly remembered the book he had written. How could she forget? It was a sensation that summer and was widely agreed to be one of the most accomplished debuts the literary world had ever read. It was a novel called *Destiny*, and its simultaneous storylines and multiple protagonists all tracked over a single twenty-four-hour period, up to the end of the book, where—as the reader knew all too well—their lives devastatingly converged at the 7/7 London terrorist bombings.

The year it was published, it became one of the novels she had most often noticed people reading on the Tube—always a litmus test of a book's penetration into the market. It meant big sales. Huge. And big sales were not a given: Sometimes even the major literary prize-winning books somehow failed to translate into actual money. This was just one other reason why writing books was the most absurd way to earn a living.

Petra stared into the fire, remembering. She tended to resist reading the books that everyone else was yammering on about, stubbornly seeking out the books for her "to be read" pile that hadn't caught the public imagination quite so well. It had always felt like a tiny gesture to remedy the capriciousness of it all, the horribly unfair element of luck, on top of talent, that dictated a writer's career. But for *Destiny* she had succumbed to the hype and made an exception. She still remembered the gorgeous but spare language, the writer's skill at giving a different voice to each character, their inner monologues shared with the reader as their secrets and motivations were gradually revealed. It had been an experimental *but* accessible book. The Holy Grail. Turning back to the article, she noticed this—unlike the others—was the briefest of notes, and then she saw why.

> A second novel from McCloud is eagerly awaited but has not yet appeared. Our journalist enquired, but McCloud's agent, Veronica Bampton, of the Bruce Bampton Literary Agency, declined to give an update. The agency also declined to confirm whether McCloud was still represented by them. Enquiries directed at the publisher went unanswered. Mr. McCloud could not be traced.

Well!

Petra sat back and blew her bangs out of her eyes. Five years and not a peep? Something had clearly gone horribly wrong . . . Had he died? No, they would have said . . . How old even *was* he? She had never been particularly interested in how old the writers who approached her for representation were, even less what they looked like; physical appearance, background, gender, and age mattered less than the writing. The writing was everything. At least to start with.

Curiously, she picked up her phone and googled "Ross McCloud."

What she saw made her throw her phone across the room in astonishment.

She skittered to retrieve it from the hearth and scowling back at her were multiple search results showing the same photograph—a brooding, handsome man, with that lock of dark hair falling over his face, and those cheekbones accentuating the eyes with their thousand-yard stare. It was a moody black-and-white image. But Petra knew those eyes were green.

Milton man. Not just "Ross," the man with the insanely beautiful cheekbones, but "Ross McCloud," a writing luminary rising high and bright before disappearing from the world altogether. Or so it had seemed.

And here he was, hiding out in Portneath of all places. And Petra had found him. Damn it, she would love to find her copy of his book, but most of her possessions were still in her little flat in London.

Too hyper to stay sitting by the fire, Petra leaped up and thundered down the stairs to the used books section. Thumbing impatiently through the shelves to find the *M*s, she scanned along and—yelping with glee—pulled out a copy of his book.

She recognized the cover instantly. It was the hardback edition, just like her own copy, still with its dust jacket intact and here—on the back flyleaf of the dust jacket—was the same moody black-and-white photo she had just seen on her phone.

No wonder she kept feeling like she had seen him before. The question now was, would she ever see him again?

Chapter Seven

Days passed, with Petra jumping every time the shop door opened. She took to scanning the streets outside too, desperate to spot him. Why was he not turning up? He knew where she was. She only wished she could say the same, puzzling over his brief description of where he lived. He had pointed at some roofs from the top of the hill.

It wasn't a lot to go on.

She kicked herself that they had not exchanged cell phone numbers, but then why would they have? As far as he was concerned, she was this mildly demented—but presumably harmless—woman who ran a bookshop and was quite possibly stalking him, given the number of times they had randomly bumped into each other. None of those assumptions would lead him to seek her out, she could see that. And the random bumping into each other thing seemed to have come to a halt, unfortunately. That was to say, unfortunately for her.

But she, a literary agent—okay, an ex-literary agent—had stumbled across the most significant new writer of the decade. That *had* to mean something. It was fate, right? Somehow it made sense of all the crap that had happened, because it had led her to *this* town, hell, it had even led her to disembark from *that* train, at *that* moment, and in *that*—admittedly unconventional—way. If none of those things had happened, then . . . It was a sliding doors moment. There had to be more to the story than "literary agent bumps into fugitive author, and then never sees him again. The end."

If Flo thought Petra was acting strangely that Saturday, she was too tactful to say anything. Petra's hopes that Ross might pop up were heightened. It was market day, so, surely, he would be in town again like last week? All she had to do was spot him in the crowds and then what? Dash out of the shop and rugby tackle him to the ground? Actually, yes, she decided. That sounded like a perfectly legitimate plan.

In the end, physical intervention wasn't necessary because—just at the end of the day—when Petra had given up hope, the bell rang and in he strode.

Petra yelped, and dived into position at the register, all but pushing Flo out of the way. "You go and get yourself a cup of tea," she gabbled to Flo, not taking her eyes off him for fear that he might dematerialize before she had a chance to speak to him. She need not have worried, as he made straight for her,

"I *know* you," she told him as he reached the desk.

He sighed and rolled his eyes. "Are we seriously going to do this every time?" he asked. "We've met," he said heavily. "A lot."

"I know, I know—I mean I *know* who you are."

"Yay! I know who I am too," he quipped, but his face had drained of color and his voice was not entirely steady.

Petra raised her eyebrows meaningfully. "So you're . . ." She glanced around to make sure no one was in earshot and then leaned in and murmured out of the corner of her mouth. "You're *him*."

She leaned back again, nodding emphatically.

He sighed again, but this time, his sigh seemed to come up from somewhere deep in his soul.

He closed his eyes. "Busted," he said, hanging his head in an attitude of abject despair. He turned to go, and then—as if he had just remembered something—he turned back. "I came to give you this," he said, reaching into his coat and producing a chunky, red leather, gold-tooled volume. "*Jane Eyre*," he said. "You told me you collected different editions, like I do with *Paradise Lost*," he reminded her.

Petra could hardly bring herself to take her eyes from his face, but she glanced down at the book he was holding out and dazedly took it from him. "Thank you," she said. "That's so kind. I didn't—"

But he was walking away, not waiting for her to finish.

"No, no, no, no," she gabbled, running after him and grabbing his arm, just as he reached the door.

"I have to go," he told her, not wrenching his arm away, but looking pointedly at her hand.

"Why?" she said. "Go where?"

"Well, I'm not going to tell you *that*, am I?" he reasoned. "Excuse me, I have to go and pack. I'll be gone by morning, so there's no point calling anyone. By the time they get here, it'll be too late."

"I'm *not* calling anyone," she told him. "Who would I call? Why would I do that? It's not like the police are after you or anything. You've made it obvious you don't want to be found, so I'm not going to give you away to—I dunno, the book police, am I?"

"You're not?" Hope glimmered in his eyes.

"Of *course* not," insisted Petra. "But I really want to—well—talk to you. Can I do that? Will you come upstairs?" she asked, seeing Flo unobtrusively switching off lights and turning off the register. "I've got tea! Wine? Chocolate hobnobs? Please don't go . . ."

There was a pause, where Petra looked at Ross imploringly, at a loss for words at last. If only silence was something she could muster more often, she thought.

"Chocolate hobnobs, eh?" he said at last, raising a ghost of a smile. "Okay, you've got me."

They started with tea. Petra plonked Ross in the sitting room and instructed him to light the fire while she put the kettle on. She was terrified that he would change his mind and run. Her ears were alert for any noises that would suggest he was leaving.

She breathed a sigh of relief to see he was still there when she elbowed open the sitting room door and put her tray down on the coffee table with a clatter.

"You've done that before," she joked weakly, nodding her head at the enthusiastically burning fire. The logs were already beginning to glow red beneath the yellow flames.

"The cottage I'm staying in doesn't have central heating," he told her. "It's a summer vacation rental primarily."

"Do you move around a lot?"

He nodded.

"So . . ." she announced, pouring the tea from a brown teapot into two generously sized mugs, "tell me everything."

"Interrogation by chocolate biscuit? You'll have to be more specific. *Everything*'s a lot."

"I'm a believer in the carrot, not the stick," she told him, holding out the plate, "and you *know* what I want to know about. What happened?"

He sighed, taking a biscuit, adding milk to his tea, and then staring, apparently unseeing, at the biscuit in his hand. "It's going to sound ungrateful," he began, addressing the biscuit earnestly. "I know how lucky I am—but I found all the fuss over that book a bit . . . much." The haunted expression on his face informed her what an understatement that was.

"'A bit much'?"

"Yeah, I mean, I wasn't expecting it. Everyone tells you you're going to get ignored, you won't get an agent, you won't get a deal, you won't sell even if you do get your book out there . . . and so—my whole experience was the opposite of all that. It was just ridiculously overwhelming . . ."

"So, the whole 'hot new writer' thing . . . ?" said Petra and then blushed. "I don't mean 'hot' as in 'attractive,' obviously."

"Obviously." He laughed. "But—yeah—I think I was just ready to be invisible—and quite right too. I thought my first book was never going to be the *best* thing I would ever write. I was supposed to be learning my craft, right? Not smashing it right out of the park."

"Nice problem to have?"

"Sure. Anyhow," he shrugged, "it turned out it wasn't just the 'best' thing, it was the *only* thing I was ever going to write."

"So, no book two?"

He shook his head. There was no laughing now. Petra glimpsed the pain behind his eyes and gasped in sympathy. "*Nothing?*" she queried.

He shook his head, staring at his hands. He had placed the biscuit down by his mug, untasted. "Nothing remotely publishable. At first, I just thought I needed to get away from all the noise and fuss, you know? Just go where the phone would stop ringing, where my brain wouldn't be being distracted by the daily bulletins from my agent. 'These rights have sold, those sales figures have come through. Do you want to write the screenplay yourself?' Blah, blah . . . And yes, I can hear myself. Entitled fool, you're thinking, yeah?"

Petra shook her head slowly. "I get it," she said softly. "You just needed to get back into your own head."

"Yeah, only—guess what? I went back in there and . . . crickets."

"Too many expectations?" Petra asked. She hadn't really thought about it before. None of her clients had ever had stunningly successful debuts unfortunately, but the whole "second book" weight of expectations was definitely a thing.

"Maybe. But also, maybe I've just said it all. Everything that was in my tiny brain came out in the first book, and now I have nothing." He splayed his hands, palms up.

Petra took another biscuit, thoughtfully. For a long moment, they sat in companionable silence, watching the flames dancing.

"So," he said briskly, "what's your story?"

"I too have nothing," she intoned, trying to make a joke of it, but he just waited calmly. Expectantly. His unfathomable green eyes resting on her face.

So she told him.

And, damn him, when she got to the bibulous pedophile bit, Ross threw back his head and laughed, on and on. "Not saying you were right about the child molestation bit," he said eventually, wiping away tears of mirth, "but—if it's any consolation—I have heard that guy is a complete tool. But then you'd know that?"

"He wasn't the easiest," she admitted.

"A relief, then?" He screwed up his face.

"Yeah, phew," she deadpanned. "I mean, who wants a career anyhow?"

"You ran?"

"I ran," she admitted. And there it was. Ross couldn't doubt the veracity of her sympathy over his own predicament. They were the same. Fellow victims of fate.

"I mean, it wasn't just that," she admitted, remembering the exquisite feeling of what she now realized might have been relief when Alistair suggested she might need a career break. Her eyes moistened again at the memory. "I kind of . . ." She cleared her throat, loosely disguising an eye dab as a nose scratch. "I had already kind of lost my mojo a bit."

She felt his gaze. She felt seen, and also—for the first time—able to perhaps articulate a feeling she had hardly dared even acknowledge until now. "I *had* started to struggle," she went on. "I . . . stopped being able to read."

"You can't *read*?" He was incredulous. "Why? Galloping myopia? Late onset dyslexia?"

Petra smiled wanly. "I don't know . . . Picking up a new manuscript, every time, the weight of expectation, the stress of finding I had overlooked a unicorn—like yours—the even bigger stress of taking on some material and then not being able to place it, or placing it and then watching it fail, not because of the work, but because of something *I'd* done, or something the publisher failed to do, and I couldn't make them, because I wasn't good enough . . ."

She glanced up and was affronted to discover that Ross was silently shaking with laughter again. "What now?" she demanded. "That's funny? Listen, I'm pouring my heart out here."

"You have to admit, it is a *little* bit funny," he said, trying and failing to stifle his mirth. "I mean, look at us! We're a writer who can't write, and an agent who can't read . . ."

Petra giggled reluctantly. He was right. It *was* absurd.

Ross was now so amused that he was wiping tears from his eyes. There was something so contagious about laughter. God knows, she'd barely raised a smile since she had left London. Whenever they had nearly managed to suppress their hilarity, they caught each other's eye and set each other off again.

There was a near hysterical component to it, Petra felt. And then something even more ridiculous struck her. "Plus," she contributed, "we're stuck, in an *actual* bookshop!"

"Oh, the irony," he agreed, clearing his throat and trying, unsuccessfully, to stop the laughter bubbling up again.

It had felt good to laugh. If there was any remaining awkwardness between them, the hysteria had melted it away. Afterward, they chatted for a couple of hours about everything except their former work: families (minimal on both sides), hobbies (same), aspirations (confusingly nonexistent). They were both—they agreed—in a liminal space where the future they dared to expect had disappeared and not yet been replaced by anything else.

So . . . same.

Petra smiled as she got ready for bed. It was a relief to have gotten past the ridiculous breathless wanting to giggle all the time at how devastatingly handsome Ross was. Now, thankfully, what came out of his mouth felt more important than the distractingly kissable appearance of his lips.

Friendship. That was what it was now. Thank goodness. Romance was the last thing she needed.

She slipped into bed and, sitting up against the pillows, opened *Jane Eyre* with reverence. It really was a lovely edition, printed in nineteen fifty-three, she saw. There were color plates with beautiful watercolors of key scenes and—better than that, even—settling in to read, Petra was immersed instantly into the life of ten-year-old Jane and the horrors of the red room.

Gripped by the familiar tale, Petra read until the early hours, waking the next morning to find the book still open on the bed.

Tears pricked at her eyes as she got up and put the book reverently on the chest of drawers beside the bed, ready for nightfall. She already couldn't wait. Ross didn't even know what his thoughtful present had done for her. It was a tiny first step—but she was reading . . .

One of the things on Petra's "Ask Flo" list next morning was the entry about the Portneath Book Club. It was in the shop diary for the coming Tuesday evening.

"I think it would be good if you were there," Flo told Petra. "Things are getting a bit fraught, and people behave better if there is a guest."

"Not sure if I like the idea of being a United Nations peacekeeping envoy," admitted Petra. "What do you mean 'fraught'?"

"Insurrection," Flo offered darkly. "You'll see . . ."

Petra was intrigued, but the day turned out far too busy to interrogate the older woman more thoroughly. She barely had a chance to get through the list of "need to knows" in between serving customers and putting book orders through their antiquated computer system. The day flew by pleasantly, and Petra was weary when she came to shut up shop, although she was pleased when Ross arrived for a chat.

"Handbags at dawn," joked Ross when Petra told him about the book club. "If you're there to keep the peace, I'd arrive armed if I were you. Those little old ladies can be vicious when they fall out over protagonist motivations."

"Will *you* come?"

"No way," he said unhelpfully. "I value my life. Anyhow, what excuse would you make for me being there?"

"You could be helping me set out the tea and biscuits. Or you could say you were joining the club."

Ross scoffed. "No thanks," he said.

"You could recommend your own book?" Petra teased.

"Because *that* wouldn't be monstrously egotistical at all," he replied, but his face clouded over, and Petra regretted prodding Ross's only sore point.

"Sorry," she said. "Tactless."

"Nah, you're fine," said Ross, but he was frowning and failing to meet her eye.

Chapter Eight

Conversation had stalled after that, Petra remembered when she was lying in bed later, regretting her quip. She had been trying hard, since arriving in Portneath, but there was seemingly no end to her talent for saying the wrong thing.

Perhaps it was because she was a literary agent—an *ex*-literary agent—but she was pining to know more. Ross had definitely been given a two-book deal, so what had happened to his advance for book two? Had he been made to pay it back? It was rare, but she had heard of that happening. He didn't seem to be working but clearly had *some* money . . . she mustn't be nosy . . . But—ooh—she wondered how much that book had made him? Probably not as much as the man on the street thought, she told herself, knowing the industry too well.

Feeling mildly ashamed of her nosiness, and not able to sleep, Petra reached for her phone. She googled his name—not for the first time—and found the *Bookseller* article about the signing, and then—of course—there had been all the coverage about the debut book's extraordinary success. These all basically said the same thing. He was from a tiny village in the Scottish Highlands. His father was a postman; his mother worked in a factory; he had been exceptional in school, receiving a full scholarship to a prestigious Edinburgh academy and then getting a scholarship to Oxford; he completed his creative writing MA with distinction by his mid-twenties, debuting his first novel at just twenty-nine years old, and then . . . tumbleweeds. He had no LinkedIn profile, or any other social media presence, come to that: no writing website, no Amazon author page, and his agent no longer listed him as a client on the agency website.

So, she concluded, putting her phone down with a sigh, as before, Ross McCloud, darling of the literary world, had deliberately and thoroughly scrubbed himself from the map. And the single thing she was dying to know was also the one topic of conversation she dared not bring up with him. People didn't suddenly lose their abilities for no reason. If she knew anything about storytelling, it was that when something dramatic changed, there was always an inciting incident. So . . . what had been his?

In the same ballpark, she admitted to herself as she snuggled down to sleep, were other hopelessly impertinent, unaskable questions such as—their now almost-daily catch-ups notwithstanding—what was he doing with himself for the rest of the time? She was *increasingly* sure he was writing again. He had hinted as much.

Now, that was something her re-emerging literary agent self was dying to read.

PETRA WOULD DO most things to avoid conflict, so when Tuesday evening came around, she was genuinely nervous. Flo's instructions were to do very little in preparation, so after closing Petra just fiddled around, clearing a space in the middle of the shop and putting out some chairs. She gave the mugs a good wash too, as they were quite stained, and dug out a couple of plates for the chocolate biscuits to go on. She had splashed the petty cash for some fancy chocolate ones, hoping to quell any violence via distraction.

Flo arrived first, with Diana and Mungo in tow.

Having only ever seen Diana from a distance, Petra discovered she was just as elegant up close: a tall woman in her sixties or seventies with an armful of tinkling silver bracelets, a glamorous mane of blond-gray hair, and a general impression of trailing chiffon scarves. She smelled absolutely delicious too.

Mungo, a man of a similar age to Diana, was also pristine, with his pressed woolen trousers and a scarlet sweater that looked so soft it could only be cashmere. He responded to Flo's introductions in a deep, gentle voice, taking Petra's hand in both his own. She would have avoided this if she could without being rude, as—through nerves—her paw was so cold and sweaty.

"You're freezing," he exclaimed, rubbing her hand between his warm, dry ones with their impeccably clean nails. Nobody got their nails that shiny without buffing, Petra thought. "You poor thing," he went on, chafing briskly and then insisting on repeating the maneuver on her other one. "Is there some heating you can put on? Would you like to borrow my jersey?" he added, making as if to strip it off there and then.

"I'm fine!" Petra assured him, but he insisted on fetching the little electric space heater from the office and then went to find her in the tiny kitchen behind the shop to help with the coffee and tea.

"I can do all this," he assured her, waving her away. "Why don't you go out and talk to Diana. She loves having new people to boss around."

Flo and Diana were deep in intense conversation. "The peasants are revolting," Diana was declaring. "There are 'factions.' There will be blood before the evening's out," she added darkly. "'Specially as it's Beatrice's turn to choose the next book and she always chooses such dreary ones."

"Goodness, so she does," agreed Flo, turning to Petra. "Well, that'll get everything out in the open, at least. Something has got to give."

"There won't be *actual* fighting, will there?" asked Petra anxiously, remembering Ross chuckling over the "handbags at dawn" suggestion. God knows what passed for normal behavior in these circles.

Diana and Flo both broke into peals of laughter. "Absolutely not," Flo said at last, wiping a tear of mirth from her eye. "Poor child. We've frightened her half to death with our dramas."

"It'll be fine," Diana reassured Petra, rubbing her upper arm bracingly. "Leave it to me. I'm used to making people behave themselves."

"It's 'do as you say, not as you do,' then," Mungo interjected cheekily as he came into the shop with a laden tray of mugs and chocolate biscuits.

Diana threw him a quelling look, but it didn't look to Petra as if he took much notice. Clearly this was all just the normal banter between the two of them, much like the relationship she had with Ross. Was she allowed to call it a "relationship"? she wondered. What was it now anyhow? A friendship? Something else?

There was no time to ponder as people seemed to arrive constantly from that point. Soon there was a circle of eight women, with Mungo as the token male. They were all chattering loudly, exclaiming over the fancy chocolate biscuits and helping each other to tea from the big tin kettle. It all seemed perfectly affable to Petra. For now.

Two women who introduced themselves to Petra as Joan and Muriel—and could only have been sisters, they looked so ridiculously alike—set themselves slightly apart from the others, chatting quietly just to each other, until Diana called them to order.

"So, the book was *The Fox Wife*; who's read it?" Diana raised her own hand and cast her eye around the circle. "Up or down, Genny?" she queried a sweetly smiling woman in a denim shirt, who couldn't have been much older than Petra.

"Ish?" Genny replied. "I didn't quite get to the end."

"Shall we avoid talking about the ending, for Genny's sake?" Diana asked the group, generating a quiet moan from more than one quarter.

"Don't worry, don't worry!" interjected Genny quickly. "I don't mind! I think I've guessed it anyway . . . I'll be interested to find out if I'm right."

Even this exchange made Petra nervous, but—after that—things seemed to go smoothly. They were a nice bunch, and the love of reading was apparent. It was delightful seeing people get excited about books, Petra thought, remembering with a pang how she too had loved reading as a hobby. Now it was her job, and there was no returning to those innocent and joyful times, not entirely.

Petra was aware of *The Fox Wife* but hadn't read it, feeling it would require too much brainpower and concentration, both things she had very much lacked in the months prior to leaving London. It was amazing to realize now how much that inability to concentrate had been panicking her. Even remembering it now was making her anxiety levels soar.

"All right?" murmured Mungo, who was sitting beside her. His expression was a mixture of concern and reassurance, making Petra's eyes flood with tears. Now he—and anyone else who noticed—would have her down as an anxious wreck, she told herself angrily. Great.

She gave him a wobbly smile, and he surreptitiously whipped out a pristine white handkerchief, passing it to her under cover of the book he was holding in his lap. She dabbed gratefully.

"Better?" he asked, out of the corner of his mouth, while looking dead ahead.

She nodded. "Thank you, you're so sweet," she whispered.

There it was again: that feeling she had had after meeting Freya, Flo, and the others. It was a community that had each other's backs. And that they had a good life out here, miles from London, where she had convinced herself the action was, several unrelentingly stressful years ago. People were happy here. And kind.

Diana had been leading the discussion with questions about the book, but now people had stopped addressing the whole room with their thoughts and were chatting among themselves until Diana clapped her hands. Silence fell instantly.

"Thank you, everyone, for your thoughts on tonight's book. I think we can all agree it was a pleasant, entertaining, and thought-provoking read. Thank you, Genny, for proposing it."

"Even though you were the only one not to finish it," quipped someone.

Genny smiled ruefully. "One word," she said. "Ofsted inspection. Okay, two words," she admitted with a shrug.

"For context," Mungo whispered to Petra, "Genny is head teacher at Middlemass primary."

At the mention of the school, Petra remembered she had wanted to ask Flo whether Capelthorne's was supporting schools. She didn't want any of Jules and Roman's initiatives to dissolve away on her watch.

"Aaanyway," said Diana, looking around the room to quell further interruptions, "our next choice comes from Beatrice, of course. Beatrice, have you chosen?"

Petra followed Diana's gaze, which was directed at a determined-looking, solid woman in her sixties, with a bowl haircut and a slash of crimson lipstick on an otherwise unmade-up face.

"Yes," said Beatrice. "I have—as some of you know—been writing a paper on the efficacy and relative environmental impact of differing plastic waste sorting and recycling protocols, and I have found a marvelous source in this treatise on the subject." As she spoke, she rummaged in a capacious reusable shopping bag before brandishing a chunky ring-bound book. "It gathers together hitherto uninterrogated data from no fewer than sixty-eight countries," she declared excitedly.

Not just a pamphlet then, thought Petra, with a smile at the barely suppressed groans emanating from the other participants.

"Was there something?" Diana said, casting a sharp eye around the group.

There was a brief silence and then, bravely, Joan piped up. "Actually," she said, "I just wanted to say that I love being in a book club, because it can make me aware of books that I enjoy; books that I wouldn't have discovered if someone else hadn't recommended them."

"Yes . . . yes . . ." came the sibilant, whispered agreement of others.

"And," Muriel picked up the thread her sister had commenced with, "I am sure we should all find out more about plastic waste disposal, because I cannot deny"—she made a nod to Beatrice—"it is an important subject we positively have a duty to understand better."

Again, there were nods around the group, and slightly less enthusiastic yeses, but Muriel wasn't done. "However," she went on, "I just feel—and I am not the only one—that I am being compelled to read things that are 'good for me.'"

More whispered agreement.

"And I am *just not* prepared to do that anymore!"

Aha, thought Petra. There it was.

"Yes!" piped up another lady, seemingly empowered by Muriel's and Joan's bravery. "I saw the new Jill Mansell on the way in," she declared. "I want to read that! I want my reading to be a pleasure!"

"Hear, hear," rumbled Mungo, before shooting an anxious glance at Diana. But now, Petra noticed, Diana was sitting back in her chair, bright-eyed, clearly happy to see the insurrection play out.

"Hands up who wants to belong to a book club for happy books," cried Flo. "I for one am perfectly prepared to say I *adore* writers like Jilly Cooper and Jenny Colgan. Always have, always will."

"And Sue Moorcroft!" declared Joan.

"And Veronica Henry," cried another lady.

"And *crime*," suggested Muriel. "I love a bloody murder and a good mystery."

"She does," agreed Joan. "You like a police procedural, don't you?" she told her sister.

"I'm *devouring* all the Kate Rhodes books at the moment; they've got *horrific* murders in them," Muriel declared happily. "She's a bit like that Shetlands crime writer."

"Ann Cleeves! I love the Shetland books," confided another lady. "I must try these ones—Kate who?"

"Rhodes," supplied Muriel, leaning toward her.

"Beach reads," suggested Mungo diffidently. "That's what I call them. Something to enjoy on a sun lounger. My favorites are Wilbur Smith and all the Jack Reacher books."

"In that case," suggested Muriel, "you might like Chris Ryan. My hubby loves a bit of SAS adventure."

"Ooh, that *does* sound good," Mungo enthused. "I already love the Andy McNab ones. Thank you."

A swell of conversation filled the room.

Diana clapped her hands again. "Okay," she said, looking around for silence. "So I propose that there will, henceforth, be a Beach Reads Book Club. Who wants to join?"

Everyone except poor Beatrice, who was now the color of a beet, raised their hands.

"Good," said Diana. "And who *also* wants to stay in the current book club."

Again, everyone—except Joan and Muriel—raised their hands.

"Fine!" said Diana. "There we go, something for everyone. Joan and Muriel, I propose that you should both lead the new club. Do I have a second?"

Mungo rumbled a response, and Diana gave him an affirmative nod.

"Settled!" she declared. "Now, someone pass me another one of those splendid chocolate biscuits."

"Drinks at The Bell tonight?" Freya popped her head in the shop to propose, one morning a few days later. "Time for you to meet the crowd, I think. All work and no play, et cetera."

"Oh, I don't know if I can make it," Petra demurred. "I've got a date with my pajamas and a good book this evening." It was true; she and Flo had started the yearly inventory, and they had at least a couple of hours more to do after closing time. Plus, she was halfway through her umpteenth reading of *Jane Eyre* and the getting-to-know-Rochester scenes were her favorites. Somehow, she had discovered, reading a deeply familiar book didn't trigger her anxiety the way a new book did.

"Nonsense," Flo said unhelpfully. "It'll do you good to get out. I'm fine on my own."

"What? You, going up and down that stepladder? I don't think so . . ." insisted Petra.

"I'll leave you two ladies to your row," laughed Freya. "Eight o'clock sharp!" she declared, pointing at Petra. Then she ducked out of the shop rapidly before Petra had a chance to reply.

"Going up and down the steps on your own *does* add a lot to the time it takes," admitted Flo.

"Not the reason why," muttered Petra. But, fine, make Flo think it was a time and motion thing, not the ridiculousness of letting a woman in her eighties climb a ladder. While alone in the shop. Although—to be fair—she was the fittest woman in her eighties Petra had ever met.

"Why don't I come in on Tuesday to finish inventory instead," Flo was continuing. "Ah no, hang on, this Tuesday is WI, now let me see." She thumbed through a little lilac diary, murmuring to herself. "Wednesday? No . . . Thursday? No . . . Friday? Mm . . . No, I have to bake that evening for the coffee morning . . ."

"Look, call me out for insurrection, but can't the inventory wait a couple of weeks?" proposed Petra. "It doesn't have to be done in February, does it?"

"Fair comment," admitted Flo. "I've always done it at this time of year, but I'm sure Jules and Roman won't mind. As long as it gets done by the financial year-end."

"There you go! Loads of time," said Petra.

Secretly, working with Flo the last two nights after closing—doing deathly dull work—she had been missing her time normally spent with Ross. They had fallen into a pattern where he would sneak into the shop and settle himself on the second floor toward the end of the day. Then when Petra closed the shop, they would sit together and shoot the breeze. At the beginning, she would bring up coffee from the little kitchen by the office, but then they both agreed the caffeine wasn't the best idea at that time of day. Instead, Ross would bring beer, and—when they got chilly in the shop once the heating was off for the day—they would retire to the fireside in the sitting room upstairs.

That evening, Petra, accepting her fate, tried to persuade Ross to come with her to the pub. She was sure Freya's friends were lovely, but she was still a little shy, plus—as she pointed out—Ross could maybe make some new friends too.

"I don't need friends," he declared.

"Everyone needs friends," Petra replied.

"*You're* my friend. I'm all friended up, thanks."

"Not a verb. Anyhow you need to get out more."

"Says who?"

"Me."

"But people always want to know what people 'do.' What do I say?"

"Tell them you're a spy," suggested Petra. "A secret agent. It's almost true. You're incommunicado. They don't have to know why."

"Actually, I'm incognito," corrected Ross.

"You're both," Petra appeased.

"And I'm pretty sure being incognito doesn't include going around declaring you're incognito," Ross went on. "*Or* a spy."

"You could perfectly well tell them you're a writer," Petra reasoned. "They don't have to know what sort of writing. Or what you've done before. Lots of people are writers. It can be loads of things."

Ross suddenly looked bleak. "Not even a writer anymore, though, remember?" he reminded her.

Petra looked at him sympathetically, her head on one side. "Why don't you want people to know? If it was me who'd written that amazing book, I'd be proud."

"Okay, well . . . I mean, I'm not *not* proud, but talking about it's something else. Also, maybe I still think like a writer: I feel like I *need* to be invisible," Ross admitted. "It's freeing not having to join in. I like to be in the corner, watching . . . listening . . . God, it sounds really creepy when I say it like that. I just need to know that people are reading my words, not watching my life."

"I get that," said Petra softly. "So . . . you *are* writing?"

In reply, Ross stood up abruptly, ruffling his hands through his hair, pulling at the roots as if he would like to tear it all out. It had grown since his dramatic makeover, with a wave appearing that just made him look even more like Lord Byron, or a brooding hero in one of Petra's favorite romances. "Maybe," he said shortly. "Now, don't you have somewhere to be?"

Chapter Nine

Time always flew when Petra was with Ross. Now it was late, and she had precisely ten minutes to get ready and present herself at the pub, or they would all think she was rudely not coming. Or—nearly as bad—they would think she was a diva who didn't think twice about showing up late. And she minded, very much, what they all thought, even if she *was* going to be gone by the end of the summer.

Half-crouching in front of the sink in the tiny bathroom, Petra tried hard to see herself in the tiny, age-spotted mirror. It was just an evening in the pub, but the whole thing felt alien and ridiculously daunting. Even though she was "in public" in the shop all day, being "in public" at the pub felt like a bigger effort was required. She gave up on mascara because her hand was shaking too much and settled for just brushing her teeth and then sticking on a bit of lip gloss.

In the bedroom, as she pulled on a slightly dressier top and changed her shoes, Petra admitted to herself that she was out of the habit of socializing. She had had a loose group of London friends once, but she was either out in the evening at work events, frantically networking, or she was too tired to meet up with people at all. On weekends, she felt she should be reading for work, not out having what passed for fun when you had no money in London. In the end, people had gradually stopped involving her, so that had been that.

It seemed the whole of Portneath was going out that Friday evening. All around her, as she walked up the steep main street, she saw groups of young people, couples holding hands, families heading into the pizza restaurant or the posh burger bar that served sweet potato fries and better-than-average cocktails.

Hardly anyone was alone.

Her heart pounding, Petra pushed open the pub door and was immediately assailed by a wall of noise and the pungent, yeasty aroma of old spilled beer. The place was crammed already. With scrubbed floorboards and a long, wooden-topped bar all along one side, the pub seemed mostly to be filled with people standing, although there were some little groups sitting at tables. Petra's heart sank. She couldn't see Freya's bright-blond hair anywhere, although that could easily be because her view was blocked by the crowds. She desperately wished she were taller so she could see over heads. Should she just turn tail and tell Freya she had developed a migraine and decided not to come? No. Apart from anything else, she knew Ross would ask, and she would sound impossibly lame if she admitted she had bailed, especially as she was hoping to maintain the moral high ground over his refusing to accompany her.

Starting to politely squeeze through the crowds, she quickly learned to gently barge with a hand on an elbow here, a dart through a narrow gap there. She was broadly heading for the fireplace that she could glimpse at the far end. When she got there, she sighed with relief to see Freya sitting in a group of five or six people on two sofas set on either side of the fire. Freya was laughing and slipping her hand through the arm of a handsome man sitting next to her. This was Finn, Petra presumed, Freya's new husband of not even a year. She was grateful that Flo had briefed her a little on who might be there.

Freya sprang to her feet and bounded over as soon as she saw Petra, enveloping her in a hug and then taking her arm to tug her over to the little group. Shouted introductions were carried out, and Finn was dispatched to the bar to get Petra a drink. She asked for a gin and tonic, as it was the first thing that popped into her head, but then felt like an idiot, as she saw the rest of the group was drinking pints of something amber-colored and slightly cloudy.

"Scrumpy," Freya told her, pointing at her own glass. "Local and lethal. You think you're fine until you stand up and realize your legs are drunk."

Given the noise levels, conversation was almost impossible, and Petra was limited to nodding and smiling and trying to look interested as the barely audible conversation bounced around the group. Still nervous, Petra drank far too quickly and then—realizing she had emptied her glass—she indicated through hand signals and facial expressions that she would get the next round, but Freya was having none of it. "New girls don't buy, it's the law," she told her, getting up instead. Being so tiny, she was immediately swallowed by the crowd as she elbowed her way to the bar.

At this, Petra sat with her knees together, feeling even more awkward. She was grateful when the woman with dark, curly hair sitting opposite came around and plonked herself next to her.

"I'm Jess," she shouted, in Petra's ear. "You likely didn't hear the intros first time 'round. Want to come to the ladies' room with me?"

Petra nodded and then instantly regretted it. Why on earth would she want to go to the loo? She didn't need to pee. Oh God, maybe it was Jess's way of inviting her to take drugs or something? She didn't seem to be the type, but there was no way of knowing, was there?

Obediently, she followed Jess down the corridor to the back of the building, glimpsing a small deserted beer garden through a glass door beyond the bathrooms.

"Thank goodness!" exclaimed Jess, as the door of the ladies' loo clumped closed behind them, and the noise levels dropped. "I didn't really need a pee," she confided. "I just thought it would be nice to be able to actually talk, rather than yell."

"It's a relief!" admitted Petra.

"We book lovers have to stick together."

"What do you do?" asked Petra, before remembering that Ross clearly despised the question. Jess didn't look as if she minded being asked at all.

"Regional reading lead for local schools," she told Petra. "It basically means I help with the libraries and reading programs. It's pretty broad, actually. I get stuck into World Book Day, competitions, sponsorship, reading schemes, grant-applications, the whole thing."

"How long have you been doing that?"

"Not long," admitted Jess. "I moved here only a couple of years ago. I put my grandmother's books in the telephone box outside my house and it kind of took off." She smiled, remembering. "Also, I met Aiden—he's the grumpy-looking guy I was sitting next to out there. So—long story short—I decided to stay, and the job came along, so . . ." She shrugged.

"But what qualifies you for all that stuff you do? It sounds like you need to be an expert in—well—pretty much everything!" Oops, rude, thought Petra. "What qualifies you . . . ?" Ouch. But Jess didn't seem to have taken offense.

"Yup, jack of all trades," admitted Jess. "But I just love books, that's my main qualification. Plus, I used to be a librarian, in another life. It's just so lovely to meet another book lover."

Petra didn't like to put her straight that, actually, she wasn't sure she *was* a book lover anymore.

"So, you're running Capelthorne's?"

"Just until the end of the summer," said Petra.

"People who come here have a habit of staying."

"Can't see that happening," said Petra. "What would I do?"

"We'll see . . ." said Jess mysteriously. "Now, I was looking forward to meeting you for a specific reason. I have a cunning plan to launch a little literary festival here at the end of the summer. Actually, it was supposed to be me and Jules, but now she's away. I didn't want to wait another year, so I thought I'd just start small."

"Because you haven't got enough to do?"

"Yeah." Jess grinned. "Anyhoo, *you* know about literary festivals."

"I do?" Petra replied anxiously. "I mean, I've been to a few . . ."

"That'll do nicely," Jess piped up. "Will you help me?"

Petra looked at Jess blankly. Did this woman not know she was a walking disaster, the kiss of death to everything she touched?

Of course, she didn't. Not yet. But then a tiny thought crept into her head. Okay, several thoughts: The first was that Jess seemed delightful, and it would be nice to spend more time in her company. The second was that she needed to broaden her skill set, seeing as she had failed as a literary agent. She was going to have to find *something* to do to support herself in the future. A book festival was distressingly "booky," which wasn't ideal, but she supposed she needed to say yes to everything that fate presented.

"Sorry, I shouldn't ask," Jess said, anxiously, clearly watching the expressions flitting across Petra's face as she sifted through the issues, ending with—Petra was sure—a look of gloom. Because these days, thinking about her future did that to her face.

"Actually, yes, why not," Petra made herself say while trying to raise a smile. "I'm honestly not sure what good I can do, but I'll try."

Jess beamed and did a little skip of pleasure. Mission accomplished, she then led Petra, arm in arm, back to the bar in triumph. Petra was relieved to see the place had emptied out a little. Patrons who had arrived to have drinks after work had disappeared off home, or on to somewhere where they could find food. It was a blessing, she decided, that the noise levels had dropped.

As a double bonus, the little group seemed to have now accepted her as part of the furniture, benignly ignoring her, which suited Petra just fine; she was done having shouted conversations with each of them in turn, repeating her name, details of her recent retreat from London—the less said about the circumstances the better—and her purpose in Portneath.

They all seemed delightful, if crazily, glamorously good-looking. Freya's partner, Finn, was one of the most handsome men Petra had ever met, and it was a high bar now that she knew Ross. Finn seemed sweetly protective of Freya too, resting his arm casually over the back of the wooden bench they were sharing and absently stroking her bare shoulder with one finger as he chatted to Gabriel about cheese. Could it really be cheese? Petra might have been mishearing. Finn and Freya checked in on each other often, locking eyes as if choreographed, Finn's slightly intense expression relaxing into a sweet smile each time as Freya silently reassured him she was okay.

Aiden and Jess were cute with each other too, Jess gently teasing her partner whenever he got too serious, to which he responded by instantly playing the underdog for laughs.

Imogen and Gabriel were the most daunting of all, though. Jess had told her that Gabriel and Imogen lived in the manor house in Middlemass, just up the road. Jess had briefly divulged that Imogen was none other than Imogen Crawley, the Carnegie-award-winning children's author and illustrator. Petra knew her agent slightly. The story of Imogen's meteoric rise was approaching legendary in publishing circles. Petra was too shy to disclose to Imogen that she was from the same world, and she was hoping it wouldn't come up. She had no impressive client names to bandy around, not anymore. In fact, she found herself too shy to speak to either of them much. Maybe next time.

Overall, she thought, glancing at the clock behind the bar, it was clear that being in Devon, with a partner who adored you, and a fulfilling job to do, made for a damned good life.

No wonder this Jules woman had defected from the London publishing scene.

It was nine o'clock already and Petra was stifling yawns. When the group thrashed out a plan to return to Finn and Freya's so that Freya could knock them up some pizzas, Petra tactfully declined. They all put up enough resistance at this for her to feel wanted, but they walked her, en masse, to the shop door and allowed her to escape equitably enough.

Lying in bed with her eyes pinned open, staring at the ceiling, Petra smiled to herself. Having a group of friends to hang out with was nice. She had been lonely in London, where friendships seemed harder to come by, let alone maintain. Maybe Jules and Roman would want her to stay for longer? The thought of returning to London in August, the summer heat making it the very worst time to be in the city, was starting to fill her with dismay, and it wasn't even spring yet. A lot could change in six months, she told herself, rolling onto her side and willing sleep to come.

Chapter Ten

Petra slept well that night. It might have been from relief.

Next morning, during a lull, she shared her latest idea with Flo.

"I'm going to ask the Beach Reads Book Club for their all-time favorite romance recommendations," she told the older woman. "I've got them all coming in for cake and prosecco in a couple of days, so I can pick their brains, and then we can order in stock for Valentine's Day."

"Excellent!" said Flo. "And can I just say how lovely it is to see you be so enthusiastic. Fresh ideas, that's what this place needs."

Settling into her stewardship of Capelthorne's, Petra realized she was waking with feelings of joy instead of dread most days. She would spring out of bed, well rested and excited, looking forward to everything in her schedule, from the first cup of tea, which she allowed herself to drink in bed while looking out at the wonderful view, to her days in the bookshop, chatting to customers; she had spent another pleasant evening in the pub with Freya and friends, was enjoying her catch-ups with Flo on Saturdays, and then there were her almost daily chats with Ross after work, which filled her evenings with laughter and companionship and inspiring conversations about anything and everything. Thankfully, she had almost stopped blushing at his ridiculous good looks too, as her understanding of him as a person deepened.

Then, by mid-evening most days, there was her retreat to bed again—pleasantly tired—usually with cocoa. This last act of the day was fabulous for another reason too: her reading habit was starting to return. And it felt like a pleasure too. She had started with the *Jane Eyre* edition Ross had given her. Its familiarity made it a brilliant gateway drug, giving her confidence to stretch her mind with other old favorites and then—with the odd lurch of painful memories from her recent career crash—some of the books that were the talk of the literary world. As Alistair had told her, working in Capelthorne's provided her with "all the books she could eat," and that was gradually becoming more a blessing than a curse as the new titles arrived in brown cardboard boxes a couple of times a week.

"Why did you choose Portneath?" Petra asked one evening, as she and Ross lounged in comfortable silence in front of the fire. "Did you know it?"

"No," he replied. "I came here because I *didn't* know it. I had no memories, no friends, no family here."

"Are they terrible people, your family, then?" This was something Petra could relate to, having no close family herself. At least, no family she chose to keep close.

Ross considered. "No, they're really not terrible at all. My mum's a sweetheart, and Dad's fine, apart from the emotional repression, which is generational, to be fair."

"Where are they?"

"Can you guess?" he laughed.

"Okay, well, Scotland presumably. I notice you contrive to maintain an impenetrable Scottish accent."

"Nothing contrived about it," he defended himself. "Although I quite like being hard to understand; it makes people think I might be saying something profound when I'm not."

"Or so you fondly assume," Petra teased.

"Tell me about *your* family," he said, ignoring her attempt to wind him up.

Petra shrugged. "Dad buggered off with another woman when I was little," she told him. "He went on to marry her and have another family. I have two half-siblings. One is less than a year younger than me, so go figure. Mum was predictably furious and devastated. Refusing to have anything to do with him myself felt like solidarity at the time."

Petra frowned. It was true, as a small child, she felt—and was possibly encouraged to feel—that asking to see her father was disloyal. As far as she was aware, he had made no attempt to maintain contact with her either. Her mother had made it clear he was doing nothing to support the two of them financially once he left. As Petra got older, she learned to despise him for this nearly as much as her mother did.

"Mum had to work really hard to support us both," Petra went on, staring into the flames, remembering. "It was tough for her. I had everything I needed. She provided for me well."

"But she wasn't around much," observed Ross. It wasn't a question.

"No. I got used to letting myself into an empty house. I made my own tea. Did my homework on my own, got myself ready for bed . . ."

"You brought yourself up?"

"I did," Petra agreed brightly. It was fine. She didn't need pity.

"Are you close now?"

"Ha!" The exclamation escaped her, expressing more than she intended to say. "We really aren't," she admitted. "Mum lives in Spain. She says I'm welcome any time, but after the first day, we've basically got nothing to say to each other. If we could just meet for a quick cup of tea, we would probably do it fairly often, but—all the way to Spain . . ." Petra didn't finish. It occurred to her in that moment that she hadn't told her mother what had happened, hadn't thought for one moment that she should escape the fallout from her smashed career in Spain. That she might flee to her remaining parent for comfort and reassurance. The possibility hadn't even registered as an option. Which said it all.

"What about your half-siblings?" Ross persisted.

Petra puffed out her cheeks. "I think they're up north somewhere. We don't know each other at all, really. Maybe one day . . . What about you? Siblings?"

"Just me," he told her. "Can you imagine? Their one and only child announces he wants to be a writer. Watching their little faces . . . the hope fading that their son would ever make anything of himself . . ."

"Except that you did," Petra reminded him. "They must have been so proud, no?"

"Yeah, yeah . . . Mum enjoyed telling all her friends when I started being talked about, winning awards . . . I'm pretty sure

I didn't come up in conversation much when I was starving in a garret for years before that."

"Do writers still have garrets?" Petra teased.

"It's the law," he said. "It's only the absence of a garret that hinders my writing now, obviously."

"Obviously," Petra agreed cautiously. Right from the beginning of their friendship, there had been an omertà over anything other than the most frivolous jest touching on his writing and her agenting. "What even *is* a garret?" Petra mused, steering the conversation away.

"God knows," he said. "But I think they have to be freezing, whatever they are, and it's so cozy in here that I don't want to leave," he said, getting up to poke the fire and shove another log on.

"Supper?" asked Petra, emboldened. Usually, Ross took himself off after two hours or less, being apparently reluctant to impose on her evening routine.

Or possibly reluctant to relinquish his.

"It's only baked potatoes with cheese and beans," she admitted.

"My favorite," Ross declared. "But I'm inviting myself . . . that's not right. I should be cooking for you."

"Then do," said Petra. "That would be very nice. But not tonight."

In truth, Petra thought later—when Ross had left, after a supper eaten in comfortable near silence—he had never even invited her to his rented cottage. Instead, they invariably met in the shop, and then the little flat. She had once proposed a coffee at Freya's, but he declined with something approaching fear in his eyes. Despite their easy rapport, there was still a guardedness about him, and as far as she knew, she was still his only friend around Portneath. However repressed he might be around her, it would seem he was even more insular with everyone else he might encounter.

Petra had lined up cake and prosecco as a treat for the Beach Reads Book Club and was laying it all out when Diana, ever glamorous, had wafted into the shop looking cool and elegant in ice blue cashmere with a matching scarf.

"Darling, I'm positively freezing," she declared to Petra as she air-kissed. "Shall we put the kettle on?"

"Of course," said Petra. "I was thinking the same."

By the time the two women had made tea for themselves and laid out the wine and fresh cream gateaux, the others had arrived, stamping their feet to warm them up and chattering about their weekend plans.

Petra and Flo, on the other hand, knew they would be working a busy Saturday in the shop, with the remains of the inventory on Sunday. Valentine's Week coincided with school vacation, and they were expecting to be busy as the population of Portneath soared during the holidays, and not just during the summer as Petra had previously assumed.

"So," declared Petra, when all had full glasses and cake plates in hand, "there is a reason for our generosity this evening. Capelthorne's is turning over its window and its most prime selling space in-store to the best romance stories ever, and we want to know from you which ones they are. *And*," she said, looking around the group, "we want a particular focus on commercial fiction, although," she added hastily, "remember, even the classics were the commercial fiction of their time, so nothing is really off limits, right?"

"Right!" they all chorused, their faces filled with eager anticipation at the task ahead. Flo, having finished distributing the cake, was now womaning the flip chart, with her marker pen at the ready.

"So who's going to start?" prompted Petra.

"*Frenchman's Creek*," declared Diana, "and we're in du Maurier country too, so it's perfect. I'm fed up with du Maurier always meaning *Rebecca*," she went on. "Not that I don't love it too, obviously."

"But *Rebecca*'s less of a love story," agreed Flo. "Although I suppose you could say Max and the Girl . . ."

"Hmm," chipped in Mungo, "not the most equal relationship. And more coercive control than love, I've always thought."

"True," said Flo, uncapping her pen ready to write. "We'll go with *Frenchman's Creek*."

"Plus, it's got an actual pirate king in it," said Petra happily. She didn't know if it was just her own personal interest or whether she was intuiting the next big thing, but she adored a pirate.

"It's got a sad ending though," piped up Alison, the leader of the group.

"Happy sad," Diana told her. "Happy because she feels empowered as a woman, looking after her children first and foremost, and seeing her pirate king sometimes."

"Exactly," Petra chipped in. "It was the only good ending she could have gone with, I've always thought. Bittersweet."

"Are we allowed sad endings, though?"

"Of course! Sad endings are sometimes the right ending, don't you think?" asked Petra diffidently. Diana had told her Alison was a romance writer, so she would normally bow to Alison's expertise, "But we can do a 'Happily Ever After' list? Totally."

"Let's just see what comes up," suggested Alison.

"*The Thornbirds*!" suggested Jess next, putting her hand up first, because she worked a lot in schools.

"That's another one for a sad ending," said Mungo as Flo wrote it down.

"*Twilight*," suggested someone else, to general sounds of approval.

"Fun fact: E. L. James's *Fifty Shades* started off as fanfic for *Twilight*," said Jess.

"What on earth is fanfic?" asked Flo, her marker pen hovering over the flip chart.

"Fan fiction—online writing, shared for free," Petra told her. "Very often it's homage—existing characters created by someone else—but with new adventures. Apparently, there are huge amounts of fanfic for Doctor Who and Sherlock Holmes too."

"I didn't know that," chipped in Diana wonderingly. "I must investigate. I always wished Conan Doyle had written more Sherlock Holmes stories."

"Okay, so just to be aware," Petra said hastily, "a lot of it's quite steamy, with Holmes and Watson in a relationship."

"That won't faze me," said Diana. "I'd always assumed Conan Doyle meant us to infer that anyhow."

Mungo nodded. "The filthier the better, for this one," he remarked.

"Absolutely," Diana agreed. "Speaking of which, I thought *Fifty Shades of Grey* was great, but people love to have a pop at it, I know."

"You can't argue with sales of more than one hundred and fifty million. I doubt E. L. James weeps bitter tears over her detractors," Petra agreed.

"If she does, at least she can wipe her eyes with her very nice royalty statements," concurred Mungo. "I think *Fifty Shades* should be on our list as well."

"Okay," said Petra, making a mental note not to order too many paperback copies even so. Not everyone would want to signal publicly what they were reading, hence the benefits of e-readers.

"And if we're talking delicious literary comfort food," said Flo, "I think the late, great Jilly Cooper deserves a slot on the list."

"Definitely," said Petra. "I just absolutely adored *Riders*."

"Which one was that?" asked Alison. "I still re-read the ones with the girls' names; they're my idea of perfect little romances. She's my biggest writing inspiration, actually."

"I love the girls' names ones too," agreed Petra. "But the Rutshire ones are amazing."

"Yes!" sighed Jess, her hand on her heart. "Rupert Campbell-Black versus Jake Wotsisname. Heaven."

"We should have that *and* the latest," said Mungo, "and *Riders* deserves a place on the list, for sure, because they've just made a TV series of it, haven't they? That's got to boost sales of the book."

Petra nodded her agreement. She barely watched television these days, as she only had her laptop and the flat's wonky internet connection.

Flo wrote down *Riders*, and then—"the latest, whatever it's called," and then looked around the group for the next suggestion.

Quickly, they all agreed on Colleen Hoover's *All Your Perfects*, because it wasn't the one that sold the most copies, but it was the most romantic. Jilly Cooper's first romance, *Emily*, made the list, as did David Nichols's *One Day*.

"Glad to see a male writer on the list at last," said Mungo. "We men are not completely devoid of romantic sensibility."

"Yeah, but you mostly are," teased Petra. She loved Mungo. "Remember all those women who had to get their books published under men's names," she told him reprovingly, as if it were his fault. "Talking of which, I'm going to vote for *Jane Eyre* because it's—well—because it's amazing," she went on.

"Can't argue with that," said Flo, writing it down.

"If we're doing the classics—and, let's face it—they're classics for a reason," said Diana, "I don't see how we can leave out something by Jane Austen."

"Agreed," said Petra, "but which one? My vote goes for *Sense and Sensibility*," she proffered.

"That's my favorite too!" piped up Alison. "That Colonel Brandon . . . just a quietly good hero, all the way through. Honestly? I think I prefer him to Mr. Darcy." She clapped her hand to her mouth.

Sacrilege indeed.

"Let's have votes for *Sense and Sensibility* versus *Pride and Prejudice*," suggested Petra. So far, this list was making her want to buy and re-read every single one of them.

"Can I make it even more complicated and suggest *Persuasion* too?" piped up Diana.

Mungo and Flo groaned. "We can't have three," said Flo firmly.

Pride and Prejudice narrowly took first place in a show of hands, but Petra was seriously wondering whether to get stocks of both, as she loved Colonel Brandon too. After all, they were going to have two Jilly Coopers.

"This list is starting to get out of hand," she observed. "Let's just agree on a couple more and then get onto our Jill Mansell." They had all read the latest Jill Mansell in advance, and Petra had loved it.

Eventually, they agreed on *The Great Gatsby* as the best example of doomed infatuation. This pleased Mungo enormously as it was another male writer. There was talk of *Atonement* too, but—in the end—the final place on the list went to Sally Thorne's *The Hating Game*, to Petra's delight, as she thought it was the most perfect rom-com she had read in a long time.

"Oh, except, hang on," said Petra, as they refilled glasses in preparation for their literary discussion on the chosen book. "This is the Beach Reads Book Club, so we can't not have its inspiration, *The Beach Reads Book Club* by Kathryn Freeman."

"Absolutely!" they all chorused. "Another book about books," sighed Diana happily. "I bloody love those."

"That's my reading list sorted for the next few weeks," agreed Mungo. "Petra, please put me down for copies of the whole lot."

"Perfect," said Petra, making a note.

"But, darling, we've got most of these at home," said Diana. "In fact, when I moved in with you, I think I brought my own copies, so we've probably got jolly nearly two copies of them all."

"No matter," said Mungo firmly. "I want new, beautiful copies," he told Petra. "The most lovely edition of each, please. Hardback preferably."

"Good idea," said Petra, who had been thinking the same. People were already going to have these books. Beautiful new editions were the way forward, she thought, remembering Ross's first present to her—that beautiful edition of *Jane Eyre*. She treasured it. And Valentine's Day was about buying romantic presents for each other, not just books for one's self.

Speaking of which, she already had her eye on the Virago Modern Classics clothbound women's literature edition of *Frenchman's Creek*.

She might treat herself.

Chapter Eleven

"Who did you insult today?" Ross asked, smiling in anticipation.

This was his favorite game, Petra had learned, getting her to amuse him with examples of her disastrously big mouth and inability to filter anything that popped into her brain. "How do you know I insulted anyone today?" she asked peevishly.

He didn't reply, just raised an eyebrow in query.

"Okay, *fine*," she conceded. "There might have been a slight misunderstanding when I rolled my eyes at a lady because we were both watching a little boy pulling all the books out of the shelf onto the floor. The little monkey."

"Parent?"

"Grandmother," admitted Petra.

"And you managed to insult her without even saying anything," Ross marveled. "Truly, this is your superpower."

"Actually, I did speak," Petra admitted. "I followed up the eye roll with something about kids not knowing how to behave because the parents don't have a clue either. He *was* being a little monster; she should have been intervening."

"*Way* to keep digging," Ross said, amazed. "And you can't make the grandparents take the rap, to be fair."

"Yes, I can!" insisted Petra. "This is generational misbehavior. It was probably *her* bad parenting that's made bad parents. She's totally responsible."

Ross cocked his head disbelievingly.

"Just speaking the truth as I find it," Petra insisted sulkily.

"Like I said," Ross replied, placating now, "it's your superpower. Never change."

Petra grunted. The superpower thing was a matter of opinion. She herself had discovered there was little enthusiasm for straight-talking.

"What are you doing tomorrow night?" he asked, as they both contentedly gazed into the flames.

"Friday? Hanging out with you here in front of the fire?" Petra hazarded, passing him the chocolate hobnobs. "Unless you've got other, exciting plans?"

"I do, actually."

"Gosh, good for you," said Petra, trying not to feel miffed. It was Friday night, after all. People were allowed to have other plans, and kicking back with your friends—okay, your one solitary friend—eating chocolate biscuits and chatting about stupid things she had said wasn't the most thrilling prospect in the world. Although she personally couldn't think of anything better.

"But you're not doing anything?" Ross persisted. "Even on Valentine's Day?"

Of course, Petra thought. It wasn't that she totally didn't know what the date was—she had just done the Valentine's Day window display—but the whole concept of romance felt very distant from her own life. Irrelevant, in fact.

"Sadly, no one is—what's the expression?—'laying siege' to me currently," she told him. "Thank you for asking—and for making me feel like a loser, by the way."

"You're welcome. 'Laying siege'? Seriously?"

"Yeah, whatever . . . it's been a while," she admitted. "I'm not up with the terminology. So anyhow, what have *you* got lined up? I want to know everything about your hot date." Petra was frankly astonished. Ross never mentioned seeing *anyone* else around Portneath, let alone a girlfriend. Or boyfriend, obviously, although she had never had those vibes from him.

"I thought it was about time I cooked *you* supper," he told her, grinning as if he was reading her mind.

Petra tried to wipe her face of all expression. "What? You mean *I'm* your 'hot date'?" The second the words blurted their way out of her mouth, without the slightest liaison with her brain, she felt like curling into a tiny ball right there on the carpet.

"*God,* no," Ross exclaimed, apparently equally discomfited.

Well, this was excruciating.

"I mean, I didn't even know you could cook," Petra burbled on, eager to put words—any words—between her and her faux pas.

"Maybe I can't," Ross said, seemingly equally keen to move the conversation on. "You can be the judge of that tomorrow. You're not a vegetarian or anything? Although it's fine if you are . . ."

"You've seen me eat a bacon sandwich," she reminded him.

"Oh yeah, so I have," he admitted. "Although some vegetarians make the exception for bacon."

"Because that's a thing," said Petra scathingly. "But—yes—I eat everything, thank you for asking. What can I bring?"

"Just yourself. Seven o'clock?" he said, getting up to leave, seemingly delighted to shrug his way into his coat and keen to escape before anything else happened.

"Oh no, I've just realized, I can't!" burst out Petra.

His face fell for a moment. "Yeah, no, of course . . ." he said automatically. And then, tilting his head in confusion "Why?"

"Because I don't know where you live, dumbo."

THE SHOP WAS busy the following day, mainly with men rushing in out of the freezing rain, grabbing last-minute Valentine's presents.

Petra dealt with them smilingly, touched on behalf of the lucky recipients, whoever they were. She applauded these men on the whole. It might all be a bit "lastminute.com" but they got points from her for picking poetry books rather than gas station flowers, where red roses, in particular, were an outrageous price for just that week. Petra had had an earnest, very boring boyfriend in her teens who insisted on buying her roses like that, with their bare, ramrod-straight stems and tightly furled scarlet flower heads that didn't so much bloom as unfurl slightly, so as to look ragged and untidy before crisping at the edges and withering in defeat. They never had any scent either.

Petra had always promised herself that one day she would have her own garden. It didn't have to be big or grand, but she was going to fill it with big earthenware pots overflowing with scent and color. She would plant stock flowers, and sweet peas in a riot of shades, and roses! Not just any roses, but the old-fashioned ones with the fat, heavy flowers that burst open on a sunny day, a riot of pinks, creams, velvety reds, and peaches, scenting the air with cinnamon and marshmallow. Petra would cut these flowers for the house, of course, going out at dawn with her scissors to cut just one perfect dew-soaked rose destined for a glass by her bedside. Or perhaps she would cut a fat fistful of sweet peas to cram into a little vase on her desk, their honey scent filling the room.

Ah, this life she would have.

One day.

"I WISH I could get someone to look at me like that," came a deep voice.

Petra jumped, startled out of her reverie. It was lovely Mungo, Diana's other half. "You were miles away," he went on, "so radiant and full of joy, as if you were gazing at the person you loved more than anyone else in the world."

"I *was* miles away," Petra admitted, taking the book he had selected and scanning it. "I would imagine Diana looks at you like that all the time."

"I'd be horrified," he retorted. "We do live together, true, but Diana and I are definitely just friends. She's . . . not my type, if you take my meaning?"

"Ah, I see, sorry!" said Petra, catching his drift. "So are you out on a hot date tonight?"

"*I'm* not," admitted Mungo. "Sadly, my most recent boyfriend has just gone back to Brazil. No, no," he added, seeing Petra's sympathetic look, "it was nothing serious. But I am sure Diana has multiple grand plans. She's generally beating them off with a stick."

Petra giggled. "I'm not surprised. She's very glamorous."

"And you, my dear?"

"Yeah, I'm *not* exactly beating them off with a stick," Petra admitted.

"Then, I don't suppose you would allow me . . . ?" Mungo said diffidently. "Freya's is probably fully booked, but I'm sure there's somewhere . . ."

He really was the sweetest man Petra had ever met.

"That's so kind," she said, "but you don't have to take me out, I'm fine. As a matter of fact, I am having supper with a friend—*another* friend," she said in deference to Mungo, "and we are going to spend the evening being completely unromantic together."

Mungo smiled. "That sounds perfectly delightful, my dear, but if it doesn't pan out, you know where I am." He gave her a little bow, tipped his splendid homburg hat, and left with his book under his arm, Petra smiling after him.

Yikes, she thought. About that supper with Ross: He had said not to bring anything but obviously she was going to ignore that. What did you bring to an un-Valentine supper?

She had very handily learned that Freya did a takeout service, selling her divine patisserie in slices to go. She could bring two slices of the raspberry gateau, with its swirly crème patisserie and layers of raspberry in jewel-pink jelly, but it was altogether too pink and white. Too Valentiney. So, what about the lemon tart? Or the chocolate ganache? But then, if he had made a dessert, they would be unneeded, she thought. Plus, they were so exquisite, whatever he had made himself would compare unfavorably so—no . . . Okay, flowers then? That was a hard no. Far too romantic.

The other difficulty was that she couldn't close the shop until five o'clock, so when was she going to get anything anyhow? It was looking like her only option was the little supermarket over the bridge, which didn't offer a lot of classy choices. A packet of wine gums? A box of Maltesers?

Ha! Chocolate . . . Now that *was* a good idea.

Chocolate didn't have to be lovey-dovey did it? Everyone liked chocolate. *And* there was that amazing-looking chocolatier, with its tiny shopfront squeezed between two tea and cake places just up the main street. Petra grabbed her phone and googled "chocolate Portneath." There it was—Maison Chocolat—and, thank goodness, it didn't close until six o'clock today. Of course, late closing on Valentine's Day, for all those last-minute lovers.

"I WANT SOMETHING manly," Petra told the exquisite French lady behind the counter, who was managing to look chic and Parisienne, even in a food-hygiene hairnet.

"*Du chocolat masculin?*" the lady queried, clearly nonplussed.

"Yes, *you* know, not . . . 'girlie,'" Petra explained, scanning the glass shelves for inspiration. There were serried rows of the most exquisite handmade chocolates; violet creams, with crystallized violets on chocolate so dark it was almost black, rose-centered ones with tiny rose petals, some with gold leaf, pyramids of cocoa-dusted truffles . . . all far too exquisite, far too—well—"love-tokeny," Petra attempted to explain.

And then, with an emphatic nod, the lady turned around and brought out a slab of dark chocolate, swirled with thick splodges of milk- and white chocolate and studded with whole nuts, Brazil nuts, hazelnuts, and heaven knows what else, chucked randomly onto its surface before it set.

"So," said the lady, producing a small hammer, "with zees, we *bouf, bouf, bouf*," she mimed shattering the slab into shards. "*Oui?*" she raised her exquisitely plucked eyebrows, seeking approval. "*C'est très viril, n'est-ce pas?*" she queried, flexing her tiny biceps and giving a little French-accented growl, for emphasis.

Petra giggled. "*Oui. C'est bien. Merci*," she agreed.

The lady made a surprisingly violent job of breaking up a considerable quantity of the chocolate and then—with a silver trowel—sliding the pieces into a black, corrugated cardboard box. It was the shape of a cube, lined with black tissue paper. Deftly folding the origami-style lid so it was closed, she then walked her fingers over the rolls of pastel-colored ribbon questioningly before selecting a dark brown grosgrain, tying it around the box and finishing it, not with a bow, but a sleek knot, more like one you would see on a necktie, all the while chattering to herself under her breath.

After being invited to wave her phone at a reader displaying a disconcertingly large sum, Petra was back out in the street with her precious parcel. It was raining now, and cars swished through the puddles, the lights of the shops spilling out and reflecting back in the wet pavements. Petra shivered. Ross's cottage, she now knew, was just beyond the outskirts of the town. That was a brisk twenty-minute walk away, which would have been a pleasure at any other time, on any other day.

Nope. Uber had not extended its tendrils as far as Portneath, her app confirmed. There was a taxi firm at the station, but she didn't know its name. Petra was just pondering, swinging the entirely "ungirly" box of chocolates, as she chewed her lips in an agony of indecision. If she didn't make some sort of plan she would be late, and that would be unforgivably rude—

"Going my way?" came a voice as a dark blue car drew alongside her and the car window slid noiselessly down.

Petra was about to give one of the withering replies she always kept handy for unwanted approaches in London—more common than she would like—when she realized who it was.

"I nearly punched you in the face," she told Ross, sagging with relief. "I thought you were stalking me."

"I kind of am," admitted Ross. "Hop in. I just saw the rain and didn't want you walking."

"Shouldn't you be slaving over a hot stove?" Petra asked, as she slipped into the passenger seat, shivering gratefully as the heat blasted her chilly legs.

"Probably. My soufflé will be ruined."

"We can always send out for food."

"In Portneath? You're kidding. No delivery apps here."

"No Uber either," Petra observed. "It's basically medieval."

"Picturesque though," said Ross, steering the car confidently back into the line of traffic snaking up the main street. "If you like that sort of thing."

Chapter Twelve

"I hope you're hungry," he said, coming around to open the car door for her when they arrived. Petra wasn't used to the whole gallant behavior thing and found it disconcerting. *Were* they on a date? She sure as hell wasn't going to ask again. There was only so much crushing casual rejection a girl could take.

"This is soooo gorgeous!" she exclaimed delightedly as he ushered her in.

A low oak door with a heavy black wrought-iron knocker opened directly into a sitting room only perhaps twelve feet square, with a stone inglenook fireplace taking up the majority of one wall. On the hearth crouched a squat black woodburning stove, a fire already at its heart. The glow from the fire was matched by low light from two fat table lamps on either side of a squishy dark-blue velvet sofa, liberally scattered with cinnamon and orange silk cushions.

"I'm renting it for the winter," said Ross, helping her out of her damp coat and hanging it on the back of the door. "It's damp as hell, and dark too, but—with the stove going—it's cozy, I suppose."

"For you," said Petra, handing him the chocolate. "I didn't know what to bring."

"Totally unnecessary, but—thank you—it looks beautiful . . . chocolate?"

Emily nodded.

"We can have some later, if you've got room," he said.

"Something smells delicious," Petra said, sitting as instructed on the sofa. It was so wonderfully enveloping with its deep, squashy feather cushions, she wasn't at all sure she was going to be able to get out of it.

"Wine?"

Petra nodded.

"White? Red? Pink?"

The transaction agreed, settled in front of the fire, clasping red wine in a glass the size of a goldfish bowl, Petra was instantly relaxed.

This was nice. Really nice.

Ross disappeared into a warmly lit kitchen just through a doorway in the middle of a wall of bookshelves. After a few minutes of clattering and banging, he poked his head out. "Forks and bowls in front of the fire, or plates, knives, and forks at the table in the kitchen?"

"Bowls, please," said Petra. Anything that delayed having to move.

". . . which is the correct answer. Bear with me . . ." called Ross.

A minute later he appeared again, balancing two laden wide white china bowls on his hand and forearm, with a pair of forks and an open bottle of red wine clutched in the other fist.

After popping the two bowls on the ottoman in front of the

fire, he deftly topped up Petra's glass, put the bottle of wine down on the hearth, and handed her a bowl with napkin and fork. Meaty steam rose from it, which smelled absolutely delicious.

"Shepherd's pie," Ross explained. "Honeyed, roasted carrots and—well—peas, as you can see," he waved dismissively as he chucked another log into the stove and then flumped down beside her.

"Oh. My. God," Petra groaned with her mouth full. The ground lamb was rich, soft, and intensely savory, redolent with wine and herbs; the mashed potato was golden and browned into crispy peaks on the top; and the carrots were the best she had ever tasted, intensely honeyed and roasted to a caramel perfection at the edges. "This is amazing! You are a fantastic cook! *You* are going to be cooking for me *a lot* from now on . . ." To think he had sat eating her baked potatoes with beans when he was capable of this.

"Fluke," insisted Ross, although he was also tucking in with relish. "Actually, I say fluke—if I'm honest—I've been on a WhatsApp video call with my mum half the afternoon."

Petra giggled. Somehow, she couldn't picture Ross with his mum. "Tell her thank you from me," she said.

"Yeeeaah, maybe not," he admitted. "My mum gets ridiculously excited if I give her the slightest hint there's a woman in my life."

"Oops, don't then, 'cause it's definitely not . . ." said Petra, because it seemed required and Ross's emphatic nod of agreement confirmed it.

In profile, as he sat next to her, with that lick of dark brown hair falling across his forehead, she was reminded—yet again—how handsome he was. Given this, why were the women not swarming like flies? And then it occurred to her they possibly were. She only saw him for a few hours a week after all. Lots of time to make his mum happy, if he chose to.

"I CHEATED WITH the dessert," Ross admitted, bringing out small plates and cake forks, then returning with a large chunk of Freya's raspberry gateau, the one Petra had rejected because it was too Valentiney. And that was without her having even noticed that Freya had decorated the top with little fresh raspberry jelly hearts.

Ross seemed oblivious, though, cutting them each a generous slice and digging enthusiastically into his. Petra didn't even think she was still hungry but found it irresistible and surprisingly light. The fire was burning down to glowing embers now, and the little sitting room, shrouded in shadows, was cozy and warm.

"So—you were saying—you've not been here long?" she asked.

"Only since the autumn," said Ross. "I've moved around a fair bit over the last few years."

"Like the Incredible Hulk?"

"Um, yeees . . ." he said doubtfully, apparently failing to see why Petra would align him with a massive green creature prone to violence.

"I mean, because he moved around a lot. To avoid people finding out who he is."

"Ah yes," said Ross, "I see your point. So—now you know who I am—I suppose I should—"

"You *know* I'm not going to tell anyone," Petra said rapidly. "Don't go. You're my only friend. At least wait until I leave in August?"

Ross thought for a moment. "I do really like Portneath actually," he admitted. "And I like this," he added, indicating himself and Petra. "I didn't think I wanted to actually 'know' people, but—well—we have a lot in common."

"Yeah, we're both failures," Petra agreed ruefully. "Misery loves company. Although actually," she added hastily, "I'm surprisingly unmiserable here, aren't you?"

"Same," agreed Ross.

"So," Petra went on, tentatively, "are you writing? At all? Even a little bit?"

Ross stiffened, and Petra's heart sank. She had upset him. She should have kept her mouth shut. It had all been going so well.

He stood, and she wondered if he was going to invite her to leave, but instead he took down the box of nutty chocolate she had brought and sat back down with it, looking thoughtful as he carefully untied the knot and offered her the opened box.

"Just give me the first line," Petra implored, taking a piece, thinking she had probably blown it anyhow. The first line of a second novel from the legendary Ross McCloud? How jealous her London contemporaries would be. But he wouldn't do it, would he? And even if he did, she wouldn't tell them.

"Okay then," said Ross.

It was so unexpected, Petra sat bolt upright. "Go on," she implored. "Give."

"So let me just . . ." Ross handed her the chocolate and stood up in front of the fire, facing her. He squared his shoulders and cleared his throat. "'It is a truth, universally acknowledged, that a single man'—" he intoned in a posh, high-pitched voice.

"Oi," shouted Petra, chucking a bit of chocolate at him in remonstration. "You're such a windup artist."

"Me?" he protested. "Whadayamean? That *could* be my first line. For all you know, it's a brave and innovative Jane Austen 'homage.'" *He* was laughing at her now, dodging the blows as she followed up the chocolate with a barrage of sofa cushions.

"Yeah, but it isn't though," Petra laughed ruefully. He had really got her then.

"I've got an idea," he said, sitting back down and taking the chocolate box away before it occurred to her to throw any more of it at him. "Here's how it works. I give you first lines of famous novels. For each one you identify correctly, I'll honestly answer a yes/no question about my own writing, agreed?"

Petra sighed happily. He must know she would agree. Which right-minded book-loving person would turn down *any* opportunity like this? "Go on then," she said, trying to sound sulky, but unable to hide her fierce anticipation and delight. This was going to be the best game ever. He would quickly discover she was a demon for first-line recognition.

"Last night I dreamed—"

"—I went to Manderley again," Petra cut in. "Du Maurier's *Rebecca*. Too easy. Right. First question: What went wrong?"

"Yes/no answers," he reminded her. "That's a Bible-length reply."

"Okay, fine," said Petra, humming as she thought, with her finger over her mouth. Tactics were required. "*Are* you writing?" she asked slowly.

"Yyyy . . . no," said Ross.

"Liar!" Petra declared.

"All right, yes," admitted Ross.

"I knew it! So come on," she pleaded, "can I read it?"

"Not so fast. You have to earn it, okay . . ." Ross tapped his lip reflectively. "All right, this one: 'It was a bright, cold day in April, and the clocks were striking thirteen.'"

Petra groaned in frustration. "Hang on, hang on . . . I know this. Ha! Orwell. *Nineteen Eighty-Four.*"

"Finally!" declared Ross. "Okay, next one—"

"Wait! What about my question?"

"Go on then."

"Um . . . Didn't you have a two-book deal with Encore?"

"Yes."

"Damn! I meant to ask, 'Are you still under contract?'"

"Ah, but you didn't," Ross observed infuriatingly. "Okay, this one's easy. 'It was the best of times, it was the worst of times . . .'"

"*Tale of Two Cities*!" crowed Petra triumphantly. "God, I love that book. 'It is a far, far better thing I do than I have ever done . . .'"

"'And a far, far better rest I go to than I have ever known,'" finished Ross, momentarily reflective, flumping down on the sofa beside her, their thighs nearly touching.

"God, I bloody love that book," Petra quavered, her chin wobbling. What? Just thinking about Sidney Carton made her want to cry? She had to get a grip.

"Need a minute?" said Ross gently, turning his body to face her. He rested his hand on her knee, ducking his head so his beautiful green eyes, with their thick, dark lashes, could meet her own. For a long moment, they gazed at each other, neither apparently able to break the connection. Next thing Petra knew, her hand was covering his. By instinct, their fingers interlinked, and electricity coursed up Petra's arm, straight to her core. She wondered what it would be like to reach up and stroke her fingers along his strong jawline, to press her mouth against his—whoa!

"Absolutely not," Petra blurted aloud, shaking her head to dispel the moment, forcing her mind to return to Sidney Carton, doing the noble thing. And that was what *she* had to do. Never mind her own increasingly disturbing feelings toward this man, their friendship was far too precious to risk ruining it with a casual fling.

With difficulty, she gathered her scattered wits. "Now, spill. Are you still under contract?" she demanded briskly.

Ross hesitated. "No," he said at last, apparently reluctantly taking back his hand and turning around to face the fire.

Silence fell.

Seriously, this was huge, thought Petra, unable to think up a response. Being released from a contract was top level "bad." It basically never happened, except when things had gone really, really wrong.

"Did you have to pay back the advance?" Petra asked at last, her face screwed up in sympathy.

"Rudely personal," Ross observed mildly. "I actually didn't, which was nice. My agent did a very good job. She had ammunition because the breakdown between me and—the publisher," he said carefully, "was . . . complicated. We sort of had a special relationship."

"Like the US and UK 'special relationship,'" probed Petra impertinently. "Or seriously inappropriate, don't tell anyone, X-rated 'special relationship'?" she asked.

If she recalled correctly, the editor who acquired Ross's debut was well-known in the industry as a ball-breaking, fast-tracking wrecking machine, currently editorial director in one of the big five publishing houses, an ascent that meant the woman had serious cojones. Plus, conceded Petra, the woman—Cassandra, was she called?—was one of those shiny, leggy, perfectly manicured women other women loved to hate. Which was fine if you liked that sort of thing. And why wouldn't he?

"Okay, let's start at the beginning," she said, keen to pry further revelations from him now that he was in the mood to talk. "Tell me about your agent?"

"Did I have a special relationship with her too?" he said, deliberately misunderstanding. "No, as it happens. I'm kind of a one-woman guy. One woman at a time, I mean, I'm not saying that I've only been with one woman," he added hastily. "'Cause, you know, I'm thirty-four, so that would be borderline weird—"

"Yeah, all right, all right, I don't need to know about your *entire* romantic history," said Petra, finding that she very much didn't want to hear about *any* of it, for some reason. "Are you still with your agent at least? It's Veronica Bampton, isn't it?"

"Yes, it is. Was. I mean, it still is, of course. She's not changed her name. But no, I'm not signed to her anymore."

"So basically," said Petra, struggling to get to grips with this monumental car crash Ross was describing, "you're a major international prize-winning debut novelist and you've now lost your publishing deal, your editor, and your agent. Correct?"

"To put it bluntly," he agreed. "But this we know," he protested. "We've talked about this, remember?"

"Yeah, but I just didn't . . ." Petra whistled through her teeth, shaking her head. Ross had clearly had a very, very bad time of it. "Oh Ross," she said, "I'm so sorry that happened to you."

"Thank you," said Ross, selecting a large piece of chocolate from the fast-diminishing stash in the box. "Catch," he said, aiming it at her mouth.

She did. "I'm not a performing monkey," she protested with her mouth full, well aware this was a diversionary tactic. Or at least an attempt to lighten the mood.

"Yeah, *I'm* not a performing monkey either," he said. "And that's kind of why the whole thing with book two happened."

Petra gave him a sympathetic look. "We ask a lot of our writers," she admitted. "People who don't know the publishing industry tend to ask us whether we are all actually frustrated writers ourselves . . . Maybe some of us are but—in all honesty—I can't imagine anything worse."

"You put your trust in your editor, for sure," he mused, not looking at her. "You have to. It should never have gotten messy, like it did."

He looked so abject, Petra felt bad for grilling him. Time for a change of focus.

"So," she said, "going back to current writing that you are—or possibly are not—doing . . . ?"

Ross sighed, staring into the fire for a long moment. "I actually really am," he admitted, squaring his shoulders. "Just recently, I started again. Since we met, as a matter of fact. First time in a long time, and it feels . . . well, it feels surprisingly okay."

"So, *can* I read it?"

"No."

"Oh, go on," Petra wheedled. "I'm a professional, remember?"

"No," he said again, but he was smiling.

Chapter Thirteen

Later that night, in her bed, Petra lay in the dark, staring at the ceiling. Poor Ross. Okay, so the sad, grinding, low-level failure to thrive that the majority of published writers experienced in their careers was soul-destroying enough, but this? This shooting-star success followed by complete disintegration? This took "messed up" to a whole new level. No wonder he was hiding out in Portneath.

And now he was writing again? Exciting! Disillusioned as Petra was with the whole book industry, she wanted to read what Ross was writing. A lot.

Ross WAS AWAKE too. Strange, he thought, how he had felt able to be so candid with Petra tonight. He hadn't shared much about that period in his life, five years ago, with anyone, not even his family or his small handful of remaining childhood friends back in Scotland. And now here he was, telling all to a woman he had known for a very short time. Though actually, perhaps not "all."

But Petra was a woman who was—until very recently—part of the machinery that had crushed him so totally. And as for the woman who had been at the heart of that damage—a woman who still often haunted his dreams—she was someone very different from Petra. He saw that increasingly clearly these days. Henrietta had been a drug he hadn't known existed until he was already addicted. The process of sharing his manuscript had created an emotional intimacy that left him wide open, and Henrietta had known exactly how to move in. Before he knew it, she had cast herself in the role of guide and mentor, someone who even replaced his agent as the facilitator to the future he so craved, as a recognized and published author. Without her, she persuaded him, he would stray from the path and become prey to all the misfortunes that snatched defeat from the jaws of victory for all the other aspiring authors. She had picked him up out of obscurity, and now she was his greatest fan and acolyte.

He could trust her. That was what she had told him.

And yet, when she touted him around the literary world on her arm, and as she persuaded him his work was nothing without her input and oversight, he also slowly became aware—too late—that neither their working relationship nor their romantic relationship was quite as it seemed: She was not the devoted acolyte to the magician creator she had told him he was. Far from being the Ariel to his Prospero, she had made him her Caliban, her Frankenstein's monster, being held resentfully in her thrall, while being emotionally dismantled so—as in Stockholm syndrome—he became infatuated with his jailor.

He had become her creature.

Monday was Petra's day to do all the shop admin: the ordering, cleaning, and decorating the shop window. Today, she was preparing her Easter window display, and she was glad Ross—not able to face more writing that day—was giving her a hand.

"How are you going to fit all these in?" he puffed good-naturedly enough as he delivered a galvanized pail of daffodils and a tray of blooming primroses in gorgeous terracotta pots that Petra had ordered from the florist up the road.

"It has to look abundant," Petra smiled. "I can't do an Easter egg hunt window without spring flowers. Just keep thinking of that coffee and pastel de nata I'm going to get you from Finn's shop when you're done," she told him.

She had borrowed Flo's lovely wicker shopping basket to fill with chocolate eggs, and she was also running an Easter bonnet competition, with the short-listed entrances going on display in the window too. There was a danger that there wouldn't be room for the books.

"Do you want some moss?" asked Ross. "There's loads on the ground in the little woods by the cottage. I can only take a little bit, of course. And maybe some big pebbles?"

"Nice!" exclaimed Petra. "Look, I've got the sweetest little fluffy yellow chicks that I can dot around too. Look! So cute . . ." She waved the basket at him, causing one of the bright yellow fluff balls to leap out and fall on the floor.

Ross rolled his eyes, picking it up, but she knew he was loving the whole endeavor, really. "We should go for a walk on the beach later," he told her. "It's beautiful out there."

"Honestly? I'm going to be so busy until this evening," she admitted apologetically.

"Early evening walk then," said Ross. "And if you're good, I'll buy you fish and chips for supper."

"Now you're talking," said Petra, her mouth watering at the thought.

An hour later, Petra was satisfied with her work. There were piles of books artfully stacked around baskets of chocolate eggs that were wrapped in jewel-bright foils. The Easter theme could be pretty broad, she had decided, mixing children's Easter stories with egg-focused cookbooks and a whole load of spring-themed crafts from yarn bombing to basket weaving. She wanted them all herself, and she only hoped her customers would think the same.

Portneath really did come alive in the spring, with vacationers pouring in as soon as schools let out for the Easter holidays. The local population—never a ghost town in the winter, but definitely quieter—must have tripled since she arrived in January. Sales had been fine so far, she thought. Flo had been reassuring, and she would know. And as a woman who professed to have her finger on the pulse of the publishing world as a literary agent, she herself ought to know what a provincial bookshop should be selling. Let's hope she was right.

"So, where's the man in your life?" Flo asked, apropos of nothing that Saturday. The two women were just sipping tea in a brief lull, as the shop had been pleasingly busy that morning.

"Whoa!" protested Petra. "Where did that come from? What if I said there *is* no man in my life?"

"Pity," said Flo reflectively. "Beautiful, clever woman like you . . . how old?"

"Twenty-eight, why?" she shot back guardedly.

"Hmm. Not getting any younger," continued Flo, ignoring Petra's expression—a mixture of outrage and amusement.

"Where's the man in *your* life?" Petra retaliated.

"Touché," laughed Flo. "I'm *definitely* not getting any younger, and—since you ask—I left Graham in bed this morning. He's not an early riser, bless him."

"Does he live with you, then?"

"God, no, I couldn't abide that. We hook up most Fridays, though, and he often stays over. But anyway, back to you."

"Goodie," muttered Petra, under her breath, but secretly impressed—and a little depressed—that this woman in her eighties had a more dynamic love life than she did.

"Impertinent of me, I know," Flo went on.

"Don't let that stop you," breathed Petra, just loud enough for Flo to hear. She was ignored.

"It's simply that it would be a tragedy if you weren't a mother one day," Flo continued, undaunted. "You're so beautiful and clever. Imagine how utterly amazing your children would be. That's my only thought. You owe it to the world to reproduce. Not that you even need a man for that nowadays, of course."

"Do *you* have children?" Petra asked her, in another attempt to get the woman off her private life, which she would rather keep private, if it was all the same to Flo.

"Yes and no," said Flo. "I've raised two girls, but neither were mine. Maggie—she's in her fifties now, was my sister's child, and then I ended up more or less raising Jules as well—Maggie's daughter—because poor Maggie was not a natural parent. Mainly because she was far too young . . ."

"That's the Jules who owns the shop now?"

"Yes, that's right. Jules who has just married Roman. He's so handsome," said Flo, starry-eyed, "and thoroughly delightful despite being a Montbeau. Really, the whole pairing was ridiculously unlikely, and yet—when I saw them both together—I simply couldn't imagine any other outcome, especially after the fire."

"Fire?"

"A fire that destroyed the bookshop opposite. Look, you can see. It's all been repaired now, of course. Where the pharmacy is now."

Petra looked. It was true, there was no sign anything had ever happened. "Two bookshops right opposite each other, though," she said. "That can't have been great. It wasn't you that burned it down, I hope?" Petra teased Flo. She was only half joking. Flo looked like one of those women who would go to any lengths if circumstances demanded it.

"It never occurred to me." Flo laughed. "It probably should have! My point being, you never know where you are going to find 'the one.'"

Funny how the conversation arrived back at the one topic she would rather avoid, thought Petra ruefully. "I haven't had time for romance," she admitted. "Work's been . . . intense. Plus, publishing actually is quite a woman-dominated industry, so there's not much talent around for people like me."

"Good news that you're in Portneath now then," declared Flo. "I will have to see what I can do. I'll ask around," she added, as if Petra might be in need of a secondhand bookcase rather than a life partner.

"Oh God, please don't," muttered Petra. She needed that kind of complication like a hole in the head. And it would be totally inappropriate to mention Ross. Whatever it was they had, it wasn't *that*. Was it?

"Talking of organizing your life for you," admitted Flo, without the slightest hint of shame, "you're meeting Jess on Tuesday. She wants to talk to you about the literary festival."

"She hasn't told me that," replied Petra, who had been hoping—since she had raised the issue in the pub—that Jess would get back to her about it. "And I'd love to, but I have to be in the shop on Tuesday."

"But that's what I'm telling you," explained Flo patiently. "You *may* meet her because I'm coming in to mind the shop. She wants you in Freya's for coffee at ten o'clock."

"Well, *that's* all organized then," said Petra, laughing. Resistance was clearly futile. And—to be fair to Flo *and* Jess—she was genuinely dying to find out more about Jess's plans.

"WHAT'S YOUR VIEW on literary festivals?" Petra asked Ross that evening when they were both sitting in the flat by the fireside, Petra on the blue sofa and Ross in the little armchair where he usually sat.

"I think they're perfectly fine, providing all the participants are consenting adults who aren't hurting anyone."

"Idiot."

"I did the rounds," Ross admitted. "Back in the day . . ."

"It was only five years ago," Petra reminded him. "You make it sound like ancient history."

"Five years is a long time in publishing," he said. "You know that. Anyway—yeah—I sat in drafty tents, debating the future of the literary novel—mostly whether or not it had one—with a bunch of other writers. That bit was quite fun actually. But then there's a lot of sitting around at signing tables wondering if anyone is going to want to even buy your book, let alone ask you to sign it."

Petra made a disbelieving noise. "Like *you* sat there wondering where the fans were," she scoffed. "I bet they had to add security to hold back the crowds."

"Yeah, okay, I was lucky," Ross admitted. "But I knew other writers—other completely superb writers—who sat for hours, signing pen poised, watching the tumbleweeds blow by."

Petra glanced over at him, alerted by the sudden gloom in his voice. He was staring, unseeing, into the fire, the flames illuminating his ridiculously beautiful cheekbones, but casting his eyes into shadow so she couldn't tell what he was thinking.

"There *are* good books that don't get the airtime they deserve," she agreed. "But that wasn't you, so why . . . ?"

"Was it even a good book though?" he demanded, suddenly animated, turning to face her, eyes blazing. "Who says it was a good book? Who decides? Do they even know? Who are the book police who decree which writer floats to the top of the pile and who spends years and years slaving away invisibly?

"When it's all so arbitrary, what does success even mean?"

Petra sighed. "I totally agree with you," she began, choosing her words carefully. "As an agent, I only represent people whose work I really believe in, but we all know good work isn't enough. There's luck in it as well, and—you're right—the mavens who control the marketing budgets, they can make a book or break it—"

"Exactly," said Ross, pointing straight at her. "Exactly. My editor. *She* made my book. Whether I felt it was good or bad—

whether *anyone* else felt it was good or bad—that's all irrelevant. My editor decided my book was going to sell well, and she made decisions accordingly." He broke off, rubbing his face in his hands wearily.

"I'm not sure an editor's as powerful as all that," said Petra, feeling that he was being a tiny bit weird. Who the hell *was* this editor? "You wrote the book after all, not her," she said gently.

"You *say* that . . ." he said, clearly not believing her for a minute, but too polite to call her out on it. "It just leaves me," he broke off, shrugging. "It just leaves me not knowing . . . Am I a good writer, or a crap writer who got lucky? A crap writer with a pretty face?" He gazed unseeing at Petra, and then he shrugged, sighing with what sounded like despair. "Not being able to answer that question is driving me a little bit 'round the bend at the moment," he admitted, smiling apologetically at Petra.

"This is *such* black-and-white thinking," said Petra gently. "Look," she said, engaging him, forcing eye contact, "what happens to all the other superb writers—all the writers who never get the time in the limelight they deserve? *You* didn't stop them from being successful. *You* didn't fraudulently take anyone else's place. The book you wrote was objectively amazing," she said firmly. "I read it. It changed my way of looking at the world, and my memory of it still makes me look at the world differently. How many other writers can do that?"

"Loads," he insisted. "You've just never heard of them, that's all."

"I *get* that," Petra told him softly. "But it does *not* detract from what *you* wrote. You've got to stop thinking that way."

Ross sighed. He raised a smile with conspicuous effort. "Thank you, Doctor Petra," he said. "Who'd work with writers, eh? Neurotic or what? Sorry . . ." He hung his head, apparently exhausted suddenly. "You're literally the only one I can have this conversation with. Anyone not in that world would—quite rightly—think I'm an ungrateful brat. Nice problem to have, right?"

"Don't apologize," said Petra. "It's understandable. You're stuck in your own head, day in, day out, finding a way to express ideas. And it's all so that readers can experience things they have never done before; so they can maybe see the beauty in something ugly; or understand their own pain better; or see their own life experiences shared by a writer in a way that makes them feel less alone . . . God knows, we all need that. We need writers to *do* that for us."

Ross scoffed. "You make me sound like a superhero."

"Yeah? Well," said Petra briskly. "I wouldn't go that far."

She was sympathetic, sure. But there had to be an end to the self-pity somewhere along the line.

By Tuesday, Petra was beginning to doubt the wisdom of every word she had said in response to Ross's disclosures. In her normal clumsy way, she had probably said all the wrong things. She couldn't help revisiting the look on his face, his despair and confusion. Whoever this editor was, whatever she did, something horrible had clearly occurred and he seemed genuinely traumatized as a result. Yes, feeling out of her depth, she had definitely said the wrong things, she decided. Same old Petra.

With friends like her, who needed enemies?

Understandably, Ross certainly seemed to be avoiding her now, texting to let her know he wouldn't be dropping into the shop that day—or the next—or the next. The texts were oblique and becoming less frequent: He "had a lot going on," he "lost track of the time," he "needed space to reflect . . ." The rejection—at least that was how it seemed—felt bruising. But it wasn't like they were "together," she told herself. He owed her nothing. And now she needed to get Ross out of her head, so she could concentrate on what Jess was so earnestly telling her about the literary festival.

"It's daunting," Jess admitted, straightening the already straight writing pad, several pens, a desk diary, and a packet of Post-it notes she had brought to Freya's to record their thoughts.

Petra admired the organization. Maybe one of the reasons she was a rubbish literary agent is because she had insufficient stationery. "You'll do great," she told Jess as the other woman took a deep, steadying breath.

"Hmm. That's what Aiden says, but . . . I mean, it wasn't even my idea, to be honest."

"Oh yeah, you were saying it was you and Jules?" Petra responded.

"Right! So I honestly don't mind, but Jules made a public announcement there was going to be this new literary festival, but right after that Roman insisted they were going to do their Grand Tour, so Jules wanted to cancel, but then she thought—well—everyone's going to be really unimpressed that she said it and then bailed . . ."

"So you picked it up instead?"

"Yes. And actually—you know what?—we are starting really small: something for the kids, a bit of fiction, memoir, a few industry professionals doing a couple of writing workshops or talks about publishing maybe. The challenge is getting people to come all this way. We're kind of out in the sticks. But then—when I heard you're a literary agent—"

"Ex-literary agent," Petra corrected her, but it was as if Jess hadn't heard.

"So you know loads of people, right?"

"Actually, not as many as you probably think." But then Petra caught herself. Everyone was being so lovely to her, they deserved her support. And there was always Alistair. He would do something, wouldn't he? "I might be able to pull some strings," Petra admitted, sparking a look of immense relief on Jess's face. "Leave it to me."

"And we've got Imo," said Jess, sounding more confident. "She's being amazing, of course. Did you get a chance to talk to her the other day?"

Petra had no idea what Jess was talking about, so she made a hopefully noncommittal face, while watching and listening for further clues.

"You know she's *the* Imogen Crawley, don't you?" persisted Jess.

Ah! Dauntingly perfect Imogen and Gabriel from the other night. "Carnegie-medal-winning children's book author, Imogen Crawley?" she said, nodding.

Imogen Crawley—like Ross—was one of those publishing unicorns whose debuts had soared to spectacular success right at the start of their careers.

"Imo, as in Gabriel and Imo, yes," said Jess. "She's a superstar—tough for Gabriel being outshone by his wife. Lucky he's not a conceited snob. I mean, he easily could be, being lord of the manor, but he's never been like that."

"He's a lord?" Now Petra felt even more that she was frantically playing catch-up in this conversation.

"Yeah, so anyway, Imo is kind of our headliner, in terms of the children's stuff," Jess went on, being clearly less interested in the whole "lord" thing than Petra was. "She's really generous with her time over my work in schools, and Jules gets on well with her too, so she's always in Capelthorne's doing stuff. We'd thought of having a children's story-writing workshop and maybe an art competition, drawing their favorite book character? But, of course, the festival's in early September, so whatever we do in the run-up, it'll end up during the school vacation, which is where you come in," Jess stopped and took a deep breath, throwing Petra an apologetic look. "Sorry," she said. "Listen to me gabbling on. On the subject of stories, do you intend to carry on doing the children's story time on Saturdays this summer? It could be a great recruitment hotbed for the festival stuff."

"Wha—? Oh, I don't know," said Petra, making a mental note to ask Flo when she got back to the shop. Mainly, she had been in a daydream while Jess chattered, imagining Ross making his heroic comeback as a headliner in the festival. Sheesh, if he did that it would put Portneath on the literary map for sure. But she would never persuade him. That is, if they ever saw each other again. The others—Freya, Jess, Gabriel . . . the whole crowd, and Flo of course—had been very welcoming, but Ross?

Ross had become a close friend in those few short weeks.

At least, she thought he had.

She missed him.

Chapter Fourteen

"Oh, and don't forget *Black Beauty*," declared Petra, advising a woman who was buying birthday books for her soon-to-be-ten-year-old, pony-mad granddaughter. "We've got a beautiful new edition, just came in last week, hang on." Petra scurried off and came back triumphantly with a clothbound hardbacked book, flicking through to show her customer the lovely color plates. "Only—trigger warning—you know it's seriously sad, don't you?"

"Gosh, it really is," said the lady, handling the book reverently. "I remember sobbing over it myself as a child. Such a wonderful book, but I don't like the thought of her reading it alone. We've always got a book on the go that we read together, and this can be that one. I'll have a second copy, if you have it?"

"Talking of sobbing, she's read *War Horse*?" queried Petra over her shoulder, fetching another copy of *Black Beauty* and adding it to the stack. There was a substantial pile of books building up on the checkout table now.

"Ah, *War Horse*," reminisced the lady. "We read it, *and* we saw the stage show with the puppets! Magical . . ."

"It was," said Petra, tearing up at the memory. "What a story."

"And then, of course, there are the endless pink, little girl pony series books, which all look the same to me," admitted the lady. "I think it's so important to have something undemanding to read along with the challenging stuff."

"I *totally* agree," said Petra, positively adoring this woman and thinking what she wouldn't have done to have a grandmother like this. "So . . ." Petra thought a moment. "We risk giving her something she's already read, but has she had the Katie Price books?"

"That woman with the boobs?" queried the lady. "I think her mother vetoed those."

"Oh no, honestly, they're fine," Petra reassured her. "I mean, she is genuinely keen on horses, Katie Price. She might not have written them herself, of course. I couldn't possibly say," she added with a wink.

"Go on, then," said the lady. "I think it's important for the child to see her grandmother subvert her parents' wishes occasionally."

Petra giggled.

Fat chance *she* would ever become a naughty grandmother, Petra thought with fleeting sadness as she went to collect the Katie Price books, or even that her own mother would take the slightest interest if she ever had a daughter of her own. And that was equally unlikely, she told herself, momentarily subdued, although she perked up when she saw the total, after whizzing the lady's books through the scanner.

"You are *so* good at this," Flo told Petra, when the customer had left. "And I consider myself pretty decent at recommendations myself."

Petra flushed, pleased to have impressed Flo, who she increasingly regarded with awe. What with Jess making her feel important earlier and Flo bigging her up now, she was going to have a head the size of a planet by the end of the weekend.

It felt good. All she wanted to do was share her minor triumphs with Ross, but he was still absent.

She could message him, of course, but pride stopped her.

"By the way," Petra said to Flo, remembering Jess's comments about storytelling, "tell me about the Saturday Stories thing?"

"Ah," said Flo. "I regret we haven't done that for a while. It used to be me, when I had Jules helping to run the shop."

"I could do that!" piped up Petra. "By which I mean, I could run the shop, not that I could read the stories . . ." she added hastily.

"The thing is, my eyesight really isn't up to it anymore," said Flo sadly. "When I read for myself, I do it either on Kindle with the font size up high or—at a stretch—with the large-print books. Reading aloud, and not knowing whether I am going to read something wrong, or not be able to make it out at all? Too stressful, my dear, I'm sorry."

Flo looked very sorry, Petra saw, and not just because she was letting Petra down. Getting old must be brutal, even though Flo made it look easy most of the time.

"I loved it, though," Flo went on, smiling at the memories. "Doing all the voices, acting it out . . . the best fun in the world."

That set Petra thinking. Who was it who was producing all the silly voices the other day . . . ? And then she realized. It was Ross, playing their daft "opening lines of books" game. Now *he* would be a brilliant children's story reader. And he needed something to do. She would ask him.

If she ever saw him again.

Throughout the following two weeks, four days, and sixteen hours—if anyone was counting, and she was—Petra was checking her phone obsessively. Now that she had deleted all her social media apps, drifted away from all her friends, and essentially "estranged" herself from family, as her mother liked to point out in her rare texts to her daughter, there was no one who would be contacting her.

This left Petra feeling anxious, lonely, and adrift. She played over in her mind her last conversations with Ross and remembered the lost look in his eye when he sought, with brutal honesty, to articulate his position: He was a writer who—like Icarus—had flown too high and come crashing down to earth. He had carefully skirted the specifics—precisely what had happened between him and his editor, for a start—and concentrated instead on how the hideous unraveling had made him feel. And she had struggled to know how to react. She had let him down. Despite her own experience of failure, she had been unable to comfort him, rally him, or even let him believe she understood him.

She had failed him.

And then, one Saturday, when she had Flo helping in the shop, her phone pinged just as the last customer had left the shop for the day. Far too quickly, Petra reached over to check, trying to give the impression to Flo that it was no big deal. She was fooling no one, especially not that particular sharp-minded old woman.

It was Ross.

Fancy a beer after closing? the message said.

What? Radio silence for more than two weeks, and then a five-word text? What the hell? Trying to be affronted, Petra felt a tremulous smile spread across her face. She was going to see him. And soon.

"Thank goodness," said Flo drily. "I take it that's what you've been waiting for?"

"Yeah . . . just a friend," Petra admitted, trying to sound airy and casual. "Wondering if I fancy meeting up for a drink, that's all."

"Well, say yes, for *God's* sake," Flo shot back, pulling on her coat and leaning down to clip on Digger's lead. "And I think we're all jolly relieved he—or she?—has finally contacted you. There we are, old boy," she murmured to Digger. "Walkies and din-dins at last, you will be relieved to know . . ."

As Flo closed the door behind her, Petra's phone dinged again. Clearly Ross felt his first text had been insufficiently compelling.

I have snacks???? 😉

Petra went and peered out of the door, into the rain-glossed street. Then she saw him. Standing on the street corner with a bulging bag from Finn's delicatessen in one hand and his phone in the other. He was wearing the khaki coat she first saw him in and an embarrassed grin. And he was soaked.

She gave him a lopsided smile and held the door open.

"Thanks," he said, coming in and heading straight for the stairs to the flat.

It was only when he was kneeling, lighting the fire, and she was returning from the kitchen with the bottle opener that either of them spoke again.

"Where have you been?" she said. "I thought you'd died."

He leaned back on his heels. "I've been a complete jerk," he admitted. "A drama queen, a self-obsessed brat, and—worst of all—a crappy friend."

"Yeah, well," mumbled Petra, "I'm still a little bit pleased to see you."

"Tell me that's not just because of the snacks," Ross teased, laying out his wares on the coffee table. There was a little pot of fat kalamata olives, each one stuffed with a whole almond, Roquefort cheese straws, thick-cut potato chips liberally dusted with smoked paprika, and some glistening scarlet sweet mini-peppers filled with goat's cheese. They were Petra's favorite. She would eat them every day, if she could afford to.

"It is *mainly* the snacks, to be honest," she replied, reaching for an olive. "So what have you been up to all this time? Writing?" As soon as she said it, she was metaphorically beating herself over the head. Of all the things to say! Would she ever train herself out of opening her big mouth? Probably not, realistically . . .

"I actually *have* been writing," Ross said, leaning back and taking a long drag of his beer before crossing one leg over the other at the knee and relaxing, beer bottle swinging between fingers and thumb, that familiar lock of dark hair hanging over one eye. He was the image of the handsome bohemian intellectual at play.

"Care to tell me more?" said Petra, raising an eyebrow in what she fondly imagined was a mirror of his own insouciance.

"What do you want to know?"

Ooh, this was promising. Unless he was just reeling her in, for fun.

"First line?"

"The cat . . ." He paused, with a faraway look on his face.

Petra leaned in, unconsciously.

". . . sat on the mat."

He *was* reeling her in for fun. Of course he was.

"You're supposed to be feeling penitent, remember," she reminded him sternly. "I didn't let you in just so you could yank my chain."

"Okay, okay, for real this time?"

Petra waited.

"It was a dark and stormy night—" he declaimed, tipping his head back and looking down his nose at a point on the far wall.

"Yeah, fine, whatever," snapped Petra. She had forgotten how annoying he could be. When was he going to stop teasing her like a kid brother? It was getting old. She was done.

There was a stiff silence.

"Look," Ross said seriously—or was he? "I know I deflect. That's all it is. I'm working on it, but it's hard, you know? I value your opinion more than anyone else I know."

"Okay—so—I'm also the *only* person you appear to know," Petra pointed out.

"True," he admitted. "But I've been working. I've been writing. That's why I haven't been around. I just needed to get into my own head. Coming out into the daylight again, seeing you, I feel kind of exposed, and my defenses go up. Forgive me?"

"If you let me read it, maybe . . ." Petra replied.

"Funny you should say," Ross replied lightly, but there was a tiny tremor in his voice that made her look at him sharply.

Avoiding her gaze, his hand went back into his carrier bag and reappeared with an A4 cardboard folder. He proffered it to her and she took it gingerly, still expecting a joke.

"I'm not going to find fifty typed pages with 'All work and no play makes Ross a dull boy' written on it, am I?"

"Only if I am now so inescapably insane, I don't even know that's what I've done." He grinned. "Fun fact: That little detail in the film was Stanley Kubrick's idea. It's not in the book."

"I didn't know that," Petra admitted. Stephen King was a genius of course, but horror was not her reading genre of choice. Being allowed to watch *The Shining* by a babysitter when she was just ten years old had left her having nightmares about twins in pink dresses for weeks.

"It's just the opening pages," he explained. "First ten thousand words, more or less."

"Sure. I'm looking forward to it," she said, totally serious now. And she was. Suddenly, she could barely wait for him to leave. "Thank you. For trusting me with it," she said.

"No need to thank me. I owe *you* a favor if anything," he replied. "Whatever I can do . . ."

"There *is* something actually," Petra said, remembering her conversation with Flo that day. "We want to resurrect the kids' story-reading session in the shop. It's just half an hour on market days. Lets the parents get on with their shopping in peace."

"And makes them come in and buy books," suggested Ross.

"Naturally."

Ross winced. "Do I really have to?"

"Don't you like kids?"

"No, it's not that. I love kids."

"Because you *are* one?"

"Yeah." He smiled sheepishly. "But my concern is, how will this play with my whole incognito thing?"

"How many six-year-olds have read your first novel?"

"Only novel," he corrected her absently. "Not fair though. They aren't the people I'm hiding from."

"Sure," said Petra, "but you've been living here for months, and—even over the last few weeks without the beardy disguise—how many people have recognized you?"

"You did."

"Okay," Petra amended patiently. "How many people—*who don't have a job where they are supposed to know this stuff*—have recognized you?"

"Fair." Ross made a face and thought for a long, silent moment. "Okay, I'll do it," he said.

"Great. Next Saturday, ten o'clock, we'll provide the book. Feel free to practice some silly voices. Kids love silly voices."

"Listen, *I* love silly voices," Ross said, looking at his watch and standing up to leave. "Will you promise me something?" he asked.

"What?"

"It's already late, so don't stay up half the night reading, okay? It can wait. And you look tired."

"Thanks," said Petra, frowning at him. Mind you, she *was* tired.

Maybe it was a little bit nice that he had cared enough to notice.

Locking the door behind him, tiredness totally forgotten, Petra raced back up the stairs to the flat and—with deliberate control—made herself brew cocoa and put her pajamas on before allowing herself even a peek at the contents of the brown folder.

"'Don't stay up half the night reading'?" she repeated aloud, as she propped herself up comfortably in bed and slid out a slim sheaf of printed text. "Ha! In your dreams," she told Ross in his absence.

Of course, the writing was beautiful.

And the premise was compelling too: A retelling of *The Tempest* from Caliban's perspective. From the very first line, Petra was lost to herself. She was immersed in a way that had been eluding her for at least the last two increasingly difficult years. The only break in her compulsion to keep devouring the words on the page was when a particularly exquisite turn of phrase would cause her eyes to mist with tears. Blinking them away impatiently, Petra read on, but this—just the opening fifty pages or so—was all too brief.

She was left jolting back to reality as she shuffled the papers tidily together. It was nearly one o'clock in the morning. She stared, unseeing, at the indigo sky beyond the window, trying desperately to draw the language around her shoulders like a cloak rather than return to cold gray reality. Her mug of cocoa sat cool and untouched beside her with a layer of puckered skin on its surface. But what a ride! She, Petra, had been the first person to read those words, the first person to share Ross's ideas, expressed with such sparkling language, since the world had read his first book. And now it was just her and Ross together in the universe. Joined. It felt more intimate than—well—intimacy.

Her phone pinged, and she scrambled to pick it up off the floor where it was recharging. Clearly, she was not the only one still awake.

Walk up to the bench with me tomorrow?

I'll be there, she typed, hesitated, inserted a heart emoji, then pressed send.

There was a pause of several minutes.

Did you hate it? Yes or no?

Only Shakespeare's words would do, thought Petra. "In dreaming, the clouds methought would open and show riches, ready to drop upon me, that when I waked I cried to dream again," she typed before pressing send.

And then, Don't leave me hanging, GIVE ME MORE!

Petra put down her phone and curled back up in bed, her head swirling with the beautiful, sorrowful images of longing and loneliness on the "island of strange noises" Ross had conjured.

Within minutes, she slept. And poor, oppressed, savage, beleaguered Caliban haunted her dreams.

Chapter Fifteen

Six hours later, Petra woke to find the haze-dulled sun was high in a pearl gray sky.

Oops sorry, she texted. See you at the churchyard in twenty minutes?

A thumbs-up came back so quickly that it seemed he had been waiting, poised.

Petra scrambled to dress and brush her teeth. Locking up the shop behind her, she risked keeping Ross waiting even longer so she could pop into Finn's shop for coffee.

"Sorry," she told him, as she approached the lych-gate to the churchyard where he stood, waiting.

She handed him his coffee.

"Well, *you* look like shit," she blurted, clocking his pale face and his eyes that were puffy and shadowed.

Mind you, she probably wasn't exactly looking radiant herself.

Sweetly, it seemed he was too gallant to reply, merely lifting his coffee to her in ironic salute instead.

It was still early enough to be misty as they went down into the valley, the cold clamminess touching their faces as if with ghostly fingers, but—as they climbed and approached the summit of their hill—they burst through the low clouds into glorious, yellow spring sunshine. By the time they reached their little bench, they were both sweaty and panting a little. Flumping down on the seat, they each peeled off an outer layer and then sat, catching their breath.

"So . . ." said Ross at last, without turning to look at her.

"So," echoed Petra carefully, gazing out over the valley.

There was a pregnant silence, while she thought about what to say. "It's beautiful," she told him at last, her voice cracking at the memory of it. "Obviously. Your writing is assured . . . lyrical but—at the same time—spare and *en pointe*. The subject matter . . ." She paused, thinking. "Well, it's stunning. Not the first *Tempest* retelling there's been, naturally, and the whole Caliban thing? It's a personal favorite of mine, I have to admit, but—yeah—it feels as if it's very personal for you too?"

She looked at Ross questioningly. He seemed to be avoiding eye contact, gazing at the view, but after a pause he nodded, just once.

"Also," she said slowly, watching his face closely, "some would feel the Caliban-Miranda vibe is problematic."

"Prospero's thinly veiled rape accusation?"

"Well, yeah."

"I want to rescue Caliban's reputation from that. To rehabilitate him. He's a victim of character assassination, in my view."

"Motive?"

"It's obvious, isn't it? Prospero creates him, and he thinks he owns him. He's bound to think poor Caliban isn't good enough for his daughter. He has Miranda on a pedestal. She's a chattel destined—as far as he is concerned—to inflate his consequence by making a strategic marriage. And—I suppose—Caliban is a chattel too. But Caliban is there to serve him, and Miranda is there to further his prestige. It's all pretty narcissistic."

"Not great parenting," Petra agreed. "But sexual assault?" she went on. Ross wasn't naïve. He must know the publishing industry would shy away from anything potentially controversial. Anything that might cause a writer to be canceled. The success of a book was already too arbitrary to risk bringing it down over something unnecessarily divisive.

"It's an *allegation*," persisted Ross, "and I want that allegation to shine a light on Prospero's behavior, not Caliban's. Caliban is an innocent. Pure of heart. The story is about love, of course—between Caliban and Miranda—but it's also about having a mentor that creates you and makes you fully emotionally dependent on them"—he swallowed, screwing up his eyes as he looked at the sky—"so they can control you."

His use of the third person didn't fool Petra. "You're Caliban?" she ventured.

He shrugged, then nodded again and hung his head as if the admission weighed heavily on him. "When I was first playing with these ideas," he told her, "I started with Frankenstein's monster, you know? The freak, the outcast, the rejected son who wants nothing more than to be loved by his creator—his parent, whose job is to protect him . . ."

Sheesh, this was heavy stuff, Petra thought. "I mean, you're ugly," she joked gently, "but you're not *that* ugly," she said, pleased to see him crack a smile.

"Then," he continued, "I realized Caliban was a better fit for this idea I wanted to explore. For me, the whole thing with my first novel was about me becoming the creature of the people who were invested in my work. I was the 'creature' of"—he hesitated—"the publishing industry, required to do its bidding. A being with no agency. Kind of a facsimile of an author, who didn't even exist outside this role that she—they," he corrected himself, "had created for me, you know?"

Hmm. She? thought Petra.

Now, at last, he turned to her, his eyes pleading for her to understand.

"I get it," she said, placing her hand gently on his forearm. "It's not as rosy in the garden as people think it is, looking in from outside. I do get it. Truly."

Ross nodded again sharply, satisfied, it seemed, by her understanding.

"But still," Petra went on, "that accusation Caliban tried to rape Miranda? That's heavy stuff to get around. People don't stop to absorb the nuances if they sense an issue . . ."

"Ah, but in this retelling I absolutely want to show how Prospero completely invents the slur as part of his cruelty toward Caliban. It's character assassination to achieve his goal of ostracizing Caliban now that he constitutes him as a threat to his ambitions for Miranda."

"Okay," said Petra. She would have to read the whole thing, but this kind of risky content could be more than enough to prevent Ross's ideas from getting out into the world. "So how does it end?"

He sighed. "Well, in Shakespeare's version, not well for Caliban, if you remember?"

"Hmm . . ." Petra frowned, trying to recall. "Ariel gets released by Prospero, doesn't he? I remember it's Prospero's final act before he leaves the island, to free the little sprite in return for his good service. I actually don't remember *what* happens to Caliban in the play."

"That's because it's left open," Ross explained. "The audience doesn't get to hear, and I suppose the suggestion is that Caliban has been surly and resentful, so he's left there, discarded and unwanted. Trapped in purgatory forever."

"Perhaps," said Petra gently, "this time Caliban can have a happily ever after?"

"Yeah, maybe," said Ross quietly, staring into the middle distance. "I don't know yet . . ." And then he seemed to gather himself. "Have you had breakfast?" he asked suddenly.

"Nope," said Petra, who had been thinking longingly of pancakes with syrup or a big, squishy bacon sandwich. She was starving.

"I know a place," Ross said, standing and holding out his hand to help Petra to her feet. She was a little stiff. It must be the climb. Or the cold. It was still just barely April. The sunshine was weak, and the wind was cutting.

Going down the hill was considerably easier than going up. Ross seemed elated now and full of energy, whereas Petra was definitely still feeling the effects of her late-night reading session, despite getting up late.

Ross didn't stop at the turning to the lane where his cottage was but slipped his arm through Petra's, marching her through the churchyard to the top of the main street and down.

"Where are we going?" she laughed, panting a little, buoyed by his sudden high spirits.

"You'll see," he told her, as they strode together in lockstep down to the quay. Out at the harbor now, the wind from the sea sliced like a knife and Petra clamped her hands to her cheeks, trying in vain to imbue warmth with her icy fingers.

Suddenly, Ross took a sharp left, grabbing her arm and wheeling her around into a little greasy spoon café on the seafront. Inside, the air was fuggy, warm, and redolent of bacon fat and wet wool. Most of the Formica tables were occupied, but Ross steered Petra to a little table that had just become vacant by the window, sitting her down and efficiently stacking the detritus of the previous occupants out of their way.

Petra blew her nose on a plasticky white napkin from the stack in the middle of the table. Ross was truly seeing her at her most radiant, she thought, wiping her eyes that had been streaming from the cold.

"Full English twice?" Ross queried, looking at Petra as the bustling café owner came to take their order.

Petra nodded. "Totally," she said, nodding at the lady. "But just once is plenty for me," she added.

"Even the lorry drivers don't manage two," the lady agreed. "I'll get you some nice hot tea straightaway, my darlings," she went on. "You look like you need warming up."

Two steaming mugs of strong milky tea arrived, and Petra warmed her hands around hers gratefully.

"I had you down as an avocado-on-sourdough kind of girl," teased Ross as two plates piled high with bacon, sausage, eggs, baked beans, tomato, and mushrooms arrived, along with side plates of sliced white bread and stacks of little foil butter packets.

"I eat avocado," said Petra defensively, before shoveling a forkful of sausage and bacon into her mouth. It was as hot as lava, and she panted desperately, fanning her hand in front of her open mouth. This must look utterly charming, she thought to herself, rolling her eyes at Ross, who was laughing at her predicament.

"Classy," he deadpanned. "Listen, I *like* to be around women who actually eat," he went on, in response to her pseudo-outraged expression. "I dated enough avocado toast girls when I was living in London."

Dated? Is that what this is? thought Petra, hoping her blushes at the word were lost in the general ruddy-cheeked-ness of chilly Sunday morning walks with no makeup on. Suddenly, she hoped that Ross was a man who liked the natural look.

"Tell me about your London life?" she said, fiddling with a butter packet and spreading her bread so she had an excuse not to meet his eye.

"Book launches, interviews, parties filled with people who don't actually like each other . . . leggy, clever women throwing themselves at me. And men."

"Must have been hell," said Petra, feeling a pang of jealousy. "And did you manage to refrain from reciprocating?"

"Yeah, mostly," he said. "I was kind of . . . 'unavailable' at the time." He gave Petra a twisted smile.

"You were in a relationship?" she hazarded.

"Yeah," he said, without elaboration.

"With Prospero?"

"Yeah, kind of . . . Dr. Frankenstein, Geppetto, choose your god/creator/whoever . . . Female in this case, if you were wondering."

"When God made man, *she* was only joking," Petra told him.

"Bumper sticker philosophizing. Profound stuff," he told her, looking away and pretending to be very busy with the ketchup.

Clearly, he didn't want to talk about it, which—of course—meant that Petra very much did.

"So about Caliban's happy ending," she said tangentially. "What might that look like?"

Ross put down his knife and fork reflectively. "I think I always saw it that Caliban's thing for Miranda was legitimate," he said. "And potentially reciprocated. I mean, why not?"

"Makes sense," Petra nodded. She had kind of had a crush on Miranda herself, after seeing the play as a teenager.

"I mean, why wouldn't he be in love with her?" Ross agreed. "Not just because she's beautiful, but because of her courage," he went on. "Her open-mindedness and determination to find beauty in all things."

"'Brave new world . . .'" quoted Petra.

"' . . . that has such people in it,'" Ross quoted back, his eyes locked onto Petra's. "Exactly. So there's Caliban, in this beautiful place, but lonely, angry, and hating everything, then there's Miranda, his childhood friend. I think she's so amazing," he said smiling, with a faraway look in his eyes.

"Because . . . ?" prompted Petra, her heart inexplicably pounding.

"She's astounding," he went on. "She's ended up on the island because of someone else's agenda, she's endured the trauma of a shipwreck, and she's got this seriously weird father. Despite all that, there she is: embracing change, driving positivity, bringing life, joy, and a fresh perspective into Caliban's world at exactly the time that he's suffering from having lost his freedom to this manipulative Svengali figure, Prospero. It's intoxicating," he said, his eyes ranging hungrily over Petra's face as he talked. "She's . . ." He shook his head, locking eyes with Petra again, smiling. "She's kind of my dream woman, I suppose."

Seconds passed, and they sat, opposite each other at the little table—knees touching—the hum and clatter of the café seemed to fade into silence.

For an insane moment, Petra was convinced he was going to kiss her. She closed her eyes and leaned imperceptibly toward him, but . . . nothing.

When she opened her eyes again, Ross had looked away. The moment was gone. He sat, gazing out of the condensation-streaked window at the heaving green-gray sea beyond. His fingers were busy, fidgeting with his paper napkin, twisting it into a rope.

Suddenly he came to, looking back at her and simultaneously gesturing for the bill.

"We should go," he announced briskly. "I have to write."

PETRA HEARD NOTHING from Ross the following day. Or the next.

On Wednesday, she received a text from him. Sorry, it said. Writing.

For someone who was all about language, sending just a two-word text felt like the brush-off Petra assumed was intended. Clearly, if he felt half the intensity Petra had experienced during their last conversation, he had thought better of it.

Enough! She was like a silly, infatuated schoolgirl and needed to get a grip.

Plus, she needed to focus on herself and her real reason for being in Portneath.

Running the bookshop was now a pleasure—okay, maybe not completely unadulterated. Lugging boxes of books around was not an unalloyed joy—but for the most part, the customers were great fun, and Petra was having the best time implementing some small changes, with Flo's approval. No, the sadness in not seeing him—she told herself—was only about not having the chance to download the day's experiences with him as a friend—a friend who was, like her, rediscovering the joy in books.

Once the shop was closed, though, Petra was alone with her thoughts.

Mostly, they were not jolly thoughts.

Like, what she was going to do with herself once Jules and Roman wanted their shop back, for example . . . Books were no longer her enemy, but going back to London and taking up the reins of her literary-agent life still felt impossibly daunting. Plus, she had a massive hole in her list where her most lucrative clients had been. Which was a problem.

It was impossible not to have a creeping thought that Ross—writing a new book at last—might be looking for representation, but then she dismissed the idea as hubris. As if a major novelist like him would seriously consider asking her to be his agent. She wondered if he would at least allow her to read more of the manuscript. In the meantime, inspired by his passion, she pledged to herself that she would "be more Miranda" in all of her endeavors. She thought that Caliban—and perhaps even Ross—would approve.

After such a strange day together, Petra had half assumed Ross would think better of allowing her to press-gang him into reading to the little ones on Saturday.

Which was why she was astonished—and delighted—when he slipped quietly into the shop that Saturday morning.

"Sorry," he said, pecking her on the cheek—which was a new habit, Petra noted—"it's been quite a week!"

"In a good way, I hope?"

"Yeah, definitely, but my brain hurts. It's great to take a break."

Flo, sharp-eyed and very obviously clocking the kiss, presented herself for an introduction.

"Flo, this is Ross—Ross, Flo—he's doing our story-reading session for us? I'm sure I said . . . ?"

"You did!" exclaimed Flo. "You are a darling! Petra says you're the master of silly voices."

"Damned with faint praise," said Ross, equably enough. "Hopefully not my only skill. What am I reading?"

"Have you heard of Jill Murphy? *The Last Noo-noo*?" asked Petra, riffling through a pile of books at the front desk for the one she wanted, with its picture of an adorable baby monster looking extremely cross on the cover.

"Of *course* I've heard of Jill Murphy," said Ross. "I'm not a complete philistine, but what, in the name of all that is holy, is a 'noo-noo'?"

"Don't panic, the noo-noo's just a pacifier," laughed Petra, handing him the book. "One of the mums popped in this week to buy a copy. She wants her little boy to stop using a pacifier before he starts nursery school, and he's struggling, poor little thing. He's called Archie. She's probably bringing him in for the session, so I thought it would be a good one to start with."

"Thanks," said Ross, raising an eyebrow in disbelief. "I think I assumed I'd be reading Tolkien or something."

"That could work," said Flo. "That's providing you are planning on doing this every Saturday for the next hundred years."

"I could be persuaded," said Ross, glancing at Petra and then decidedly looking away. "I can think of worse things than spending the next hundred years trapped in a bookshop."

"Welded to a swarm of snotty children clamoring for more?"

"Yeah, maybe not that bit," he admitted.

Flo settled Ross in the corner of the children's section with an adult-sized chair and a fresh cup of tea and—within minutes—he was off.

Who knew that a handsome man like Ross could appear even more attractive when he was putting on a bossy granny voice, thought Petra, finding herself gazing at him between customers, something that she spotted Flo noticing too. She would be interrogated later, that was for sure.

"So . . ." said Flo heavily, in a brief moment when Ross had left and they were in between flurries of customers. "Ross, eh?"

"Hmm?" Petra replied, noncommittal, but she was fooling no one.

"I, for one, feel *much* better knowing you have a nice young man looking out for you," said Flo complacently.

"Don't need a man looking out for me," muttered Petra gracelessly.

"Didn't say you did," Flo retorted. "But life is much nicer with, than without. I would miss Graham if he wasn't there . . . and you would never have caught me saying *that* just a year ago," she added, sounding astonished herself at the revelation.

Chapter Sixteen

Perhaps it was never too late for love, Petra thought, back in the flat that evening as she sat in front of the fire. She was still two years short of thirty herself. There was loads of time. Although—that said—she hadn't dated for years: being a struggling student, then working various low-paid editing jobs, and then as a rookie literary agent, frantically working and networking in the evenings and weekends. Life hadn't seemed to allow the time or the energy for romance. She hadn't even had time to maintain her old friendships.

No wonder she had been so lonely.

It was hard to be lonely in a busy bookshop, she found. Another lovely thing was how, when the shop was closed at five o'clock, Petra really did feel the work was done for the day. Life was so much more pleasant even in the little ways, she thought contentedly, sipping her tea and opening her latest book with pleasurable anticipation.

On Thursday, Petra—locking up the shop after another good sales day—was looking forward to the evening. It was to be the first time that Capelthorne's hosted the local writing group.

Alison, the leader of "Write Club" (first rule of Write Club is you do not talk about Write Club) was the only member Petra had already met. Clearing a space and pulling the chairs into a circle, she suddenly found herself suffering a fit of nervous excitement at the thought of being with actual writers for the first time in ages. Hearing a knock at the door, Petra was relieved to see Alison was the first to arrive.

"This is so kind of you," said Alison, looking around the shop nervously, as if expecting someone to be lurking in the shadows, ready to leap out and tell her Capelthorne's wouldn't be hosting the group after all.

Mind you, thought Petra, she hadn't double-checked with Jules that it *was* all right. She had been loath to interrupt the honeymoon, but Flo was enthusiastic when Petra mentioned it to her as a fait accompli a few days ago.

"Mrs. Hamilton at the library was so relieved when I told her we had managed to find another venue," Alison told Petra, bobbing her head in gratitude.

Alison was a thin, nervous woman in her sixties, given to wearing anoraks and bobble hats. She reminded Petra of the little mouse seamstress in Beatrix Potter's *Tailor of Gloucester* with her earnest head-forward posture and habit of wringing her hands.

"You are all very welcome," Petra reassured her. "It was such a shame the library couldn't continue," she went on, "but I know how difficult funding is these days. Here, look, we have some biscuits," she went on, getting out the tin with the chocolate biscuits left over from the most recent Beach Reads Book Club, "and all the tea- and coffeemaking bits are in the kitchen here, so do just help yourselves."

"Thank you, we will," said Alison anxiously, "but—I confess—we were also hoping you would stay and give us your thoughts? When I told the crew you were from publishing in London," she practically put "publishing" in quote marks, such was the majesty she conferred to the word, "we were hoping you would join in?" She screwed up her face as if feeling the request was very significantly too much to ask.

"Of course! I'd love to," exclaimed Petra, who was secretly hoping she *would* be asked but hadn't wanted to volunteer herself.

THEY WERE AN eclectic bunch, Petra decided, looking around the little circle when they had all convened and were settled with mugs and chocolate biscuits in hand. They had clearly exchanged material by email in advance and were already leaning in solicitously, heaping each other's work with praise as they chatted quietly among themselves.

They all nodded and smiled as Alison made introductions, which gave Petra a chance to apologize for not having read anything beforehand. At hearing this, they all diffidently handed over sheafs of printouts showing the work they were going to discuss that evening. Petra promised that Alison would provide them all with her email address so she could study up in advance of the next session, prompting an outburst of gratitude from them all.

The range of writing projects and styles was huge, Petra discovered.

Simon was a bear of a man who reminded Petra of Hagrid from Harry Potter. He wore a thick Arran sweater that smelled faintly of sheep and had the facial hair of a grizzled old sea dog. Simon was writing his memoirs of a life spent crisscrossing the world's oceans on his single-handed yacht.

"I adored your descriptions of the Balearics," said Sylvia diffidently. "I thought the use of metaphor was inspired."

"Melvillesque," breathed Alison, who had submitted the newest chapter of her romance novel.

"I wondered if I had gone a bit too far on the old descriptions," admitted Simon modestly, but they all rushed to politely disagree.

Sylvia, another member of the group, was a poet, Petra discovered, and she had written some genuinely fine verse, judging by the one set in the churchyard on the top of the hill, which they were all reading that evening. Her description of imagining wedding and funeral parties convening at the lych-gate for several hundreds of years made the hair stand up on the back of Petra's neck, and she said so, while also admitting she had never worked on poetry in a professional capacity. "There are so few opportunities to work with poetry in today's publishing scene," she said apologetically.

"Oh, gosh, I know!" Sylvia rushed to reassure her. "I'm not even seeking a traditional publisher, although I've entered the odd poetry competition here and there," she admitted.

"And won some of them too," Alison chipped in, "although Sylvia's too modest to say."

Sylvia blushed. "I confess, I did get excited about a poetry competition Portneath Books set up last year," she told Petra. "But then there was a fire, and the bookshop was gone, although I don't know if Jules and Roman will reinstate the competition when they get back. Perhaps they will . . ." She trailed off, bright-eyed with hope.

"I *know* they will," Petra reassured her, knowing no such thing, of course.

The evening had flown by, Petra mused as she brushed her teeth that night. They were all so lovely. Alison, writing romance, was seriously good, which Petra had *not* been expecting. In another life, she would have been asking for the full manuscript. She had been surprised to notice how excited she was to read good work. She had always relied on the physical signs . . . the feeling of something pushing upward in her throat, like a laugh wanting to bubble up, the sense of wanting to sit up straighter. There were so many things a writer had to get right: language, plot structure, hooks, topicality *with* originality, and—when it was all there, or nearly there—Petra had the thrill of the chase, the hunger for acquisition.

But then she gave herself a stern talking-to: She had been a *bad* literary agent, letting her clients down by not always getting their work sold, and it was no good telling herself—as Alistair always had—that no agent sells everything. The stakes were high for her writers, and she had failed them. So she knew better than to listen to the instincts she was feeling again now. The last thing she wanted to do was raise—and then dash—the hopes of any more writers who were unlucky enough to cross her path.

Ross's thoughts that evening, sitting alone in his cottage, were—like Petra's—mixed. He had had a great day of writing. The sticky middle was as "in shape" as he could get it for now, and the final act was mapped out in some detail, to the exclusion of the ending itself. Could he really pull off a happy ending for Caliban? What would that be? It seemed a stretch for him to "get the girl" unless he played it that Miranda, with her courage and optimism, had managed to civilize him a bit. Otherwise, she really was too good for him. The happy ending would not be believable, he feared.

No, it was no good. He lacked the writing skill to make it plausible. And he was more than aware of the parallels with his own life. The Caliban character he was writing was about as autobiographical as he could get. He could no longer ignore that he was drawn to Petra as his real-life Miranda. But the best thing he could do for her was keep his distance, he told himself gloomily as he brushed his teeth. Let her escape at the end of the summer and return to her life in London, with a chance to find someone who would be good for her. Someone who wasn't a writer—and a complex, damaged, emotionally fragile writer at that.

On which note, there was one thing he might bring himself to ask her before she disappeared from his life, and that was about representation. He could not bear the thought of anyone else being his literary agent. And that was another excellent reason why he needed to detach the two of them from any suggestion of an emotional tie. It was unfair of him to ask her, and selfish too, but he had no choice: He couldn't be entangled romantically—or even as a friend—with a woman who was responsible for his career.

He had made that mistake once. He wasn't going to make it again.

"PETRA!" ROSS ANNOUNCED heavily as he approached the front desk where she sat.

"Ross!" she declared, echoing his tone with a grin. "What gives, big man?" He looked anxious, she noted, with dark circles under his eyes and heavy stubble. It seemed the grizzled look she had first seen him rocking was coming back into fashion.

"We need to talk."

"We are," she pointed out.

"Later. Properly."

Petra put her head on one side, pretending to consider. "That would be very nice," she said. She tried hard not to show hurt that he had been absenting himself from their daily chats again. "Beer and peanuts after I close the shop? I may even have some tortillas and guacamole, if you're very good?"

"Snacks would not be mandatory," he bantered back, with visible effort. Rather than his proposing a catch-up between friends, he looked more like she had proposed the final hearing of a death sentence appeal.

"'Snacks are not mandatory'? Are you quite well, sir?" she enquired. It was one of their shticks, lapsing into Austen-speak. This time, it barely raised a glimmer.

"Five o'clock then," he merely said in reply, sketching a salute and turning away.

Watching him leave, she saw that even his back view radiated depression. What could it be? Perhaps his writing was not going well. Yes, that was it. She would find a way to restore his confidence, she told herself, as she flitted around the shop, tidying a stack of books here and straightening a shelf label there. There was always a point in writing a novel where the writer felt like they were wading through quicksand. She knew nothing if she didn't know that. One thing her literary agent experience had taught her was how and when to give a mired writer a boost to their confidence. And also to know when they just required a swift boot up the backside.

She would decide later which one Ross needed.

"Right," Petra said, when they were both sitting in their usual places, she on the sofa and he on the little chair. There were open bottles of beer and a generous array of snacks on the coffee table, and the fire was blazing cheerily. "How goes it, noble scribe?"

"Writing-wise?" he said, sighing. "Well. Very well, in fact."

"Yeah? So that *totally* explains why you've got a face like a slapped arse," declared Petra with a performative sigh of relief. "Always a bit shitty when writing is going 'very well,' I've found. I don't know how you stand it. Imagine how much worse everything would be if it was going amazingly . . ." Frankly, Petra could have carried on riffing on this vein indefinitely, and Ross seemed to know it, because he leaned forward to silence her, his expression still unrelentingly grave.

"I've nearly finished my first draft," he told her.

"Oh no! Boo . . ." she countered.

"Yeah! Actually, it is 'boo' because you know what this means?"

"Um, that you might—actually, probably will—have a stunningly successful novel on your hands? Nice problem to have, I'd have thought." But he was not to be jollied along.

"No," he replied. "It means I need you to read it—soon—and then decide whether you will represent me."

"Ohhh!" said Petra, throwing up her hands, as if that explained everything. "Well, that's easy," she said. "I won't."

"Read it? Or represent me?"

Petra wavered. She was craving to read more, in a sickly way that made her think about crack addicts.

"I'll read it," she said, more gently. "Of course I will. But represent you? No. I'm not going to do that."

At this, Ross looked even more dejected, which was ridiculous, Petra thought. He was dodging a bullet. He should be pleased.

"Why won't you?" he said.

Because I'm terrified, thought Petra. Because this particular book, written by this particular writer, matters too much. Because I'm scared that I'll fail and damage his career, she thought, gazing at him and picking up her beer with a shaking hand.

Because hurting this man in any way at all would be totally unthinkable.

"Because I'm not a literary agent," she said at last. "Not anymore."

"Coward."

"Ouch, not fair," she protested, stung. "You weren't there. It was grim."

"It was a TYPO!" he shouted, waving a tortilla chip loaded with guacamole in a way that put the hearth rug in significant danger. "You literally threw away your entire career because something awkward and embarrassing happened. Have you any idea how awkward and embarrassing it is being me?" he demanded. "To have to go crawling back to the publishers, the reviewers, the readers, and explain why I absented myself for the last five years?"

"Sure, it's gotta be pretty bad," said Petra, her voice laced with sarcasm, "being a devilishly handsome debut novelist with a first novel achieving stellar success, the darling of the literati, and now being ready to come back to them with more of the same? They're going to hate you . . . I mean *I'd* be embarrassed if I were you," she told him. "Anyway, it wasn't just the typo thingy—although it was genuinely bad," she went on, hearing and hating the self-pity in her voice, "I was disillusioned by then anyhow."

She declared, "I've lost my mojo, and my clients deserved better than that. So do you."

"Read it," said Ross, handing over a folder he had just pulled out of his coat. "Just read it. If you hate it, fine. If you love it, then *you tell me* why you're not the best person to represent my work. Deal?"

Despite almost every fiber in her body begging her not to, Petra reached forward and took it. Then she sighed performatively, flopping back on the sofa cushion in capitulation. *"Fine,"* she said, clutching the folder to her chest.

"And there's something else I need to tell you," Ross said quietly.

"Oh, goodie," replied Petra. Jeez, the fun was just going on and on this evening.

"This bit's difficult," he muttered, hanging his head before raising it again and looking her right in the eye, his entire body tense, as if he was bracing himself. "I need you to be my agent, but—if you decide you are prepared help me, and I hope you will—there is a price to pay."

"*Now* he tells me," joked Petra, furious to be unable to suppress the tremble in her voice.

"You and me. Being . . . friends," he said. "Or whatever this—thing—is, between us?"

Petra nodded, an icy trickle running down her back. She had been here before. She knew what being dumped looked like. And—hell—this wasn't even a romance. Being dumped *before* a romantic relationship even began had to be a new low.

Chapter Seventeen

Later, after leaving the folder in the kitchen—it felt contaminated now that she understood it was part of such a Faustian pact—Petra lay on her back in the pitch-black bedroom, her eyes glued to the invisible ceiling. "Whatever this—thing—is," he had told her. And now her mind kept repeating his words on a death loop. "Whatever this thing is," "whatever this thing is . . ."

What was this "thing"? What was it to Ross? Friendship? No. If he thought it was just that he would have said so, which indicated it was more . . . Which was good, because if Petra asked her heart what her relationship was with Ross, she would call it more than friendship too.

A lot more.

But then he had solemnly announced that if she represented him "it" would end. And that was fine, she tried to reassure herself, because she definitely, definitely wasn't going to represent him. Especially now that she knew the deal. So . . . all good. No?

Petra groaned. Sleep was impossible. She picked up her phone. Just at three o'clock. She had to get up in four hours. Despite that, accepting the impossibility of rest, she snapped on the light and went off to the kitchen to fetch the folder.

When her alarm went off, Petra discovered she had been staring sightlessly into space for some time, the individual pages scattered on the bedspread, the final scenes of the manuscript he had given her still held loosely between her fingers. Although, of course, they were not the final scenes. Not quite.

The gray dawn had warmed fully into daylight now, with a watery yellow sun casting its cool rays across the rooftops. A perfect late spring day, chilly and bright. The dawn chorus had died away, leaving just a solitary thrush serenading, its quicksilver notes rising and falling through the air.

Petra looked down at last, struggling to persuade her strained, gritty eyes to focus on the manuscript. She rubbed her face and sighed before rolling her head to try to iron out her stiff neck.

It was good.

It was *more* than good; it was superb: Sweeping but intimate, elegant but raw . . . She had decided to re-read the beginning before continuing with the new pages Ross had given her and—despite the story being familiar, of course—the reframing of it with Caliban as protagonist was totally convincing.

Even better than that, the narrative drive was somehow also irresistible, which was a tricky feat to pull off in a retelling. Of course, he had smashed it, on this and every other point.

As before though—when she just had the opening chapters—the story stopped abruptly. It was perhaps sixty thousand words in total—a full-length literary work—but it was not yet complete. The critical decision of whether Caliban's ending was a happy or a tragic one was still to be made it seemed, although any reader, however dull of spirit or hard of heart, would be longing for an uplifting finish. The two unanswered questions—which had been posed and explored with exquisite skill—were whether Caliban's release from Prospero's domination would feel like freedom or abandonment, and whether his seemingly hopeless crush on brave, inspiring Miranda was reciprocated or ultimately rebuffed.

Petra couldn't remember a time when she had cared more about how a book ended.

Later, in the shop, Petra's lack of sleep, and the horrible quandary she now found herself in over her relationship with Ross, had left her strung out and exhausted. She sat crouched on the chair at the cash register, numb and devoid of rational thought. She was completely unable to rouse herself to do any of the tasks she would normally be doing when not serving customers. Even escaping to the kitchen to make herself a really strong instant coffee was like scaling Everest. And it tasted vile.

She was just wincing over the dregs in her mug when the doorbell clanged and Freya rushed in, looking as adorable as usual, with her face prettily flushed, and tufts of her bright blond hair sticking up at all angles where it had escaped from her ponytail.

"Sorry," she stage-whispered as she trotted in, nearly at a run. "I'm sneaking out to grab Finn a birthday present," she confided, glancing guiltily over her shoulder. "I've left it horribly late, and I'm worried you'll have to order it in . . ."

"What did you have in mind?" asked Petra dully, relieved that she wasn't being asked to come up with suggestions.

"I was thinking that going wild book—it's, like, a memoir, I think?—about encouraging diversity by letting farmland revert to the wild? They are thinking of giving it a whirl at Hollytree Farm," she told Petra. "It's by Isabella somebody?"

"Isabella Tree," furnished Petra, faintly astonished that her dulled brain had managed to come up with the facts. "Nominative determinism, I suppose you'd call it."

"I have no idea what that is." Freya laughed. "But do you have it in stock?" She bit her lip anxiously.

"Um, I actually think we've sold the last copy; it's on order, but I suppose next week is too late?"

Freya looked crestfallen.

Then Petra had a brainwave. "Hang on," she said, scurrying as fast as her leaden limbs would take her, quickly returning from the stockroom waving a large, slim hardbacked book with a beautiful woodcut of a hare on the cover.

"Now, this is the children's version," she warned, handing it to Freya doubtfully.

"That's perfect. Finn's just a big kid," said Freya. "Wow, it's beautiful!"

The two women looked at the book together, exclaiming over the spectacular illustrations, a mix of sketches, watercolors, and woodcuts, featuring the re-wilded estate at Knepp, the farm where the whole experiment had started.

"Perfect," declared Freya, putting it on the table and reaching for her wallet. "I think he's going to love it—wowsers, you look terrible," she exclaimed, looking Petra full in the face for the first time as she handed over her card. "What on earth is the matter?" She placed her hand gently on Petra's forearm, her face a picture of concern.

How to explain? "Oh, it's nothing," Petra said, dropping her gaze so Freya wouldn't see the sudden tears. "I didn't sleep. I'll be fine."

"Come over for supper," said Freya decisively. "On the house. As soon as we open. Before, even, and then—as soon as you've eaten you can go straight off to bed."

"That's so kind," said Petra, "but—you know what?—I think I'll just skip the food and hit the sack as soon as I close."

"Sure?" Freya screwed up her face anxiously.

"Yeah, totally," Petra insisted. If she was desperate for sleep, she was even more desperate to get away from people. All people. Not even just Ross . . . Although she *definitely* wanted to get away from Ross.

When the longed-for closing time finally arrived, following an afternoon that dragged so badly she had started to feel stuck in a complete paralysis of the space-time continuum, Petra was sure she would crawl straight upstairs to bed, but then—arriving in the flat at last—she found she couldn't settle.

The horrible double bind Ross had put her in—a quandary she had been pushing away from her thoughts all day—immediately swamped her consciousness again, followed by repeated waves of physical anxiety. She found herself wandering twitchily around the little flat, utterly preoccupied, sweating but cold, making tea but forgetting to drink it, scrolling on her phone but then chucking it down in despair as even the mini-dopamine hits of Instagram and TikTok failed to amuse. The pink walls of her west-facing bedroom were glowing like copper with the falling sun, but dark was still some time away. It was barely six o'clock. Going to bed before darkness fell was a complete impossibility, she realized.

What she needed was profound physical fatigue. A tiredness of the body so overwhelming that even her mind would be quiet.

Deciding in a moment, she shrugged on her thin waterproof coat and—not even stopping to change her sneakers for something more robust—she locked the door and strode up the hill to the churchyard. She remembered halfway up that she didn't even have her phone, but that was fine. Phones were for speaking to people, and the point was to avoid that. She could watch the sunset in solitude from the bench at the top of the hill.

Their bench.

Getting into her stride felt good. She found herself counting "1, 2, 1, 2" like a mantra as she walked, the hypnotic rhythm and effort driving out all thought. Instead, she concentrated on the physical sensations: her breath, the rocky ground beneath her feet, the feel of the increasingly cold evening air sharp on her cheeks and nipping her nose.

She arrived at the bench, panting, and sat down—right in the center—to watch the sunset paint the sky, its rays grazing the rooftops of Portneath far below. As a meditation to replace the walking, she focused her gaze on the golden orb dropping lower until it touched the sea on the horizon. It wasn't enough. The thoughts intruded again, swirling and coalescing: their friendship, their connection, the exhilaration of reading his work, but then the lurch of fear she felt every time she replayed the moment when he asked her for representation.

It was impossible. Going back to that world? Unthinkable . . . and to have to face doing it without even this "thing" with Ross to sustain her? Even more unthinkable.

She pined for a return to their easy banter, the freewheeling conversations, the laughter, and the excitement of lighting upon yet another shared love, be it poem, novel, or even a piece of art.

They were soulmates.

And, of course, he was so beautiful, and she no longer meant just on the outside. Was it any wonder she had allowed herself to daydream that the two of them might one day share something deeper?

Ridiculous.

It even struck her then, with a physical wail of pain, that he might even have fostered their friendship with a view to what she could do for him professionally. Otherwise, what would an absolutely stunning and talented human being like him be doing with a pseudo-goth, career-failed basket case like her? Petra stared, unseeing, at the glorious view, unblinking for so long her eyes started streaming with tears.

Also, she tortured herself, there *had* to be a good reason why he was no longer with his previous agent. Was he unrepresentable? A raging despot? He must be . . . Perhaps she was the only person in the industry not to know it. That would be it . . .

But—no—she *knew* him. He was funny, fallible, kind, and insightful—a good friend. Of course, if she refused him, he would no longer be a friend anyhow. She would have let him down in his moment of greatest need. How could they possibly be friends after that? He would—quite rightly—want nothing more to do with her.

And that was the whole thing, wasn't it? She had a stark choice, if you could even call it that. The friendship was at an end whichever way she turned. Tears leaked from the corners of her eyes. And it wasn't from not blinking enough this time.

The friendship was done.

If she cared about him at all—if she had ever been a true friend to him—then helping him now would be her last act of love for him. It was the only decision a true friend could come to.

And if representing him—returning to that world—felt too unbearable to contemplate, then she would simply do her best. She would try. In any case, she told herself, all she really had to do was agree to help but then gently offload him onto Alistair. What writer wouldn't want a real, proper, experienced agent like Alistair—an agent who carried a little weight within the industry. Unlike her.

So really, although the situation was *terrible* for her, in order to show her care for him—which was what mattered most—she could only do one thing.

Say yes.

Petra gave a shaky sigh, her shoulders dropping a little at last. It was horrible. It was bleak. But at least she had decided . . .

How LONG HAD she been there, staring unseeing at the view? Longer than she should have been, she realized with a flicker of unease. The sun was gone. The horizon was invisible now. A paler patch of sky showed where the moon was attempting to shine, but the stars were absent, swallowed up and swaddled in a dense layer of clouds, descending so low they had blotted out the town below. It was as if the mountaintop were an island protruding from a sea of fog.

Without her phone, she had no idea what time it was, but the temperature had dropped several degrees.

It was definitely late.

She made two attempts to stand before she succeeded. Her limbs felt stiff with cold and fatigue. She longed for her bed, with her electric blanket and a cup of tea, and desperately wished she wasn't separated from those things by a dark, chilly, and lonely walk. Despite the looming depression, Petra also felt hungry for the first time that day. She would distract herself from her current discomfort by planning what she would eat that was hot and comforting on her return.

Channeling Flo's no-nonsense pragmatism, she set off.

She and Ross had climbed this hill so often together over the past few months. These had been, she realized more keenly in retrospect, happy, optimistic times—times she would never have anticipated having after her crestfallen exit from her life in London. "You don't know what you've got 'til it's gone," Joni Mitchell had always told her.

If only she had listened.

The first bit of the descent from the peak was always the easy bit of the walk, jolty, sure, but easier on the thigh muscles than the walk up. At night, in the mist, the jolts seemed a bit more—well—jolty, thought Petra, but she was making good progress until a misstep took her feet from under her and deposited her hard onto her backside. Getting up and brushing off her hands, she reached for her phone to use the flashlight, but—of course—she realized it was sitting uselessly on the kitchen table at home. Not a problem, she told herself, it was just this steep bit and then the path leveled out a little. God, it was cold though. No wonder she had fallen. Her feet were completely numb now, and she could no longer feel her face either. Cold as it was with no gloves, she needed to keep her hands out of her pockets in case she fell again. She cursed herself for not taking the time to put on warmer clothes. Going slower now, she was puzzled more than shocked when she fell again, harder this time, hearing a clatter of dislodged stones skittering a long way down the hillside after she landed.

Uh-oh.

She was in trouble, she thought, her heart accelerating. Somehow, in her preoccupied state and in the darkness, she had deviated from the steep, narrow path, not much more than a rabbit run, really. She made herself sit for a moment, assessing her options. Her thought processes felt dull and slow. There were some sheer drops on the steeper side of the hill, she thought groggily, and somehow, she realized now, this was where she had ended up in the dark, while preoccupied. Time passed as she assimilated. Bemused, she then realized she had lost track of how long she had been sitting there, not moving. It was as if time were simultaneously slowing down and sliding away from her.

Grasping at fleeing thoughts, Petra understood that staying there was not an option. She was thoroughly chilled to the bone now. Continuing down, in the dark, with the cliffs ever present and loose material under her feet would be suicide. She took some deep breaths, willing herself to think clearly. So sleepy. It must be late.

What would Ross do? Funny and silly although he could be, in a crisis he became stern and authoritative. Hadn't that been the first thing she had seen about him, in that ridiculous first meeting on the station platform? She smiled hazily at the thought. In this situation she had to "be more Ross" she told herself, feeling momentarily more focused. Okay, she had to get off the mountain, or she would freeze. The mist was still dense, and the visibility almost zero, but her safest plan was to turn around and go up again. Somewhere along the journey she would almost certainly find herself back on the path. At worst, she would get back up to the bench at the top. Then she could carefully descend again with greater concentration.

Hot toast and a steaming cup of tea were even farther away now, she thought with dull-witted dismay.

On the seemingly endless journey back up the hill, the universe contracted: There was only the dark, the rocky path, and the cold, all seemingly stretching on for eternity. She fell often, and her hands were soon bruised and scraped, but they were so numb she barely felt it. Vaguely she wondered whether she had become even more lost, the journey seemed so interminable, but she no longer trusted her judgment of time, and she was still going upward . . . When I get to our bench, she kept telling herself, I'll be safe.

Chapter Eighteen

Ross sat in front of the glowing stove, but all evening he had been unable to relax in its soothing warmth. He held his phone in his hand. Still no reply to his text. Was she sulking? No, that wasn't like her at all. Was she so deeply distressed she was left without words for him? God, he hoped not but—he realized with a fist-clench of guilt around his heart, if she was, it was because of him. He replayed their conversation in his mind on a punishing loop. It had been less of a conversation and more a monologue from him, he thought bitterly; on reflection, he had been telling her how *he* would like the world to be. He had selfishly put his own priorities first: for her to represent him with this new work, for them to end their relationship because—well, absolutely not because he wanted to—but because his terror of repeating past mistakes had made even relinquishing one of the most precious things in his life seem a price worth paying.

Now he wasn't so sure.

He texted her again. Just a question mark this time. A nudge to remind her of his earlier text, simply asking if she was okay.

Then, despite it being—of course—a rude and unwelcome imposition, he called her. With his phone on speaker, he sat staring at her name on the screen, listening to the ringtone, willing her to pick up.

It rang out. Not even a mailbox message. Not even a chance to hear her voice.

So she wasn't okay. Obviously.

He held this thought painfully in his head for a few minutes. And then he stood, despite having no clear plan other than going down to Capelthorne's to hammer on the door and insist that she speak to him face to face. Even though her silence made it very clear that he—the cause of her distress—was probably the last person on earth she wanted to see.

Striding down the main street, he was surprised to see Flo standing by the door to Capelthorne's with Digger at her feet. Even from a hundred yards away, her anxiety was visible.

"She's not with you, then?" Flo called, recognizing him as he approached.

"No," he told her as he arrived at her side. "What do you mean? You're looking for her too?"

"I arranged for her to dogsit while I was at choir practice," Flo explained. "She always does it on a Thursday night, the lovely girl. He gets separation anxiety and becomes destructive, so I don't like to leave him. It's just not like her to forget."

"What have you tried?" he asked.

"Knocking . . . phoning . . . but—nothing. No sign of her."

"Could she have gone out?" he suggested. "Perhaps to get something to eat? She sometimes meets friends in the pub for a drink, doesn't she?"

"Only on Fridays, generally," said Flo. "And I've been in and spoken to Freya. She hasn't seen her this evening either."

"Maybe the supermarket over the bridge?" he said, almost as if he were talking to himself.

"What, for an hour and a half?" said Flo.

"You've been here that long?" he asked curtly, looking at his watch. Nearly half past nine. The little supermarket had been closed for half an hour already, and it was only a five-minute walk.

"Then she *must* be in the flat," said Ross. "Something's definitely wrong . . . Do you have a key?"

"I didn't bring it," admitted Flo. "I wouldn't have needed to, but I was wondering about driving back to Middlemass to get it."

"No time," said Ross, assessing the door critically. The lock on it looked pretty robust, but he could break one of the glass panes and reach in.

"There are bolts top and bottom too," said Flo, following his gaze. "If you're planning to break in, I think your best bet is to go around the back."

She was already walking away, assuming he would follow.

On Flo's instruction, Ross clambered over the wall into the little courtyard garden at the back of the shop, then extracted a brick from below a terra-cotta planter and used it to smash a window in the back door. As Flo had promised, he made quick work of gaining entry.

Not pausing to assess the damage to the door, Ross ran up the stairs to the flat, his pounding heart being only partly because of the exertion. He searched the rooms upstairs rapidly, throwing open doors and not allowing himself to think of the horror of finding Petra slumped on the floor, unconscious. Or worse.

"She's not here," he barked, as he rejoined Flo outside. "And she doesn't have her phone. It's on the table. Is there *anywhere* else you can think of that she might have gone to?"

"There's no Write Club or Beach Reads tonight," said Flo. "And, in any case, that would mean her being in the shop . . . I did wonder if Jess was meeting up with her to talk about the literary festival this evening, but I bumped into Jess in Middlemass this afternoon, and I happened to mention the dogsitting. If she had plans with Petra tonight, she would have said so then."

They stood silent, at a loss, for a few seconds, both looking up and down the street as if willing Petra to approach by sheer force of determination.

"Could she have decided to go and see you?" ventured Flo at last.

"I was thinking the same," said Ross grimly. It wasn't impossible. He could quite imagine Petra coming to the cottage, having decided to give him a piece of her mind for his selfishness. It was just about conceivable that she could have gone another route, missing him as he walked down to the shop.

"I can't think of anything else," he said, his eyes narrowing in concentration. "Right, let's go there," he said, setting off, but Flo grabbed his arm.

"My car is just over there," she said. "We'll drive."

AFTER A MILLION years of dull, cold, exhausting effort, the slope became gentler in a way Petra recognized. The summit at last!

She numbly reached for the bench in the darkness, lowering herself onto it stiffly, a single tear leaking from her eye. She sniffed. Now was not the time for self-pity. This was *their* bench. The location of many happier times, just her and Ross. At that thought, the misery of her current situation consumed her again. She allowed herself a minute of weeping, wearily wiping her running nose on her sleeve.

Sheesh, it was hot now. The climb to the top of the peak must have raised her body temperature, unlikely though that sounded, as she was still unable to feel her hands and feet. It was *really* boiling, though. The thin jacket and sweatshirt she was wearing suddenly felt unbearably constricting.

In a near frenzy, she tore them both off, dropping them on the ground at her feet before lying down stiffly on the hard bench. She needed to rest. Just for a minute. And then—she promised herself—she would start the slow descent.

Time drifted.

Her cheek was painfully cold, resting against the bench as she gazed dully at her clothes on the ground. The thought of using them as an impromptu pillow arrived slowly and the impetus to enact the thought was even slower. She balled up the fabric and then lay back down again, snuggling into the softer surface. That was better.

Petra closed her eyes.

THERE WAS NO sign of Petra at the cottage. Ross groaned in worry and frustration. He imagined he could feel her presence close by as he stood, indecisive, willing her to put into his mind an image of where she was. Flo was standing at his elbow, looking equally concerned.

And then Ross knew. "She's gone up to the bench," he said.

"Where?"

"Top of the hill, the bench on the summit, she—we—go there . . ."

"You can't go up there in the pitch black," Flo told him.

"I damned well can," he said as he let them both into the cottage. If she were indeed at the bench, then *she* was up there in the pitch black without even the flashlight from her phone. She could be injured. Or ill. Either way, she needed him.

"Wait here," he instructed Flo, chucking another couple of logs into the stove to keep her warm while she waited. Digger was already settling on the hearth, lying down and resting his head on his paws, his eyes swiveling anxiously to Flo and Ross in turn.

Ross grabbed a blanket from the back of the sofa and then dived into the cupboard under the stairs, coming back out with a huge black waterproof flashlight.

"I've got my phone," he told Flo as he went to the door, tapping the screen to add a new contact. "Quick, shout out your number? I'll call you."

Flo obliged. "If you can even get a signal," she added, anxiously. But he was already gone.

Ross's mind was spiraling into various disaster scenarios as he half-walked, half-ran up the steep slope, his thigh muscles burning, although he was barely aware of the pain. It was all his fault. He had been an idiot, thinking they could morph like that, from friends—more than friends—to just another business relationship. Faced with the horror of losing her, he realized Petra was so much more than that to him. He knew that now.

He just hoped it wasn't too late.

The flashlight illuminated swirls of freezing mist in front of him, casting the rest of the landscape into velvet black darkness. His breath came in heavy plumes, and he could discern a sparkle to the gray-white tussocks of grass. Frost. In May. Unlucky, but not that unusual. If she was lying somewhere injured, she would not last long in these temperatures. The thought spurred him on even harder. What if he walked straight past her, unaware? He began to call her name, punching it out into the void, and then listening, trying to hold his breath, terrified he would miss any faint reply.

He was nearly at the summit now. Just one last push. If he got there without having found her, he didn't know what he would do next. But he couldn't afford to worry about that now.

Calling and listening was slowing his progress. He stopped briefly to push his screaming muscles into a final effort and then . . . he was at the summit.

Just for a second or two, he leaned forward panting, his hands resting on his agonized thighs. The bench was just yards away now but all the flashlight would show him was the swirling fog.

Hardly daring to breathe, he walked the last few steps, the high back of the bench blocking his view.

She was there.

In his relief, Ross nearly collapsed to the ground, his legs like water. As he gazed down at her sweet face, illuminated by the beam, her cheek cupped in one hand, eyes closed with her lashes fanning her cheeks, another unspeakable thought struck him. Why had the light not woken her?

"Petra? *Petra!*" Now his knees did buckle beneath him, and he found himself kneeling beside her, unable to take a breath, unable to make a further sound. He took her hand in his—so cold!—and stroked her cheek with the back of his other hand.

And then she stirred.

First she seemed to push her cheek into his hand, nuzzling, like a cat, and then her eyes flickered open, and her expression changed to one of horror.

"I missed my stop!" she slurred. "I have to get off. Am I in Penzance?" she asked, her eyes meeting his as she started to struggle upright in her agitation.

"You're not in Penzance, my darling," said Ross, barely able to speak with relief and with the rush of emotion that filled him, overflowing into a tidal wave of love. "You are exactly where you need to be," he soothed her. "You're with me." He slid his arm around her shoulder and gently lifted her upright so he could slide in beside her on the seat. He rested her against him and pulled her tightly against his body, his relief quickly giving way to the need to plan his next actions. She was wearing practically nothing. He was amazed she hadn't already frozen to death, but the danger was not over yet.

While holding her with one arm, he reached for the blanket on the ground and pulled it over her, but—even with his body warmth—it wasn't enough.

He had to get her out of here. Fast.

He looked briefly at his phone, holding it up to the skies. One bar. He called Flo, who seemed to answer, but he could hear nothing. Briefly outlining their situation and his plan in the hope she could hear him, even if he couldn't hear her, he then persuaded a reluctant, barely conscious Petra to put her sweatshirt and jacket back on before wrapping the blanket around her shoulders.

"*Hot!*" she complained, her voice slurred and weak.

Hypothermia. Ross's heart thumped hard in his chest.

"Your body is playing tricks on you," he told her, holding her face in his hands, commanding her attention. "You need to trust me, okay?"

Petra nodded, her eyes meeting his and then flickering closed again.

"Oh no, you don't," he told her firmly. Pulling her to her feet, he immediately had to prevent her from falling, and she was groaning, mumbling, her eyes drooping back down into deadly sleep.

"Petra, no," he beseeched her. "No sleeping on my watch."

Even if he could persuade her to stay conscious, there was no way she was going to be able to get herself back down the hill quickly enough, even with his help, he assessed, forcing himself to think tactically.

Picking her up in his arms, and thanking the fates she was so slight, he snuggled her head in between his shoulder and cheek, with an arm around her body and the other arm holding the flashlight tucked under her knees. After checking that she was secure, he started the slow, careful descent.

It was at least a half hour's walk in daylight. In the mist and darkness, he was going to be lucky if he could get her safely to his cottage within an hour. Poor Flo would be worrying. He could only hope she had been able to hear him when he called.

"Tell me about your clients," he ordered Petra as he navigated the rocky path.

"*Ex*-clients," she drawled.

At that, Ross smiled. She was still in there, just very, very cold . . . As he jolted along, panting, he fired a series of questions at her. Anything to get a response. Irritation—which is the response he mainly got—was fine. He just had to keep her talking. To keep her awake. He blanked from his mind what could have happened if he hadn't found her, already drifting away. Without him arriving when he did, it was doubtful she would have woken again, and her story would have ended right there. Yes, the local community might have been shocked to hear that a woman had been found dead on that bench. People would have wondered at it. They would have felt distress, regret, sadness . . . but then their lives would have continued, and her passing would have been a sad postscript to what she told him had been a failed London career.

But this was *not* the end of her story.

It was the beginning of *their* story.

Okay, so he couldn't ask her to represent his book, but she didn't need to. She was a talented, funny, amazing woman who would have been returned to her rightful place in the publishing firmament soon enough anyway. As for his own career, at this point in time, it couldn't matter less to him.

He now understood that fate had decreed they would meet, not—as he had arrogantly thought—so she could represent him, but so they could be together. It was his destiny. Her destiny.

Such was his driving desperation to get her into the warmth of the cottage, that the journey down the hill took little longer than a Sunday afternoon stroll on a sunny day might have done.

Flo leaped up as he shouldered his way through the door with Petra in his arms.

"I switched on the heater in your room," she said, bustling to take the flashlight from him and wrap the blanket around Petra a little tighter. "The kettle's just boiled. Do you think she could manage some tea?"

"Maybe," he said, already halfway up the narrow wooden

stairs, turning sideways to protect his precious load from bumps and bruises.

Flo had done more than put the heat on, she had turned back the bedcovers, found an extra blanket to put on top of the duvet, and even—miracle of miracles—managed to find a hot water bottle that she had freshly filled and nestled in the bed, waiting.

He laid Petra down tenderly on the double bed, tucking her in, and then turned to Flo as she came into the bedroom, a steaming cup in each hand.

She gave one mug to Ross and put the other on the bedside table. "Best to let her sleep, perhaps," she whispered, looking down at Petra fondly. "She owes you her life," she told Ross. "Who else would have known where she was?"

Ross wrapped his hands around the mug gratefully and took a sip.

"I'll go now," said Flo *sotto voce*. "I've got to get Digger home. Call me if you need anything?"

Ross nodded, touching Flo's arm in thanks, all the while gazing down at Petra as she slept.

After he heard the door close downstairs, he stood drinking his tea, thinking. But then he roused himself. She needed as much warmth as possible, as quickly as possible. He put down his mug, sat on the edge of the bed to remove his shoes, and then—gently so as not to disturb her—he molded himself into her back before wrapping his arms around her and pulling her close.

Petra stirred, nestling against him and sighing before the gentle, regular breathing of sleep resumed.

It was hardly surprising that she was exhausted, he thought, his fears now totally allayed that this time it was sleep and not an incipient coma. It was late, and he was exhausted too, not only by the physical challenges but also by his endlessly circling thoughts.

But now, all that ended. She was safe and she was with him. All was well.

Chapter Nineteen

There was a woodpecker in Petra's dream. It was summertime and she was in the churchyard at the top of the hill, sitting on the grass and leaning against the sunbaked wall, which was warm against her back. She was alone but—somehow—not lonely. The dream—and she knew it was a dream—felt so vivid that she could feel the sun's rays on her face and hear the woodpecker tip-tapping away in the ancient yew tree by the church. For reasons she could not grasp, the sickly anxiety of recent days had dissipated, and she was bathing in a newly acquired serenity and calm—a feeling of absolute safety and quiet happiness.

And then, as her sleep phase lightened, her conscious mind, worrying at the puzzle of this new mindset, insisted on flooding her mind with brutal lucidity, and she groaned with dismay as the delightful dream rushed away from her.

She lay, unmoving and unwilling, with her eyes still closed but—dammit—that woodpecker was still tapping like a mini pneumatic drill. What the hell was that? Could it be that the little flat at the top of Capelthorne's had deathwatch beetles in the roof timbers? She had read somewhere that they were audible in the spring, tapping their way out of the wooden beams. She should let Jules know. Groaning again audibly at having to impart bad news, thereby ruining someone else's day as comprehensively as her own, she reluctantly opened her eyes.

But what was this? The curtains at the window were blue linen, not the blowsy rose chintz pattern she had gotten to know so well. And the window was smaller too. Lower. With an entirely different view of grazing black-and-white cows rather than the Portneath rooftops. Where the hell was she?

At least the tapping had stopped.

"Morning, Rip Van Winkle," came a deep, familiar voice.

The feelings of absurd happiness and security returned in a rush.

"Um," said Petra, turning over in bed to see Ross sitting in a little armchair in the corner of the room, his laptop on his knees.

Ah. The tapping noise explained. Typing.

"What do you remember?" he asked. "About last night?"

"Er . . . not sure," said Petra, playing for time. She definitely now remembered the sensation of being in his arms. It had been lovely, but—like everything else—the circumstances were a bit hazy. She peeked under the bedclothes. Fully clothed. Hmm. "Did we . . . ?"

"*God,* no," Ross replied. "I mean, I would never . . ." He gestured. "I'm not massively into necrophilia, for a start." He smiled self-deprecatingly. "Also, I'd like to think it would at least be a *little bit* memorable."

Petra chuckled. "You'd like to think," she teased. And then the despair of last night filled her again—more an emotion than a memory.

"I found you on the bench at the top of the hill," he said.

Petra stared ahead, frowning. It was coming back to her now. "I went up the hill after work," she said. "I needed to get my head straight."

Ross nodded. "And then?"

"It got misty," she admitted. "So I couldn't really see where I was going. Somehow, I came off the path. Then it was dark as well—I didn't have my phone, so I had no light—I went back up to the top again so I could find the path. Then I realized I was going to have to wait 'til dawn . . . I think I went to sleep."

"Not sure sleep is the right description," said Ross evenly, but then his frustration overcame him. "What kind of an idiot are you, going off walking at that time of day, anyhow? And with nothing on you? When I found you on the bench, you were freezing. You wouldn't have made it 'til morning!"

"Sorry," said Petra in a small voice. "Sorry to put you to the trouble. You could have hurt yourself."

"I would have done worse to myself than that if I hadn't been there to bring you down safe," said Ross in a low voice, rubbing his temples distractedly. "Petra, I—"

"—I did some thinking," said Petra, interrupting. Not wanting to let him say it. "While I was walking last night. And I realize I *do* want to represent you. More than anything."

That was a lie. If she were doing what her heart was telling her to do, she would be refusing to work with him, choosing to have him in her life in an entirely different way. But then the world would never read that beautiful book. And he would never have the chance to shine again. If she cared about him less, she would be happy to deny him that.

"But I've been thinking too," said Ross. "And I don't want you to do it. Not anymore."

Petra nodded slowly, catching her scurrying thoughts. That was fair enough. He had had time to reflect and—naturally—decided that appointing her as his agent would be disastrous. Career suicide. As if things hadn't been bad enough already for him.

"Then, of course, I will do what I can to support you in finding someone else," she said, trying to sound measured but unable to suppress the wobble in her voice. Rejection was rejection, however you looked at it. And she had had more than her fair share of that in the last few months.

"Yes, good, thank you," said Ross. "Obviously, I would have loved for you to do it—and I appreciate it would have been good for your career, so I am hugely sorry about that."

Petra made a dismissive gesture.

"But," he went on, "I really can't allow myself to break my rule of mixing business with my private life. You have to trust me—it's a really bad idea."

"Oh, okay, so . . ." Petra was struggling to keep up, her brain felt foggy and full. "Does that mean that we . . . ?"

"If you want to give it a go?" said Ross anxiously, coming over to the bed and pulling her into his side. He gazed down at her, a sweet smile spreading across his face.

"I think we could 'give it a go,'" said Petra, sighing a happy sigh.

And then, oh so slowly, Ross bent his head down and brushed her lips with his own.

Petra gave fleeting attention to the thought that she very likely had smudged mascara, bird's nest hair, and morning breath, but then she dismissed her chattering negative brain, allowing those delightful feelings she had experienced in her dream to suffuse her body once again. And there was more. A warm glow started in her core and spread as she pushed herself against him, deepening the kiss, and reaching up to run her hands through his thick silky hair, pulling him down against her.

For a long while they communicated without words, exploring and basking in their physical nearness. Touch was enough. It was as if the months of growing friendship had been missing this one piece of their relationship, and now their need to catch up was a gentle but persistent hunger.

Eventually it was Ross who pulled away, sitting up and resting Petra back against the pillows. "You need to take it easy," he told her as he got to his feet. "I'll get us some food."

Disappointed, and not at all feeling like taking it easy, Petra gazed after him, yearning for him to stay near, but comforted to hear the everyday sounds he was making in the kitchen below.

She was no longer in any doubt about how close she came to losing everything the night before, and that realization drove her to a revelation. She had to lose no more time living her life to the full. Books were great, work was—well—becoming a little more attractive, but this? This meeting of minds and bodies had had "inevitable" written all over it, right from the moment they met on the station platform, if only she had known . . .

It would be like this now, she told herself, astonished that her happiness could be so profound and yet the feeling should exist with this calmness she felt—a quiet "rightness" that she had never experienced before. So, this was what it felt like. This was "true love," not the edgy, anxious excitement, the stomach-churning roller coaster of her past relationships, but this.

This.

Ross returned with a laden tray. There was fresh coffee, a pile of hot sourdough toast, a jar of thick-cut marmalade, and a pat of daffodil yellow butter.

"I wasn't expecting guests," he grinned. "I didn't have a lot in. But get this into you and maybe later I'll let you get up. We can go to our café and have bacon and eggs."

"Our café," said Petra dreamily, spreading her toast thickly and taking a huge bite. She was suddenly starving.

"I thought love was supposed to make you too preoccupied to eat," she said apologetically. "I'm going to get massive at this rate."

"Good," said Ross. "I don't think *real* love stops you from eating. Sounds like something else does that . . . And also," he added fiercely, "eat whatever the hell you like. I'm not in love with your backside being its exact current size," he went on. "I'm just—well—in love with your backside generally . . ."

"Such a way with words," teased Petra.

"And it's not just your backside either," Ross went on. "I'm in love with all of you."

Suddenly he was serious. He held her gaze. "I'm in love with you, Petra," he said quietly.

"I'm in love with you too," she replied with a happy sigh.

Later that day, Flo texted Petra to ask after her and to confirm (insist, really) that she was taking charge of the shop until Petra was up to it.

Ross went to Capelthorne's to collect some bits and pieces for her, having made it quite clear to Petra—and also to Flo—that he and Petra would be living together at the cottage from that day onward.

By Wednesday morning, Petra was raring to get back to work, insisting that she walk back down to Capelthorne's in time to open up. There was a delivery due that day, and she didn't want Flo humping boxes around. Plus, she had a meeting scheduled with Jess about the literary festival in the shop after closing. She was determined not to let her new friend down.

It was a late spring morning, and it felt as if the world had been unwrapped all brand-new just that day. The sky was cerulean with cartoonishly perfect fluffy white clouds, and the birds sang so loud in the churchyard that they drowned out the sound of cars beginning the rush to work.

Petra walked down the main street, reveling in the warmth of the sun on her back. Portneath felt like her town now. There was the little flower shop, with the lady owner placing tall galvanized buckets filled with blooms on the pavement outside. There were bunches of bright tulips, the last of the narcissi, and early apricot-colored roses unfurling and releasing their heady scent into the air as Petra passed by. The chocolate shop was still dark and shuttered, but the windows of the bakery next door were piled high with fresh crusty loaves and trays of huge croissants. A short queue had formed already as retired people collected their bread along with their newspapers and milk from the corner shop farther down.

The windows of Capelthorne's winked in the sunshine as Petra slid the key into the door. She knew its foibles now, a little twist to the left, a push, a twist around to the right, and the door opened sweetly for her, not like her precipitous entrance that first evening just a few months before.

Walking in, and humming contentedly, Petra whizzed around the shop, switching on lights, firing up the register, running her eye over the displays to make sure all was as it should be. Flo had been in the day before, so everything was—of course—perfect.

Petra cast an eye over the receipts. Once again, it had been a good day's trade yesterday, she noted with satisfaction. The little shop was doing well under her care, despite her initial morose predictions.

Petra was in the habit of sending Jules and Roman a brief weekly update, and they had been professing themselves delighted with her work too. Not for the first time, Petra wished her six months' stewardship was not whizzing by quite so quickly. It would be summer soon, and time for her to leave. And now, with Ross in her life, what would become of them both? Okay, so he had professed his love, but would it be enough to persuade him to leave this charming town and come with her?

Would he even want to go to London?

Would she?

Chapter Twenty

"So," Jess announced as soon as she arrived and placed her folder on the table between them. "You and Ross, eh?" She was grinning widely.

"Good grief, news travels fast," Petra muttered, unable to wipe the smile from her face. Ross had been messaging, promising her a delicious supper on her return to the cottage after this.

"Fast work, eh?"

Petra laughed. "I met him before I met any of you," she said in her own defense. "It's just been nice having a friend . . . and now . . ."

"It's luuuurve!" declared Jess. "Fabulous. We need to see more of this beautiful man. Bring him on Friday? Usual time and location?"

"God, poor Ross," laughed Petra. "You will be gentle with him, won't you?"

"*I* will," promised Jess, "but you know what Freya's like. Also—this is great—because it saves me having to find you a 'plus one' for Jules and Roman's wedding party. I've been racking my brains, to be honest."

"Hang on," said Petra nervously. "I haven't actually RSVPed

on that yet. I'm assuming Jules and Roman are just being polite . . . They want me to be out of here as soon as they get back, surely? I'm only covering while they're away. That's the deal."

"Of *course* you're welcome to come," said Jess firmly. "And anyway, you can't rush off, because I need you for the festival, so it's going to be at least the beginning of September before you go. Plus"—Jess's face fell—"well, I thought you'd *want* to stay. We blow-ins need to stick together."

"Yeah, well . . . it's not even June yet. Let's see how things go," said Petra, flipping open her laptop and opening up her festival "to do" list. "So . . . let's talk about responses to our speaker invitations, because we need to get the final lineup confirmed asap."

Closing his laptop with a sigh, and—more important—another thousand words of the novel safely in the bag, Ross was thinking about Petra coming home, and how they would cook supper together. Maybe they would sit in the tiny garden with a beer while it cooked, shooting the breeze, exchanging news about their respective days . . . They never ran out of things to talk about.

Just as he went to stand up, his phone pinged, and he reached for it, smiling. Petra's texts were always so funny. Really, she should write a book too. Maybe a rom-com . . .

When he saw the notification, his heart clenched like a fist, a rock, heavy in his chest:

Rossie! read the message. It's been too, too long, lover-boy . . . Call me?

When they were apart, Petra longed to be with Ross.

Had they ever *really* been "just friends" she wondered now as she walked back up the main street to Ross's cottage—home—at the end of another satisfying day's work. How had she not seen this sooner? It must have been more than simple friendship that caused her spirits to lift so euphorically when she saw him slip in through the bookshop door at the end of the working day. And on the days when his writing was going well and he hadn't shown up, she had been so downcast. Ridiculously, she had not recognized the cause of her seesawing mood.

It was as if their love for each other had been hiding in plain sight. Even from themselves. Flo's predictions about the two of them had been right all along. She was a wise old bird. Petra smiled; she would give her that. And they were good for each other too. It wasn't just the not being able to keep their hands off each other bit—which was fun—it was also the deep shared interest in all things related to books. Ross was so confident of his abilities again now. His editing was underway with a sure touch, and Petra's work for Jules and Roman had become inspired: She had the writing club, the *two* book clubs, and—best of all—her reading recommendations were becoming so legendary that she was getting strangers coming into the shop asking for her by name.

Yes, the Beach Reads Book Club, in particular, was thriving, she mused as she walked. And it was even becoming a useful bellwether for her commercial fiction buying.

Write Club too was flourishing under her tender stewardship, which gave her an idea.

"You should come to Write Club next week," she said to Ross as they cooked supper together, squeezing past each other in his tiny kitchen. Not that close proximity was any kind of problem.

"What? I could never be a tutor, if that's what you mean? I'm a crap teacher."

"That's actually not what I was talking about. You're in another stratosphere to them careerwise, but I meant you should join in. Actually, you probably wouldn't want to lower yourself. Forget I said anything." He was in a weird mood tonight, she told herself. Negative, which wasn't like him. Okay, it *was* like the old Ross—

"That is *absolutely* not what I meant," Ross said hastily. "Of *course* I don't want to pull rank on other writers." He sighed. "I feel like I'm not ready to share. Except with you," he added. "I wish you had been my editor first time out."

He looked stricken at the mention of his editor, Petra noticed. He really had had a rough time. It was important to make sure he was happy with his relationships this time around, she thought.

"You say that about not sharing," she challenged him, "but you're still not happy with the first three chapters," Petra pointed out. "We've talked them over a million times. Would it not be helpful to have a fresh pairs of eyes? They're never mean. You could be a visitor," she suggested. "One session only. So if you don't like it . . ."

Ross didn't demure, so Petra pressed on. "We all submit some work for review by Sunday evening, and then talk about it together on Thursday, so you'd still be in time for this week."

"Could I use a pen name?"

"'Course you could," encouraged Petra. "Except why? Someone is going to work it out eventually, and then they might feel they've been manipulated. That's maybe the only issue . . ."

"I worry people won't be honest if they know," said Ross, staring sightlessly at the pan he was stirring. "I mean, this novel is so completely and utterly different from the first, I was actually wondering about whether to change my writing name anyhow . . ."

With her literary agent hat on, there would have been no way Petra would allow him to waste the platform he had built with his first book by doing that. It would be madness. But she wasn't his agent—so . . .

"Sure. Do that," she said.

Whatever it took to get this particular horse to the starting gate, she thought. Clearly, whatever had happened to Ross the first time out had been bad enough that he needed—even more than other writers—the validation of honest criticism. He still hadn't really talked with her about what had happened. She smiled ruefully, thinking of her client—ex-client—Isabella May, in contrast to Ross. That woman was such a raging narcissist, her editor had learned it was better for a manuscript to go unimproved than for her to suggest changes and deal with the seismic meltdown that invariably resulted.

Petra duly emailed Write Club to ask their permission for a new member. Of course—they were such a lovely crowd—the affirmations came flooding straight back, so she submitted his opening chapters just in time for discussion at the meeting the following week.

PETRA TRIED TO get into the shop before Flo that Saturday. It had become a weekly good-natured battle, and Petra rarely won, especially now that she found it hard to leave Ross. On this particular morning, by the time she and Ross had reluctantly gotten out of bed at the cottage, had breakfast, repeatedly said goodbye to each other (as if, Petra remarked, she was going into a war zone for months rather than Portneath for a single day), Petra was virtually jogging down the street to make up some time.

"Dirty stop out," Flo remarked with a cheeky smile when Petra arrived to discover the door already unlocked and Flo in position behind the front desk.

Petra smiled, abashed. She and Ross being an item was still a new enough thing for her to feel awkward, and Flo was clearly going to extract every ounce of delight from the situation.

"So . . . you and Ross, then?" Flo remarked, in a lull later that morning.

Petra smiled. *Here it comes,* she thought. "What about me and Ross?"

"Only that I can't think why the two of you took so long," Flo told her. "And he's a good one too. Brave. Kind. Devoted to you."

"He speaks highly of you too," smiled Petra. "You could form a mutual admiration society, the two of you." Petra paused a moment. "When did you know?" she asked.

"My dear . . . I had my suspicions—and thoroughly approved too—but the deciding point for me was when you were missing that night. The look on his face will haunt me," she remembered. "And when he finally arrived home, carrying you in his arms, so pale . . . blue, literally," she told Petra, "he looked as if he would never let you out of his sight ever again. It was beautiful to see him caring for you," Flo said, with the utmost sincerity, all teasing gone now. "He loves you, child."

"The feeling is mutual."

Flo sighed happily. "How *wonderful*," she said with relish. "Another Portneath triumph."

"Hmm," said Petra, loath to kill the mood. "It's not as simple as that unfortunately," she cautioned, busying herself tidying the table so she didn't have to meet Flo's eye.

"Oh?"

"He asked me to be his literary agent."

"How perfect! No wonder you both have so much to talk about. I hope you said yes."

"Actually, I said no," Petra explained. "Before the hill thing, he wanted us to stop seeing each other because he wanted me to represent him. He has a strong aversion to combining work and pleasure."

"Very wise." Flo shrugged. "So you said no because you didn't want to stop seeing him?"

"Yes."

"You said yes?" Flo looked confused.

"No, I said no," said Petra, starting to get confused herself. "Also, it's partly because I'm not at all sure I want to be a literary agent anymore. And then, when I went up the mountain and got stuck, I realized that I *had* to say yes, because—caring about him so much—I would never forgive myself if I didn't help him. He refuses to contemplate working with anyone else."

"Okay, so now you *will* be his agent?" asked Flo, frowning.

"No," said Petra. "Because by the time I said yes, he decided he didn't want me to be his agent after all."

"Good grief, I wish you would both make up your minds," said Flo.

"I know, sorry," said Petra.

"So he still needs an agent?"

"Yes. *Very* much so," said Petra fervently, remembering her extraordinary excitement at reading the Caliban story.

"What are you going to do?"

"I think," said Petra, "the only thing I can do is very gently persuade him to find other representation."

Flo put her hands up to hold her head as if it was hurting. Which it probably was, thought Petra. Her own head was hurting while pondering these difficulties too.

"On to other matters," Flo said, understandably giving up. "I was wondering if it would be too awful of me not to come in on Tuesday next week?"

"Of course it wouldn't, that's totally fine," said Petra immediately, although inwardly she gave a groan. Flo had taken to coming in twice a week since Easter, and Petra had been grateful for the extra help.

"I wouldn't ask," said Flo, "but I must get my sweet peas in if they are going to have any chance of being in full bloom for Jules and Roman's party. I've got a couple of hundred plants on the go. She wants them everywhere. On the tables, on the pew ends in church, mixed colors . . ."

"Oh, for the wedding party," said Petra, catching on. "Church? I thought they were already married."

"They are, but the church in Middlemass is very special to them both. They're having a blessing there, and then back to Roman's house for a tented wedding breakfast with a ceilidh in the evening."

"That'll be fun!" said Petra, thinking it sounded anything but. She was sure that everyone else attending—the people she was now proud to call her friends—would have a much better idea how to behave, and dress, and what sort of gift to bring. She knew Roman's family was wealthy. What could she possibly give the couple who either had everything or could go out and buy anything they wanted themselves?

"I don't suppose you've brought anything suitable to wear," Flo guessed. "I would love for you to come and have a rummage through my wardrobe? I've practically got a whole room full of pretty frocks I don't wear anymore. And we are about the same size, I would say . . ."

"That would be really kind," said Petra gratefully.

One problem solved at least. She loved vintage.

"And I do believe my father's morning coat would fit Ross," Flo went on. "It's ancient, but fantastic quality. I'm assuming Ross is going to be your plus one—" she broke off enquiringly.

"Who knows?" admitted Petra. "It's a long time between May and August . . . Anything could happen." She felt like saying it out loud kept her safer. If anything happened to their new relationship, she didn't know how she would survive it—that was the truth.

"Might be smelling a bit mothbally," Flo mused, tactfully ignoring Petra's gloomy outlook on her romantic affairs. "I'll dig it out and drop it off at the dry cleaners."

"I can do that," Petra said quickly. "Thank you, that's so sweet of you."

Maybe this thing will be fun after all, Petra thought.

"What if they figure out who I am?" said Ross anxiously.

Petra had him putting the chocolate biscuits on the plate while she boiled the kettle. They were expecting the other members of Write Club any minute.

"Hardly anyone recognizes writers," she reminded him. "Even the really high-profile ones. Also, what if they do?" she reasoned with him, giving him a reassuring squeeze. "What's the worst that can happen?"

"Okay, well," Ross looked at the ceiling and counted off his points on his fingers. "The worst that can happen is that they hate it and they'll be too nice to say so, and *then* I'll get falsely confident, and publish, and *then* the critics will hate it, and *then* the public will hate it . . . Actually—I say that—they won't even *buy* it, and *then* the publisher will make me pay back the advance, because it was so terrible it literally contravened the contract . . . and *then*—"

"You are talking such—" protested Petra, and then she saw the expression on his face. He was just teasing her. Again.

She was secretly relieved that his mood was more level these days, most of the time at least. He had seemed painfully anxious the last few days though, twitchily checking his phone and jumping whenever a notification came through. It was strange, she pondered, as he had cut himself off from the world so completely, she couldn't even think who he could be in touch with.

As pre-agreed, Petra introduced Ross just by his first name and not a pseudonym. The whole group greeted him warmly, without an impertinent level of curiosity. There was no lack of insight when it came to feeding back on his writing, though.

"Well done, lad," said Simon gruffly. "Stunning opening. I wish I could write half as well as you."

"Yes, stunning," said Alison, the romance writer, fanning herself at the memory. "Such a strong opening—the whole premise of the novel laid out in the first soliloquy. Clever stuff."

After this initial praise, Ross seemed to relax a little, and the whole group was soon having a lively discussion about Ross's decision to write in the first person, and the various pros and cons of the approach. They toyed with the idea that Ross should alternate with Miranda's point of view, before deciding that Ross would probably do better to show Miranda's autonomy through the lens of Caliban's twisted understanding of the world. Ross, the group mused, had to have sufficient faith that the reader could be trusted to intuit, something it could be hard for a writer to allow.

"How does it end?" asked Alison. "I hope the boy gets the girl. I don't like books that don't have a happy ending," she admitted.

"I hope the boy gets the girl too," said Ross, casting a darting glance at Petra. "I actually don't know yet . . . it could go either way."

"I'm frankly astonished you don't have an agent, lad," said Simon. "You seem like a very assured writer to me."

Petra and Ross exchanged a look, but Ross just shrugged and Simon—thankfully—let it go.

Although he was right, thought Petra. Ross *didn't* have an agent.

She was touched to see that Ross had somehow—despite his intense writing schedule—also had made time to read and offer feedback thoughts on the work of the rest of the group. They were so generous and kind with each other, she mused, not for the first time. How sad that group members who were seriously seeking representation and a publisher would learn soon enough that the rest of the writing universe was not always as delightful.

Chapter Twenty-One

"See?" Petra told Ross as they washed up the mugs. "You're not as recognizable as you think you are."

"Yup, ego only a little bit dented," Ross acknowledged ruefully. "Five years is a long time."

"How will you sell it—this lull—when you get back out there with this one?" asked Petra. "Are you going to admit to writers' block or something? I think there's an important message about mental health support and managing expectations. You could be the poster boy for change . . . if you wanted?" Petra added, as Ross declined to respond.

"Or on the other hand—you could just say it was all a massive publicity ploy," Petra proposed. "Like Agatha Christie."

"I think she only disappeared for a few days," Ross told her. "And wasn't it about escaping a failing marriage? Which is understandable . . . I didn't think it was generally thought of as a ruse. You're too cynical for a woman your age," he teased.

"But people *will* ask . . . You'll need to be ready," Petra insisted.

"Not yet . . ." said Ross quietly, hanging up his tea towel to dry.

And Petra left it at that. For now.

Ross didn't reply to Henrietta's text, or to the email that followed. What could he possibly say? He mulled over whether to block her, but that seemed childish and cowardly. Plus, she wouldn't even recognize that she was blocked, and—for all he knew—she would carry on messaging without him even seeing them. Somehow, rendering your enemy invisible didn't make things better, it made things worse.

"I'm just so nervous that Jules is going to come back and be disappointed," admitted Jess when she and Petra were poring over the festival plans, fortified by multiple cups of tea and a lemon drizzle cake that Freya had dropped off for them both earlier.

"*How* would she be disappointed?" Petra demanded. Jess had already done an amazing job of compiling speakers, workshops, signing events, and media interviews. Petra was hugely impressed and frequently said so. "You know what?" she said. "I can see one of the London publishing houses wanting to snap you up for their publicity department when they see what you are capable of."

"Really?" Jess blushed, clearly abashed. "Although obviously I would hate to work in London," she added hastily. "I want to stay here with Aiden and Maisie—Maisie has GCSE mock exams this autumn, so there's no way . . ." she mused, squashing all her remaining cake crumbs onto the end of her finger. "Really, though?"

"Definitely," said Petra firmly.

"Although I've had zero interest from the London publishing scene for this festival," Jess went on, frustrated. "We've got a local crime writer—he's a big cheese—and it's like getting blood out of a stone, persuading the marketing team to produce some collateral for him."

"I suppose they're waiting to see whether we are worth the bother," soothed Petra. "This is the guy doing the crime-writing workshop?"

"Yes. I'm really worried no one will sign up to take part. Poor man."

"Write Club will probably all come," Petra said, but Jess was beyond reassurance.

"And book signings!" she went on, as if Petra hadn't spoken. "I hate them. I get so stressed that the writer won't sell any books. Jules is used to all this stuff, with the publishing job she had before she came down here to live."

Petra thought again how lovely it was going to be to meet Jules and compare notes, but then her stomach lurched in its now too familiar sign of anxiety. Jules and Roman appearing back in Portneath signaled the end of her time at Capelthorne's. What she was going to do next was becoming an extremely vexing question.

"You should get involved," Petra told Ross when she was reporting back about her meeting with Jess. "It's going to be great. Quite low-key, local, gentle stuff . . . brilliant for getting your feet back under the table."

Ross was opening a bottle of wine and delayed his reply until he had dispensed with the cork and poured for them both.

"I'm actually seriously thinking about it," he said as he handed Petra her glass. "Jess lobbied me when we met for drinks the other day."

"She didn't tell me!" said Petra, oddly put out.

"Well, it wasn't like she was putting her case to 'award-winning debut writer Ross McCloud,'" he reminded her. "I know you told them I was a writer," he said, "but Jess seemed to think I was—what was it?—a UX writer for a US tech firm . . . ? Don't even know what that is," he admitted.

"I have *no* idea why she said that," fibbed Petra, who had admittedly told them all something vague about Ross being a website copywriter. It wasn't a complete lie. "But you've written website copy, no?"

"*Years* ago," Ross insisted. "When I was a starving writer in a garret."

"Ah yes, then," said Petra ironically. "Aren't you still one of them?"

"Not really," he admitted. "I might not have been completely straight with you," he went on. "I'm actually still getting quite a decent income from royalties, and rights sales are still popping up too."

"Why not be honest?" said Petra, puzzled, as she had—frankly—been wondering how Ross was making the rent.

He sighed. "It's going to sound silly, but I'm kind of embarrassed to be making so much more than most. Do you even *know* how little the average writer makes a year in the UK?"

"There was a survey," said Petra. "It's something absurd like seven thousand pounds. Which is crazy, obviously. How can anyone live on that? And how are we going to have diverse voices in writing if no normal person can afford to do it? But you're not average, thankfully."

"No," said Ross. "I'm not. I'm incredibly lucky."

"So," said Petra, pressing her advantage, "going back to Jess and the festival, why don't you pay forward some of your luck and get involved?"

"You're right," said Ross. "I'll lead that writing workshop Jess was hitting me up for, why not? I'll have to google whatever the hell a UX writer is before then if that's what I am."

"That would be *amazing*," Petra told him. Okay, so he wasn't breaking cover with who he really was, but it was something. She was dying to let Jess know right away.

Alone again, after Petra left to speak to Jess, Ross tried—and failed—to unclench his jaw a little. He was so tense, he was giving himself a headache. It was such a joy sharing everything in his head with Petra these days, but she could do without knowing about these messages from Henrietta. This little complication he would bear alone for as long as he could. He knew the woman too well to think she might give up. And—he had already had the thought—if she was going to hunt him down anyway then he might as well beat her to the punch and come out into the open. Maybe the festival would be the time and place? That way, he could help his new friends at the same time, which was a bonus. But it was a grim thought all the same.

Jess and Petra were sitting in the little office at the back of the shop, cramming in a bit of work on the festival pre-publicity while the shop was quiet.

Jess, when Petra admitted Ross's true identity, was staggered.

"You mean, I've been in the pub having a pint with Ross McCloud, and I didn't even put two and two together," she wondered in awe. "You said he was a UX writer," she accused Petra.

"Actually, *you* said that," corrected Petra. "*I* said he wrote website copy."

"Which is basically the same thing and also not true," Jess protested. And then the six-million-dollar-question occurred to her. "Is he writing something now?" she demanded, but Petra wasn't to be drawn. All he had agreed to was hosting a workshop as Ross the website copywriter. It was a start.

"We definitely do need some sort of attention-grabber, though," Petra said, scratching her head anxiously. "We need a big announcement."

"I've been following some of the talks and workshops on our Insta feed," Jess agreed, "but the only one that gained any traction was the illustration workshop with Imo. I mean, obviously, Imogen Crawley is such a big name around here . . ."

"Around everywhere," observed Petra.

"Right. And her publisher and agency kindly added it to their stories, which was cool. We got a surge of new followers from that."

"And how is our lineup looking?"

"Not bad," said Jess, "but we're a long way from London. It's seriously hard to attract big publishing names to do presentations or even just to attend. Actually, Imo's agent is very sweetly coming down to present a seminar on getting representation, which is proving really popular . . . it's nearly fully booked up! Goes to show how many people secretly want to write a book—"

"—or already have," Petra chipped in.

"Plus, she's going to do some one-on-ones, which is so kind," said Jess, looking relieved at the thought.

"That's amazing," Petra told her. Jess was doing an incredible job. Whereas, her . . . ?

She felt like she ought to be able to hook in some big names from the London publishing scene, but really? She had only ever been a bottom-feeder in the publishing world. And what sway she used to hold with the bigger writers on her list was nonexistent now.

Petra caught Jess stealing a look at her and then vaguely looking away, for all the world as if last year's planner, up on the wall, was the most fascinating thing in the world.

"I could ask," she said.

"Ooh, would you?" Jess replied, far too quickly. "I mean clearly he doesn't like being in the limelight. But it would be amazing. Honestly? He could totally be the keynote speaker. And he can talk about whatever he likes: being a successful debut author, the writing process, his experiences in the publishing world as a big seller . . . whatever. And even if he does have something written, he doesn't have to say so, does he?"

Although the expression on Jess's face told Petra everything she needed to know about how much Jess hoped he would.

Ross was collared by Flo as soon as he had finished hugely enjoying himself reading *The Gruffalo* in the children's reading corner that Saturday.

"A little bird tells me you're writing a beautiful book, Ross," was her opener. "Or should I say 'award-winning debut author Ross McCloud,' to use your full title?"

"Bit of a mouthful, for every day," he deadpanned. "Just Ross will do fine, thanks for asking."

"Hmph," said Flo, narrowing her eyes. "And I gather you and Petra . . . ?"

"Yeah," said Ross, smiling at the thought. "She's great, isn't she?"

"She certainly is."

"God knows what she's doing with a basket case like me. I don't deserve her."

"I don't suppose you do," Flo agreed. "So make sure you look after her . . ."

"Yeah, stopping her from finding new and inventive ways to accidentally kill herself is part of my job, for sure," he said. "After that whole nighttime hiking fiasco," he went on, looking grim as he remembered.

"Not one of her best decisions," agreed Flo. "Although she's a talented woman, of course," she continued. "Quite the high-flyer. What will you do when she wants to go back to agenting? Presumably you would want her to represent you?" she said, looking sharply at him.

"Ah," said Ross, taken aback. "So, that's er . . . um . . . it's complicated."

Flo continued to look at him expectantly, telling him she had absolutely heard from Petra on the subject too.

"So I asked her to be my agent, but she refused," he admitted.

"I see."

"Ah, but you don't," insisted Ross. "I was disappointed she said no, but I was also really relieved because that meant we could be together, which was good."

"And now . . . ?"

"I'm starting to understand how much it would do for her professionally if she represented me with this next book to sell. It's making me wish I could break my cardinal rule."

"Combining work and pleasure?"

Ross nodded, his brow knitted.

"And—just to clarify," Flo pressed on, "Petra turned you down when you asked her in any case because . . . ?"

"I think because she's lost confidence in herself," Ross hazarded. "Although, just recently, she's been pushing me to keep writing, and I can tell she's intrigued to think how to sell this book. I feel like she's getting her mojo back, and I'm wondering if I can't change her mind about the agenting, for her own sake. I flatter myself, I know, but it would be a bit of a comeback for her."

"So you want her *not* to represent you, because you personally don't want to muddy the water in your relationship, but then you *want* her to represent you for the sake of her own career?"

"Yes."

"And—just to clarify—she *doesn't* want to represent you because she thinks she isn't good enough, but maybe now she's thinking she *is* prepared to represent you, for the sake of *your* career. Yes?"

"Yes," said Ross, delighted that Flo seemed to be following. "Make sense?"

"No," said Flo bluntly. "I think you're both totally cracked."

Petra was seeing a lot of Alison, the—as yet—unpublished romance writer, but that was hardly surprising: Alison was in Write Club *and* the Beach Reads Book Club, plus, she was in the shop at least twice a week, buying what Petra felt was an admirably broad selection of books.

"I'm dying to read this myself," she told Alison as she brought a hardback copy of *Onyx Storm* by Rebecca Yarros over to the register.

"Have you read the others?" Alison asked. "I adored *Fourth Wing*. It was my first romantasy, actually."

"I haven't yet," admitted Petra. "I hate getting to the end of a book in a series and having to wait for the next one, so I save them up. That reminds me—I have to pick the group's brains about romantasy when we next meet. I've got a few, but I'd like to stock other writers in the genre, and it's not my specialist subject."

"I can tell you everything about romantasy," declared Alison happily. "We can have a heated debate. Any and all things romance, that's me. And thank goodness Capelthorne's actually stocks romance."

"Of course!" said Petra, thinking of her pleasing sales data from the Beach Reads Book Club books, which were mostly romance.

"Exactly," chimed in Alison, shaking her head. "Whenever I travel, I always visit the local independent bookshop to check what they do and don't have. I mean, they seem to grudgingly have the really big hits, but only after they've gone huge on TikTok and become unignorable. The romance writers *I* love don't get a look-in. And I challenge them about that too, you know?"

"You do?" said Petra, smiling. Alison was the sweetest, quietest, most gentle woman she ever met. She couldn't imagine her picking a fight with anyone.

"I do!" Alison declared fearlessly.

"And what do they say?"

"It goes like this: First I ask them why they don't stock a good range of romance. Then they give me some rubbish that there isn't much call for it. I even had a man tell me they only stock 'proper books.'"

Petra made an outraged noise.

"I know! What he—they—*actually* mean is they think romance is below them."

"Their loss," opined Petra.

"Exactly. I mean, it doesn't go unnoticed that the majority of romance is read by women, so what does that mean? And don't even get me started on how underrepresented queer romance is," Alison added, frowning furiously.

"And how do you reply when they say romance doesn't count?" Petra smiled.

"I ask them if they stock Jane Austen and the Brontës," Alison said stoutly. "Of course, they always say yes to that. And then I watch it slowly dawn on their silly little faces."

"Brilliant!" applauded Petra. "Not much call for it," she scoffed. "How can they ignore that romance book sales are beaten only by crime. They're *huge*. Who wouldn't want a slice of that market?"

"Romance readers, out and proud!" agreed Alison. "But maybe those snooty bookshop owners are right, though," she added doubtfully. "Is it an online thing maybe? Perhaps romances *don't* sell in physical bookshops."

"Self-fulfilling prophesy, if they refuse to stock them," snorted Petra. "It's the classic circular argument. That's why you all at Beach Reads Book Club are *so* helpful to me."

"I did feel like Diana's book club was sometimes a bit too much about wading through hefty books to demonstrate your intellect or how cultured you are," admitted Alison.

"Hmm, book clubs can be a bit . . ." Petra wrinkled her nose, ". . . performative. People don't talk about their commercial fiction reading habits."

"Which is crazy. Why shouldn't they?" said Alison firmly. "It's just the same as having a Snickers bar rather than something fancy from Maison Chocolat. Some days you want one, some days the other . . . *Both* are fantastic."

Chapter Twenty-Two

Petra brought it up with Ross that evening as they ate and, although he seemed a little distracted, his response was robust: "What you're *really* asking is whether bookshops should be selling commercial fiction or just literary," he proposed.

"No, I'm not," protested Petra. "Of *course* they should sell both. I mean, we're selling the latest Costa winner, sure, but if we weren't pushing the books the Beach Reads group recommended, our last three months' turnover wouldn't look anything *like* as rosy as it does."

"Exactly," said Ross. "So the question is not whether romances are serious books—whatever that even means—but if there's another reason why bookshops don't generally stock them." He waited patiently for Petra to catch up, but she was puzzled.

"Okay, who reads the most romance, men or women?" he postulated.

"I want to say both, but . . ."

"Yeah, but you can't because it's primarily women, isn't it?" Ross went on.

Petra nodded, annoyed, but she started to see Ross's point. "So it's misogyny," she admitted reluctantly.

"Pure misogyny," said Ross, topping up Petra's glass. "And, before you ask," he went on, "I like reading a good romance myself. I am the exception that proves the rule."

"I would expect nothing less," said Petra.

"So how are we going to change the world?" prompted Ross, smiling in expectation.

"How are *you* going to change the world first?" said Petra, buying time.

"How about I write a romance?"

"Done."

"Good, because I already am," said Ross, delighted that Petra had fallen for his little trap.

"You are?" said Petra, flushing with pleasure at the thought. But of course he was! Caliban and Miranda . . . it was the greatest love story never told . . . "That Shakespeare was a sappy old thing, wasn't he?"

"He was. Although he didn't always deliver on the happy endings."

At that, his expression darkened.

"This is nicer than holing up in the used books section," said Petra quickly to divert him, cuddling up for warmth. Even in early summer, the evenings could be cool, and the stone cottage was a little damp, if Petra was honest.

This was how they spent their evenings now, she mused happily, curled up together on the sofa in the cottage, drinking endless cups of tea, sometimes watching a film on Ross's laptop, but—as often as not—just chatting about work and life.

"Doesn't four months ago feel like forever," said Ross, gazing into the flames, his dark thoughts apparently forgotten again as he idly stroked Petra's cheek.

"Yeah, time's been kind of dragging since I met you," Petra joked.

They both sat in contented silence for a minute or two, and then: "About the festival—" they both said in unison and then laughed.

"You go," said Petra.

"Okay, so I'm thinking it's a bit silly to do that workshop incognito," Ross told her. "And I'm going to look like a total weirdo if people find out later."

Petra stiffened. He was right, of course, but the last thing she wanted to do was push him.

"Plus, you and Jess are doing an amazing job, and I know bandying my stupid name around will help, which is ridiculous, but . . ." He trailed away.

"If you're sure?" ventured Petra.

He nodded firmly.

"Okay," said Petra, looking at him anxiously, but she was reassured by what she saw. "I'll get Jess to draft an announcement that you're our keynote speaker for the launch then," she said. "And we'll need a publicity photo . . . This is the kind of thing you should be talking to your agent about, really," she said, biting her lip.

"Who needs an agent when I've got you as my . . . 'unagent.'"

"Kind of like the 'undead' with fringe benefits?" queried Petra.

"Oh yes," said Ross. "*Aaaall* sorts of fringe benefits. Like, I would never do *this* with my agent," he said, pulling her onto his lap and kissing her on the neck, just behind her ear, where he knew it would drive her wild.

"Yup, that would be seriously unprofessional behavior," she sighed, slipping her hand inside his shirt and leaning in for more.

Petra was anxious. She was glad to be in the shop alone today because Flo would definitely weasel it out of her, but the truth was, she was out of her depth. She was well aware how incredibly brave Ross was to agree to be part of the festival. He was, she knew, doing it out of loyalty to her—and to Jess and the gang who had sweetly taken him into their friend group as one of their own.

But this unease was making her feel isolated, because none of the crowd in Portneath would understand what was causing it. Not even Ross. She wasn't the most experienced literary agent in the world, but she wasn't totally green. Once Ross broke cover, it would be a complete fracas, especially if they got wind that there was a manuscript too. Not only would the trade media be all over it, she was fully expecting a flock of influencers to descend. And social media was powerful but fickle . . . His TikTok fans might have helped to make Ross, but they could break him just as easily. If they didn't buy his story—his reasons for disappearing (and even *she* didn't really understand what they were)—then the condemnation could be personally and professionally crushing.

There was only one person she could turn to, and she knew she could trust him to keep a secret.

"Petra!" cried Alistair. "What a pleasure to hear from you. It's been so long I thought you might have gone native down there in Devon—forgotten all your London friends."

"My London friend, singular," she reminded him. "Pretty sure everyone else was happy to see me go."

"Not at all," he said gallantly. "If anything, people have been missing your entertainment value."

"Ouch," said Petra. That was mean! She had actually been making a real effort and insulting people less often, these days. Although Alistair wouldn't know that, of course.

"Sorry," said Alistair, sounding genuinely contrite. "Still too soon?"

"Hmm . . . no, you're fine," Petra reassured him. "I fully accept my blurting problem is amusing for everyone. I am glad to be of service. I *am* starting to like it down here, though. People live well. There's a lot to love . . . the beach, the people, the shop! The shop is amazing, I love the shop. Obviously I'm only temporary, though, but—yeah—I'm kind of envious of Jules, not going to lie."

"So, to what do I owe the considerable pleasure?" Alistair enquired gently.

She could picture him sitting at his huge walnut desk, perhaps fiddling with one of his bonsai trees, or casting his benign gaze on the garden square that the offices overlooked. As London venues went, the agency's offices were not bad. The silver birch trees would be fully in leaf now, she thought, casting their delicate, dappled shade.

But Petra still didn't miss it. Not one bit.

"So a quite exciting thing has happened," she said slowly, choosing her words.

"Hmm?" He would have his gently bemused face on, Petra knew, the mild, bumbling, literary creature with a vagueness that was entirely illusory. Alistair had a mind like a steel trap, Petra knew, and his judgment was rock solid. It was those attributes she needed now.

"Um, do you remember a writer called Ross McCloud? He wrote a—"

"—of course I do," Alistair broke in. "Who could forget? Debut author, stunning first novel, and crazy young too, makes me wonder what I've been doing with my life. Didn't he win the Booker too that year?"

"He did," Petra confirmed.

"Haven't heard of him for—what?—five years?" Alistair mused. "Strange . . . It's like he dropped off the face of the earth, now that I think about it. Why? What about him?"

"He's here," Petra said simply.

Alistair made a noise. She could picture him sitting bolt upright now, all pretense of dusty, vague establishment figure banished.

"What do you mean? You've seen him? Are you sure? Do you actually know him?"

"Yes, I actually know him quite . . . well," said Petra carefully.

"Is he writing?" Alistair demanded, razor sharp now.

"He is."

"Is there . . . is there a manuscript?"

"Nearly. Yes, there is. It's not quite finished . . ."

"Doesn't need to be. We could sell Ross McCloud if he just scribbled down his shopping list," said Alistair rapidly. "But wait a minute, does he have representation? He must have . . . Wasn't it Eleanora Francis?"

"Veronica Bampton," said Petra. "But—no—he doesn't have representation currently."

"He's going to need it," Alistair said curtly. "If anyone gets wind that there's another manuscript going begging. This could be the deal of the decade. Have you offered?"

"Yes and no," admitted Petra. "It's complicated. But here's the thing—he's been incommunicado for years, but he's now agreed to front up the Portneath Literary Festival in a few weeks, his first public appearance since he disappeared, so . . . people are going to notice."

"They most certainly are," said Alistair, "and he's going to need a team around him. A publicist, and an agent obviously, and the publishers are going to be buzzing around like flies as soon as they get wind of it—when's the festival?"

"End of August," said Petra.

"Good," said Alistair crisply. "Then there's time. I envisage we'll make the announcement, open the bidding, and tie up the deal just in time for the winning publisher to have it as the jewel in their crown at Frankfurt. They'll have sold translation rights to the world and its wife by the end of the show. I hope very much you are telling me he would like our help?"

"I can persuade him," said Petra, thinking she very much doubted that she could, actually. "It would be for you to represent him, not me, of course."

"Absolutely not," said Alistair. "Listen, I'm happy to back you, happy to talk through every step you take, but you're taking the lead on this. It's your win."

"But—like you said—it's huge . . ."

"Yup. It's a career-maker," Alistair agreed. "And it's just what you need and deserve. Don't worry, I've got your back. You're an *excellent agent*, Petra. You can do this."

Life was good, thought Ross one morning, staring out of the kitchen window toward "their" hill as he polished a glass absently. If it wasn't for Henrietta's increasingly insistent messaging, which he was trying and failing to ignore, he might even declare himself—well—"happy"?

With his and Petra's relationship sustaining him, he had found new energy and purpose as the summer wore on. He would write through the daytime, and then by evening, when Petra came back to the cottage, tired from a long day in the bookshop, he was there with supper already prepared. They would eat, share news of their respective days, and then talk, read, and listen to music late into the night.

It was idyllic.

But all the while, he was painfully aware of time ticking away. In just a few weeks Jules and Roman would be returning to take back control of the bookshop. Petra would be staying on until the end of the festival, as she had promised Jess, but then?

Whatever happened to Ross after his reappearance on the literary scene, it seemed inevitable that this charmed existence in Portneath would end. Especially if Henrietta delivered on her barely veiled threats. She had been dangerous enough before, and her messages indicated she still felt as if she held a sway in Ross's life. As she used to tell him, she knew him better than he knew himself. And maybe she was right. Strong as Petra made him feel, he feared that the sickly, enervating gravitational pull Henrietta could wield might be too overwhelming to resist if he were to see her again. And what damage could she do to him if he angered her? Plenty, he feared . . . What about when she discovered she was officially "a woman scorned"?

What then?

On the same day, Petra, walking down the hill through the fresh, cool morning air, was having similar fears about the time when their current idyll would come to an end. She dreaded how a return to the limelight might affect him, after last time.

And as for their relationship . . .

But—as Flo repeatedly told her—there was no point meeting trouble halfway. Petra was loving running the bookshop, putting more and more of her creative energy into little initiatives she hoped Jules and Roman would approve of. She would message them about anything big, of course, and Flo was a wise mentor, but Petra was growing in confidence at last and having a lot of fun.

"I *love* a ghost story!" Petra told a local self-published author she knew, later that day. Rosalie, a retired college lecturer who had taken up writing history books in her retirement, had sidled into the shop to show Petra her latest book, with its tales of local folklore.

"Five copies to start with, please," Petra told her. "We're steadily selling your other one, by the way, look!" She pointed out the little table where she had displayed the books by local authors. It made sense to have them together. People were always coming in asking for them, and stories about the ruined castle on the top of the hill were especially interesting to vacationers.

"I'm so grateful," Rosalie was telling Petra. "Not all bookshops want to deal with writers who don't have a traditional publishing deal, but Jules and Flo have been so supportive . . . Now, about this latest, I uncovered some fascinating information about how the castle was used as a lookout post for wreckers—"

"Wreckers?" squeaked Petra excitedly. "Yes! *And* ghosts?" This was getting better and better. "Pirates too?" she asked hopefully.

"Well, no," admitted Rosalie, "although I am sure pirates did come here, with Portneath being such a significant port at the time. There's not much written about the pirates, maybe I should—"

"You definitely should," said Petra firmly. "But I'm also keen to read about the ghostly wreckers."

Rosalie handed her a copy of the book. "Do have a read, and I'll bring the other copies next week. I am happy to sign them, if you think I should?"

"Actually, let me have ten copies," said Petra, flicking through the book excitedly, "and—yes, please—do sign them. Um, Rosalie . . ." Petra began diffidently. "I don't suppose I could persuade you to do an event at the festival in August?"

"Me? Oh no," Rosalie said, blushing. "This writing thing is just a hobby to stave off the dreaded Alzheimer's. You don't know how much it takes me just to come in and talk to *you* . . ."

"I could make it *so* easy for you though," pleaded Petra. "And—I tell you what!—I have an idea . . . Why don't I convene a panel for you," she suggested. "This other local writer Tony is kind of a local ghost-hunting skeptic, he's less about the history and more about the science, like whether the appearances can be explained by electromagnetic fields, and—I dunno—cold drafts, and things."

"Drafts?" asked Rosalie, looking perplexed.

"Yeah, maybe not actual drafts," admitted Petra, who was hazy about the details. Science was so not her thing. "But my point is you can both talk about the same areas but from different perspectives. Also, the Tourist Information Office has a booklet on the castle, do you know it?"

"I do," said Rosalie enthusiastically. "It's brief, but it's good."

"So we could get the author of that to join in—don't you think it would be fun? I'll host it, and ask you all questions. And the audience can ask questions too. Honestly, people who come in here are always interested."

Rosalie was starting to nod. Petra had her. "It would probably mean selling quite a few copies," she persuaded, to clinch the deal. "Maybe a little slot on local radio too?"

"I *would* like to find a way to support the literary festival," said Rosalie. "Which I think is a splendid idea, by the way. Why not? I'll do it!"

The schedule for the festival was now packed to bursting, with daytime and evening events in Capelthorne's, the town library, and town hall. The museum, it was decided, would host the panel discussion Petra created, as it was where all the history-related activity was going on.

Petra began to doubt the wisdom of limiting the festival to three days.

"BEST TO START smaller, though," said Jess that evening, as they compared notes in the shop again.

Petra was checking her watch, knowing Ross was waiting for her at home. "I'm sure you're right," she said, wondering how soon they could wrap up.

"Jules will pick up the threads when she gets back. Next year's will be bigger."

"What are ticket sales like?" Petra asked.

Jess grimaced. "Slowish," she admitted. "But we only started putting the program up on the website a couple of weeks ago. Um, when are we going to announce Ross as our keynote speaker?"

"Not a peep about Ross yet, remember?" said Petra anxiously. She had been lying awake at night, running through all the scenarios as to when and how they would publicly announce that he would be there *and* that he would be declaring the existence of his manuscript. He was going to have to. Every time she thought of it, her insides gave a little lurch, leaving her wondering whether it was fear or excitement. She didn't know whether it would be worse for it to be huge and uncontrollable, or whether she would feel even more terrible if she mishandled it, and the whole thing was a damp squib.

"I'm nervous about announcing the Ross thing," admitted Jess, voicing Petra's own fears. "He's so kind to get involved with our teeny tiny little festival. I want to do him justice."

"We will," Petra reassured her, wishing badly she could reassure herself.

Chapter Twenty-Three

"You're all fired up," observed Ross, looking pleased as they had a late supper after the meeting.

"I am," admitted Petra. "I've just done the orders, and I've had so many helpful recommendations and requests from customers, I'm starting to feel like I might actually know what I'm doing."

She was acutely aware that Jules and Roman's money needed to buy books that would actually sell. It was a responsibility. And, as she repeatedly reminded herself, Capelthorne's wasn't her plaything—it was Jules and Roman's livelihood. Whatever she personally thought about any individual book, it was sales that mattered in the end.

"I'm so proud of you," said Ross quietly, putting down his fork and smiling across the little supper table at her.

"Why?" said Petra.

"Fishing," he teased, laughing at her perplexed expression. "Don't look at me like that! I'm allowed to be proud of you! You're smashing the whole running-a-bookshop thing, you're doing the almost impossible job of giving me the emotional support to keep me writing, you're making good friends locally—everybody loves you . . ." He shook his head, clearly struggling to think of more.

"What? Running out of compliments so soon?" said Petra, pretending to be offended. "What about my stunning talent for always saying the exact right thing at all times?"

But Ross refused to rise to it. "Do you think that you might just be able to be a tiny bit proud of yourself?" he asked her quietly, serious now.

Petra sighed. "Mmm . . . maybe," she said. And, as Ross continued to gaze at her steadily, "Look, I'll try."

"That's all I ask," Ross told her. "Because I might not always be there to remind you to be."

And the expression on his face when he said it was so wistful, and so forlorn, Petra didn't dare to ask him what he meant.

THE SHOP WAS busy that weekend. Being Saturday, it was market day and also changeover day for most of the tourists. Flo and Petra were busy from the moment they opened, selling to the crowd who were leaving—mainly last-minute children's books to help distract on the journey home—and also to the crowd who were arriving, blissed out at the thought of long days ahead to read and daydream on the beach.

The weather was expected to be fair for the whole week, although today there was a brisk wind coming in from the sea. Flo, usually a paragon of efficiency, was distracted. She was, Petra discovered, fixated about her sweet peas.

"I planted two enormous lots from seed," she told Petra. "Way back at Christmastime—they were all over the kitchen windowsills—but they've all made the transition from the greenhouse to the garden now. The trouble is, the second lot might have gotten put out a bit late. I'm worried they won't be in full bloom in time for the wedding, although this lovely sunshine will help."

"Sweet peas don't last long, once they're picked, do they?" said Petra, realizing just as the words came out of her mouth that she had inadvertently made Flo's anxiety even worse.

"Absolutely right," she fretted. "They have to be picked on the day, and we need tons for the tent with tables. Roman's mother is calling it a small wedding—I'd love to see what she thinks is a large one—but it's still ten round tables for ten, so that's ten big glass jarfuls for the centerpieces. And then there are going to be these silver ice buckets on stands at the entrance with loads more, plus a few of my roses too, if a rainstorm hasn't wiped them out just before."

Petra made a sympathetic face at Flo, but she also faced her own anxiety about the party. She loved those regular pub evening drinks with the Portneath crowd—they had been so welcoming to her, and now to Ross—but this event of Jules and Roman's was daunting. A hundred people they mostly didn't know, but who knew each other really well? It seemed a nerve-wracking prospect. It shouldn't be, though, she told herself sternly. She had routinely attended all those professional receptions in the London publishing scene, book launches and industry shindigs. Of course, that was before her massive faux pas . . . She was becoming insular.

"We *must* get your dress sorted," said Flo suddenly, in a brief lull. "It's only a couple of weeks away now."

"Gosh, so it is," said Petra, with a wave of sadness. Jules and Roman were returning in just a few days, making her departure significantly more imminent. She had to find another job, but leaving Portneath—and all her new friends—potentially leaving Ross, felt like the most dispiriting thing in the world now.

Responding to Flo's comments with an effort, Petra allowed Flo to arrange for her to come and rummage in Flo's wardrobe one evening that week.

"And don't let me forget to give you the morning coat for Ross when I see you," Flo reminded her.

I'll be a bit late, Petra texted Ross as she and Flo closed up the shop that Tuesday. I've got to go back to Flo's to find a dress. She had told him this that very morning, but he was so vague these days, his story of Miranda and Caliban filling his head. Surprisingly, he had politely declined Flo's offer of a morning coat, telling Petra he already had something to wear for the wedding party.

The evening air was warm and sweet as Petra and Flo drove, windows wide open, through the narrow country lanes to Flo's cottage in Middlemass, a pretty little village a few miles inland from Portneath. It was also, Petra learned, where Roman and Jules lived, and where the party would be in a couple of weeks' time.

"What is it?" said Flo perceptively as she drove.

Petra sighed. There was no hiding anything from her friend. "Jess wants to go ahead and announce that Ross will be headlining the literary festival."

"And . . . ?"

"I mean, it's fine that he's going to be there. Actually, I think it's good. He's in such a great place now," gabbled Petra. "He's writing . . . the book's nearly finished, as a matter of fact . . ."

"It's good?"

"Outstanding," breathed Petra. "Truly . . . No, I mean, it needs to find an audience."

"So . . . ?" prompted Flo.

"So when we make the announcement, everything is going to explode. It's going to feel like I'm trying to suppress nuclear fission."

"Sure?" probed Flo.

"Yes," said Petra with conviction. And that was not just because *she* thought it, hadn't Alistair said as much himself? And he would know, with his wisdom and experience.

"I fail to see a problem," said Flo. "You want to make a splash, presumably?"

"No, I mean, yes, it's all good! It's all good," declared Petra.

"But . . ." nudged Flo.

"He *says* he wants me to represent him, and he refuses to go with my old boss Alistair instead," Petra burst out.

She gazed unseeing out of the car window, breathing in the straw scent of the sun-warmed meadows they were driving past as they entered the outskirts of Middlemass, over the stone bridge and past an old stone church, with its square Norman bell tower.

"But he wants you," said Flo at last. It was a statement, not a question. "So do it," she added with finality, pulling into the driveway of an exquisite little stone cottage with towering hollyhocks in the tiny front garden. "Good talk," Flo continued, switching off the engine. "Now, on to other matters."

NIGHTINGALE COTTAGE WAS a study in cozy cottage perfection. Flo opened the back of the car and Digger popped out, trotting to the front door and looking at the two women expectantly.

"He's settled so well," said Flo fondly. "You would think he's been here since he was a pup."

"Has he not?" asked Petra.

"Rescue," said Flo succinctly. "Bless him. Not saying we didn't have our teething problems, but they were understandable really."

"He landed on his feet, coming to you," said Petra, following Flo into the little house.

"He knows when he's home," said Flo simply. "You do too, don't you?"

"How do you mean?"

"Dear girl," said Flo, "I think you know. I've seen you settle and change so much since you arrived . . . your confidence, self-belief—apart from this silly wobble about representing Ross—your happiness . . ." Flo gave her a sweet, wistful smile, quite different from her normal brisk manner. "Don't tell me you aren't happy here," she challenged. "I can see you positively glowing with it these days. This is home for you now, don't you both see?"

"Home is where the heart is," said Petra. "I suppose. That's just a saying, though . . ."

Flo laughed. "Sayings tend to become sayings because they're true. Now, gin and tonic or wardrobe dive?"

"Both?" said Petra.

"—is the correct answer," said Flo, beaming.

When the women were both furnished with large glasses of icily delicious gin and tonic, so strong the first sip made Petra wince a little, they went up the narrow stairs together.

There was little more than a cast-iron bed and a huge brown

wooden wardrobe in Flo's guest room, the low casement window casting golden summer evening light across the bare waxed floorboards. On the stone windowsill, a day of sunlight had warmed the bowl of dried rose petals, which was releasing a heady scent.

Flo threw open the doors of the wardrobe with a flourish, releasing a waft of dust and lavender.

She began pulling out clothes and laying them reverently on the bed. Dress after dress materialized, each one neat, pressed, and impeccable. The vibe was Audrey Hepburn, and it was clear Flo had bought—or at least kept—only the best.

"Can't do black for a wedding party," said Flo, regretfully disregarding an enchanting black minidress with a white collar and cuffs. "I loved that one to bits."

Then she disappeared back inside and reappeared holding a stunning dress covered in the most enchanting purple pansies, with yellow buds and green leaves. The dress was a classic fifties shape, with a full skirt, neat waist, boatneck, and no sleeves.

"You would need a little cardigan with it," said Flo doubtfully. "Even in August, it can get nippy in the evenings. I used to have one specifically for this very frock . . . Why don't you pop it on, while I go and see? Just a moment . . ."

The dress slipped off the hanger with a quiet swish. It was surprisingly heavy and—Petra quickly realized—pure silk. It was hand-painted by the looks of it too. The label was for a fashion house Petra had never heard of, but it claimed to have outlets in London, Paris, and New York. So—*fancy*.

She dropped her T-shirt and jeans on the bed and carefully stepped into the dress.

It was beautifully constructed. Petra had never worn anything like it and had never expected to, except perhaps on her wedding day.

If she ever had a wedding day.

Carefully pulling up the side zip and then opening the wardrobe door wider so she could see herself in the mirror, Petra gasped. It was stunning. The boatneck and the full, flared skirt made her waist look tiny. Her neck, with the nape exposed, looked long and delicate, but the front of the dress was high and surprisingly demure. She twisted her raven black hair up and held it there while she turned one way and the other. Being an avowed lover of trousers, Petra rarely wore even a skirt, let alone a dress, but in this she felt delicate, feminine, and—yes—pretty.

Normally barely glancing in the mirror except when she was brushing her teeth and hair, Petra was entranced by this new and glamorous version of herself. It might have been the flattering evening light, but her skin—bare of makeup—had lost its gray London pallor at last. Instead, perhaps from her regular walks on the beach and the hills with Ross, she was prettily flushed and lightly freckled. Lugging boxes of books around had toned her arms and kept her fit too. Also, Ross was determined that she should eat well and made sure she did by cooking for her most nights, so her body had lost all of the angular awkwardness she was used to covering up with baggy clothes.

"You look gorgeous!" exclaimed Flo, as she came back into the room, holding a purple wisp of something.

"It's a stunning dress," Petra replied shyly, looking away from her reflection at last. "Are you sure? I promise to take the best, best care of it."

Flo made a dismissive noise. "It will be a pleasure to see it worn," she said. "I'm hardly going to parade myself in something like that these days. It's too good to be shut away in the dark, waiting for the moths to eat it for lunch. Ross is going to adore you in it," she added slyly. "He won't be able to keep his hands off you."

"Flo!" said Petra, blushing scarlet.

"Just saying," replied Flo unrepentantly. "Now, it's a shame to cover those elegant arms, but you'll need this with our English summers." She held out the wisp, which turned out to be a sweet little cropped bolero cardigan with delicate beading along the edges. It matched the purple of the hand-painted pansies perfectly.

Flo nodded her satisfaction when Petra slipped it on. From its lightness and softness, Petra realized it must be cashmere.

"Shoes?" Flo enquired.

"I've got big feet," admitted Petra. "Bigger than yours anyhow, but there are some lovely summer sandals in that shoe shop on the main street. Perhaps I'll pop out when you're in next Tuesday and see?"

"Splendid!" Flo exclaimed. "Now, bring your drink, and humor an old woman while I give you a tour of the garden."

Chapter Twenty-Four

Back at the flat later that night, Petra sat on the bed gazing at the pansy dress that was hanging in front of the wardrobe door. It was one of the increasingly rare nights she and Ross spent apart these days. She had had a dusk tour of Flo's garden, which was magical, and then shared a simple supper of scrambled eggs on toast with the older woman. It had been late by the time she was ready to leave and—after messaging Ross—they had agreed to reunite the following evening so Ross could pull a late one tonight and work through. He had been writing at such a frantic pace that the manuscript was now complete, barring the final chapter, and he was immersed in rewrites and editing, smoothing the rough corners off the already sparkling prose.

When she was at the cottage, she would sometimes wake in the night and find herself alone in the bed. She would turn to look and there he would be, sitting in the chair in the corner of the room, his laptop on his knee, totally immersed, just like he was the morning after he rescued her.

Sometimes he would work all night and then go to bed at dawn. Mostly, on the nights when she knew he was planning to do that, she would stay in the flat alone, so as not to risk waking him when she got up.

Their lives were molded around each other now. Petra had started to imagine there could be no other way of living. Slowly, almost by stealth, she had found herself completely committed to this man.

Petra sighed, putting the dress away in the wardrobe and contemplating putting her pajamas on. It was late.

Instead, she stood in front of the window for a while, gazing out at a view that had already become very dear and familiar. Across the rooftops and out to sea, she could see the bright white light of a lonely fishing boat working its way across the mouth of the bay, kept safe from the rocks by the lighthouse on the promontory.

She and Ross had walked up there together once during a summer storm, laughing as the wind gusted fiercely, stealing their breath, and then gazing silently out to sea together for a long while, with Petra wrapped safe in Ross's arms.

The lines of a Shakespeare sonnet came to her. What was it again? Something about a little boat being guided by the constancy of true love . . .

(love) is an ever-fixed mark,
That looks on tempests and is never shaken;
It is the star to every wandering bark . . .

And yet, she just couldn't convince herself that Ross saw their love in the same way as she had started to. For her it was truly a "marriage of true minds," that never "alters when it alteration finds." What if—for him—their relationship was a summer fling that would make him look back fondly on her, and Portneath, long after he had moved away and moved on with his life?

Time was ticking steadily on, whether she wanted it to or not. The months had flown past, and her time in Portneath was coming to a close. In just a few days, Jules and Roman would be returning, and as soon as their party was over, the literary festival would be racing toward them. The thought of it reminded her—in a moment of practicality—that she must follow up with Alistair over plans to announce Ross's return to the literary world.

And after the news was out, what then? She dreaded the announcement. Realistically, Ross coming out into the open—and with a new book too—would immediately destroy this private, special, magical time they were enjoying. Was their love an "ever fixed mark"? Or would the spell be broken?

Who was she kidding? Of course it would.

Could she ever convince herself that handsome, supremely talented Ross McCloud would settle for plain little her, when he was being feted by the entire literary world? With all those glamorous, clever groupies gathering around him, as of course they would be, he would instantly be tired of her.

No, she couldn't assume their little affair was ever more than just that for him.

He wasn't cruel, though, and she knew he cared for her. He called her his muse, after all. His Miranda. No. She flattered herself that he might refer to her obliquely in some of the many interviews he would inevitably end up doing. He wouldn't mention her by name; he was too classy for that. But it would be a sop to her, to their little summer fling. What happens in Portneath stays in Portneath. That's what he would say. They would both give a little smile at the secret message, designed to soothe her pain as he inevitably moved on. Hell, she might even find he dedicated this new book to her! Could she hope for that at least? Perhaps . . . She had done more than enough to make sure he finished it.

It was good to rehearse these thoughts, she told herself as she turned away from the window, an icy shaft of regret settling in her chest. At least this way she could practice the pain of loss and prepare for its intensity. The main thing for her dignity—which was all she would have left—would be to hide her distress.

She could do that by focusing on the professional stuff. It had always worked for her before.

"WE NEED TO time the announcement so *The Bookseller* can break the news first. We'll go to the culture pages on the nationals simultaneously. If we do it before, someone's bound to leak it," Alistair told Petra on the phone.

"Sounds like a plan," replied Petra, trying to match Alistair's brisk professional tone.

"Yes, and you know the second it goes out we'll be fending off interview requests," he warned her. "I suggest we use Louise. She's pricey, but she's the best publicist in the business."

"Agreed," said Petra. "And they'll all want an exclusive, but I say we go wide. With their long lead times, we will have sold the manuscript by the time they go to press. They'll be announcing the lucky publisher and probably a publication date for the book at the same time, if they haven't done it already."

"And how do you see the literary festival sitting in all this?"

asked Alistair. She could hear him tapping away on his keyboard, making notes.

"Well, Ross is keen that the festival gets a boost out of the story breaking," Petra reminded him, "so I thought we could promise a press conference with Ross on the first day of the festival, down here in Portneath. In the bookshop, probably. That way, everyone gets what they want in public and at the same time, which seems fair. Plus, they have to come down to Portneath in person to do it. Fingers crossed, that way the festival will get a mention."

"Smart," said Alistair. "Right! Well, we haven't got that long really, so if you could please put together some copy for us to use in our email to acquisition editors, you can leave briefing Louise to me, okay?" suggested Alistair.

"So I'll be . . ." hazarded Petra.

"You'll be dealing with the editors yourself," he confirmed.

"And it'll be an auction?" she asked.

"Almost certainly," said Alistair. "Unless we get the mother of all preempts. You know the drill. And we'll help here in the office too, of course. As I say, your baby but with full agency support."

It was kind of cool, Petra had to admit, having these conversations, when so much of her job in the past had involved desperately trying to get acquisition editors to take her calls.

Chapter Twenty-Five

"Don't get a big head," Ross teased when she relayed Alistair's conversation to him that evening.

"If anyone's going to get a big head . . ." she shot back pointedly. "Although, I suppose this is all same old, same old for you?"

"Ah, but no," he reminded her. "You've clearly not read the ballad of Ross McCloud," he told her. "First off, it was a tiny deal—a sink or swim number, far from a lead title. Although, yeah, it was from a respectable publisher. Then—somehow—it went viral on TikTok. We hit the literary festivals too—God, that was exhausting—I was turning up to bookshops lucky if I sold and signed one book at first . . ."

"And then you got short-listed for the Booker," Petra took up the tale, "and everyone said you wouldn't win."

"Exactly," said Ross. "And quite right too, there were some fantastic authors on that list, I was—well—I was amazed it was me, actually."

"Yours was the best book, end of story."

"Ah, so you *do* know the ballad of Ross McCloud," he told her, ruffling her hair, as the two of them slumped on the sofa in front of the fire, draped across each other and basking in the heat. Earlier they had been outside in his tiny garden with its view of the hill with their bench on it, but sunset had driven them inside, shivering in their summer clothes.

The bleak January day when they had first met seemed a world away now, Petra remembered. Not the most edifying of occasions.

"Remember when I thought you were a tramp." She smiled.

He chuckled. "And the day you blew up the internet," he reminded her.

Petra struggled to smile in reply. She certainly did. And soon she would be pitching herself right back into that world.

"Imagine if we could just stay like this forever," she ventured, "with people not knowing who you are, and not remembering who I am—what I did . . ."

"You didn't murder anyone," he pointed out, giving her a comforting squeeze. "And no one can pause time. Imagine how bored we'd get . . . the same few months over and over?"

"Not me," Petra said fiercely. "I would *never* get bored of this. Never . . ."

"So let's just keep doing this," Ross said gently, "forever and ever . . ."

"Hmm, not feasible, sadly," Petra admitted. "Money, for one thing. I quite like eating."

"Yeah, me too," he agreed. "I do need to publish something else one day soon," he admitted. "Either that or get a proper job."

"*I've* got a proper job," said Petra. "I could keep us." But even as she said it, she knew, of course. She was only borrowing this job. It wasn't hers. And it didn't pay that much either. "I could get another job around here," she said with a hint of desperation.

"We can't just stop," Ross said gently. "We're like sharks, we humans. We need to keep swimming forward or die."

They both stared into the flames for the longest time. Then into the silence Ross's phone bleeped with a notification.

He didn't move.

"Who's that?" asked Petra sleepily.

"No one," said Ross. "Now let's go to bed. You need to get some rest."

PETRA WASN'T GREAT with uncertainty. The future was a mystery, but one thing Petra *was* sure about was that the encompassing and comforting bookish arms of Capelthorne's had wrapped themselves around her and restored her love of literature. She was excited to come into work in the morning; excited to speak to the customers, to divine which books they would love; to unpack the boxes of new stock arriving twice a week, feeling like Christmas every time; to listen to the visiting sales agents as to what was hot and what was not. At first, she had known full well which books they would tell her about, knowing from upstream the titles that were going to be traveling down the line with publisher support. But just recently, the books she was encouraged by the agents to get behind were titles she didn't recognize, and that had ignited a wistful longing to be back in the London publishing world—to be preparing, even now in July, for the Frankfurt Book Fair in the autumn, where the big deals would be done, and the behemoth publishing companies, alongside the smaller independents, would go to preen and hustle and show off their acquisitions.

And this autumn, one of those acquisitions would be Ross's new book. She, of all the literary agent mess-ups, was to be entrusted with the stewardship of that sale.

What if she screwed it up?

What then for this precious relationship? Their love was blossoming here in Portneath, in the liminal space between their respective worlds, but would it be crushed by the disappointments she routinely brought to her writer clients?

How could it not?

Wise, kind Alistair had foretold it of course, on that hideous day—her last day in London that January. He had known that Petra needed this sabbatical—a chance to fall back in love with books—but how was he to know that she would fall in love even more profoundly than that?

"WHAT?" ASKED Ross that evening as they waited in the chip shop, a heavy, mouthwatering aroma of fried food filling the air.

She loved stealing glances at him, unwatched: the way the heavy lock of hair fell over his forehead as he stood, the way he pulled her against his lean body, steadying her. This time, amused, he met her analytical gaze.

"What happened?" she said, her heart pounding in response to her daring, to the danger of hearing something she didn't want to hear. Something he couldn't take back.

"Care to narrow it down a bit?" he replied lightly. "What happened when? With what? Or who? Are we talking big bang, or something more recent?"

"You've never really told me what happened before?" she went on, in too deep to stop now, even if she wanted to. "What made you so sure you couldn't be romantically involved with anyone you were working with? Was it your agent? It was Veronica Bampton, wasn't it? Were you in a relationship, you and her . . . did you . . ."

Stop talking, stop talking, thought Petra, seeing Ross's face go blank, as if she had wiped it clean like a blackboard. She managed to make herself shut up by physically putting her finger on her lips, like her primary school teacher Mrs. Grafton used to make the whole class do when they got too noisy.

She wished she was back there now. Back in her childhood where life was simple, and the grown-ups were in charge, and she didn't feel like she was going to blow her life to smithereens by opening her big mouth. Again.

With a sigh, Ross turned to face her now, placing his hands heavily on her shoulders. His expression was bleak.

"I told you," he said gently, but with studied patience. "I detached myself from my agent when it was clear she was going to have nothing of mine to go out with—that there wasn't going to be another book. That was a long time after . . ."

He hung his head, shaking it, as if trying to shake away the memories.

Petra stayed silent. Motionless, hearing the chatter and clatter of the chip shop fade as they became enclosed in their own intense little bubble.

"I was having an affair with my editor," he said at last. His voice was a monotone, like he was the most bored newsreader in the world, reading from a teleprompter. "Her name is Henrietta.

We began an intense relationship when we were communicating about edits. I felt she really *got* me," he admitted. "She got my story . . . and it was intoxicating. I was flattered that she was taking so much care and excited that she was so committed to making the book a success, knowing it was a tiny deal as far as this publisher was concerned. I felt lucky. I felt seen."

Petra stayed very still, looking up at him, giving him space to talk. A clumsy intervention at this stage would be a disaster. For once she managed to keep her mouth shut, and Ross continued:

"Genuinely, she helped me make it a better book but—at the same time—she was prescriptive. Overly prescriptive. Gradually, I realized that I had let her take control to the point where I was being *told* precisely what to write, down to individual words and phrases. And then we started having creative differences, but she was making it very clear it was her way or the highway. If I insisted on my own perspective, then I was told I was sacrificing the success of the book. So I went along with it. I didn't know how *not* to. Of course, the book was published, it did well . . ." He shrugged. "But, by that time, rightly or wrongly, I felt like it wasn't my book, so—obviously—it wasn't even my success. Not entirely.

"Next thing I knew, she withdrew emotionally. I asked what was wrong. She told me I was being paranoid. Again and again, she lied. She gaslit me. It eventually turned out she *was* in a relationship with another young writer. He was just like me, starting out, a bit younger than her, talented but inexperienced, naïve . . . He was me, basically. Anyhow, when I learned she had been lying to me for months, there was a huge row, and we went our separate ways," he explained wearily. "And I think it was only then it slowly dawned on me how Faustian the whole affair had been.

I loathed her. I was glad I was free. But—when I sat down to write, I discovered . . . I had nothing. It was as if she had wormed her way inside my creative mind and trained it to think she was the creator, not me. I was second-guessing and shooting down every idea before it even crystalized. I was self-sabotaging. I couldn't stop.

"Anyhow," he shrugged, staring unseeing at the plastic chip shop menu on the wall, "I realized that without her, I was *nothing*. I could write *nothing*," he declared, giving Petra a sad little smile. "I thought she was my muse." He gave a hollow laugh. "The things—it turns out—we are prepared to do for what we think we want . . . There's a cost," he declared, straightening and squaring his shoulders. "And it's not a cost I am prepared to pay again."

How desperate! thought Petra. No wonder he had been so broken when she met him.

"Petra?" he said softly, reconnecting with her gaze as her eyes filled with tears for him.

"I would *never, ever* do that to you," she choked, slipping her arms around him and resting her head on his chest. He enfolded her in his embrace, his chin resting on the top of her head. This was their thing. Their "go-to" position. She sometimes felt she could spend the rest of her life just being held like this, by him.

"I know you wouldn't," he said. "This thing we have is *so* different," he went on with quiet intensity, squeezing her with a fierceness that made her want to groan. "We can't break this. Whatever happens with the book—good or bad—we will still have this. Right? Because," he told her, leaning back so he could fix her gaze with his own, "if we don't have 'us,' *then I don't think I can do this.*"

Long after Ross had fallen asleep, breathing deeply and evenly beside her, Petra lay awake, looking at the silver moon through the little cottage window. The cottage was so remote, they rarely bothered to draw the curtain at night.

She knew, without question, that what Ross had told her about Henrietta was true. There had been whispers for years: She had a penchant for young, beautiful men; she got too close to her writers; she exerted a level of creative control that bordered on coercive; she damaged the careers of anyone—writers, staff, agents—who dared to cross her.

You made an enemy of Henrietta at your peril. And Ross had done just that.

As well as pondering what Ross had told her about the reasons for his long absence from writing, Petra had been increasingly nervous about Jules and Roman's return. Grilling Freya and Flo for details—because she didn't want to pester the couple by texting them every five minutes—she was under the impression they were flying back into the country at the beginning of the following week.

Flo had chatted to Petra often over the months about Roman and Jules, and how Roman was the details man, the hardheaded business brain, fresh from a top-flight career in New York. What he brought to the table was an analytical mind and an iron grip on the financials. By contrast, Jules was the creative one. Flo related fondly how Jules was a mass of energy and enthusiasm, and an ex-London publishing editor herself, with a passion for books that had been all-consuming since she was a child.

Petra had thought, over the months, that she and Jules had much in common. But now that she was going to meet her properly, she felt hopelessly colorless and dull.

When a tall, handsome, black-haired man with piercing blue eyes, and a lithe, pretty young woman burst into the shop that Saturday mid-morning to cries of delight from Flo, Petra assumed at first they were Flo's favorite customers. Then the woman wrapped Flo in a fierce and all-encompassing hug, to the accompaniment of much chatter and many exclamations.

Seconds later, the young woman released Flo, and the man replaced her in grabbing Flo for a tight squeeze.

The woman then turned to Petra and gave her a noisy air-kiss on the cheek, before holding out her hand.

"Jules," she announced. "And you're Petra, of course."

Petra could not deny this, tempting though it was—for a nanosecond—to pretend she was nothing more than a passing tourist.

"We are *so* grateful to you for doing what you've done," Jules declared.

Jules was glowing, Petra observed. She could only imagine this was what a person looked like when they had the love of a good man, a stable career that no longer included schmoozing in the torrid London publishing scene, and the wherewithal to take a six-month vacation on a whim. In fact, the pair of them were radiant, so in love, and so bright and shiny, in the way most people in Portneath seemed to be, it must be the effect of happiness, Petra supposed . . .

"I *love* the window!" Jules went on. "You are *so* creative. I knew you'd be amazing. Am I allowed to confess? I've had the most incredible feedback from Flo and everyone about how well you've been doing *and* . . ." Jules leaned in conspiratorially, "you're going out with Ross McCloud!" Her *sotto voce* rose to a squeak, and then she stopped herself, glancing round to make sure they were alone. "I mean . . . oh my good God!" she went on, slightly more quietly. "He's my hero . . . I can't wait to meet him. Now," she went on, not giving Petra a chance to draw breath, "tell me you're both available for dinner tonight. Freya's at six, yes or no?"

Dissent had not even been an option, mused Petra, carefully applying mascara in the little bathroom of the flat as she waited for Ross to arrive. He had been of two minds when she told him the plan but—understanding that Petra was dying to make a good impression—he agreed to come and was popping into the shop to pick her up a few minutes early.

It was nice to have a chance to dress up, Petra thought, smoothing her new navy blue dress with her slightly sweaty palms and stepping back to judge her appearance. School mistress, she decided, with a subtle overlay of goth teenager. God, she was going to look so colorless next to Jules with her bright, floaty scarves and expensive, globe-trotting tan.

Roman had—oh so politely—asked to see the spreadsheets when they met in the shop too. He spent an hour in the back office, bringing himself up to speed, although Jules had excused herself, claiming jet lag and the need to nap before dinner. Petra fiddled around on the shop floor, too nervous about possibly being interrogated to go into the office where he was. She knew the figures weren't bad. Flo had a good sense of the turnover they should be aiming for, even if Petra didn't, and she had raised no concerns over the last six months. But Petra was still nervous to hear what Roman had to say.

Petra's phone pinged—just Ross letting her know he was outside—so she smoothed her straight black bob one more time and checked that none of her scarlet lipstick had transferred onto her teeth. It would have to do.

"Pretty!" exclaimed Ross instantly when Petra opened the door.

"Yeah, sure," Petra replied, making a face.

"Listen," said Ross, pulling her against his chest and dropping a kiss onto the top of her head, "you look gorgeous, and you rock. They're going to love you just as much as I do, okay?"

Petra grunted in reply. If she doubted the sincerity of the message behind the words, then his eyes told her otherwise. He locked her gaze, eyebrows raised in query, and she gave him a reluctant smile.

With his arm resting heavy and comforting across her shoulder, Petra let Ross shepherd her safely across the street to Freya's.

Opening the door, they were greeted with a swell of chatter and a glorious waft of delicious savory smells from the kitchen.

Roman and Ross shook hands in a friendly fashion, but Jules pulled Ross in for the whole "air-kisses on both cheeks" treatment, accompanied by a quiet outpouring of delight over Ross's first novel, which Jules had adored, remembering all the fuss about it from when she was working at Farquarson and Trimble in her London days.

"Didn't you guys at F & T make a bid for it when it went to auction?" asked Ross, narrowing his eyes in an effort to remember.

"Well, I mean *I* didn't," admitted Jules, sitting back down and taking her napkin. "It was a while ago, wasn't it? I would have been responsible for tea-making and letter-opening at the time.

I wouldn't even have been in the room, let alone been in charge. You must have been so young!" she exclaimed.

"He was twenty-eight and sickeningly precocious," Petra told her as Ross slid her chair back for her. "I mean what *normal* twenty-eight-year-old has anything to say?"

"I'm not normal," admitted Ross ruefully.

"I'll drink to weird," replied Petra, taking a gulp of the wine that Roman had just poured for her.

"Hey, hang on," Ross remonstrated, "Weird? I wouldn't go that far."

Roman laughed. "And I gather from Flo"—here he lowered his voice and leaned in toward Ross—"that you've got another manuscript on its way. That's going to be quite the event. If you're looking for a contact in the US publishing houses, I know an editor who would love to see it."

"Thanks," said Ross. "I've got Petra representing me, so—yeah—do pass it on to her, that would be great."

"Ah," said Roman, and he and Jules looked at each other meaningfully.

"What?" asked Petra.

"We did wonder whether you'd be going back to London, to pick up the agenting thing," admitted Jules, "but we were really hoping . . ." She looked at Roman again, and then back to Petra. "The thing is, we were really hoping we could persuade you to stay." She looked at Petra, biting her lip. "Shall we just tell them?" she asked Roman, who nodded.

Jules leaned in, darting glances to left and right. "I'm eating for two," she confessed.

"Oh wow!" exclaimed Petra loudly—and then, more quietly, "That's so exciting!"

"Yeah," acknowledged Jules, looking delighted, but trying not to. "It's a honeymoon baby—what a cliché," she said, rolling her eyes.

"How are you feeling?" asked Petra.

"Mostly really hungry and really sleepy," confessed Jules. "I've been lucky, I know. I'm actually already four months gone, so I'm definitely starting to need baggier clothes, even if it's only to accommodate all the eating I seem to be doing . . ."

"So—the thing is," Roman picked up the thread, "we were hoping you would help run the shop for the next year at least, while Jules is busy with the baby? I'll be around too, of course, but we really want to persuade Flo to rest more, and we've got a few other projects we want to explore, so it would be super helpful to not be running the shop all the time as well. You've done such a great job for us. We couldn't be more grateful, but—if you're not staying . . ."

"We're definitely *potentially* staying, though," said Ross hastily. "There's a lot we need to talk about. What you're proposing sounds really interesting, doesn't it?" he said, catching Petra's eye.

"Sure!" said Petra, who had been dreading going back to her old job, something that had seemed inevitable. Now this? Staying in Portneath longer? Petra floated the idea in her head and the resultant surge in hopefulness—a swelling sense of joy—was unmistakable.

"By the way, do keep Jules's condition under your hats for now," Roman added quickly. "We thought we'd maybe announce it at the party."

"God, of course!" Petra reassured them. "And I just need to say, Ross's manuscript is a secret too, although we *totally* don't mind you knowing."

"Don't you just love sharing secrets?" Jules said. "That's what they're for, right?" She sighed happily.

"That's *literally* the opposite of what you are supposed to do with secrets," deadpanned Roman indulgently, reaching over and tenderly tucking a loose lock of Jules's hair behind her ear.

"Flo tells me you've gone on the most amazing honeymoon," said Petra wistfully. "All the most incredible bookshops in the world?"

"Yes!" declared Jules. "It's been the trip of a lifetime, so now I am totally ready to spend the rest of my days in Portneath."

Chapter Twenty-Six

"Could you spend the rest of *your* days in Portneath?" asked Ross when he and Petra were chatting about the evening in bed later.

"Could you?"

"Yeah, maybe," said Ross sleepily. "I feel like I've been everywhere, moving around to stay invisible . . . Now I'm starting to feel like I want to be found. I want to—I dunno—belong somewhere . . ."

"Hmm . . ." said Petra, snuggling in to go to sleep. "I think maybe I do too. I'd need to talk to Alistair, though. He's expecting me back soon."

Petra grabbed her chance to phone Alistair just before opening the shop, hoping to catch him before his secretary arrived and started intercepting his calls.

"You should accept," he said immediately, when Petra filled him in on Jules and Roman's offer.

"You don't want me back?" said Petra, feeling rejected.

"Of *course* I do," Alistair replied. "But you don't have to be physically here. You don't have to be in London at all. This is the WFH revolution, remember? And—even if you do relocate to London—you don't necessarily have to take all your clients back."

Ah, there it was.

"They don't want me back, do they?" said Petra, lifting her chin and refusing to be downcast. "They've gotten used to having you instead. Any sensible client would want the agent with the most experience."

"You know how we work," Alistair reminded her. "Our client agreements make it quite clear that they sign with the agency just as much as the individual."

"Have they all walked?"

"Not at all!" Alistair replied quickly, and then he paused. "I mean, one or two . . ."

She didn't need him to spell it out to her. "So, yeah, I think I'd like to stay on here," she said, letting him off the hook. "Jules and Roman have kindly said I can remain in the flat as long as I like too, so . . ." So even if she and Ross didn't last the course, she wouldn't be homeless, Petra thought. She had to be realistic. It would be unwise to hope for too much in life. And she had told herself how lovely the life seemed to be here in Portneath, hadn't she? She could retreat. Run a bookshop. Have a quiet life. Not everyone had to conquer the world.

"I'll tell you what, though," Alistair went on. "Even if you let a couple of your smaller clients go, you're not getting out of selling Ross McCloud's manuscript. Where did you get to on the submission package?" he asked. "Do you want to float the email copy by me? I'll ping you over the list I suggest you submit it to?"

"Sure," said Petra crisply, echoing Alistair's businesslike manner. She could do that for Ross. It was the least he deserved.

"There you go," Ross said later as they ate supper together at the cottage. "That Alistair sounds like a top bloke. Run the bookshop for Jules and Roman for a few months *and* represent me. Simples."

"*And* the literary festival, don't forget," Petra said, ashamed of the slight whine she could hear in her voice. "So much for escaping to the seaside for a less stressful life," she went on, trying to make it sound like a joke. "I thought you were on my side."

"I *am* on your side. And don't forget supporting me to actually write my book, in your list of amazing achievements. I'm your biggest fan, remember? I just want to know when you're going to stop underestimating yourself," Ross said gently.

Uncompromising words maybe, but when Petra met his gaze, his green eyes were ablaze with love.

Petra asked anxiously, "I mean, supporting you to write your book, critiquing it and whatnot . . . You don't think I'm like Henrietta do you?"

At this, Ross guffawed. "*God* no," he exclaimed. "Apart from all the other stuff she did . . . You? Tell a lie? You couldn't if your life depended on it."

"Listen, telling the truth isn't always the best strategy either, remember," admitted Petra, recollecting the many, many times her big mouth had got her into trouble.

"You tell it like it is, and you couldn't be less like Henrietta if you tried," said Ross firmly. "Thank goodness."

"Gosh, clever me then," she deadpanned. "By the time we get

to September I'll either be in sole charge of the known universe or expired from stress and exhaustion."

Flo told Petra there was no time in living memory—and that included hers, which amounted to a *very* long time—that Capelthorne's was closed on a Saturday. Everyone agreed, though, that for Jules and Roman's post-wedding party, closure was essential. Petra had offered to cover the shop so Flo could go, but Jules was having none of it. "You're part of the Capelthorne's family now," she told Petra. "You *have* to be there."

Petra and Ross agreed that she would stay in the flat the night before, just so she could work late and make sure all the admin was completely up to date. That way, if she didn't do much on Monday, she wouldn't fall too far behind. With Jules and Roman trusting her to keep their precious business running smoothly, the last thing she wanted to do is be seen taking her eye off the ball so soon after their return.

Petra had a late night working in the office, but then—despite no longer being used to sleeping alone—she slept soundly and woke late. With little to do until it was time for the party, she lay in bed enjoying the sunshine as it burned away an early mist, heralding another hot August day.

She had a bath and then ate toast and marmalade in her dressing gown—not trusting herself not to spill food or coffee on the precious silk dress.

Being a klutz, she put on the dress carefully and then—for extra security—tucked tissues into the neckline before she dared to put on her makeup. She wished, just that morning, that she had spent longer on YouTube and TikTok learning fancy makeup techniques. Her usual mascara with a slick of sheer red lipstick would have to do.

The green sandals she had bought were perfect, neat and pretty, making even Petra's big feet look dainty, she thought, checking out her reflection. All she could do with her jet black hair was scoop it up into a messy knot, fixing it with so many pins she hoped it would stay up all day and make her look a little more elegant and feminine than usual. The overall effect was so much less teen goth now that she had a light tan too.

Waiting nervously in the shop for Ross to appear, Petra felt bad seeing would-be customers reacting to the "closed" sign on the door. To be fair, they unanimously looked understanding on reading the reason why. Even the vacationers—who couldn't be expected to care what the locals were doing when they weren't providing a service—seemed to approve.

Weddings made people smile though, didn't they? The whole "happily ever after" thing . . . ? Even if it ended in divorce, years down the line, people still hoped for the best at the beginning. Failing to be optimistic that a couple might have a happy future felt like casting yourself as the bad fairy at the feast, cursing and condemning the happy couple to disaster. It was a bad omen. A self-fulfilling prophecy. Petra did *not* want to be the bad fairy today, she decided, plastering on a grin and practicing making elegant, inconsequential small talk with whatever strangers she was going to encounter.

Just then, Ross knocked sharply on the glass door, making her jump and then scurry to let him in, closing the door rapidly for fear a determined customer should take the opportunity to sidle in behind him.

"Why were you standing there grinning and talking to yourself?" he enquired.

"I—er—just acting out a scene," she burbled. "From *The Tempest*. I was curious whether I could still remember the lines."

"You never told me you acted in *The Tempest*," he said.

"No? Well, I haven't told you absolutely everything about my life before we met," she replied. "It would take too long, for one thing . . . plus, quite a lot of it is fairly boring."

"Yes, but *The Tempest*," he persevered. "Who did you play? Were you Miranda?"

"Actually, no," Petra admitted. "I was Caliban."

Ross put back his head and laughed.

"Why are you only telling me this now?" he asked, giving another incredulous laugh.

"Ooh, I don't know, maybe it's because I thought you might laugh?" she snarked, scowling at his mirth.

"How did it even happen?" he asked, still chuckling. "Hardly typecasting."

"What can I say!?" she told him defensively. "It was an all-girl's school, and I was five foot nine at fourteen."

"So you're pretty well qualified for critiquing this novel of mine. You are a fount of intrigue, woman, no wonder I love you so much. And I especially love you in this dress," he drawled, pulling her toward him and leaning down for a kiss.

"You do?" said Petra, smiling for real now and melting into him for a long, slow, gentle kiss that set up a wholly disconcerting ache of longing in her core.

"I do," he said, his lips pressed against hers, his words buzzing against her mouth.

"*Well*," she said, leaning back at last to study him, "I think you're looking pretty good yourself. In your skirt . . ." she added teasingly.

"Not a skirt," he reprimanded, the corner of his mouth quirking up despite his efforts to repress a smile.

Ross was wearing a fitted black jacket with polished silver buttons and—the big shock—a green-and-black kilt, complete with sporran. He didn't even look a complete idiot, she was pleased to see. In fact, he wore it very well indeed, she decided, looking him up and down. The kilt beautifully showcased his narrow hips and muscular legs, and the severe black jacket over a white shirt complemented his chiseled jaw and flopping forelock of hair.

"I like . . ." Petra murmured.

"Seemed a shame not to give the McCloud tartan an outing," he told her, sounding self-conscious. "Why don't we take a moment, or maybe longer, for a private appreciation of each other's attributes and—if you're lucky—I might even show you what a Scotsman wears under his kilt," he proposed, with an eyebrow raise. "We can always join the party later. Will they even miss us?"

Petra groaned. God, it was tempting. But they couldn't. It would be so rude. "They *might* notice," she said regretfully. "Actually, it's a sit-down lunch, so they will *definitely* notice. Come on, I can see the taxi waiting."

Sweeping around the circular gravel drive to the front of the house—a mansion, really, thought Petra—she wished they were traveling in a vehicle more salubrious and appropriate to the setting than Terry and his taxi from the railway station.

Women were wearing hats, Petra realized in horror—sweeping, swooping, feathered concoctions in a riot of colors and shapes. She suddenly felt her head was as shockingly underdressed as she would be if she had forgotten to put her knickers on.

"Hats!" she rasped to Ross. "Why were we not told about hats?"

"They look ridiculous," observed Ross, giving Petra a comforting squeeze. "You're fine. I just hope I can have a pint and that they don't just want us all to drink champagne," he muttered, as multiple neat-uniformed staff shepherded guests not toward the house's grand front door, but to a gate that led to the rear of the house.

Here, Ross and Petra found themselves in a slow-moving queue of people who all seemed to know each other, if the calls of "over here!" and "hello there!" were anything to go by. The focus of the queue, Petra could see by bending to look down the line, was a huddle of six people, first Jules and Roman themselves, then an older couple who Petra assumed were Roman's parents. The woman, a neat, spry, elegant brunette in an immaculately cut dress and coat of ice blue, was greeting guests charmingly with lots of air-kissing. Roman's father, a bluff, red-faced man with plentiful swept-back hair, largely gray, was booming welcomes so loudly Petra could hear every word. Craning even farther, she could see that Flo was bringing up the rear in a neat, flowery turquoise dress that looked like vintage sixties, which Petra suspected Flo would have owned from new. She smiled to see that Digger had taken up his usual position, lying heavily and contentedly across Flo's feet. Finally, beyond Flo and Digger was a grumpy-looking middle-aged woman in a purple dress. Jules's mother, Petra assumed.

"Heyyy," exclaimed Roman, when they got to him at last. "Loving this, er . . ." He gestured at Ross's attire.

"It's a skirt," Petra jumped in mischievously, before Ross had a chance to answer.

"We've put you guys at the same table as Freya and Jess and the crowd," Jules confided in Petra's ear when she leaned in for an air-kiss that turned into a hug, "but I'll introduce you to a load more fun people when I manage to escape from this conveyor-belt hell."

Staff in black with crisp white-cotton aprons were greeting guests with trays of drinks as they were funneled into the main garden in the back of the house. It seemed to go on for miles, thought Petra, gazing around. There was a huge central lawn, striped like a rugby sweater and studded with mature trees that provided welcome shade—the sun was fierce now. Clusters of brightly dressed women reminded Petra of parakeets, chirping and chattering, while somber gray-suited men stood by, looking bored. Gazing into the distance, Petra could see her and Ross's hill. Despite the danger of that night, she still saw it as their place. Their happy place. She wished she was there, alone with Ross, right now.

As if she had spoken aloud, Ross turned to hand her a glass of champagne and caught her eye.

"Hey," he said. "It's all good, right?"

"'Course!" she replied, summoning a wide smile. "Isn't this stunning?"

An enormous cream canvas party tent, pointed like a circus tent, had been erected to one side, partly shaded by a pair of mature oak trees. To the other side, Petra could see the ground sloping gently away to a tennis court and then to the cow-studded fields beyond. They had gravitated toward the shelter of an arbor twined with roses, jasmine, and honeysuckle. A gentle breeze wafted the scent of the sun-warmed flowers all around them and mingled it with the astringent, medicinal aroma of the rosemary bushes at their feet.

"Do you think we'll do all this one day?" asked Ross. "Would you like that?"

"Oof, no thanks," Petra shot back. "I'd rather elope."

Then she closed her eyes tight. *Whaaaat???* Had she seriously just assumed he meant a wedding? Like there weren't a hundred other reasons why people might have a party.

Ross put his head back and laughed. "I think my mum would have something to say about that," was all he said in reply, smiling down at her indulgently.

And so that was how it was first brought up, Petra thought as they stood companionably side by side and sipped their drinks. Could true love be as simple as that? Did it not have to be fraught and terrifying, and laced with drama? Petra honestly didn't know. What she *did* know was her kind, gentle, comfortable—yet still passionate—relationship with Ross felt better than any romantic entanglement she had ever had before. The potential future for this love, slipping naturally into conversation as if the discussion had already been had? So easy . . . inevitable, almost.

How complacent they had been, she thought later.

Seated at the table under the tent at last, Petra surveyed the scene. The noise level was rising as the wine flowed; the light filtering through the canvas was golden; the grassy smell of the sisal mat flooring mixed with the heady, honey scent of Flo's sweet peas. These were—in the end—an absolute triumph, despite Flo's anxiety. Each table had fistfuls—armfuls—of sweet pea blooms in low glass vases, a riot of purples and pinks—a simple generosity and abundance that summed up everything Petra had been drawn to in Portneath.

Of course, the table where Ross and Petra were seated for lunch was easily the most riotous, thought Petra, sitting back and smiling at Jules and Roman's friends—hers and Ross's friends now too.

Happy just to watch, with Ross catching hold of her hand under the table, she observed their interactions fondly as they bickered and teased, all so comfortable and assured. Petra wasn't used to being part of the cool crowd. Instead, she had always been the awkward goth child—too inclined to gloominess, the adults around her declared—always with her head in a book. Channeling that childhood obsession for stories and working hard enough to secure a toehold in publishing had felt like vindication for her sadly solitary childhood.

All the while, though, she had secretly longed for this. This group of friends made life look easy, even though she knew they worked hard and had their challenges. Really big stuff too. No, if life looked golden for this crowd, it was because they had the support of each other.

Chapter Twenty-Seven

The afternoon wore on with high spirits, inconsequential chatter, and delicious food. As coffee and petit fours were dispensed by the smiling but nigh invisible serving team, all eyes were turned to the head table. It might not be Jules and Roman's actual wedding day, but it seemed the tradition of speeches was going to be observed.

Roman's father stood first, declaring he was going to be brief and then droning on interminably. Standing in for Jules's father, he declared himself delighted with his new daughter-in-law and approving of his son's choices in this, at least, although jovial comments about being in competition with his son over business matters sounded more heartfelt than Petra thought he meant them to.

Petra was pretty sure he eventually wrapped up hurriedly because his pretty brunette wife with the kind brown eyes had given him a look. She warmed to him then. He may be full of bluster and self-importance, but it was touchingly clear that—actually—his gentle, sweet wife was the boss of him.

Roman was next and—even with Ross sitting beside her so handsome in his kilt—Petra's heart gave a little flutter at the sight of him: handsome, assured, and clearly deeply in love with Jules, who beamed up at him all the while.

And then Jules indicated that she would like to speak, and Roman helped her to her feet, holding her protectively against him. He handed her the microphone, pretending to be alarmed at what she might say, eliciting nervous giggles from the crowd.

"Like all my favorite romances," Jules began, "our story was a classic 'enemies to lovers'—my favorite trope. Much has been made of our names and our families—the whole Romeo and Juliet *thang* . . ." She paused for a comic beat. "Hilarious."

There was a wave of gentle laughter.

"But!" she continued more briskly, "I would like to think Roman and I took that tragic tale and turned it on its head—I mean, thank goodness, right?" she asked the crowd. "Double teen suicide versus happily ever after? It's time to change the narrative. So? Roman isn't my Romeo, he's my Mr. Rochester. He's my decent, principled, brave, sometimes grumpy storybook hero . . ." she made a face at him, "and I love him. And he loves me. So maybe Capelthorne's is our own Thornfield Hall? You know what? There was even a fire in our story too, now that I think about it—" She scratched her chin, in a parody of thought.

"But hardly any mad wives in the attic, honest," Roman quipped into the microphone.

"Nope, no mad ex-partners lurking," Jules agreed, joining in the laughter, "but maybe that's just because you don't know me well enough—yet . . ." she quipped in sepulchral tones.

And then Jules was serious, turning back to Roman and taking his hand. "I *know* you, Roman Montbeau. You are a good, kind, loyal man, who I am certain Charlotte Brontë—a supremely gifted writer of romantic heroes—would approve of." She turned to the crowd, "And *this* story definitely has a happy ending because," she paused for a beat, "reader, I married him."

The crowd good-naturedly cheered again, even though most of them had been denied the chance to see it for themselves.

"Yeah, and she definitely did the marrying bit first," interjected Roman over the last of the cheers. "I just want to get that in, before this other thing . . ."

And then Jules, with her hand on her gently swollen belly, broke the news about the baby, sounding a little nervous, Petra thought. But the noisy cheering, applause, and outbreak of joyous chatter must have reassured her that the guests were nearly as excited as she and Roman about the wonderful things next year held in store.

How lovely, thought Petra, wiping away a tear. Seeing it, Ross handed her his napkin and squeezed her waist as she dried her eyes, laughing at herself.

Happily ever after . . . wasn't that what everyone longed for? For the first time in her life, it even occurred to her that she might have found hers at last, here in this beautiful place, with these wonderful people.

Maybe next summer this would be her and Ross.

Maybe.

Next morning, Petra woke in the gray light of dawn with a lurch of panic. She consciously calmed herself, settling back into Ross's arms and matching her breathing to his, slow and steady . . . Ross was nothing if not a sound sleeper. He could certainly sleep for them both, which was great because Petra's sleep could be ruined by the tiniest thing. She had decided Ross's propensity for near coma-level sleep—even if there was a battle raging all around him—was admirable. Impressive even.

But also, deeply annoying.

She put her hand over her racing heart, stifling a groan of frustration. She tried to tell herself it was excitement, but the fear over her return to the literary scene was unconfined now that the distraction of Jules and Roman's party was over.

Now all that was done. And the inaugural festival was kicking off with the big "Ross reveal" in just four days.

Petra carefully disentangled herself from Ross and the bedclothes and sat up, looking down anxiously to check that she had not woken him. But, of course, she hadn't.

It may be Sunday, and she dearly hoped Jules and Roman were having a well-deserved lie-in, but she knew that Jess would be absolutely losing it fretting about what needed to be done to put the final arrangements into place.

Petra would call her and suggest breakfast.

If nothing else, she and Jess could stress about it all together.

Ross WAS LYING in bed awake looking tousled and extremely desirable when Petra came back out of the bathroom after a hasty shower.

"It's the weekend," he drawled. "Come back to bed?" He held up the covers enticingly, but Petra refused to engage.

"You stay in bed all day, sleepyhead," she chided. "I've got breakfast with Jess at our café. She needs a morale-boosting bacon sandwich."

"The festival?"

Petra nodded. "You nervous?"

"Nope," said Ross instantly. "I would be, but I've got this fab agent handling *every*thing for me."

"So I hear," said Petra. "Why get a dog then bark yourself?" But she was smiling when she left the cottage, promising to bring him back one of the café's breakfast buns—essentially a full English breakfast stuffed into a brioche, a heart-stopping concoction, but with a legendary status as Portneath's best hang-over cure.

"I THINK I should have made that last one a decaf," admitted Petra, setting her third mug of strong coffee back on the table with a tremor that set it reverberating onto the Formica table of the greasy spoon like a kettle drum. She was wide awake now, so at least there was that.

Jess, spearing the final bit of her eggs Benedict muffin and using it to mop up the last of her hollandaise sauce, seemed irritatingly calm by comparison, Petra thought.

"It's all basically fine," she told Petra. "We've sold a good number of tickets for all the events now—I'm glad we kept it small-ish this year—and all our participants have their accommodation lined up. I'm so glad Candida Bertolli is bunking up with Flo. I know she'll be spoiled rotten, which she seems to need, if my friend who did a book tour with her is anyone to go by."

"Is she a monster?" asked Petra understandingly.

"Wouldn't go that far—actually, scrap that—yes, she's a monster. And how about our launch panel mystery guest, how is he this morning? Not that *he's* a monster," she added, apparently hearing how the juxtaposition had sounded.

"Still in bed, having a lovely lie-in," reported Petra. "I think he's okay. I'd be terrified. Actually, I think I *am* terrified, on his behalf."

"When are you going to set off the fireworks?" asked Jess.

Petra knew Jess was keen to get the story out there. It was the jewel in the crown of the whole festival, having Ross come out of the shadows as its star turn.

"Soon," she reassured Jess. "Timing is critical, our publicist says. You've had the draft release from her?"

"From that Louise lady?" replied Jess. "Yes. It looks fine to me. I've signed off on it."

"Me too. First thing tomorrow, *The Bookseller*, Society of Authors, and all the national newspaper literary editors are informed and given an invitation to the launch," said Petra, with a confidence she didn't feel.

Once it was out, it was out, and then her real job—supporting and protecting Ross from the fierce, overwhelming interest—would begin. It was her job to harness that interest and turn it into a stunning offer. It was going to be like reaping the whirlwind. Or harnessing an earthquake.

Petra hadn't even read it all herself yet because there was still no final chapter. Most evenings, she had been casting an eye over the pages Ross had edited that day. The ending—the final fate of Miranda and Caliban—was still missing, but that didn't matter. It was brilliant. She reckoned she could sell it on Ross's reputation plus a concept written on the back of a cigarette packet alone, just like Alistair said.

So why did she have this vile sense of unease?

Louise, the publicist, messaged Petra almost as soon as the release went out, but she needn't have bothered, because Petra's phone had already started to ring.

First, it was *The Bookseller*, the trade magazine for UK publishing. *Publishers Marketplace* in the US called too, which didn't surprise her, knowing Ross's first book had sold more in the US and Canada than in any other market worldwide.

In fact, her phone rang all day. All these conversations were brief as Petra politely and regretfully explained. Yes, Ross was going to be headlining the Portneath Literary Festival, yes, there would be a chance for press to ask questions. No, they would not be offering an exclusive. Blanket coverage was the aim. Yes, there was a manuscript—well, there was a sample of a manuscript, at this stage—yes, she would be inviting offers, naturally . . .

And, of course, the acquisition editors had been emailed too. It was no time at all before individual editors started to call. It wasn't the junior staff members who were calling Petra either, even though these were usually the ones Petra liaised with. Instead, it was the great silverbacks in the top five publishers, the publishing directors in charge of multiple imprints and serious money. If they felt that they were lowering themselves by calling little old Petra, they were polite enough not to show it.

Relating stories of her day to Ross later, she was hyperaware of his body language. Where he would normally lounge on the sofa beside her, idly stroking her hair as she lay with her head on his lap, this evening he sat bolt upright, hand clutching the sofa arm like a claw, determined—it seemed—to keep an inch of distance between them.

"So, who else?" he kept saying, as she ran him through the names—big names—although he seemed sweetly unaware of just exactly how much of a big deal these people were.

"Anyone else?" he said, as she reached the end of her litany.

"Um . . . I don't think so. I mean—I'm pretty sure it's everyone who's anyone—"

"Are you *sure*?"

This was getting weird. "Was there someone in particular . . . ?" she queried gently, but Ross looked away.

"Nope," he said. "No one at all . . ." As if she had reminded him of something, he reached for his phone and switched it to silent before staring, apparently unseeing, into the middle distance. And then he seemed to snap back into gear. "Bloody well done," he said. "I knew you'd be brilliant at this. And Petra?"

She looked at him enquiringly.

"Thank you. I mean it." He reached out his hand and captured her own, bringing it up to his lips for a kiss. "Whatever happens . . ." he added vaguely.

"Mixing business and pleasure?" she teased and then wished she had kept her mouth shut.

His eyes went dull, just for a moment, and then he summoned a smile with visible effort. "Your pleasure *is* my business," he said, pulling her over onto his lap.

"But his first publisher is the one best placed to build on his existing readership," Alistair made his point. "You know that."

"They have to offer the best package too, though," Petra replied. "And she's not even called so far. Plus, I happen to know Ross is keen for a fresh start."

"Of course," said Alistair, "I get that. But, like it or not, Henrietta is one of the key players in the industry, even more so than she was when she worked with Ross the first time. Are you *sure* he wouldn't work with her again?"

Petra wasn't. How could she be?

"He has to be allowed to choose for himself," she told Alistair firmly. She knew already there would be plenty of contenders. "Plus, I just think it's important to go to all the players equally," she told Alistair. "It's been a long gap, you know how it is . . ."

"I do," said Alistair, "but—don't forget—it's your job to advise him on where *you* feel his best option lies, when the proposals are in, so I hope you won't shy away from recommending his previous team, if they represent the best deal."

"I'll tell it like it is," Petra promised her mentor. And she would. She wanted the best for Ross, whatever that looked like.

Over the next couple of days, she and Jess were frantically busy racing around Portneath. Not to say it was just them, though; they were directing their brilliant team of volunteers, who consisted of most of the Beach Reads Book Club and Write Club. There were several venues, each with their own logistical challenges. The main stage, which was where Ross's Q & A was happening, was in the beautiful town hall, a stunning Regency building with a colonnaded front. This, Flo had told Petra, was where Freya and Finn had had their wedding breakfast.

Used to the venue being hired out for functions, the events organizer there was not remotely fazed by Petra wanting a raised stage area, microphones, a decent sound system, whiteboard, and projector. Petra was terribly nervous that something fundamental would go wrong, and the event would go down in bookish history as the worst festival ever. Not that she was going to be doing any more of them. Jules's baby would be born, and her maternity leave would be over before autumn next year. If she tanked the Portneath Literary Festival at its first outing, at least she would not be here to explain its absence the following year.

She would be long gone by then.

Whether it was late-onset nerves or something deeper and more mysterious, Petra and Ross were unnaturally polite to each other as they moved around the kitchen in the cottage making supper, apologizing if they bumped, and having ridiculous "you first, no *you* first" interchanges over everything.

Later, sitting in front of the fire with bowls on their knees, Petra could barely swallow her vegetable chili. It was usually her favorite, and Ross had even taken the trouble to make fresh guacamole, which was even better than the stuff from Finn's deli.

"Is it okay?" Ross asked her anxiously, as she put down her bowl only half eaten.

"Great, thanks," said Petra, making the effort to smile. "The guac's amazing. I'm just not that hungry tonight."

Ross sighed. "Me either," he said, picking up Petra's bowl and getting up to take them both into the kitchen.

Listening to him loading the dishwasher, hearing the regular domestic chores that she usually found so comforting, Petra found herself biting back tears. What on earth was the matter with her? The submission concept had gone to editors, and she had invited them to express interest. Tomorrow, the full submission package would go out to those who had requested it, and they would have a further couple of days to prepare their bids. She was poised to launch into the most spectacular submission round of her entire career. The man she adored was about to achieve a deal on a stunning new novel, and *she* was going to help him do it. She had work in Portneath for at least the next few months, with time off for the Frankfurt Book Fair already agreed upon. She ought to be happier than she had ever been in her life! Sure, she thought, the next few days were going to be stressful, but in a hugely exciting and productive way. This depression she was feeling? It was a projection. From Ross.

"You *have* to tell me," she demanded when he sat back down after handing her a mug of tea she hadn't asked for. She hadn't needed to, he knew her so well.

"Don't know what you mean," he tried unconvincingly.

"Yes. You do," she insisted. "*What's wrong?*"

"You haven't told me whether any of the other imprints on the submission list contacted you today," he said, apparently changing the subject.

"Yes, I have," she insisted firmly. "I sent you the spreadsheet, with all the up-to-date notes. And you opened it. I got a read receipt."

"So you did," he said quietly. "So you did," he said again, more loudly. "And it was good, right?"

"It was *great*!" Petra said. "And the festival is going to go great too. Right? Right," she answered herself. She waited for him to respond, but there was nothing.

"Now, let's go to bed," she said. "We need to be wide awake and on it tomorrow."

Chapter Twenty-Eight

Every time Petra had a spare minute while she raced around Portneath, she would pop into Capelthorne's.

As soon as the wedding party was over, Roman and Jules had taken over the reins in the shop so that Petra could focus on the festival, but she felt compelled to check in, terrified that—by now—Roman would have spotted some terrible blunder that would cause them to belatedly regret ever getting her involved.

It was mainly Roman she was dealing with, but Jules had also insisted on rolling up her sleeves. She was unable to hide that her early pregnancy was leaving her hopelessly exhausted and queasy. Consequently, Roman was usually in the shop, with Jules resting upstairs in the flat, padding down in her socks every five minutes to see if Roman needed another pair of hands at the front desk, or if he wanted her to make him a cup of tea.

This morning, though, it was Jules she encountered. On seeing Petra, she immediately jumped up and insisted Petra sit down for a coffee and one of the cinnamon buns Roman had fetched from Finn's shop earlier.

"*Love* the Beach Reads Book Club," Jules told Petra, as they sat down with their coffee, which—for Jules—was actually peppermint tea. "Eating helps with the nausea," she explained cheerfully through a large mouthful of cinnamon bun. "So I understand it's a spin-off from the Portneath Book Club, right? That must have been an exciting coup to watch. Who started it?"

"Diana," admitted Petra, causing Jules to burst into laughter.

"Why am I not surprised." She giggled. "That woman could start a fight in an empty house."

"I was terrified it was going to be war," admitted Petra.

"Small town life," explained Jules. "What you'll learn is everyone *has* to have an opinion about everything. It's the law. And even the smallest thing is life and death too. Every. Single. Time."

"Horrible?" ventured Petra.

Jules laughed again, shaking her head. "At first it's a bit alarming," she admitted. "But you learn not to mind."

"In London people just bitch behind each other's backs. Here . . . I dunno. People—people like Diana at least—are braver, I suppose. Bolder."

"Portneath changes everyone," mused Jules. "It's the security of belonging, I think . . . So Diana can be a pain in the arse," she explained, "but she's *our* pain in the arse. And she makes things happen too. Good things, on the whole."

Petra nodded soberly. If she had learned one thing from her sabbatical here, maybe it was "*be more Diana*."

"And love. Love does that too," mused Jules. "I'm bolder and braver than I once was," she observed dreamily, stuffing in another huge mouthful of cinnamon bun, chewing ecstatically. "The baby wants it," she explained to Petra, wiping her sticky fingers on her napkin. "Everyone loves you," she went on. "You *and* Ross. You fit in."

Petra said nothing, not wanting Jules to notice that tears had sprung to her eyes at her words of praise and acceptance. After a lifetime of feeling like she had her nose pressed to the glass, watching everyone else with their busy, fulfilling lives, with their friends and their careers and their lovers . . . here in Portneath she had all of these things.

Life was good.

Suddenly, her phone vibrated, shimmying its way across the table.

Jules caught it just before it threw itself on the floor and handed it to Petra. "Jess in a flap?" she suggested, glancing at the screen.

"I can't find the folder with the VIP hotel reservations," Jess blurted as soon as Petra greeted her.

"That's because you left it in the office when we were going through the ticket sales numbers last night," Petra told her soothingly. "Why don't I drop it at the reception desk at The Swan later, and you can pick it up from there, when you meet them for dinner, right?"

"Oh, thank God, that would be amazing," Jess told her. "Urgh, yes, dinner is terrifying. I tried to get Aiden to come too, but he just threatened to put on an impenetrable Devon accent and lecture them about ash dieback all night."

Petra laughed. As a tree surgeon, Aiden knew everything there was to know about ash dieback, but he was also extremely knowledgeable about many other subjects and definitely didn't talk with an impenetrable local accent. "It's because he's got faith in you, and so have I," said Petra. "You'll be great."

She would offer to help Jess herself, but her mission that evening was to make sure that Ross was mentally on track for his big day tomorrow. The nerves about coming back out into the open seemed to be getting to him. At least she had to assume that's what it was.

In the end, it was hours before she got a chance to walk the file over to the hotel. Setting off at last, she saw it was a balmy, golden summer's evening. The sun was dipping down low on the horizon now, casting its glowing rays across the broad, flat sands of low tide, where sheets of sitting water reflected the sky, and the rippled sand gave the appearance of wavelets frozen into stillness until the sea returned to free them.

Petra tilted back her head, closing her eyes and basking in the warmth on her face, Jess's missing file binder under her arm. The Swan Hotel was on the far side of the footbridge that crossed the river mouth and as she walked across, feeling as if she was suspended between sea and sky, she recalled walking across this very bridge as night fell on the January day she arrived. Who was that young woman? Stressed, lonely, frightened . . . She could hardly remember. What she *could* remember was her first meeting with Ross, the bit where she faceplanted on the railway platform and then tried to press money into his hand.

"What are you smiling at?" came a warm, deep, familiar voice.

She opened her eyes, and there he was. Ross. Standing before her in silhouette, in front of the setting sun.

"Just thinking what a fool I made of myself the day we met," she told him, as he linked arms with her and turned back the way he had come. "What are you doing down here?" she asked, falling into step with him so naturally it was as if they had been doing it their entire life. "I thought you were up at the cottage. I was going to come up as soon as I delivered this." She showed him the folder.

"Jess told me," he explained. "I thought I'd meet you and buy you supper. It'll do us both good to have a square meal, whether we feel like it or not. I bet you haven't eaten since this morning."

He looked down at her, eyebrows raised, and she ducked her head. "You've got me," she admitted. It had been a very long time since her cinnamon bun with Jules. "And—you're right—I'm starving!" she said, delighted to see him apparently relaxed and happy again at last. Whatever the issue had been, it appeared to be resolved. "I'm going to have sweet potato fries and mayonnaise and a huge glass of viognier," she told him happily. "And garlic bread. And sticky toffee pudding."

"Hmm. Carbs with your carbs?" he chuckled. "Good thinking. I'm in, although I reckon I'll have to roll you back up the hill to bed."

"Listen, don't appetite-shame me," said Petra, jabbing her finger into his biceps. "Remember I know *all* about the potato chip sandwiches and the full English breakfast buns."

"True," admitted Ross. "You know so many of my secrets now, I'm either going to have to kill you or marry you."

"Ha!" said Petra, a little too loudly, just to show she *totally* knew that what he had just said was a joke. Until he was prepared to propose to her properly, she was determined not to jump to conclusions.

It was a relief to push through the heavy oak double doors at The Swan, escaping the slight chill of the breeze on the seafront. Petra was immediately enveloped in the quiet luxury of low lighting, wooden paneling, and thick carpets that muffled the sound.

She shivered at the sudden warmth, and Ross put an arm around her shoulders.

"Cold? Have my sweater."

"I'm fine," protested Petra.

But he was already taking off his moss green cashmere sweater, light and soft as gossamer. "Just have it around your shoulders," he cajoled, tying it around her neck for her as if she were a toddler.

Petra had learned, to her amusement, that although Ross could look like a scruff, in truth all his clothes were the quiet, unbranded luxury only truly affluent people wear. It wasn't surprising. That first novel had made serious money in translation sales alone. His second novel would be considered a failure if it did less well than the first, even if it was one of the fastest-selling books that year. Such was the curse of the second novel for anyone who had hit the jackpot first time around.

"It'll be fine," Ross said, seeing the anxiety on her face.

"I'm supposed to be settling *your* nerves," Petra said apologetically.

"Drink at the bar before dinner?" he asked.

A large reception area with low, comfortable sofas grouped companionably also incorporated a long, backlit bar with smoky mirrored glass reflecting what had to be the most comprehensive gin selection anywhere in Portneath. Or possibly the whole of Devon.

The room was humming gently with the chatter of people enjoying predinner drinks.

"Actually yes," Petra told Ross. "Good idea. Jess is nervous about her guests. We can lurk and see how things are going as they walk through."

"Sounds like a plan," said Ross. "As long as we don't have to eat with them. I want you all to myself. Dirty martini?"

Ross settled Petra on a deep, squashy velvet sofa with a view of the sunset, which was painting the bay every shade of pink, red, and orange.

Gazing at the view, Petra nearly forgot she was supposed to be spying on Jess and her guests, but then she saw her leading three people up the esplanade to the hotel. Thankfully, Petra noted, Aiden had been persuaded to provide support after all. It looked like he was behaving at his most charming too, with a tall, skinny woman on his arm who had huge dark glasses obscuring most of her face. Petra observed her curiously. She looked forbiddingly perfect, with her endless legs, a clearly expensive black-and-white-striped trouser suit worn with a cropped leather jacket, and a slash of perfectly applied scarlet lipstick. Against the background of breezy, informal Portneath, she looked predatory and sophisticated, with her short dark hair swept back to reveal impressively jutting cheekbones.

Jess had mentioned managing to line up a powerful editorial director, plus a literary agent—who Petra knew vaguely—for their panel discussion with Ross tomorrow. The idea was that they—an author, an agent, and a publisher—would talk about the state of the publishing industry.

The agent, who Petra recognized walking alongside Jess, was a kind, serious man in his sixties, longtime friends with Alistair, Petra knew. The woman must therefore be the editor, Petra thought, chastising herself that she should really know the woman's name. She had been so distracted by all the other arrangements . . . the whole opening session of the festival had been firmly on Jess's "to do" list, not Petra's.

No matter, Jess would introduce them all soon enough. Clearly Jess was doing a fine job, Petra thought, as she and her party came into reception, chatting happily.

Reassured that all was going well, Petra ducked her head down and turned away. Perhaps she and Ross could just pop over to Jess's table for coffee after everyone had eaten, she decided. That would be friendly and supportive without having to give up her quiet, intimate dinner, which was something she thought they both needed.

Jess and Aiden ushered their two guests straight into the restaurant as Petra watched. They had disappeared by the time Ross walked back to her with a dirty martini in each hand, but Petra briefed him on her coffee after dinner plan.

Ross nodded. "We could do that," he agreed. "I suppose we mustn't have too much fun."

"Busy, busy," admitted Petra. "Once the festival's done, you won't be able to get rid of me."

"Good," said Ross, holding up his glass in salute. "To us!" he declared.

"And to the book," added Petra. "God bless her, and all who sail in her."

By the time they were ushered through to the restaurant, Petra was feeling liquid limbed with the deep relaxation brought on by sun, sea air, and a decent slug of neat vodka. Wine with dinner was going to totally tip her over the edge, she thought, as the waitress led them to their table. Ross pulled out her chair and, as she sat, Petra caught Jess's eye across the room and smiled, giving her a discreet thumbs-up. She was just turning away to find her napkin, when there was a cry, cutting through the polite chatter and clinking cutlery. There was a surge of movement from Jess's table, catching Petra's eye.

"Rossie!" hailed the scary woman with the scarlet lipstick, as she reared to her full height.

Oh God, thought Petra, she was coming over. Damn it! So much for her quiet dinner with Ross. And another thing, why the hell was this woman—this stranger—calling him "Rossie"? Hadn't Ross told her that nobody called him that?

Petra glanced up toward the still-standing Ross, but her hoped-for explanation would not be forthcoming. Instead, her heart froze in her chest to see his face had gone pale beneath his tan and was entirely without expression except for a tiny muscle beating in his jaw.

By now, scarlet lips had reached them and was performatively kissing Ross squarely on the mouth, before running her finger suggestively down his chest.

Ross reached up, still dead-eyed, and wiped a smear of scarlet lipstick off his face. "Hello, Henrietta," he said quietly.

"Seriously? *Hello*?" Henrietta pouted, wagging her finger at him coquettishly. "You disappear off the face the earth, you don't answer my messages, and—after all that—you just say *Hello*?" she chided. And then she put her head on one side, like a raptor regarding its prey. "You know what, Rossie?" she said. "I'm not even angry with you. You're a creative. You're special. I'll forgive you everything, because now we're both here together again, and that's all that matters . . ."

"What do you want, Henrietta?" said Ross, seemingly calm, although Petra thought she could discern a tiny tremble in the hand nearest her face as she sat beside him. Something stopped her from reaching up and grasping it. Instead, she glanced across at Jess, who was still sitting at the table with Aiden and the literary agent, all three of them staring over at the scene with curiosity but no apparent alarm.

"What do I want?" Henrietta cooed, echoing Ross's question. "Well, a little bird told me you would be here, and so I just thought you and I should—perhaps—have a little catch-up, shall we say?"

"It wasn't a little bird," said Ross evenly, "it was a press announcement, but I am here to talk to the public and to the media. I'm not ready to talk to editors yet, and—even if I was—I would expect all communications of that nature to be managed through my agent."

"But, darling," Henrietta seemed stupefied, "this is me. This is *us*," but then she gave a mirthless laugh. "You want to play with—how would you put it, with your funny little sports analogies—with 'a straight bat'?"

Ross gave a curt nod.

"How very *you*." Henrietta chuckled, as if Ross had said something extraordinarily endearing. "Well, of course, I would fully expect your agent to be consulted in these matters, but—if you have something to sell . . ."

Here, Petra saw Henrietta lick her lips, clearly salivating at the thought. It was a nearly reptilian flick of the tongue, accompanied by a shrewd hardening of her expression. Immediately Petra knew who Henrietta reminded her of. It was like watching Cruella de Vil drooling at the sight of puppies.

". . . and, in any case," Henrietta was continuing, "you can't deny our special relationship transcends any silly business issues like agents and contracts. *Plus,* darling," she went on, running her finger down his cheek, "I am given to believe you no longer have any recognizable representation, which is a situation *easily* remedied. I happen to have an in with Henry Atherstone, no less . . ."

Henrietta gave Ross a moment to express his awe and amazement at this. Which he did not.

Petra—on the other hand—was more daunted than offended at being dismissed as unrecognizable. Henry Atherstone dealt with the biggest writer names in the business. His acumen and heft were legendary, and she had lost clients to him before. Ross would be insane not to take up the opportunity, she realized with a breathtaking wave of grief at the thought. She dragged her eyes to Ross's, dreading his response.

"That is kind but unnecessary," Ross was telling Henrietta, still with that level, quiet, dangerous tone. "I am more than adequately represented by Petra here. Please allow me . . ."

He gestured to Petra, who shot out of her chair and held her hand out to Henrietta, almost as if she had been electrocuted into action.

Henrietta studied Petra's hand suspiciously and then diverted her gaze to assessing Petra from head to toe, her expression indicating she was entirely unimpressed with what she saw. And then, something dawned, and a sickly, patronizing smile spread across her face.

"Little Miss Malaprop, no less," she sneered. "The woman who broke the internet 'bigging up' her clients." Hatefully, Henrietta used the air quotes gesture to express her opinion of Petra's talents, or lack of.

"Darling, it's important you and I talk about this manuscript of yours before anything else happens that can't be undone," she continued briskly, pointedly turning her back on Petra, who had by now dropped her hand back down to her side, "and—by all means—show our contract to—" She glanced at Petra disparagingly, but seemed unable to produce a label of any sort, settling for a dismissive hand gesture. "Before you sign anything . . . but this is just little old me." She widened her eyes in a parody of innocence.

It looked grotesque, thought Petra. Surely the woman no longer held any power over him? Did she?

"Darling, remember who I am to you," purred Henrietta. "Remember what we have, you and I."

"Had," corrected Ross.

Henrietta's face fell for a microsecond, followed by a flash of anger, and then she regained her savoir faire. "Ross," she said more firmly, like a labrador owner calling her recalcitrant dog to heel, "I don't know what's been going on with you, and I don't know what—*this*—is all about," she waved contemptuously at Petra. "If you want to reestablish yourself in the literary world, then let me be clear: You. Need. Me. I made you, and I . . ." She gave him a forbidding look and then glanced again at Petra. "I *made* you," she repeated, raising an eyebrow and nodding at him meaningfully.

Her inference was clear: She made him. She could destroy him.

LATER THAT NIGHT, Petra would replay this conversation on a loop in her mind's eye. It seemed to her that time—in that dining room—had slowed to a standstill. She was acutely aware of the interest of the other diners, the sweet sea breeze wafting gently in through the French window, bringing with it the smell of ozone and fresh air, mingling with the roasting meats and frying garlic emanating from the kitchen. And then, all her other senses seemed to fall away, and her entire universe was this single moment when Henrietta commanded Ross's obedience. Petra gazed up at Ross, and then at this woman who had had such power over Ross five years before. The woman who had done so much damage to him.

"Come to my room, my darling," murmured Henrietta, triumphant at something she perceived in Ross's face. "We have *so* much catching up to do."

Ross transferred his gaze with apparent effort from Henrietta to Petra, and the look of utter bleakness and despair made Petra gasp in pain. Wordlessly, she queried, but he just closed his eyes and gave her a tiny shake of the head.

"Let me . . ." he began quietly. "I need to . . ." he began again, but swallowed, apparently unable to continue, his eyes, fixed on Petra's face, full of pain and confusion.

Henrietta knew then that she had won, Petra told herself later. It was the moment when she tilted back her head and looked disparagingly at Petra from under lowered lids.

Feeling that hours had passed as Ross waited for her response, Petra gathered herself. It was the hardest thing she had ever done, but why compound the humiliation by making a scene? What would be the point in that?

"Of course," she said crisply, putting down her napkin. "You have my number, Ross. Call me when you need me."

"Don't hold your breath, darling," Henrietta snarked over her shoulder as she threaded her arm through Ross's and bore off her prize in the direction of the lifts. In her triumph she failed to even acknowledge Jess and her other dinner mates, who sat looking stupefied, much—Petra thought—as she must look herself.

For a very long time after Ross and Henrietta had left, Petra sat frozen, staring unseeing through the French windows and out to sea. For the first time since her very early days in Portneath, she felt bereft, alone, and very, very small.

Eventually, after what might have been just minutes but felt like a lifetime, Jess came over and made Petra join her, Aiden, and their guest for dinner. It was a convivial meal, considering, but—as she chatted and even joked—Petra felt she was observing herself at a distance, as if some other woman was asking sociable questions and making polite responses to the answers.

Chapter Twenty-Nine

It was karma, Petra told herself.

It was nearly midnight when she was finally able to escape and walk alone to the flat above the shop, because to go to the cottage was unthinkable. Out of habit rather than desire, Petra made tea. Waiting for the kettle to boil, staring unseeing out of the little kitchen window over the rooftops of Portneath, she shivered—as much from shock and fatigue as from the chill of the solitary walk home.

She tried hard not to picture Ross and Henrietta alone in her hotel room talking about—and doing—God knows what.

There was no message from him. She had sent a carefully worded text, just checking in—as a professional agent would when their client is talking to a top editorial director *without* their agent. She had her phone permanently in her hand, longing for the vibration of a response. Petra was trying hard to deny the observation that if a writer was meeting with an editor without their agent, then it was presumably to engage in an activity that the agent was not required to take part in, an activity that *wasn't* business . . . What else was she to assume?

Reflexively, Petra clapped her hand over her eyes and groaned aloud.

It was a shame Ross didn't think to check whether his heart and mind were truly free of Henrietta's malign influence before he allowed—even encouraged—Petra to fall in love with him, she thought, impatiently wiping away a tear. She tried to feel angry instead of devastated but lacked the energy.

And still there was no reply. She stared at her phone screen, watching the gray checkmarks for the moment they would turn blue, but there was nothing.

Why would she think she could offer professional support to a writer of Ross's standing? This Henrietta, although tonight was the first time Petra had met her, was one of the most powerful editors in the London publishing houses. She was the maker—and breaker—of careers. If she wanted a book, she would get it. If she publicly declined a book, then that manuscript would be forever tarnished in the eyes of the market. And a writer's reputation might never recover from being dropped by their publishing house. *Ross's* reputation might never recover.

Petra just wanted him to be happy and fulfilled, she realized bleakly.

Because she loved him.

And, unfortunately, his apparent rekindling of a relationship he had declared over didn't change that.

But she still had her professional duty to him, she told herself, straightening and pulling her shoulders back. As his agent, she had to advise him to tread with extreme caution. He may have no current contractual obligation, but a previous publishing imprint casts a long shadow, especially when the book has been a success. Even after five years, his second book could be argued to be a de facto Hamilton House book, or people would want to know the reason why not. There was nothing like a book being wanted by one publisher to make other publishers pay attention. And the reverse. Which was ironic, Petra reminded herself, as she waited for the kettle to boil. Readers would barely notice who had published a book. Why should they care?

It was a long night. At three in the morning, the checkmarks on her message to Ross turned blue.

At five in the morning came his reply.

I'm sorry.

Petra stared at it, adrenaline pumping so hard that the hand holding her phone jerked in time to her heartbeat.

She was relieved when the sun rose.

"Do YOU KNOW how many of our list requested to see it?" Alistair asked, when Petra—giving up on sleep—called him at eight o'clock that morning. "Would you *like* to know?"

"No," said Petra dully. "I mean, no, I don't know, and yes, I would like to know."

"All of them," he declared. "I don't think we've ever had that happen. Not with a list as extensive as this."

"When are you sending it out?" asked Petra, wondering when

her phone was going to start ringing. Wondering when she was going to have to start pretending to be a competent literary agent. She imagined she wouldn't have long before Ross told her he was switching to Henry Atherstone. She wanted to make the most of it while it lasted.

"Already gone," said Alistair. "Being read as we speak, I reckon. Stand by."

Petra told Alistair about Henrietta's claim and her fear she would not be representing Ross long enough to get the deal done.

"He won't go for Henry Atherstone," Alistair told her. "They're chalk and cheese. Also, Henry hasn't taken on a new client for years. Erase it from your mind."

"He took Isabella May from me just a few months ago," Petra reminded him, wincing at the memory of that appalling day.

"Apart from that," admitted Alistair. "And—let's face it—no great loss. Isabella was a nightmare."

"Talking of nightmares, what about this Henrietta woman who's got her claws into Ross again now?" asked Petra, unable to keep herself from prodding the open wound.

"That Henrietta's a piece of work," Alistair agreed, which didn't make Petra feel any better. "I could tell you some stories . . . And, the rumor is, she and Henry Atherstone are *very* close . . . if you get my meaning."

"You know you're not helping, don't you?" Petra told him dully.

"Good grief," said Jess, when Petra arrived at the Town Hall. "Did you sleep at all?"

Petra shook her head silently. She had even bothered with

makeup, getting ready in the silent flat that morning, but no amount of mascara and blusher could disguise her pallor, or her squinty, puffy, sleep-deprived eyes. All the crying hadn't helped either.

"Get yourself some coffee," suggested Jess sympathetically. "We're all set up. It's a sell-out, by the way."

"Yay!" responded Petra without energy.

"I thought you'd be bringing Ross," Jess added anxiously, looking behind Petra as if she might be concealing him. "Tell me he's on his way?"

Petra shrugged, furious with herself that Jess's innocent enquiry caused fresh tears to well up. She turned away, clearing her throat furiously. "He—he didn't come home last night."

Registering Jess's shock, Petra thought about relaying Ross's five a.m. message too, but she didn't seem to be able to make the words come out. What did his message even mean, anyway? "Sorry" for what? Sorry that he left her alone at dinner (rude)? Sorry that he was leaving her forever (devastating)?

Maybe he was now going to do a disappearing act for another five years. It wouldn't seem like the Ross she had gotten to know, to let people down. But did she ever really know him anyhow?

"He'll be there," she told Jess firmly. "Who else is on the panel again?"

Jess looked apologetic. "Um, well, there's lovely Gordon from last night," she said, and then Petra guessed the rest.

"Henrietta," she said.

"I had no idea," Jess told Petra miserably. "She was a last-minute replacement for a really quite junior editor who works on their crime imprint. I actually couldn't believe it when I got the message just yesterday that it was going to be Henrietta instead. I was thrilled to get someone so senior. I honestly had no idea she was Ross's editor before, or I would have said something."

Petra shrugged. A reply seemed pointless.

"Did she? Did they . . . ?" probed Jess, her face a mask of sympathy.

Petra shrugged again. She couldn't speak.

"Petra?" came a deep and familiar voice just behind her.

Great.

"Ross?" she said, turning. He looked—if it were possible—even worse than she did.

"Are you all right?" he asked.

"I don't know," Petra replied, unable to meet his eyes.

She was thankful when the guy Jess had found to do the techy stuff popped up and wanted to fit the three people taking part in the panel with microphones so he could do his sound checks.

At the other end of the room, he had already set up the projector that was showing the Portneath Literary Festival banner and logo.

Not long to go now. Just long enough for Jess to put in another call to Alistair, who—she noticed—had been trying to get through.

"We have a pre-empt," he announced without ceremony as soon as he answered.

"From?"

"Henrietta at Hamilton House."

"You. Are. Kidding," Petra said, angry now. That bloody woman! No wonder she was so confident she had a hold over Ross, even though he was *absolutely* not under contract to her.

"How much?" she asked warily.

When Alistair told her, it felt like someone had punched her in the stomach. She doubled over and then straightened, forcing herself to take a breath.

"That's ridiculous," she muttered.

"Yeah," said Alistair happily, "you don't see pre-empts like that these days."

"So we advise him to accept it then," said Petra. "Professionally, we can't say anything else, I imagine."

"You think?" Alistair replied. "Forget that, I reckon we hold out for an auction. Have you had any other editors contact you yet? They've all had the material since yesterday."

"No one's called me," she told him.

"That's because we asked them to email in the first instance."

Alistair waited on the phone patiently while Petra quickly logged in to her emails. She could picture him sitting at his broad oak desk, overlooking the bench in the London garden square where Petra had so often sat to eat her solitary lunchtime sandwich.

Riffling quickly through spam, Petra scanned and reported on several emails. "Okay, we've got another pre-empt offer," she said, "but it's much lower than—um, the other one," she found she couldn't say Henrietta's name, "and then there are several expressions of interest . . . What should I tell him?"

"*You're* his agent," Alistair reminded her, "but—okay—if it was me, I would advise him to hold out for an auction. Best bids by the end of the day. If you don't like what comes in, we can almost guarantee the pre-empt will still be on the table. It's a case of who blinks first."

It made sense. "The end of today, though?" she queried doubtfully. "That's very quick, isn't it? They have to consult . . ."

"I like to drum up a bit of urgency. We're talking directly to the top bods. And they only have the first three chapters and the concept to read," Alistair reminded her. "How long do they need?"

When Alistair had let her go, Petra took a deep breath and wiped away two more tears that seemed to have sprung to her eyes against her bidding. She would *not* cry in front of Ross, but there was no escaping speaking to him.

She found him pouring two cups of coffee from the thermos in the little anteroom put aside for VIP guests.

"I was just going to bring you a coffee," he said, busying himself with milk and little packets of sugar.

"I've had a pre-empt," she told him, steeling herself.

"Who from?"

This threw her. Surely it would have come out in the pillow talk she assumed he had been having. "From Henrietta," she said. "It's high."

"Should I take it?" he said, staring at the teaspoon on his saucer as if he had never seen one before.

So now he couldn't even look at her? Petra wanted to take the stupid spoon off his saucer and throw it out of the window. A little bit of wanton destruction might ease the boulder lodged in her chest.

"Up to you," she told him. "Alistair and I think you should hold out for an auction."

He still hadn't looked at her. Petra wasn't sure she could cope if he did.

"Then that's what we do," he told her.

Just then, the door flew open, and Henrietta entered in a flurry of designer tailoring and an oxygen-suckingly strong cloud of a musky, woody perfume that made Petra's head swim. Or maybe it was the sleep deprivation.

"Thank you, darling," she drawled, taking one of the coffee cups from Ross's hand. "I think they're ready for us." She gestured to the stage area, where Jess was standing anxiously watching the little trio as the audience for the opening session filed in and took their seats.

"Petra!" came a cry, and Petra turned to see Jemima—a friend from her London life all those millions of years ago. "I saw your name on the email. Representing Ross McCloud, eh?" said Jemima excitedly. "Wow! I mean, when I saw that, I had to come."

Petra duly returned Jemima's air-kiss. It was good to see her. Jemima was one of the good guys. She represented some of the better times from Petra's junior—very junior—editor days. Unlike Petra though, Jemima had progressed in accordance with her superb ability and was now something big at Penguin Random House.

"You mean, you came all this way because of our submission?" Petra asked, scanning the crowd to see if any other editors had done the same.

"Of *course,* I did," said Jemima, rather undermining her own assertion that she came because of Petra. "I'm hoping to acquire," she muttered, tapping the side of her nose. "Nothing like being on the spot to put a good word in."

It seemed that Jemima and Henrietta had that in common at least. In every other way, though, the two women could not have been more different. As an editor, Jemima ruled by consent. Her authors, Petra knew, felt supported and produced good books partly as a result. Henrietta? Not so much.

"It's okay to speak to Ross after this, right?" asked Jemima.

"Of course! I'll introduce you," said Petra rapidly, just before Jemima scurried to a seat. Jess, microphone at the ready, was stepping forward, and a hush descended.

PETRA BARELY HEARD a word of the panel discussion, she was so intent on watching the body language between Ross and Henrietta. The woman was basically unable to keep her hands off him. Every few seconds she laid her hand on his arm to make a point or approve of something he had said—not that he was talking much. At one point, Petra thought she was going to pat Ross on the head but instead took a piece of fluff off his shoulder in a proprietary manner and then stroked the nape of his neck as if soothing an anxious horse.

If Ross had returned to the silent, taciturn man she had first met those months ago, Henrietta, on the other hand, was commanding the attention of the whole room. And she was good, Petra had to admit, reeling off figures and quotes about the publishing industry, talking authoritatively about market sectors and growth. Gordon, the agent, was more amusing, though, managing to shoehorn in the odd anecdote, when he got the chance, as Henrietta alternately declared, gushed, and simpered.

Jess had been nervous about chairing the discussion, Petra knew, but she was doing an excellent job, to the obvious pride of Aiden, who was sitting next to Petra at the back of the room.

"What the hell's going on with Ross and that bizarre woman?" he hissed to Petra under cover of a burst of laughter at Gordon's latest story.

Petra just shook her head numbly. Gazing at Ross, she was

reminded of hostages paraded publicly at gunpoint: stoic, rigid, and dead behind the eyes. Desperate to run to the front and rescue him, she could do nothing to intervene. Nothing. And—in any case—she told herself, flinching with the pain, who was to say he even minded? Did she honestly feel she knew him well enough to be able to tell? In that moment, she doubted she even knew him at all.

There was a break for coffee after the panel discussion, and people drifted to the coffee table, chattering.

Henrietta—Petra saw with a sinking heart—was making a beeline for her: "You've seen the pre-empt then?" she asked Petra coldly. "I take it we can proceed with the formalities?"

"Actually, Ross and I were discussing it earlier," said Petra, relieved to hear her voice coming out sounding cool and collected. "I have recommended, and Ross has agreed, to proceed with a best bids auction," she told Henrietta. "We have interest from a number of publishing houses, as I am sure you can imagine."

Henrietta's eyes bulged, making her look rather like a cod fish, Petra decided, suddenly realizing she was staring, fascinated. Coughing into her fist to distract, she looked away as Henrietta collected herself, freezing Petra with an icy stare. "In that case, my pre-empt is withdrawn," she said, dangerously quietly. "You have just lost your client a superlative deal. I *do* hope you know what you're doing," she spat, making it perfectly clear that she was certain Petra did not.

And maybe she didn't, to be fair, thought Petra as she scuttled off, trying not to whimper audibly, seeking a quiet place where she could put a call in to Alistair.

"Hold your ground," he told her. "We're busy here, just about to send out the instructions for the best and finals."

"How many?"

"Six," Alistair told her. "All the big ones, plus Hamilton House, plus a couple more."

Petra made him list them, and her spirits rose as he went through. The biggest publishing houses in the world had all taken the bait. Ross's book had gone right to the top echelons. And now—by the end of the day, when the bids had to be in—they would see the result. One thing was already for certain: This was a book that was going to sell, and sell wide. For agents and editors across the industry, it would be one of those "it was this big" tales they told each other at parties.

Petra nearly smiled, in spite of it all, remembering the immortal line from Dustin Hoffman's agent in *Tootsie*, informing his client that his job was not to find work for his client but to "field offers." If this was the "fielding offers" end of submissions, then Petra liked it. If only all agenting work was like this. If only it wasn't Ross. If only Ross wasn't being so weird, she reminded herself, the boulder in her chest returning,

Petra duly introduced Jemima to Ross, and she could tell Jemima found him hard work. She hoped it wouldn't put her off from trying to acquire the book. Jemima and her team would provide a good home for him, and they would care for him too. Or was it just that she desperately wanted the gig to go to absolutely anyone else in the world but Henrietta? That could also be it. Partly.

In the flurry of mini-problems requiring solving, along with the in-person, phone, and email chats with the editors who were planning to bid, and the journalists who were rushing to cover the story, the day flew by without Petra having time to sit down, eat, or even go to the loo. She welcomed the distraction but was constantly refreshing her email inbox for updates.

With her pre-empt declined, Henrietta had disappeared in a huff, and Ross seemed to have disappeared too. Petra assumed he was in the cottage. Possibly not alone. She did not feel confident enough of her role in his life now to just turn up there at the end of the day. Instead, she went back to the flat and collated a professional email to him, listing the bids received—they were all in, every single one—and sketching out what needed to happen next.

Surprisingly and depressingly, Henrietta had rallied from her pre-empt rejection and submitted a bid too. Rather than putting in a lower offer, punishing them for declining the pre-empt, Petra was disturbed to see that she had now bid even higher. As promised, all the other publishing houses, including Jemima's, had submitted punchy bids as well. Jemima's came with a full and detailed marketing and publicity commitment. It was impressive. But Henrietta's bid was the highest by some margin. These were telephone number figures, extraordinary for the UK market, thought Petra.

She dithered over how to sign off her email. "Love" felt presumptuous. Even "yours" was problematic. Petra settled on "best wishes" and deleted the kisses that appeared after her name without her volition.

Petra pressed send on the email and then spent another long, lonely, largely sleepless night, mainly sitting in the little window seat reading nook, resting her head against the glass. For hours she gazed up the darkened street, toward his cottage at the top of the hill. She couldn't see it, of course, but she could imagine him there, restless, like her. Or maybe he was fast asleep, thrilled to go for the highest bid, with the bonus that Henrietta was back in his life. He was, as Petra sat there, probably dreaming happily of working together with Henrietta to make his book so brilliant it would surpass his first.

She kept her phone against her heart so she could not miss a text from him.

There was nothing.

Chapter Thirty

Ross got up stiffly to chuck another log on the fire. It was a mild August night, but he couldn't get warm. Of course, he could always go upstairs to crawl under the duvet, but being in bed alone made Petra's absence feel even worse. He was desperate to speak to her but had no idea what he would say and didn't think he was entitled to contact her, not even to reply to her email. What would he tell her? I just thought I would wake you up in the middle of the night to ask your advice as a friend, about the utter mess I'm making of my relationship with the woman I love, who is—incidentally—also you.

God knows what she thought about Henrietta coming back so obviously to claim him. He wished he knew what *he* thought about her turning up, this woman whose presence was indivisible from those heady days when his first novel was published. There wasn't a memory of those giddy months that didn't have her in it. She was like a metastasizing cancer, strangling the life force from his body while pretending that this parasitic relationship was actually symbiosis. But was that even abnormal? Surely all writers realized that—on some level—the publisher and the writer formed an uneasy alliance. Introducing emotions—romance—into the mix had made it even more toxic.

And then, when it ended—when *he* ended it, that evening—she had been incredulous at first, and then angry. Very angry. He had sat on the emerald green velvet sofa in her flat—*their* flat—sinking into a dark abyss in his head as he listened to her tell him that without her he would not survive one week—that his writing, his sales, his place at the epicenter of the literary firmament were all entirely due to her gifts. And that she would destroy him just as quickly as she had made him, elevating him above all the other talented writers. The chosen one.

He had believed her.

And now, desperate to explain to Petra but unable to even begin to articulate his own thoughts, he stayed silent.

"You look appalling," remarked Flo to Petra, when she came to open the shop the next morning. Jules, Petra, and Flo had all agreed Flo would run the shop for the duration of the festival. "How's it going?"

"Festival? Great," replied Petra. "Life? Terrible."

Flo sighed, looking at her appraisingly. "He's a good man," she told Petra. "You are *good* together."

"Were," remarked Petra, frustrated at the tears that immediately flooded her eyes and spilled onto her cheeks. She rubbed them away impatiently, sniffing.

"I don't believe that," said Flo, handing Petra a tissue. "Now dry your eyes, my darling, and be brave. All will be well. Speaking of which, how goes it with the man-child's book sale anyhow?"

"Best and final bids came in last night," said Petra, blowing out a breath noisily, in an attempt to calm her nervous system. How could it be that she was so exhausted and so jittery at the same time?

"Big?" queried Flo, her intelligent dark eyes inquisitive.

"Very," confirmed Petra, her heart sinking at remembering, again, that Henrietta's was the biggest. It was no contest. As his agent, her advice should be nothing but a formality. Apart from anything else, out of her loyalty to Alistair and the agency she should be advising him to take it. The agent's commission from a deal that big would be the bonus of the year. It covered the salary Alistair paid her and more besides.

"Well done, you. So," Flo continued briskly, "you and Ross will *have* to talk. Get through today. And then . . . ?" she made Petra meet her eye.

Petra nodded. Flo was right. When all else failed, keep going, Alistair would always say. If you stay with it for long enough, something will change. And at least she would perhaps be seeing him this evening. They could talk.

Then she received his text. Just sent you an email, it said, with a kiss. Just one. Fingers trembling, Petra fumbled to her emails. There it was.

Thank you, it said. You have done a stunning job. I could not have asked for more, and I don't deserve you (as my agent, or in any other sense).

Please tell Jemima she's got the gig, it went on. Petra sagged with relief, but there was more. Events of the last two days show me I need to go away and think. Cliché alert, it's not you, it's me, he went on. Henrietta returning to my life is stirring up complicated feelings, and I need to get my head straight once and for all. I know I'm hurting you, and I'm sorry. This is about me trying to find a way not to hurt you any more than I already have because you mean the world to me. Of course, I will be available for professional stuff, but would ask this is kept to a minimum and limited to email?

Love, Ross. xx

So that was it, Petra thought. Ross had chosen Jemima's team over Henrietta's, and she was so pleased and relieved for him. Jemima was in it, heart and soul. If anyone could take Ross's book to stellar success, it would be her. But had he done it so he could be with Henrietta without breaking his life/love cardinal rule? It looked like it to Petra. The wording was so careful. "You mean the world to me." Not "I love you." She felt numb, and yet she slowly became aware tears were trickling down her cheeks. Tears that were making Flo's face crumple in concern. "Bad news?" she asked.

"No," replied Petra, despising the wobble in her voice. "He's made the right choice, I'm glad for him."

"But what about you and him?" Flo insisted, affronted.

"I suppose maybe it was just one of those summer things," Petra said, making it clear to Flo that this was the end of the conversation on the matter.

Thankfully, Petra and Ross had few real reasons to communicate directly in the coming weeks. Petra chased through the Jemima contract and made sure everything was as it should be. Then it took just one email to let Ross know that he needed to sign.

By mutual unspoken consent, Ross did not divulge where he went, but Petra knew he was no longer in the cottage at the top of the hill. A crushing fatigue had largely prevented her from going on her usual walks, but—just occasionally—Jules and Flo chucked her out of the shop, instructing her to go and get some fresh air. The only walk that seemed remotely attractive was the one that took her to their bench at the summit of the hill. On the days she could summon the energy, she would climb up and sit there for hours, staring out across Portneath to the sea, wondering what Ross was doing. Was he editing? Chatting with Jemima? Doing one of the many interviews the book media were determined to extract from him?

Perhaps he was even writing his final chapter?

The publication date was set far enough into the future, at Petra's behest, that he was not under intense pressure, but Caliban and Miranda were going to have to have their finale eventually, and much was made of how Shakespeare had left ends untied.

It was down to Ross now.

That early October morning, the Indian summer seemed as if it would go on and on. Starting at dawn, Petra had taken a thermos of coffee to the bench and was sitting there checking email on her phone and tapping out a couple of brief replies. She and Alistair had been working hard to set up meetings in Frankfurt to sell translation rights. The weeks between finishing the festival and the Frankfurt Book Fair in October had seemed interminable.

Now that it was just days away, Petra was panicking. She checked her watch. Just after eight. Her mind made up, she phoned Alistair, who picked up straightaway.

"Alistair, I really think *you* should go to Frankfurt to do the rights," she told him briskly. As she talked, she was watching a low gray cloud chasing the sunshine away. She was going to get caught in the rain if she didn't go back to the shop soon.

"Why ever would I do that?" he replied patiently. "Everyone's expecting you. Our favorites from Sweden and Lithuania have just confirmed that they want to meet. You're Ross's agent, and they know it. They won't settle for anyone else."

"Nonsense, they won't care one bit," protested Petra. "And"—she took a deep breath before she could get the next words out—"has Ross confirmed he will attend? It can make such a difference . . ."

"He says he's all yours. Oh, and he's had tickets for his onstage interview in the main arena couriered over. He especially wants you to be there for that. I'm making sure everyone you are meeting knows about it, just in case they don't get a chance to ask their own questions if he bails on the meetings."

"Will he?" asked Petra anxiously. She honestly didn't know whether the thought of seeing him was worse than the thought of *not* seeing him.

"I don't think he will," Alistair reassured her. "Ross is one of the good ones. He delivers what he promises."

THE MORNING ARRIVED, and Petra was anxiously packing. In reality, all she needed was comfortable shoes, a few changes of underwear, and her laptop with charger. She wasn't even going to attempt "glamorous." Frankfurt was an intense experience, made even more so by having to pretend to be calm and businesslike around Ross when she felt anything but.

She came down from the flat with her backpack to find Flo and Jules already bustling around getting ready to open. Jules's gently rounded tummy and rosy cheeks signaled that she had reached the "blooming" stage, to Jules's relief after her early exhaustion. Even so, Petra was fretting. Who was going to manage deliveries? Flo was too elderly, and Jules was too pregnant.

"Are you *sure* you can do this?" she asked anxiously. "You and Flo? I wish I wasn't away so long."

"It's three days," said Jules. "We've been running Capelthorne's for decades. We'll cope. And Roman can step in if we need muscle," she added.

Jules had a point.

"Hang on, I've got something for you to take with you," said Jules, remembering. She hurried into the office and came out with a printed copy of *The Bookseller*, which was delivered to the shop weekly.

"Very pretty," said Petra, seeing the front cover was entirely dedicated to a publicity shot of Ross, looking every inch the successful young novelist. "Who is Miranda?" blazed the headline.

"Never mind the cover, it's what's inside that counts," said Jules. "You can read it on the plane. I think you will find it *very* interesting."

"Thanks," said Petra, rolling up the magazine with Ross's face on the inside and stuffing it into the outer pocket of her backpack. She didn't tell Jules she generally read the online version on her phone. Except that now she wouldn't bother. She had no interest in reading a puff piece that rehashed the same old publicity anecdotes. She was going to have to cope with the man himself soon, which was bad enough.

Predictably, the plane was delayed, and the airport was packed. Petra, already exhausted by the long trip from Portneath to Heathrow Airport, had drunk too much coffee and eaten too many pastries. Feeling wired and slightly sick, she found a wall and slid down it, plonking her backpack next to her on the floor. The magazine was poking out of the side pocket, and, in a spirit of masochism, she thought she might as well make herself even more miserable by reading the article. Maybe it would get the emotion out of the way so she could be cool and collected when she saw him.

> The halls of Frankfurt are buzzing, and all the talk is of Ross McCloud's long-awaited second novel, to be published as a lead title by Darcy Press next year. With world English rights sold for a "significant sum" by six-way auction, translation rights are set to be hotly contested at FBF this year. And all without publishers even having the final chapter of the manuscript. As Ross McCloud explained, in an exclusive interview with *The Bookseller*, this deeply personal work is—as yet—unfinished. He credits the inspiration for his Shakespeare retelling with a real-world Miranda who he says persuaded him to return to writing. The untitled novel tackles the relationship of Miranda and Caliban from *The Tempest*, an oft-reworked Shakespeare play. Scholars frequently consider the Caliban character problematic as the manuscript suggests that he molests Miranda, his childhood friend. However, Ross McCloud has a more sympathetic take on the story.
>
> "Caliban is a troubled soul, as I am myself," he admits. "But I believe he is transformed from this brutish character into something more noble by Miranda, who he adores and idolizes. My own Miranda came into my life

> when I was broken by my first foray into publishing, and I credit her with all the good things in my life since. I don't believe Shakespeare intended his audience to believe Caliban did what he was accused of. To me it is obvious the accusation, which comes only from Prospero's say-so, is simply a sign of the magician's determination to control the agenda by gaslighting all who he seeks to control. I have been in a controlling relationship myself and maybe that is partly why I have the zeal to redeem the reputation of Caliban in this way."

Then the interviewer returned to Ross's first book and its extraordinary success, but Petra skipped down the page.

> "My real-life Miranda showed me a brave new world. She inspired me to believe in myself, to write again, and—critically—to show me how even a damaged character like Caliban could be brought into the light, through steadfast love."
>
> But who is this Miranda to whom the reading public will owe so much? There are rumors that McCloud declines to confirm. But, whoever is his muse, the publishing world—and then the world of readers—await this book and its final chapter with breathless anticipation.

Sitting on the hard stone floor, Petra was immune to the discomfort. She read the entire piece from top to bottom. And then she read it again. And then she carefully rolled up the magazine and placed it back in the pocket of her backpack.

Chapter Thirty-One

The rest of Petra's journey passed in a dream. Hours went by, and Petra allowed herself to be funneled through the public transport system until eventually she arrived in her beige hotel, with its beige hotel room that was so anonymous it could be anywhere in the world.

Alistair's secretary had set up text reminders for Petra's schedule, and her phone duly pinged to tell her she was expected at the main stage to see Ross's live, onstage interview, a coup secured by his publicist to help ensure bidding around translation rights would reach a fever pitch.

She barely had time to splash water on her bare face and swipe her deodorant under her arms, fearing her long, sweaty journey might have made her stink. Fleetingly, she wished she had brought something smarter to wear, but her trusty navy trousers and blazer, with chunky sneakers for all the walking from one hall to another, would have to do.

Petra remembered her first trip to the Frankfurt Book Fair as a very junior member of her editorial team. The arrival at the airport, the study of the hall plans and the seminar timetable, the insane meeting schedules, and the effects of living with minimal access to daylight for several days while subsisting on Danish pastries and bad coffee . . . It felt like something that could be fun only in a past life.

She was exhausted.

But then, she was always exhausted these days. It had been tempting to skip day one of Frankfurt and just arrive for the meetings, but she had to face him eventually. After this one event, she was reckoning on an early return to her hotel, a glass of wine, a hot bath, and early bed, in preparation for all the meetings she had scheduled the following day.

Marching through the interminable conference spaces to her destination, the thought that she and Ross might inevitably have to be in the same room, seeing each other for the first time in the six or so weeks since the Portneath Literary Festival, filled her with queasy excitement—or possibly dread. She slipped into the back of the hot, stuffy room, packed full of shiny-faced, slightly sweaty humanity, and—because she could see no empty chairs at all—propped herself against the back wall.

Checking her phone for last-minute schedule updates from her assistant, Petra missed the moment when Ross and his interviewer walked out on the stage and took their seats. She looked up and there he was, perhaps sixty feet away. He was clean-shaven, she noted, and was wearing a blindingly white cotton shirt, open-necked under a black jacket with dark blue jeans—new, Petra thought. He looked so handsome, and so very agonizingly dear and familiar, Petra had difficulty swallowing.

The applause died down, and they were off. First, the interviewer, an esteemed Radio 4 arts presenter known universally as simply "Declan," bigged up Ross's career to date, while he bashfully stared down at his feet. Then they were into his early influences: an inspiring English teacher, a primary school success with a national writing competition. Petra was soothed, hearing this now familiar story play out. The room was warm, and she had not slept well. Seeing Ross up onstage, being charming, handsome, and clearly "together" gave her the first peace she had felt in weeks. He was okay, thank goodness. And Henrietta was nowhere to be seen. Also thank goodness.

"So tell us what it was like when your first book became so remarkably successful. How did that feel from the inside, looking out?"

"'It was the best of times, it was the worst of times,'" Ross quoted, shaking his head. There was a silence while he stared at the floor. It felt like the whole room was holding its breath. Petra was definitely holding *her* breath. "Okay, so . . ." he said at last, raising his head again and fixing his eyes directly on Petra at the back of the room. "It's the fairy-tale ending, isn't it? I mean, it's what everyone here in this room wants, for a book to be published that does well. As an author, writing a book, getting it published, having it be a huge success, ''tis a consummation devoutly to be wished,' but—not to be ungrateful—for me, at that time, it was anything but a fairy tale. I felt as if I had made a Faustian pact, where I sold my soul . . ." He stopped, put his hand to his mouth and then used it to ruffle his hair distractedly, "So—yeah—I know now that I believed I could only be successful if I capitulated to this 'romance'—at least, I thought that was what it was at the time. I realized later—much later—it was an unhealthily controlling relationship where I mistakenly believed I owed this person my success. I gave them a lot of power. Which they then abused."

At these words, the room collectively gasped, and then hummed excitedly, and then—straining to hear Ross's next words—it fell silent again.

Petra was relieved that Henrietta was not present. If she could hear herself be described in such a way in front of a roomful of her industry peers, Petra feared Henrietta would lose her shit. Which would actually be quite exciting, she admitted to herself, with something approaching schadenfreude.

Her heart swelled with pride that Ross was brave enough to talk about it in such a public arena. At the center of Henrietta's world, of all places.

". . . and I carried a lot of shame from that situation," he went on, his eyes still resting on Petra as if he and she were the only people in the room. "I had this idea my success was a fluke, a construct created by this woman in return for my obedience. I was beguiled. But I was also kind of trapped. I began to think this woman's input was necessary for me to be able to create and that meant I was paralyzed. I was basically suffering from a terminal case of imposter syndrome."

"We can all relate to that," joked Declan, and there was a ripple of laughter. "But what happened next?" he probed. "It seems you disappeared for five years. What was that all about? Writer's block? Publicity stunt?"

"A hell of a publicity stunt," contradicted Ross. "Lasting five years? No. I was in a dark place, all right. I got myself out of this destructive relationship, but that wasn't the entire solution. Without that prop, I was in a hell of my own creation—a dark, lonely, isolated existence . . . I was lost in my own head. And that wasn't a great place to be at the time," he added with a self-deprecating smile.

Petra couldn't feel her feet. There had been too many revelations that day—first the *Bookseller* article, and now this?

And if Miranda was . . . No. Petra wasn't yet ready to tell herself that she was Miranda. With difficulty, she made herself focus on the rest of the presentation.

As soon as questions were invited from the floor, someone stood up and asked who Miranda was.

Ross laughed aloud. "She knows who she is," he said, his eyes boring into Petra's and then looking away hurriedly as members of the audience turned to follow his gaze. "I'm not going to drag her into the limelight. That's her decision to make. Next question."

Of course, someone also wanted to know who his destructive relationship was with, and he demurred over that too, to Petra's relief. He could hardly name her because of the slander laws. More or less everyone in publishing would know already, of course.

Despite her dawn start and her exhausting journey, Petra felt light and full of energy. As the audience filed out, her phone buzzed. It was Ross.

Cocktails to celebrate? it said. Meet me at the Eiserner Steg 7pm?

Petra texted back a thumbs-up, put it into Google maps, and checked her watch. Forty-five minutes' walk away. There would be no time now to go back to her hotel room to get glammed up unless she took an Uber instead. No. She needed to walk off this fizzing nervous energy she felt. Frankfurt—and Ross—were going to have to take her as she came.

She set off straightaway, invisible to the chattering, smiling hordes who were meeting and kissing and finding their way into the bars and restaurants that would be mobbed right through until the fair was over.

She would get to the bridge first if she was quick. There she could gather her thoughts and calm her mind.

But she was too late. There was a solitary figure right in the center of the bridge, and there was no mistaking that height and those broad shoulders. Ross had his back to her as he gazed out at the city, twinkling with light and spreading either side of the river under a navy sky.

Petra's legs shook as, unobserved, she quietly walked to his side, gazing at the barnacle clusters of padlocks that had been attached to the bridge by thousands of lovers. Taking up position, facing the view, she asked: "Am I Miranda?"

Ross made a sound that was somewhere between a laugh and a sob. "What do *you* think?" he said, turning and looking down at her with a sad smile.

"I think I thought you had gone back to Henrietta," she said.

"As if I would go back to the hell I spent five years escaping from," he said softly, his eyes blazing with love.

"You were damned well flying *very* close to the sun in that conference hall back there," she scolded, changing the subject. "Jemima's lot will be panicking that their latest acquisition is just about to be sued for libel."

"Slander actually," Ross corrected her. "And I named nobody, remember? If Henrietta wants to cast herself in that role, she's very welcome to. If I know her, she'll seethe a bit, but she'll have the sense to keep her head down."

Petra nodded. She hoped he was right. "So, what about your final chapter?" she asked. "Does your guy get his girl in the end, or what?"

"I don't know," Ross whispered at last, gazing down at her tenderly. "Does he?"

Epilogue

Petra and Ross were inseparable from that day on.

Ross's cottage on the hill had been rented to another tenant, so they both returned to the little flat above the bookshop after a stunningly successful fair. There had been extraordinary interest in the book, now titled *I Cried to Dream Again: Caliban's Story Retold*. Ross's honest disclosures around his struggles and inspirations helped to create the story's success, as well as generating a valuable discourse about mental health issues in publishing.

Ross and Alistair continued to insist that Petra deal with everything, and by Christmas she had sold rights to eighteen countries with more to follow.

In the months that passed, back in Portneath, Ross berated himself constantly over what he had put Petra through. Over time, with lots of talking, they managed to puzzle out how the destructive and unhealthy relationship between him and Henrietta had formed, how Henrietta had exploited her power and his naïvete, and how her reappearance had instantly brought him back temporarily into her thrall.

Slowly, with Petra's patience and understanding, he forgave himself.

Thanks to Petra and Ross, Alistair's agency was set to achieve its best year ever, and the monies due from fees allowed him to recruit an excellent assistant whose sole job was to support Petra. This allowed Petra to stay in Portneath, where she had Ross, her friends, and a whole new life.

However, the fatigue that had consumed her during Ross's weeks of absence turned out not to be just depression after all. Jules—being pregnant herself—spotted it first.

On hearing he was going to be a father, Ross immediately went out and put his whole advance payment on a darling little fisherman's cottage right on the seafront. It was in the curved row of ice cream–colored Georgian houses that faced out over the harbor—the ones Petra had loved gazing at from the bedroom window of the flat over all those months.

Petra and Ross's cottage was the rose pink one, with blue hydrangeas crammed into its little front garden and a glorious climbing honeysuckle around the door.

There was a little sitting room at the front with a wooden floor, an open fire, and bookshelves in the alcoves on either side of the fireplace. At the back was a kitchen with a glass-windowed conservatory, providing just enough room for a dining table and chairs overlooking a gorgeous little walled garden. Ross took the bare, empty attic room as his writing space, placing a plain wooden table under the dormer window, so his only distraction was the constantly changing weather blowing west to east across the horizon over the sea.

Before he even started on novel number three, Ross built Petra a cozy window seat in the bay window of the sitting room. Piled high with feather cushions and throws, it was her favorite spot, where she could read to her heart's content and gaze out at the sea. She never felt alone, because she knew Ross was looking out at the same views in the room above. Also, as it happened, Petra saw a huge amount of Jules. Being pregnant together—spending whole days either in the cottage or the converted chapel in Middlemass where Roman and Jules lived—the two women shared everything, including much of the sleep-deprived fug of early motherhood. They were delighted that their daughters Esme and Harriet—just five months apart in age and destined to go through school together—showed every sign of becoming firm friends.

Speaking of friends, Petra and Ross quickly became close to all the others, but especially Roman and Jules.

Roman took on the main responsibility for Capelthorne's while the babies were tiny. He was ably assisted by Flo when she wasn't working in her garden with Digger for company. If Flo wasn't available, Petra and Jules took turns looking after the girls while the other helped out in the shop. This suited Petra perfectly, because having Ross as her sole client—and with such an able assistant in London—she had little to do until he finished his next book. In the meantime, *I Cried to Dream Again* continued to break sales records in all of its markets.

Readers were especially touched to see that Caliban—his reputation fully restored—got his happy ending with Miranda at last.

Acknowledgments

Yikes, here we go again! I can hardly believe it is time to look back on another book and to make my usual inadequate attempts to thank everyone in the complex, ever-shifting ecosystem that keeps me on track.

Friends and family—you know who you all are—thank you for putting up with me. God knows, I even bore myself sometimes as I fret, complain, and—probably worse—enthuse to the point of tedium over every character quirk and plot twist to whoever will listen. My husband gets the worst of it, to be fair, but friends, aunts, grown-up children, and even the dog have also had to show extraordinary grace when I am in the midst of writing another novel.

My wonderful agent, Kevan Lyon, and the fabulous editorial, production, and publicity teams at Avon, in the US *and* the UK, are all a joy to work with, being faultlessly charming and patient as well as being extraordinarily clever and good at their respective jobs. Thank you to all, but particularly to Tessa Woodward, Madelyn Blaney, Mary Interdonati, and Serena Stent. Additionally, many thanks to Taryn Fagerness and her fabulous team for introducing my work to other territories. It is a joy to get feedback on social media from readers in other countries, even if I end up relying heavily on Google translate in order to reply.

Confession: I love inhabiting the world I create in my books, and—if I didn't have another reader anywhere—I would probably still spend my life there. That said, thank you to the growing band of readers who enjoy these books, especially those who are kind enough to reach out and tell me so. I hope there will be many more stories for us all to escape into together.

About the Author

Poppy Alexander—who also writes as Rosie Howard—is the author of *The Battle of the Bookshops, The Littlest Library*, *Storybook Ending, 25 Days 'Til Christmas,* and *The 12 Days of Christmas*. She wrote her first book when she was five. There was a long gap in her writing career while she was at school, and after studying classical music at university, she decided the world of music was better off without her and took up journalism instead. She takes an anthropological interest in family, friends, and life in her West Sussex village (think quintessentially British radio soap opera *The Archers* crossed with *Twin Peaks*), where she lives with her husband, children, and various other pets.